THE LONG CON™

ONI PRESS

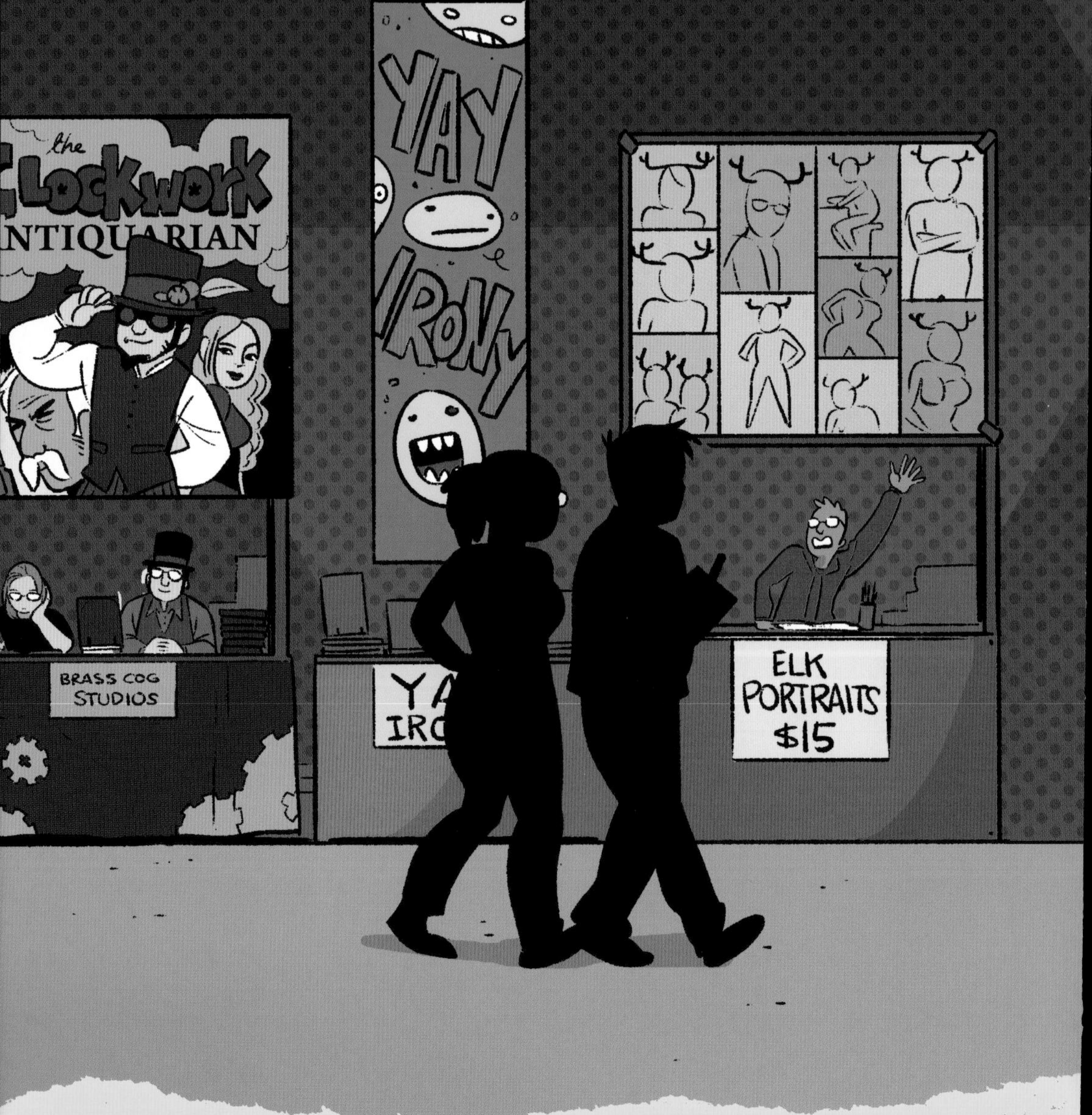

the
CLOCKWORK
ANTIQUARIAN
YAY
IRONY
BRASS COG
STUDIOS
ELK
PORTRAITS
$15

THE LONG CON

WRITTEN BY

DYLAN MECONIS & BEN COLEMAN

ILLUSTRATED BY

EA DENICH

COLORED BY

M. VICTORIA ROBADO

LETTERED BY

ADITYA BIDIKAR

ONI PRESS

DESIGNED BY
KEITH WOOD

EDITED BY
ROBIN HERRERA & ARI YARWOOD

Published by Oni Press, Inc.

Joe Nozemack, founder & chief financial officer

James Lucas Jones, publisher

Charlie Chu, v.p. of creative & business development

Brad Rooks, director of operations

Melissa Meszaros, director of publicity

Margot Wood, director of sales

Sandy Tanaka, marketing design manager

Amber O'Neill, special projects manager

Troy Look, director of design & production

Kate Z. Stone, senior graphic designer

Sonja Synak, graphic designer

Angie Knowles, digital prepress lead

Ari Yarwood, executive editor

Sarah Gaydos, editorial director of licensed publishing

Robin Herrera, senior editor

Desiree Wilson, associate editor

Michelle Nguyen, executive assistant

Jung Lee, logistics coordinator

Scott Sharkey, warehtouse assistant

1319 SE Martin Luther King, Jr. Blvd.
Suite 240
Portland, OR 97214

onipress.com
facebook.com/onipress
twitter.com/onipress
onipress.tumblr.com
instagram.com/onipress

@dmeconis · dylanmeconis.com
@OhColeman · about.me/OhColeman
@ghostgreeen · ghostgreen.tumblr.com
@shourimajo · shourimajo.com
@adityab · adityab.net/lettering

First Edition: February 2019
ISBN: 978-1-62010-571-9
eISBN: 978-1-62010-572-6

1 2 3 4 5 6 7 8 9 10

Library of Congress Control Number: 2018947002

Printed in China.

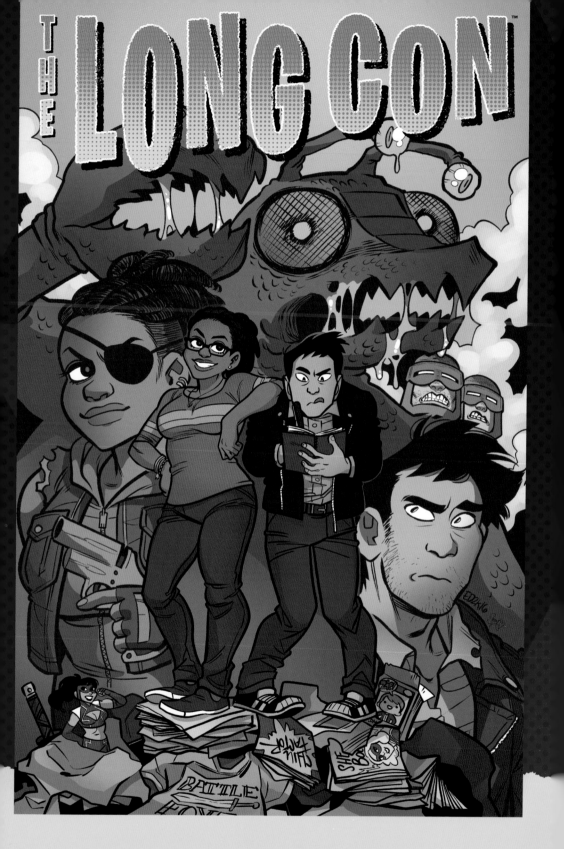

CHAPTER 1: FIVE YEARS AND ONE APOCALYPSE AGO

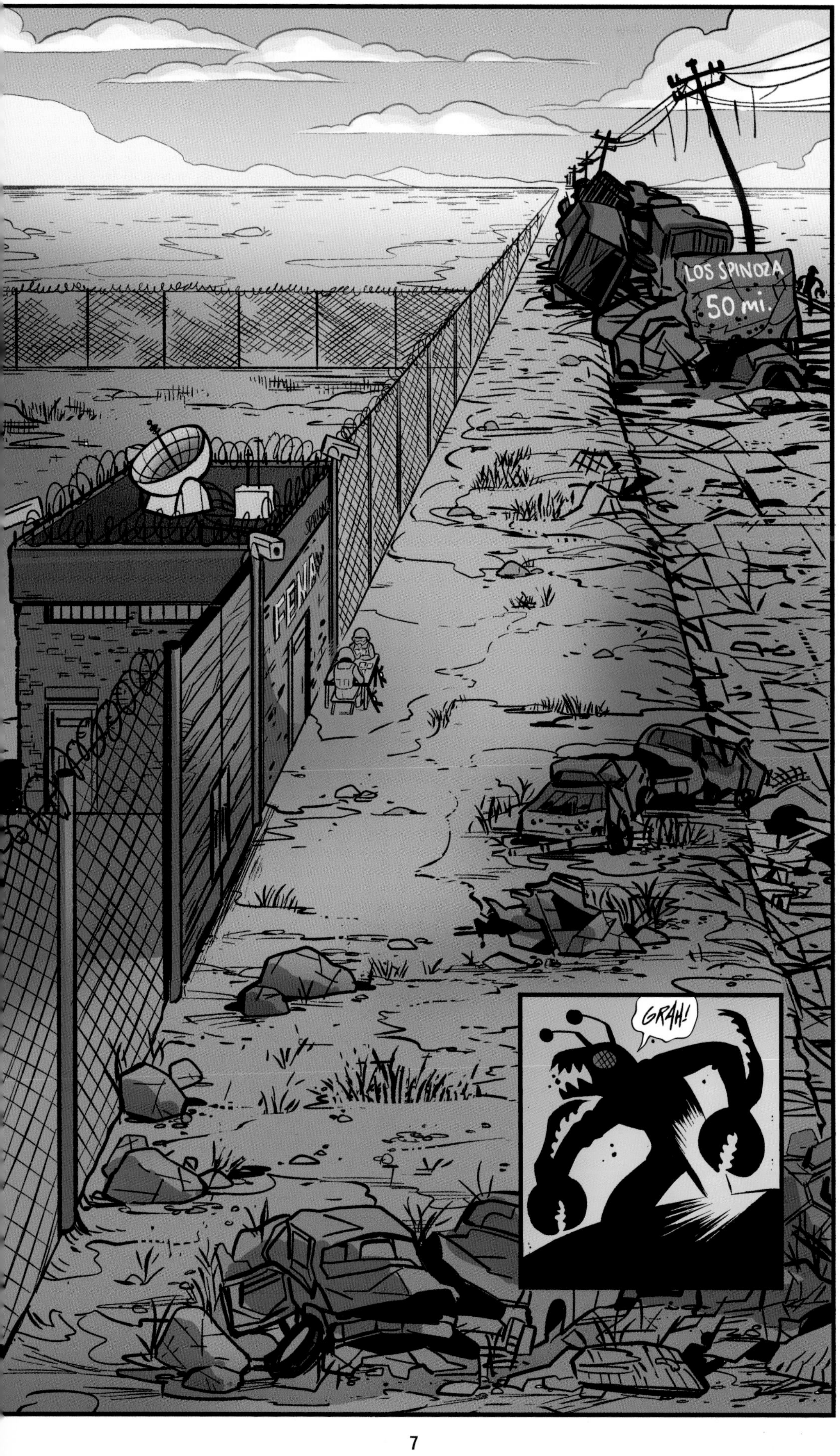
FEMA
LOS SPINOZA
50 mi.
GRAH!

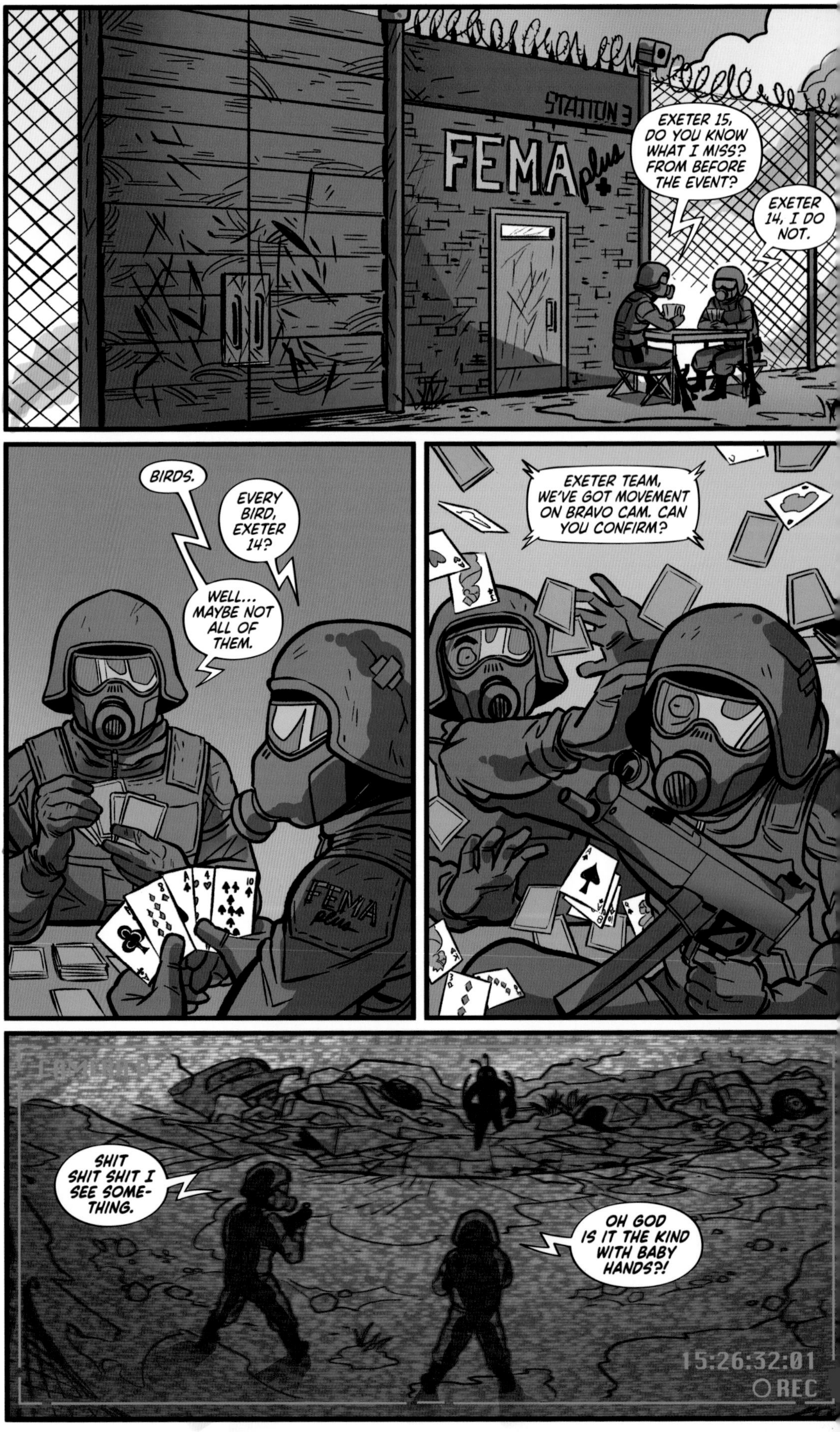
STATION 3
FEMA plus
EXETER 15, DO YOU KNOW WHAT I MISS? FROM BEFORE THE EVENT?
EXETER 14, I DO NOT.
BIRDS.
EVERY BIRD, EXETER 14?
WELL... MAYBE NOT ALL OF THEM.
FEMA plus
EXETER TEAM, WE'VE GOT MOVEMENT ON BRAVO CAM. CAN YOU CONFIRM?
SHIT SHIT SHIT I SEE SOME-THING.
OH GOD IS IT THE KIND WITH BABY HANDS?!
15:26:32:01
REC

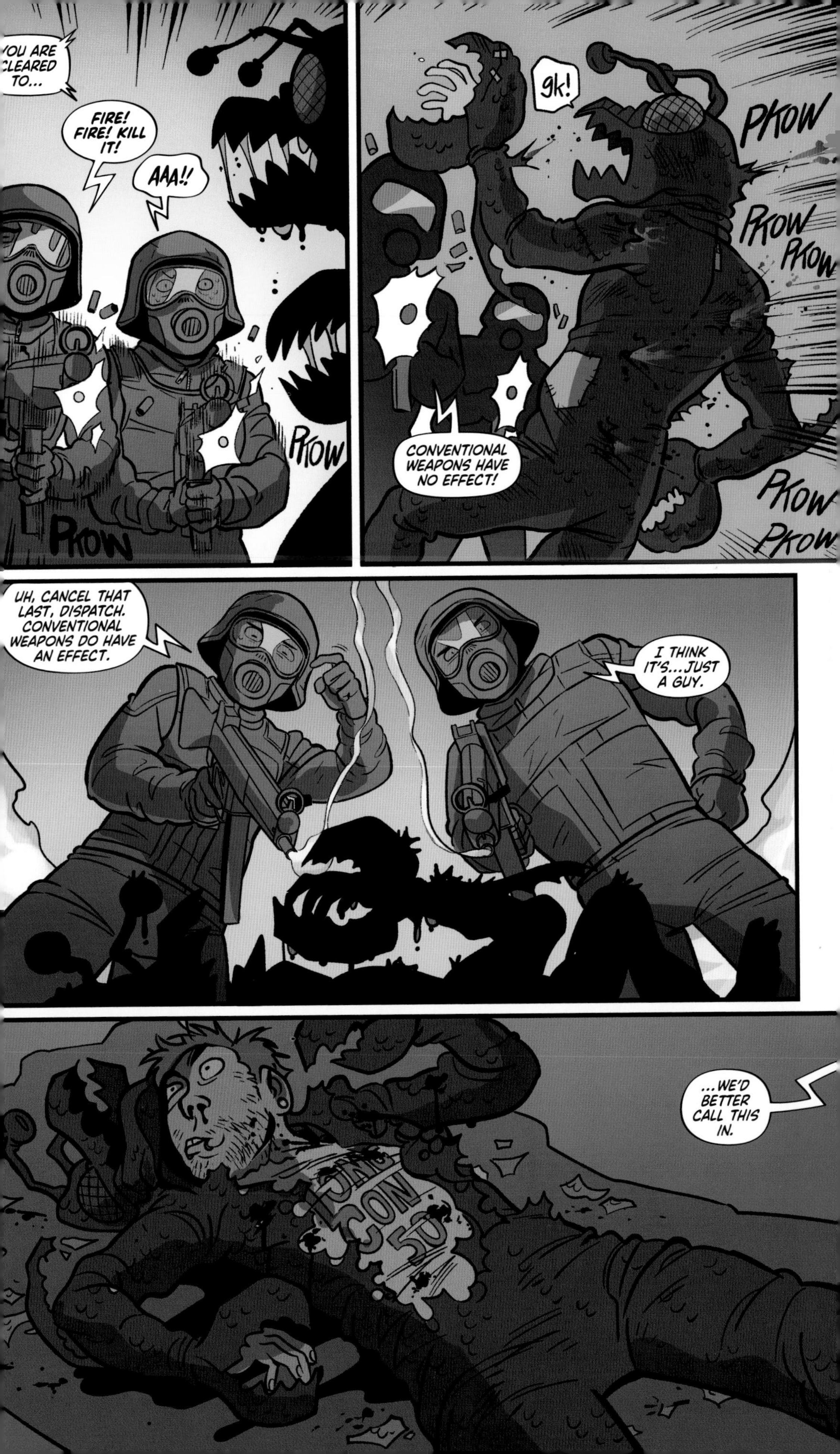
YOU ARE CLEARED TO...
FIRE! FIRE! KILL IT!
AAA!!
PKOW
PKOW
gk!
PKOW
PKOW
PKOW
CONVENTIONAL WEAPONS HAVE NO EFFECT!
PKOW
PKOW
UH, CANCEL THAT LAST, DISPATCH. CONVENTIONAL WEAPONS DO HAVE AN EFFECT.
I THINK IT'S...JUST A GUY.
...WE'D BETTER CALL THIS IN.

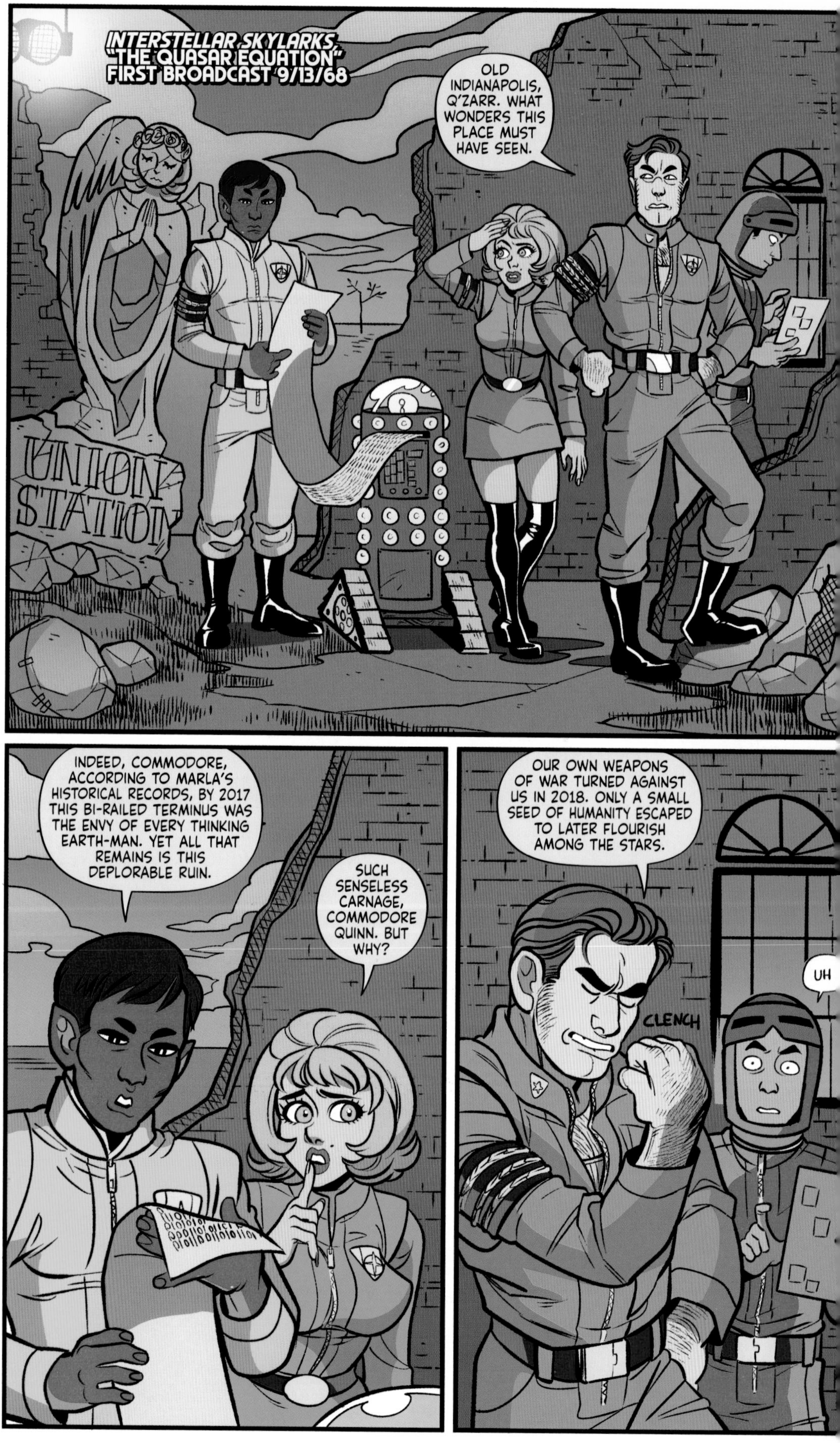
INTERSTELLAR SKYLARKS "THE QUASAR EQUATION" FIRST BROADCAST 9/13/68
OLD INDIANAPOLIS, Q'ZARR. WHAT WONDERS THIS PLACE MUST HAVE SEEN.
UNION STATION
INDEED, COMMODORE, ACCORDING TO MARLA'S HISTORICAL RECORDS, BY 2017 THIS BI-RAILED TERMINUS WAS THE ENVY OF EVERY THINKING EARTH-MAN. YET ALL THAT REMAINS IS THIS DEPLORABLE RUIN.
SUCH SENSELESS CARNAGE, COMMODORE QUINN. BUT WHY?
OUR OWN WEAPONS OF WAR TURNED AGAINST US IN 2018. ONLY A SMALL SEED OF HUMANITY ESCAPED TO LATER FLOURISH AMONG THE STARS.
CLENCH
UH

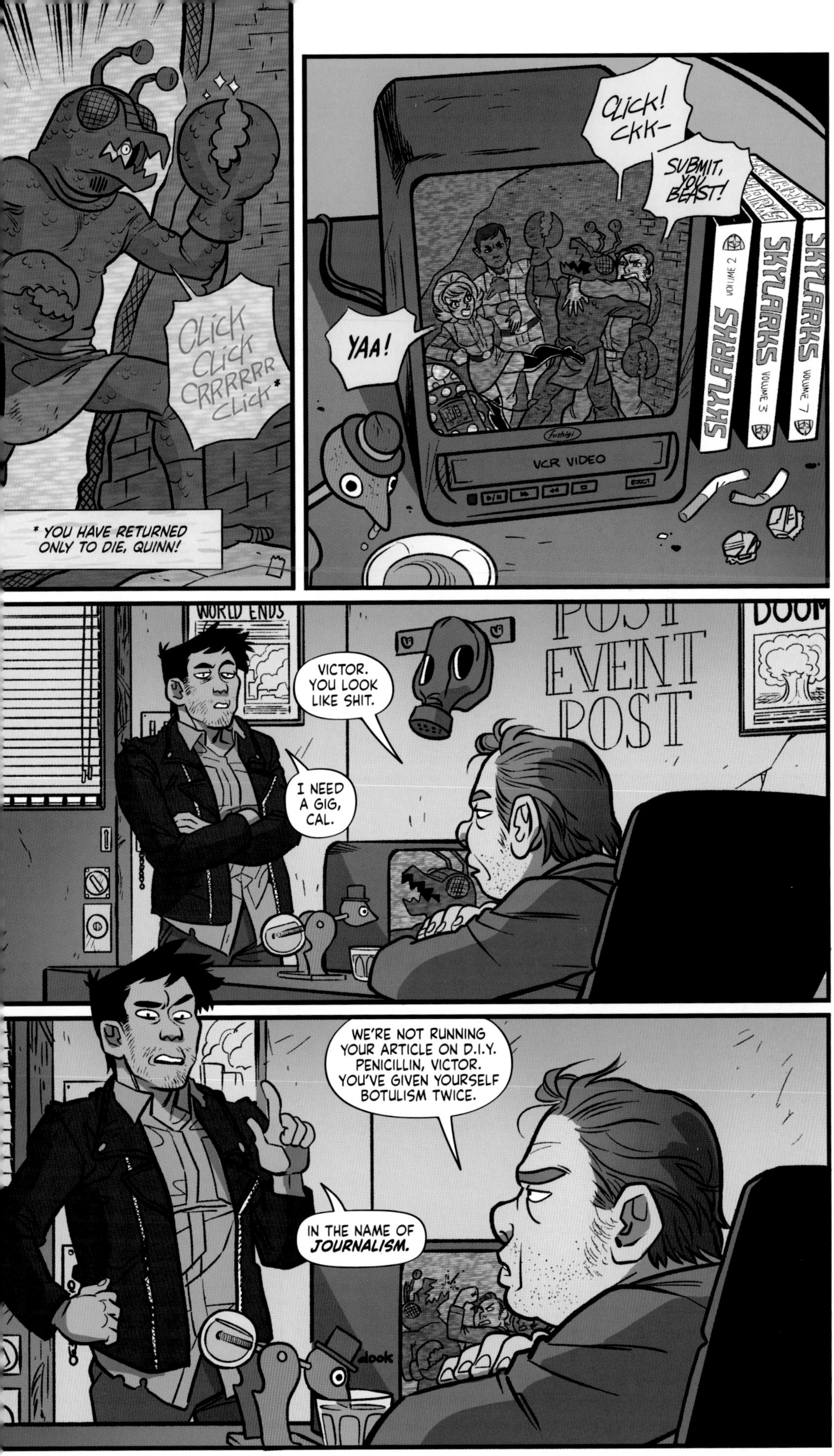
CLICK CLICK CRRRRRR CLICK*
* YOU HAVE RETURNED ONLY TO DIE, QUINN!
CLICK! CKK-
SUBMIT, YOU BEAST!
YAA!
VCR VIDEO
SKYLARKS VOLUME 2
SKYLARKS VOLUME 3
SKYLARKS VOLUME 7
WORLD ENDS
POST EVENT POST
DOOM
VICTOR. YOU LOOK LIKE SHIT.
I NEED A GIG, CAL.
WE'RE NOT RUNNING YOUR ARTICLE ON D.I.Y. PENICILLIN, VICTOR. YOU'VE GIVEN YOURSELF BOTULISM TWICE.
IN THE NAME OF ***JOURNALISM.***

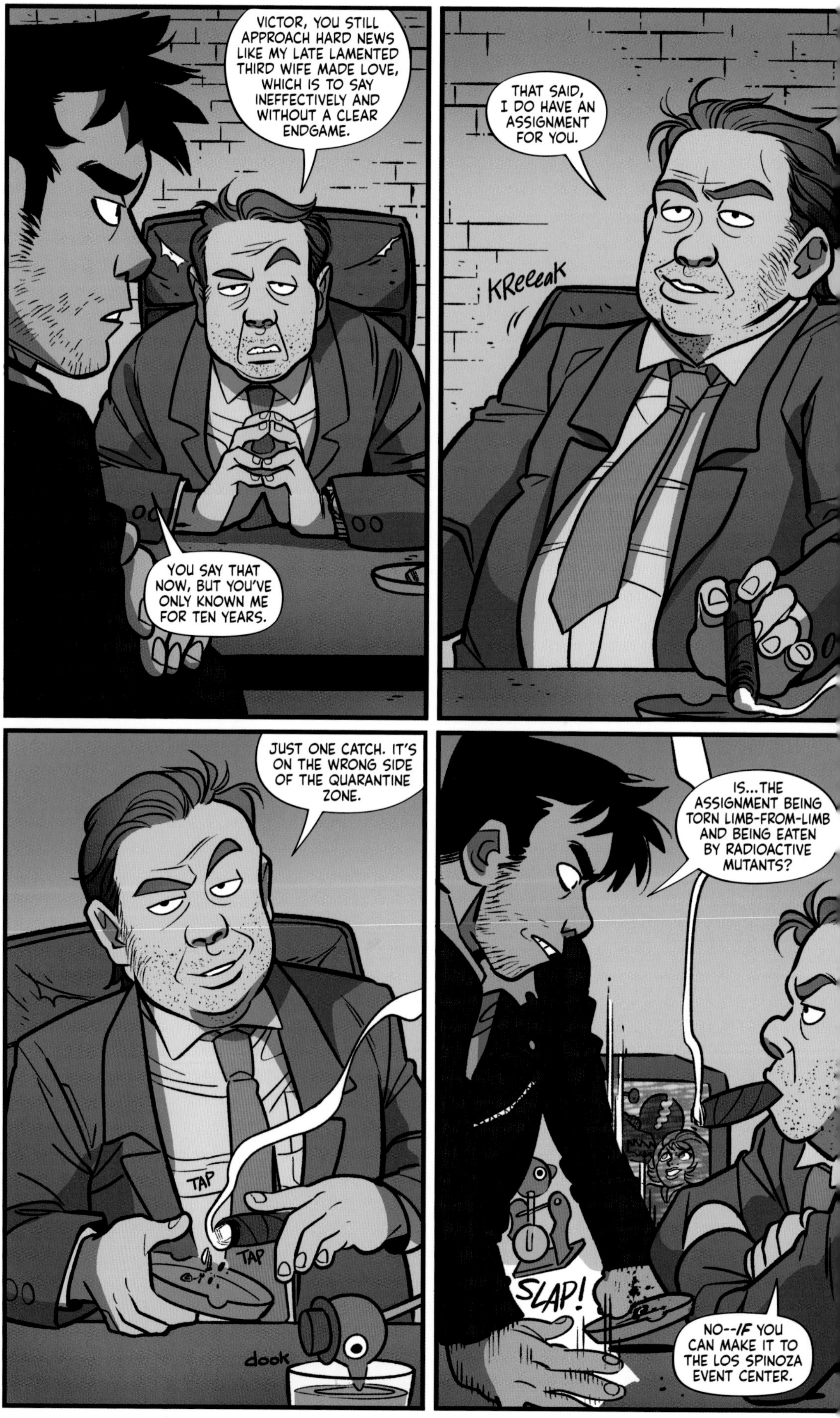
VICTOR, YOU STILL APPROACH HARD NEWS LIKE MY LATE LAMENTED THIRD WIFE MADE LOVE, WHICH IS TO SAY INEFFECTIVELY AND WITHOUT A CLEAR ENDGAME.
YOU SAY THAT NOW, BUT YOU'VE ONLY KNOWN ME FOR TEN YEARS.
KReeeak
THAT SAID, I DO HAVE AN ASSIGNMENT FOR YOU.
JUST ONE CATCH. IT'S ON THE WRONG SIDE OF THE QUARANTINE ZONE.
TAP
TAP
dook
IS...THE ASSIGNMENT BEING TORN LIMB-FROM-LIMB AND BEING EATEN BY RADIOACTIVE MUTANTS?
SLAP!
NO--*IF* YOU CAN MAKE IT TO THE LOS SPINOZA EVENT CENTER.

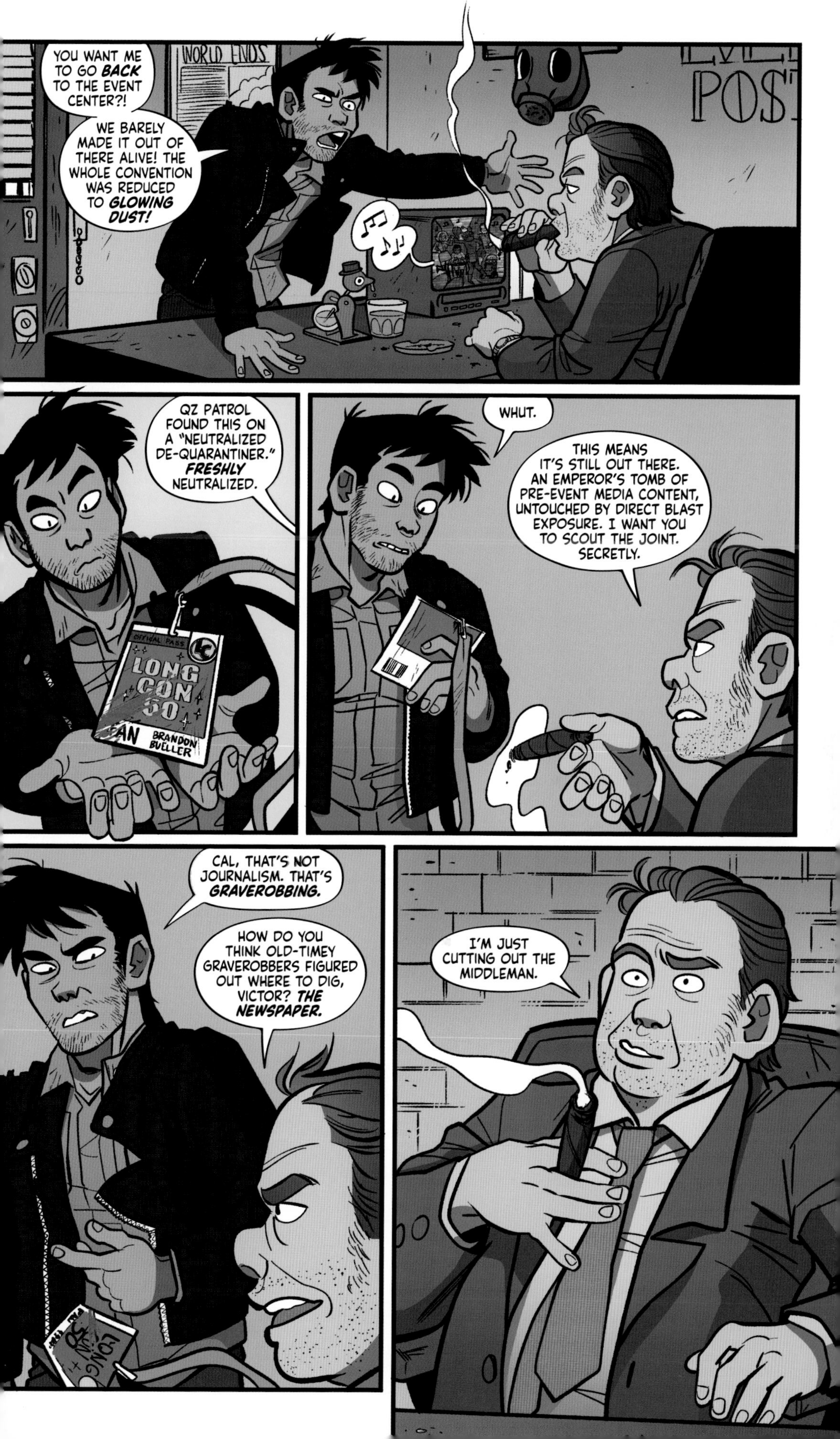
WORLD ENDS
POST
YOU WANT ME TO GO *BACK* TO THE EVENT CENTER?!
WE BARELY MADE IT OUT OF THERE ALIVE! THE WHOLE CONVENTION WAS REDUCED TO *GLOWING DUST!*
QZ PATROL FOUND THIS ON A "NEUTRALIZED DE-QUARANTINER." *FRESHLY* NEUTRALIZED.
OFFICIAL PASS
LONG CON 50
BRANDON BUELLER
WHUT.
THIS MEANS IT'S STILL OUT THERE. AN EMPEROR'S TOMB OF PRE-EVENT MEDIA CONTENT, UNTOUCHED BY DIRECT BLAST EXPOSURE. I WANT YOU TO SCOUT THE JOINT. SECRETLY.
CAL, THAT'S NOT JOURNALISM. THAT'S *GRAVEROBBING.*
HOW DO YOU THINK OLD-TIMEY GRAVEROBBERS FIGURED OUT WHERE TO DIG, VICTOR? *THE NEWSPAPER.*
I'M JUST CUTTING OUT THE MIDDLEMAN.

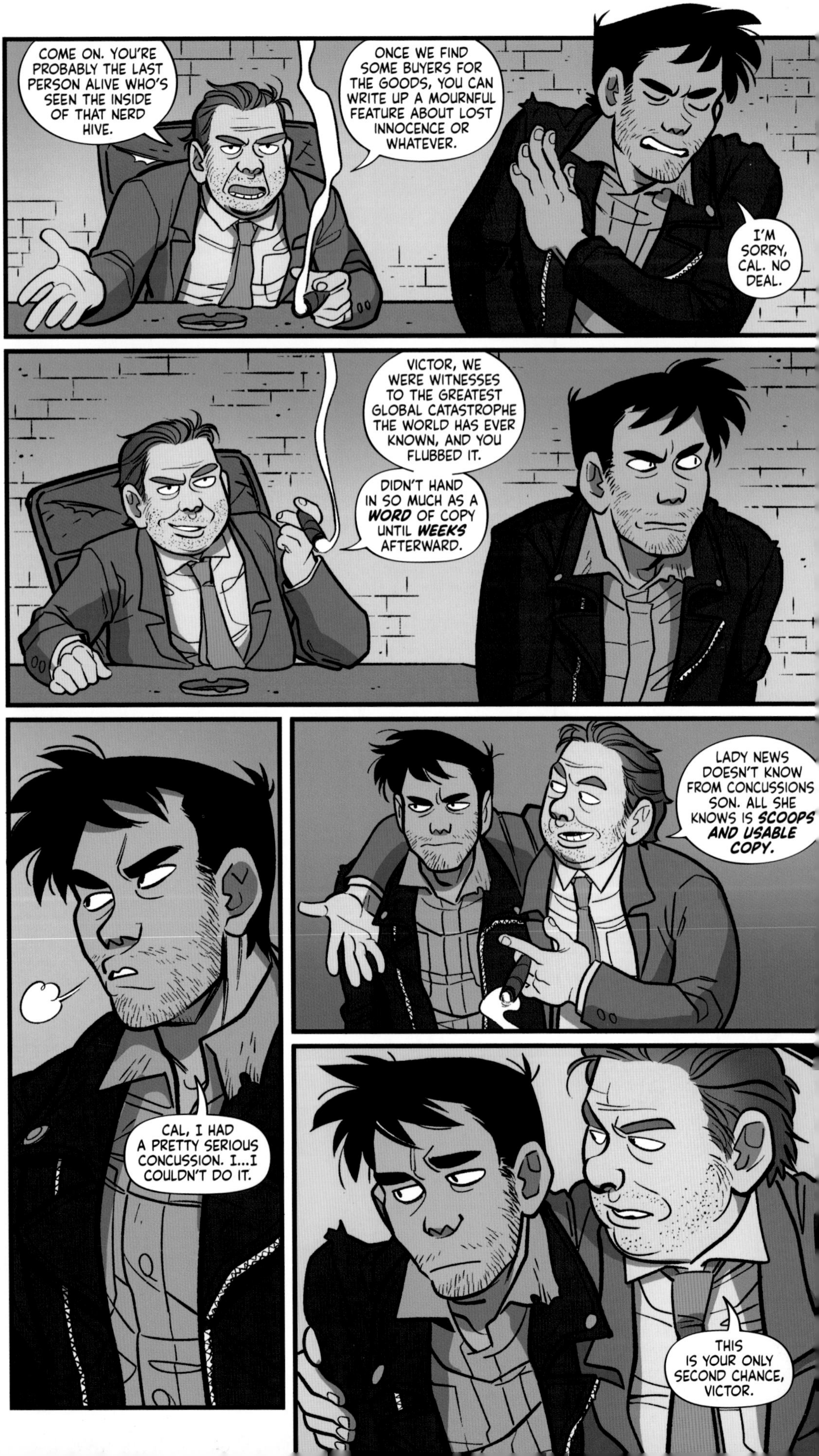
COME ON. YOU'RE PROBABLY THE LAST PERSON ALIVE WHO'S SEEN THE INSIDE OF THAT NERD HIVE.
ONCE WE FIND SOME BUYERS FOR THE GOODS, YOU CAN WRITE UP A MOURNFUL FEATURE ABOUT LOST INNOCENCE OR WHATEVER.
I'M SORRY, CAL. NO DEAL.
VICTOR, WE WERE WITNESSES TO THE GREATEST GLOBAL CATASTROPHE THE WORLD HAS EVER KNOWN, AND YOU FLUBBED IT.
DIDN'T HAND IN SO MUCH AS A **WORD** OF COPY UNTIL **WEEKS** AFTERWARD.
CAL, I HAD A PRETTY SERIOUS CONCUSSION. I...I COULDN'T DO IT.
LADY NEWS DOESN'T KNOW FROM CONCUSSIONS SON. ALL SHE KNOWS IS **SCOOPS AND USABLE COPY.**
THIS IS YOUR ONLY SECOND CHANCE, VICTOR.

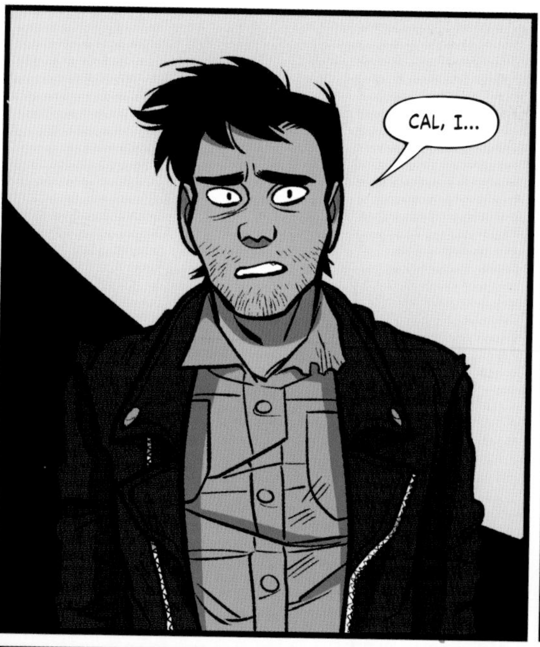
CAL, I...

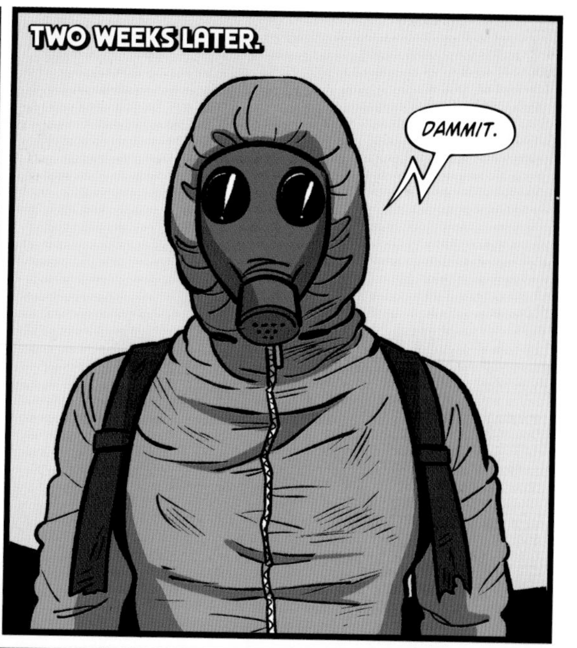
TWO WEEKS LATER.
DAMMIT.

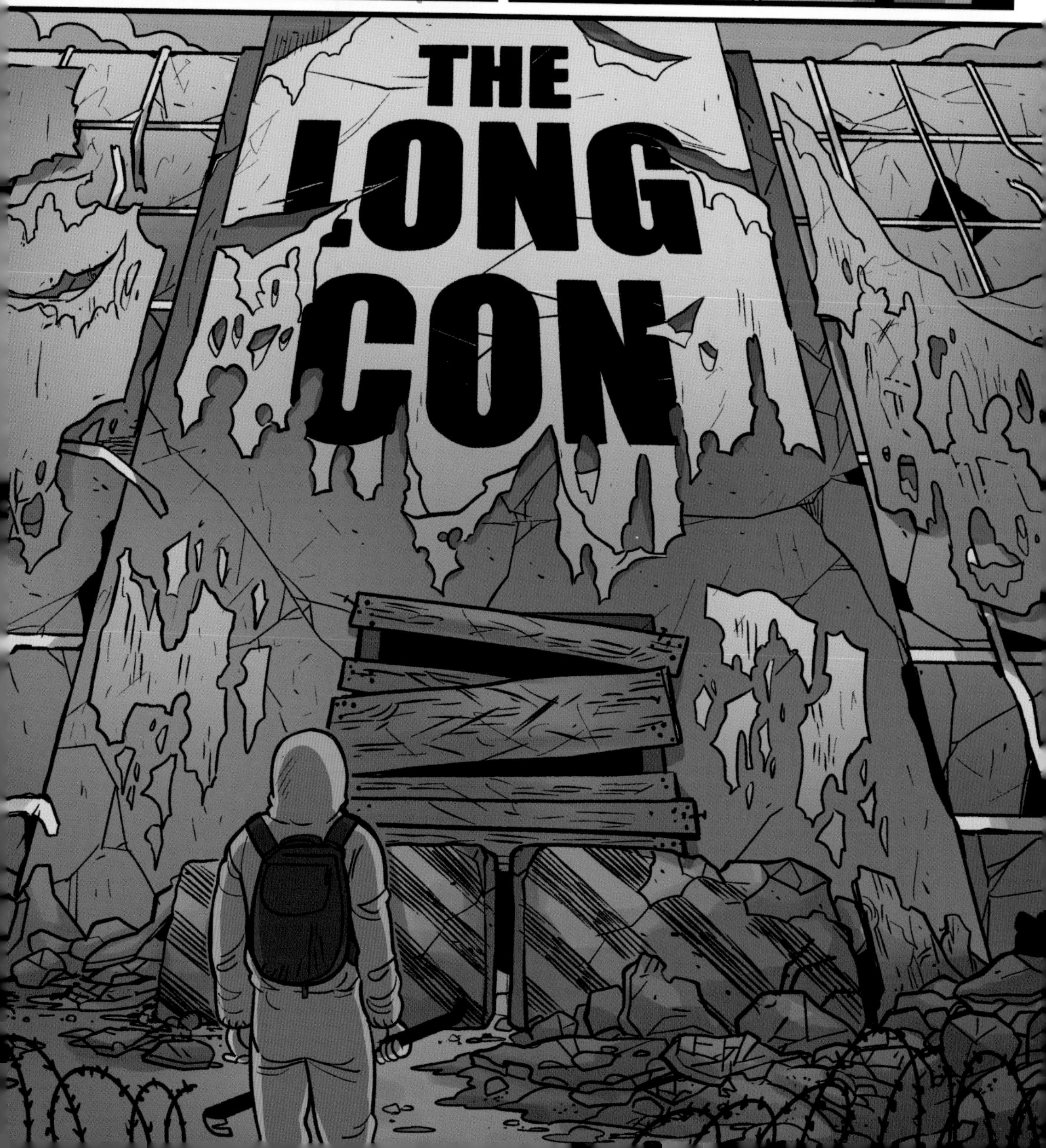
THE LONG CON

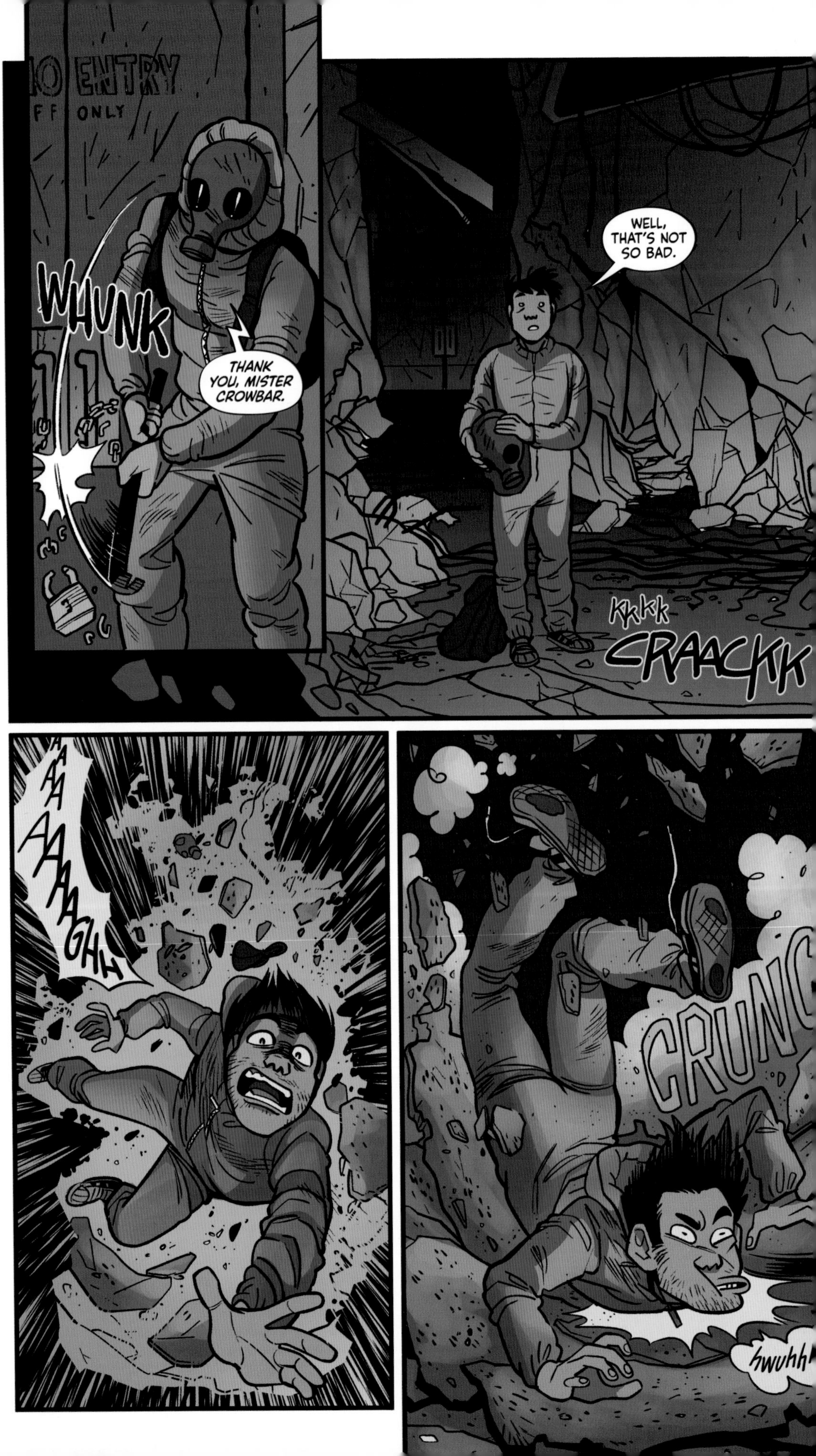
NO ENTRY
FF ONLY
WHUNK
THANK YOU, MISTER CROWBAR.
WELL, THAT'S NOT SO BAD.
KKKK
CRAACKK
AAAAAAAAGHH
CRUNC
hwuhh

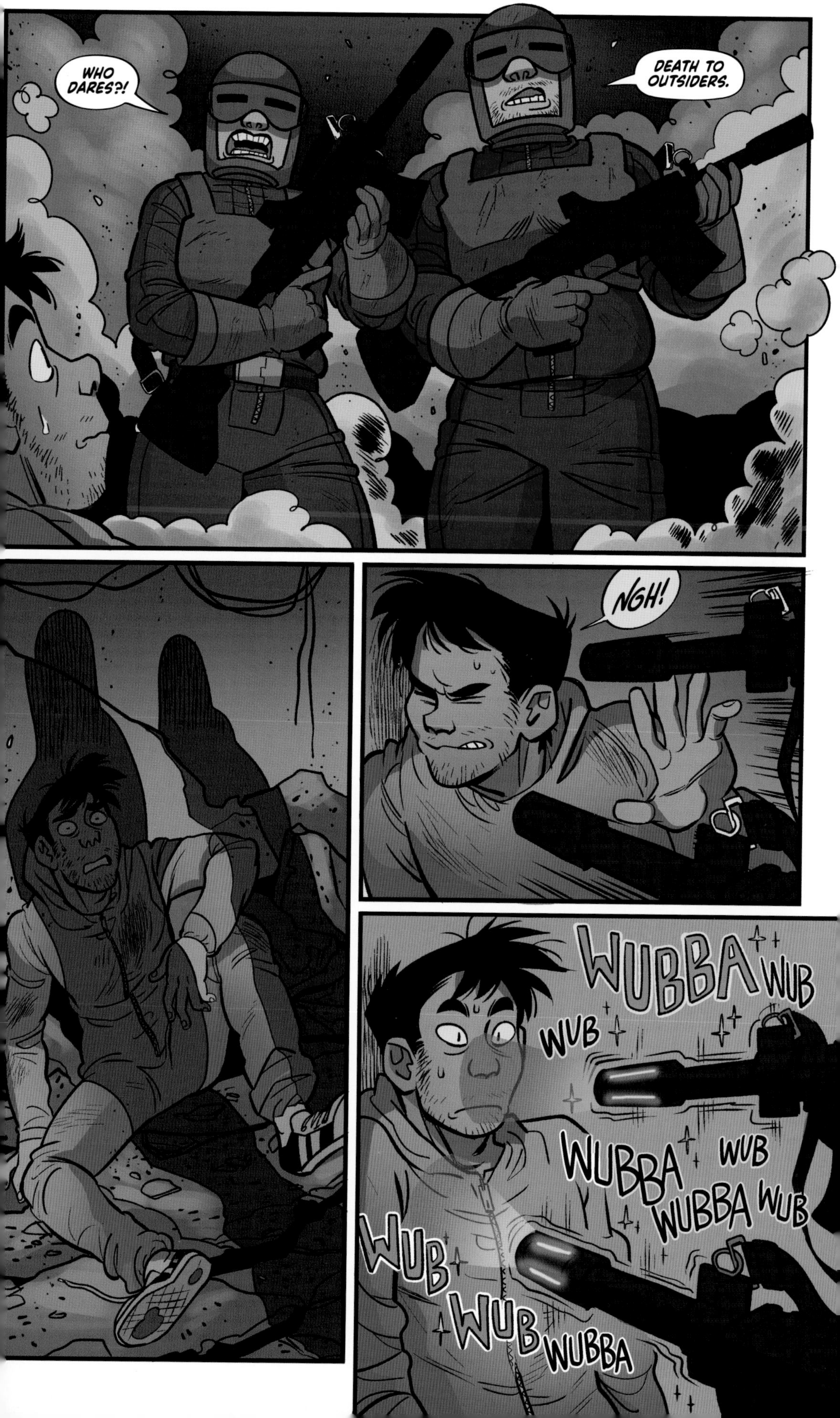
WHO DARES?!
DEATH TO OUTSIDERS.
NGH!
WUBBA WUB
WUB
WUBBA WUB
WUBBA WUB
WUB
WUB WUBBA

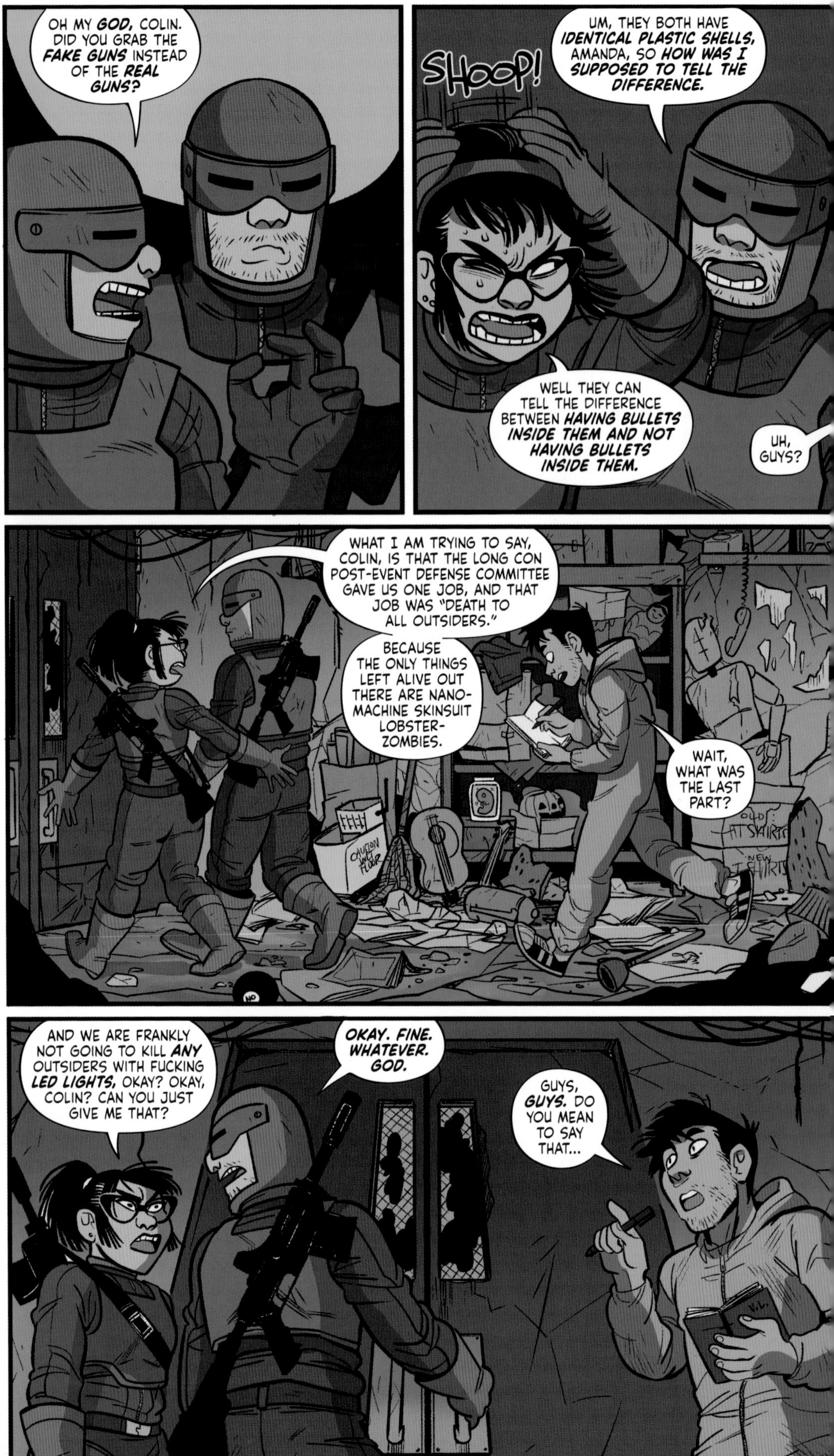
OH MY GOD, COLIN. DID YOU GRAB THE FAKE GUNS INSTEAD OF THE REAL GUNS?
SHOOP!
UM, THEY BOTH HAVE IDENTICAL PLASTIC SHELLS, AMANDA, SO HOW WAS I SUPPOSED TO TELL THE DIFFERENCE.
WELL THEY CAN TELL THE DIFFERENCE BETWEEN HAVING BULLETS INSIDE THEM AND NOT HAVING BULLETS INSIDE THEM.
UH, GUYS?
WHAT I AM TRYING TO SAY, COLIN, IS THAT THE LONG CON POST-EVENT DEFENSE COMMITTEE GAVE US ONE JOB, AND THAT JOB WAS "DEATH TO ALL OUTSIDERS."
BECAUSE THE ONLY THINGS LEFT ALIVE OUT THERE ARE NANO-MACHINE SKINSUIT LOBSTER-ZOMBIES.
WAIT, WHAT WAS THE LAST PART?
CAUTION WET FLOOR
OLD T-SHIRTS
NEW T-SHIRTS
AND WE ARE FRANKLY NOT GOING TO KILL ANY OUTSIDERS WITH FUCKING LED LIGHTS, OKAY? OKAY, COLIN? CAN YOU JUST GIVE ME THAT?
OKAY. FINE. WHATEVER. GOD.
GUYS, GUYS. DO YOU MEAN TO SAY THAT...

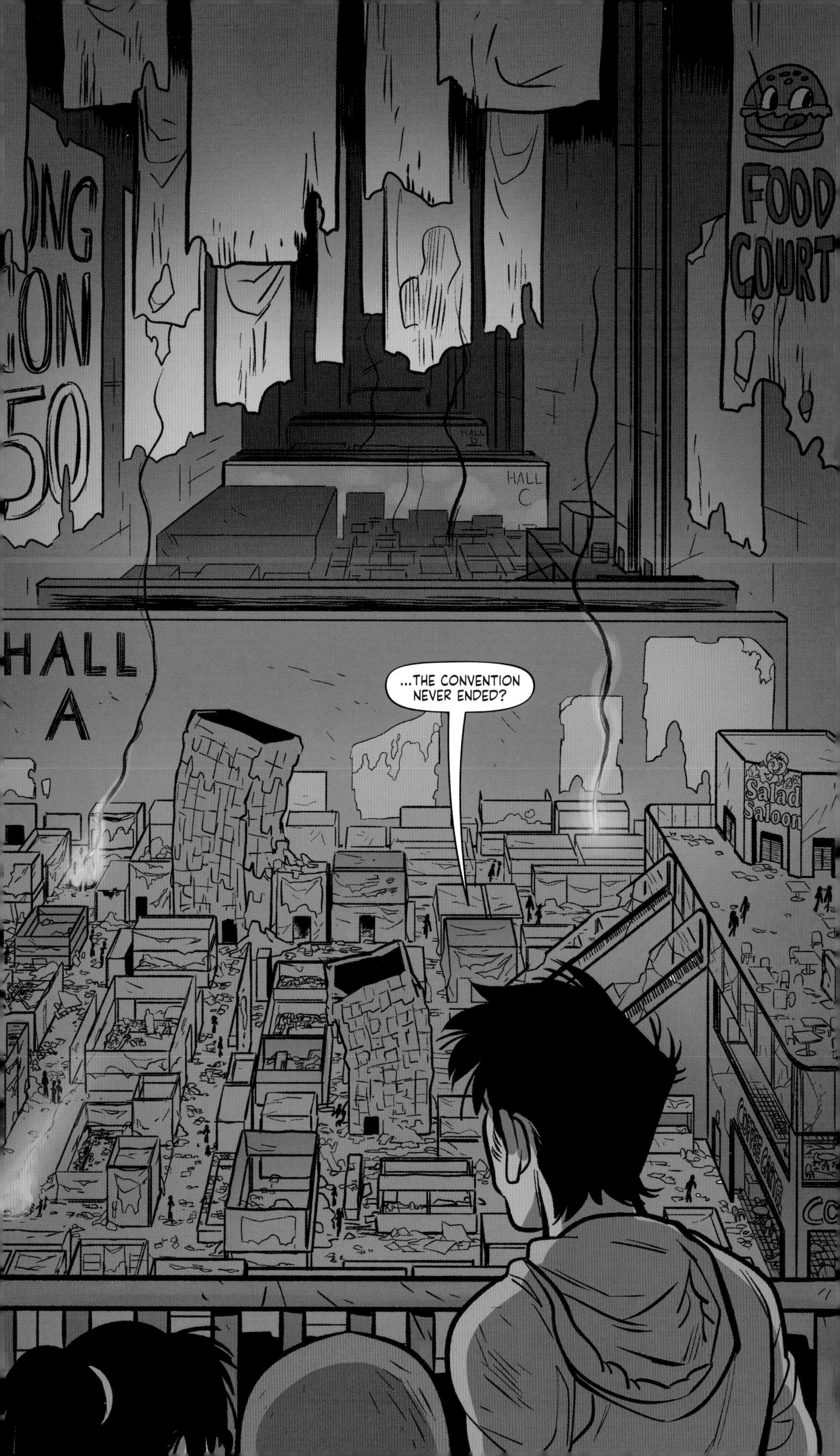

ONG
CON
50
FOOD
COURT
HALL
D
HALL
C
HALL
A
...THE CONVENTION NEVER ENDED?
Salad Saloon

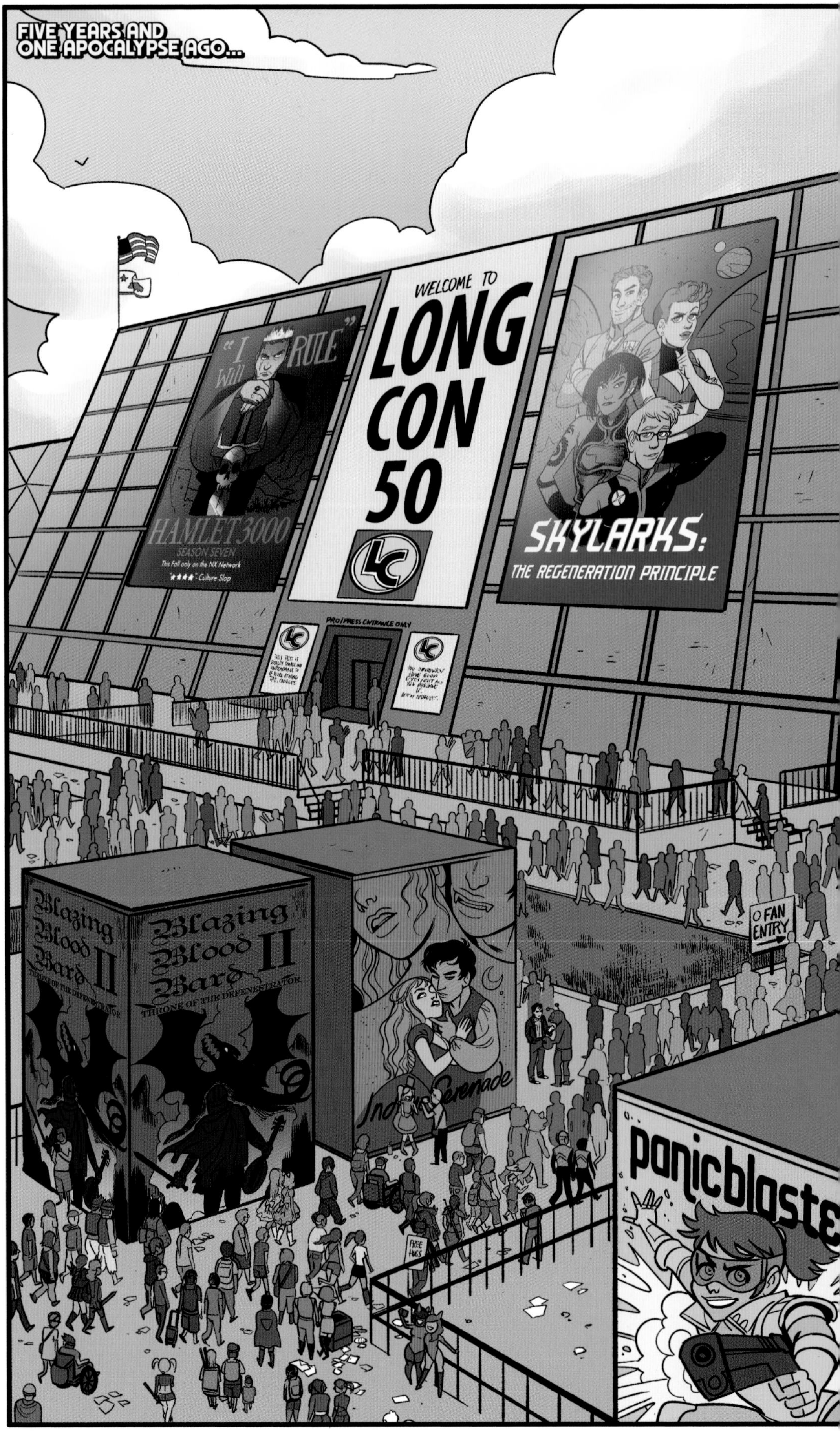

FIVE YEARS AND ONE APOCALYPSE AGO...
"I Will RULE"
HAMLET3000
SEASON SEVEN
This Fall only on the NX Network
★★★★ Culture Slop
WELCOME TO
LONG CON 50
SKYLARKS:
THE REGENERATION PRINCIPLE
PRO/PRESS ENTRANCE ONLY
FAN ENTRY
Blazing Blood Bard II
THRONE OF THE DEFENESTRATOR
Blazing Blood Bard II
THRONE OF THE DEFENESTRATOR
Serenade
FREE HUGS
panicblaste

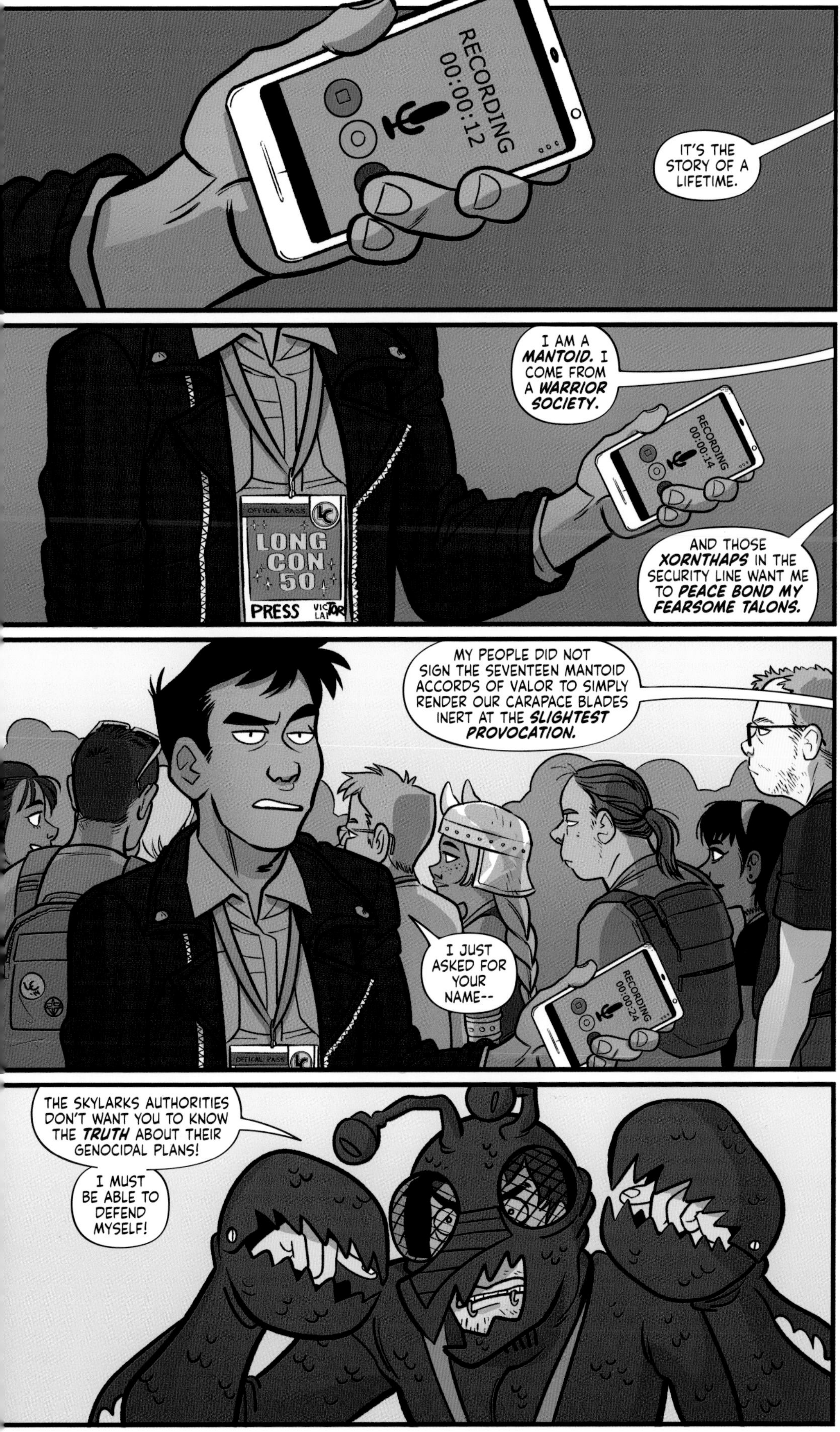
RECORDING
00:00:12
IT'S THE STORY OF A LIFETIME.
I AM A MANTOID. I COME FROM A WARRIOR SOCIETY.
RECORDING
00:00:14
OFFICAL PASS
LC
LONG CON 50
PRESS
VICTOR LAI
AND THOSE XORNTHAPS IN THE SECURITY LINE WANT ME TO PEACE BOND MY FEARSOME TALONS.
MY PEOPLE DID NOT SIGN THE SEVENTEEN MANTOID ACCORDS OF VALOR TO SIMPLY RENDER OUR CARAPACE BLADES INERT AT THE SLIGHTEST PROVOCATION.
I JUST ASKED FOR YOUR NAME--
RECORDING
00:00:24
OFFICAL PASS
THE SKYLARKS AUTHORITIES DON'T WANT YOU TO KNOW THE TRUTH ABOUT THEIR GENOCIDAL PLANS!
I MUST BE ABLE TO DEFEND MYSELF!

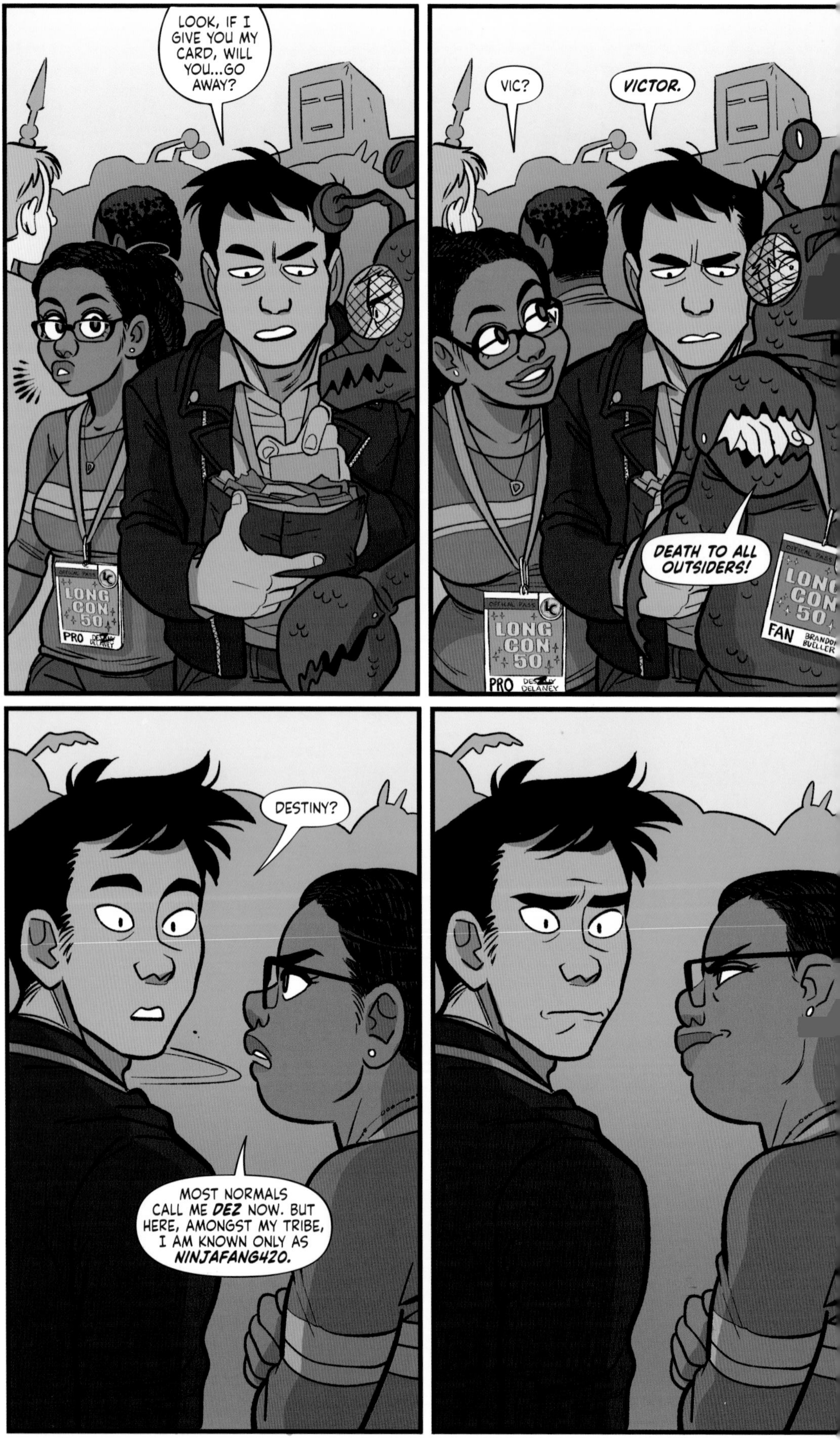
LOOK, IF I GIVE YOU MY CARD, WILL YOU...GO AWAY?
LONG CON 50
PRO
VIC?
VICTOR.
DEATH TO ALL OUTSIDERS!
LONG CON 50
PRO
DELANEY
FAN
BULLER
DESTINY?
MOST NORMALS CALL ME DEZ NOW. BUT HERE, AMONGST MY TRIBE, I AM KNOWN ONLY AS NINJAFANG420.

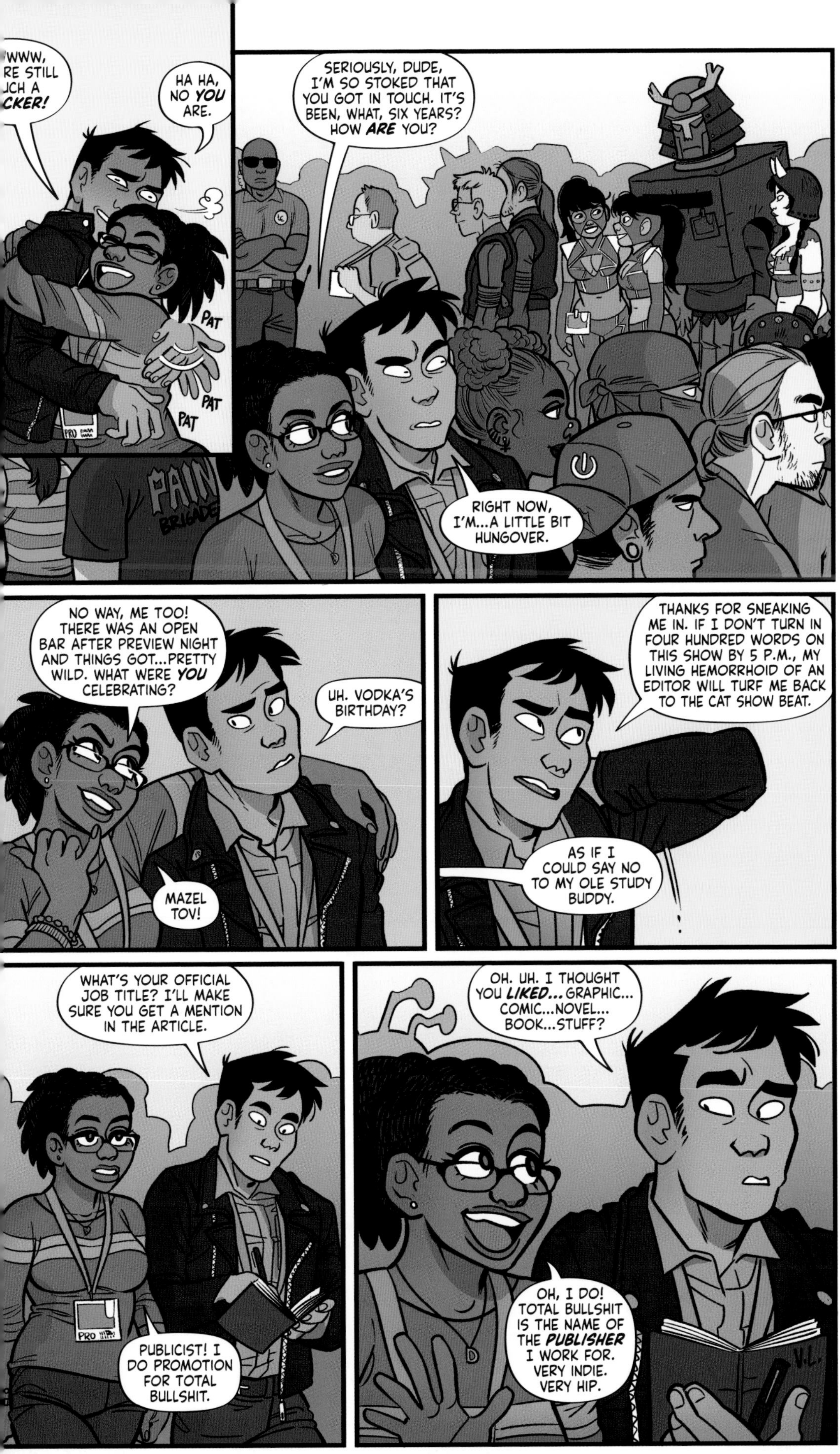
WWW, RE STILL CH A CKER!
HA HA, NO YOU ARE.
PAT PAT PAT
PRO
SERIOUSLY, DUDE, I'M SO STOKED THAT YOU GOT IN TOUCH. IT'S BEEN, WHAT, SIX YEARS? HOW ARE YOU?
PAIN BRIGADE
RIGHT NOW, I'M...A LITTLE BIT HUNGOVER.
NO WAY, ME TOO! THERE WAS AN OPEN BAR AFTER PREVIEW NIGHT AND THINGS GOT...PRETTY WILD. WHAT WERE YOU CELEBRATING?
UH. VODKA'S BIRTHDAY?
MAZEL TOV!
THANKS FOR SNEAKING ME IN. IF I DON'T TURN IN FOUR HUNDRED WORDS ON THIS SHOW BY 5 P.M., MY LIVING HEMORRHOID OF AN EDITOR WILL TURF ME BACK TO THE CAT SHOW BEAT.
AS IF I COULD SAY NO TO MY OLE STUDY BUDDY.
WHAT'S YOUR OFFICIAL JOB TITLE? I'LL MAKE SURE YOU GET A MENTION IN THE ARTICLE.
PRO
PUBLICIST! I DO PROMOTION FOR TOTAL BULLSHIT.
OH. UH. I THOUGHT YOU LIKED... GRAPHIC... COMIC...NOVEL... BOOK...STUFF?
OH, I DO! TOTAL BULLSHIT IS THE NAME OF THE PUBLISHER I WORK FOR. VERY INDIE. VERY HIP.
V.L.

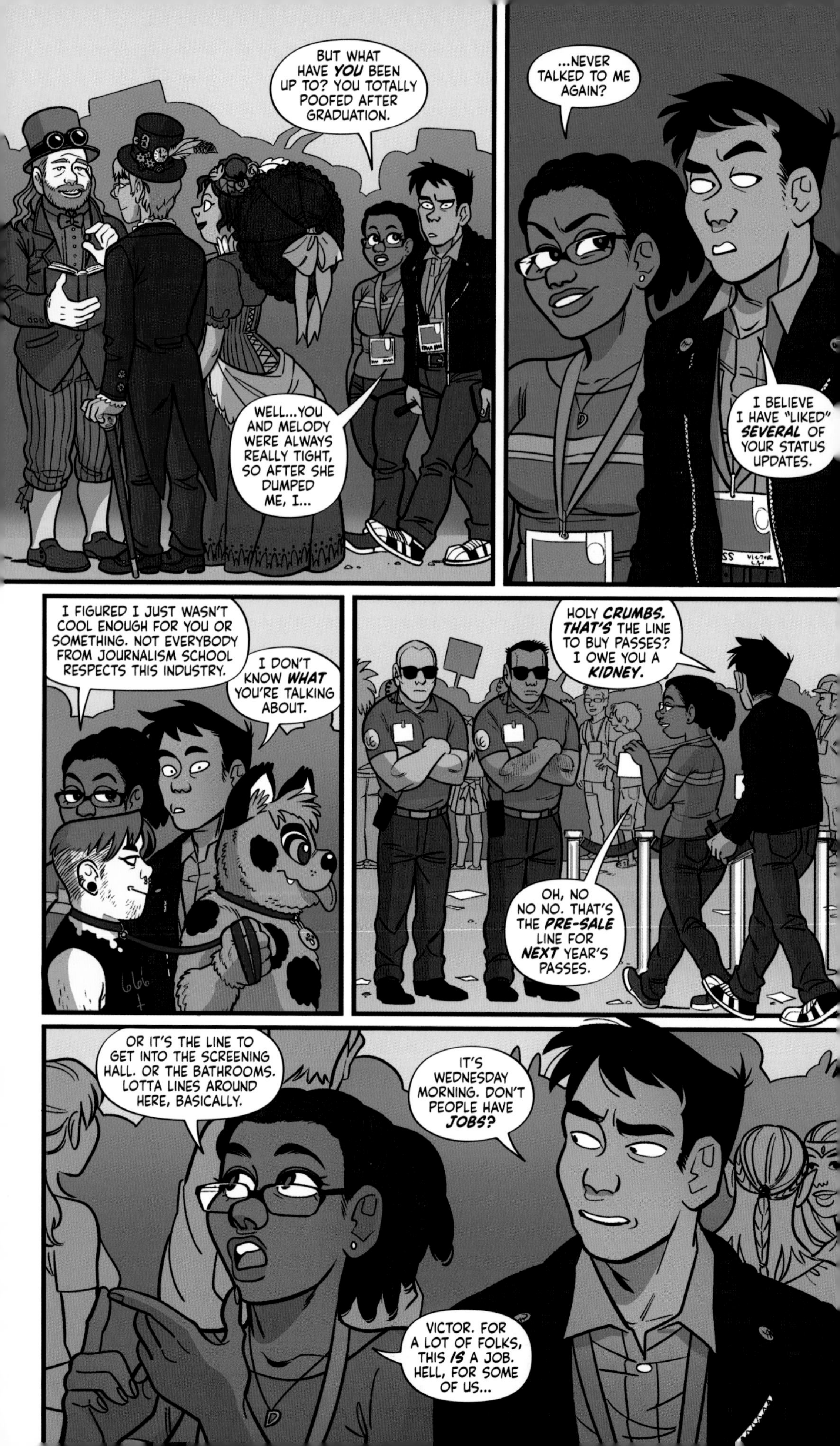

BUT WHAT HAVE *YOU* BEEN UP TO? YOU TOTALLY POOFED AFTER GRADUATION.
WELL...YOU AND MELODY WERE ALWAYS REALLY TIGHT, SO AFTER SHE DUMPED ME, I...
...NEVER TALKED TO ME AGAIN?
I BELIEVE I HAVE "LIKED" *SEVERAL* OF YOUR STATUS UPDATES.
I FIGURED I JUST WASN'T COOL ENOUGH FOR YOU OR SOMETHING. NOT EVERYBODY FROM JOURNALISM SCHOOL RESPECTS THIS INDUSTRY.
I DON'T KNOW *WHAT* YOU'RE TALKING ABOUT.
HOLY *CRUMBS. THAT'S* THE LINE TO BUY PASSES? I OWE YOU A *KIDNEY.*
OH, NO NO NO. THAT'S THE *PRE-SALE* LINE FOR *NEXT* YEAR'S PASSES.
OR IT'S THE LINE TO GET INTO THE SCREENING HALL. OR THE BATHROOMS. LOTTA LINES AROUND HERE, BASICALLY.
IT'S WEDNESDAY MORNING. DON'T PEOPLE HAVE *JOBS?*
VICTOR. FOR A LOT OF FOLKS, THIS *IS* A JOB. HELL, FOR SOME OF US...

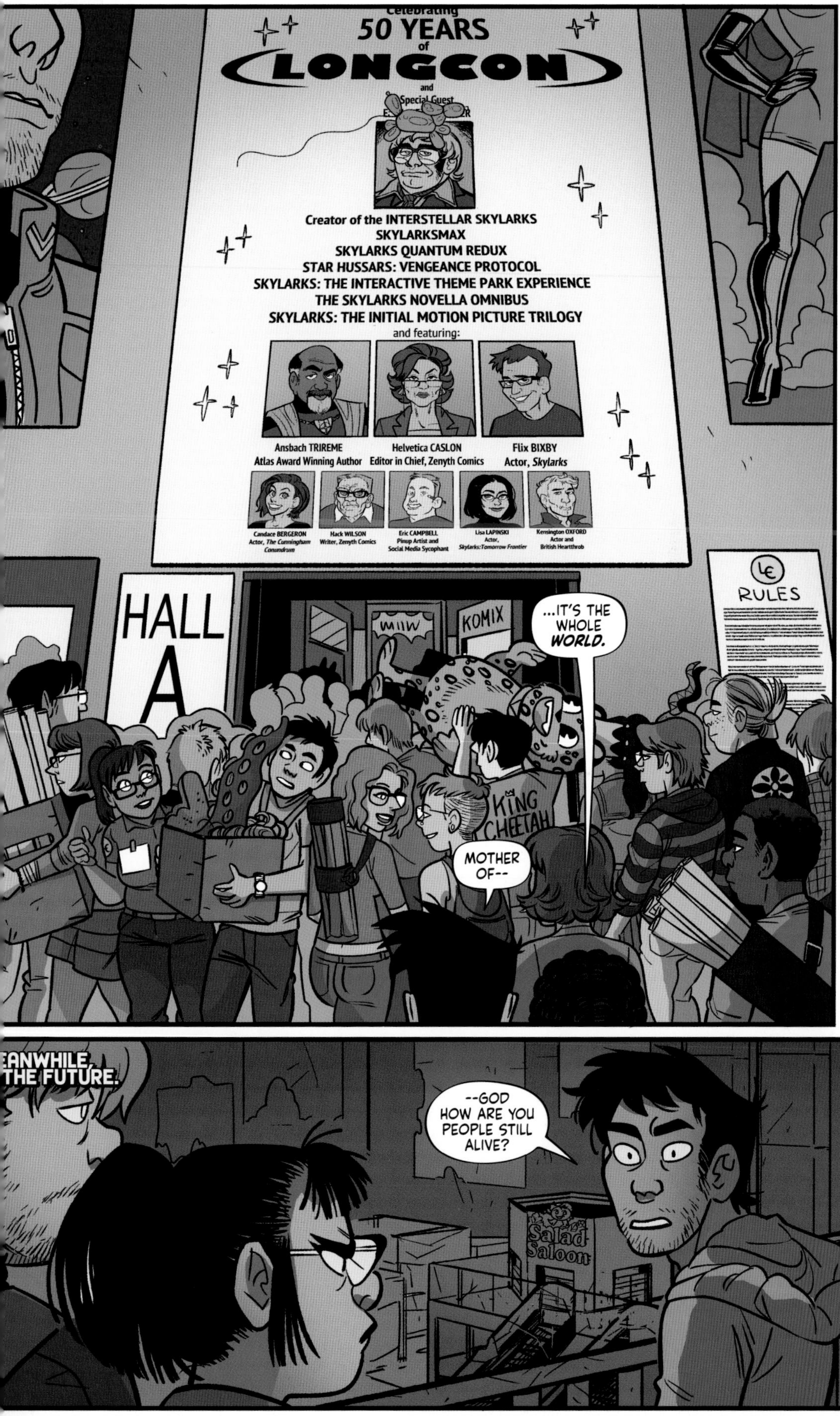

Celebrating
50 YEARS
of
LONGCON
and
Special Guest
Creator of the INTERSTELLAR SKYLARKS
SKYLARKSMAX
SKYLARKS QUANTUM REDUX
STAR HUSSARS: VENGEANCE PROTOCOL
SKYLARKS: THE INTERACTIVE THEME PARK EXPERIENCE
THE SKYLARKS NOVELLA OMNIBUS
SKYLARKS: THE INITIAL MOTION PICTURE TRILOGY
and featuring:
Ansbach TRIREME
Atlas Award Winning Author
Helvetica CASLON
Editor in Chief, Zenyth Comics
Flix BIXBY
Actor, Skylarks
Candace BERGERON
Actor, The Cunningham Conundrum
Hack WILSON
Writer, Zenyth Comics
Eric CAMPBELL
Pinup Artist and Social Media Sycophant
Lisa LAPINSKI
Actor, Skylarks:Tomorrow Frontier
Kensington OXFORD
Actor and British Heartthrob
HALL A
KOMIX
RULES
...IT'S THE WHOLE WORLD.
KING CHEETAH
MOTHER OF--
EANWHILE, THE FUTURE.
--GOD HOW ARE YOU PEOPLE STILL ALIVE?
Salad Saloon

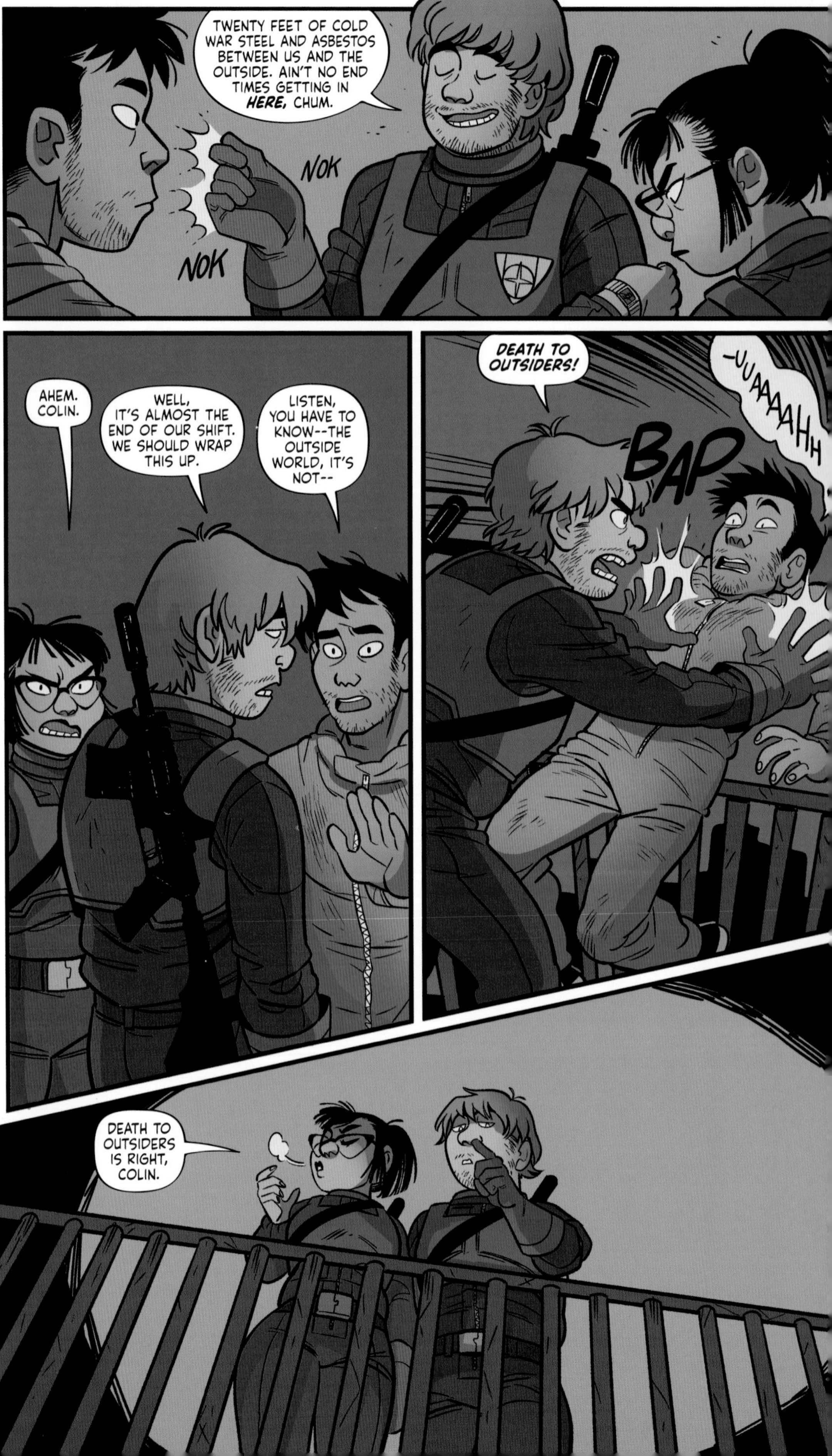
TWENTY FEET OF COLD WAR STEEL AND ASBESTOS BETWEEN US AND THE OUTSIDE. AIN'T NO END TIMES GETTING IN **HERE,** CHUM.
NOK
NOK
AHEM. COLIN.
WELL, IT'S ALMOST THE END OF OUR SHIFT. WE SHOULD WRAP THIS UP.
LISTEN, YOU HAVE TO KNOW--THE OUTSIDE WORLD, IT'S NOT--
DEATH TO OUTSIDERS!
-UUAAAAAHH
BAP
DEATH TO OUTSIDERS IS RIGHT, COLIN.

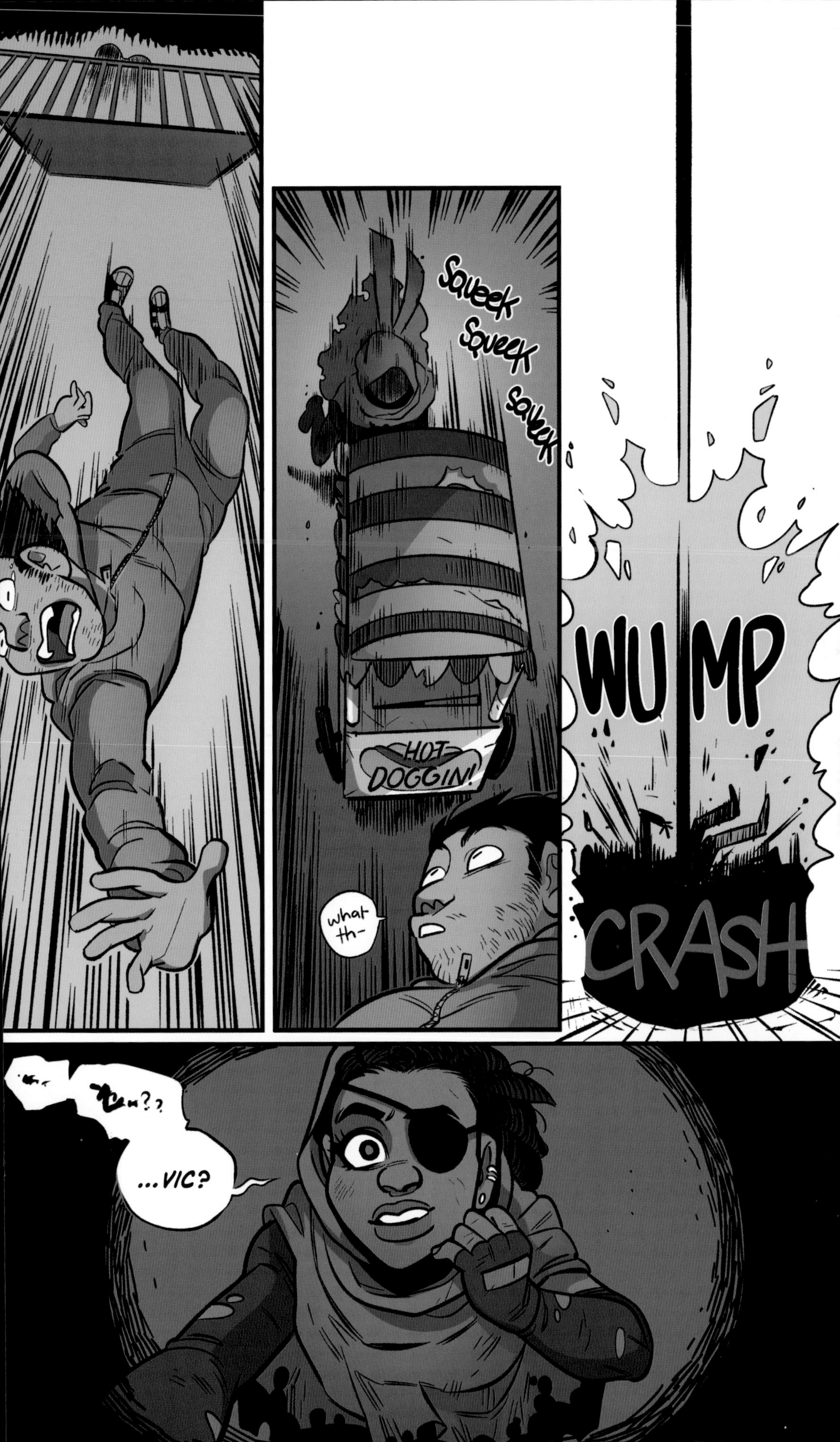

Squeek
Squeek
Squeek
HOT DOGGIN!
what th-
WUMP
CRASH
...VIC?

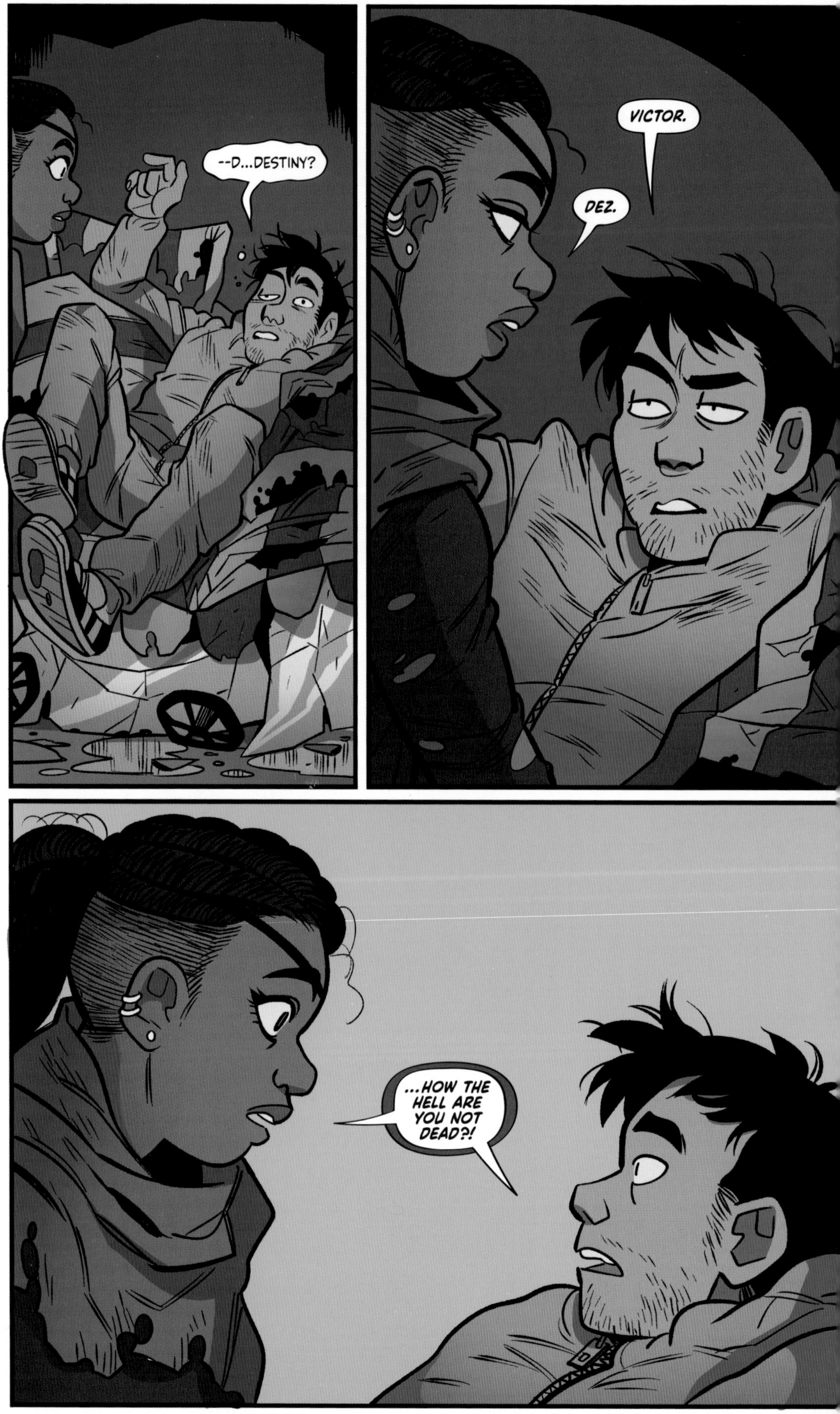
--D...DESTINY?
VICTOR.
DEZ.
...HOW THE HELL ARE YOU NOT DEAD?!

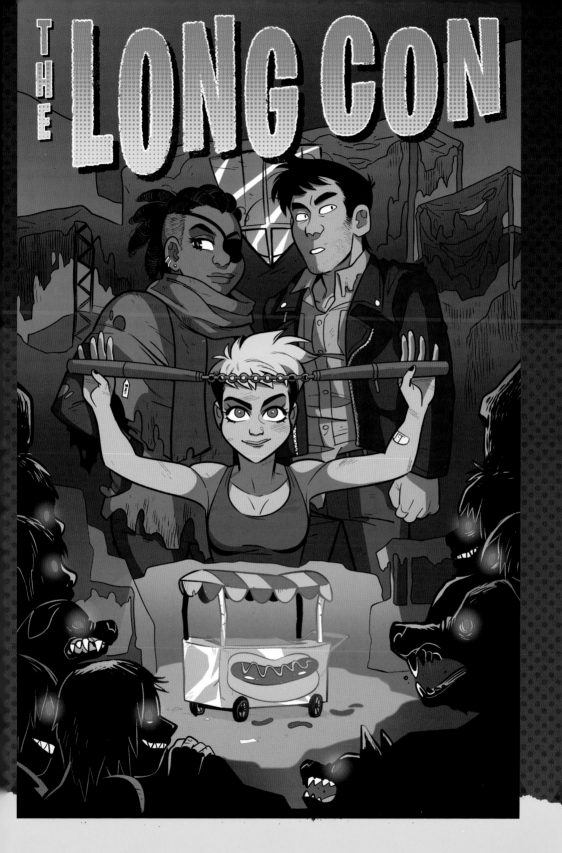

CHAPTER 2: AN APPOINTMENT WITH DESTINY

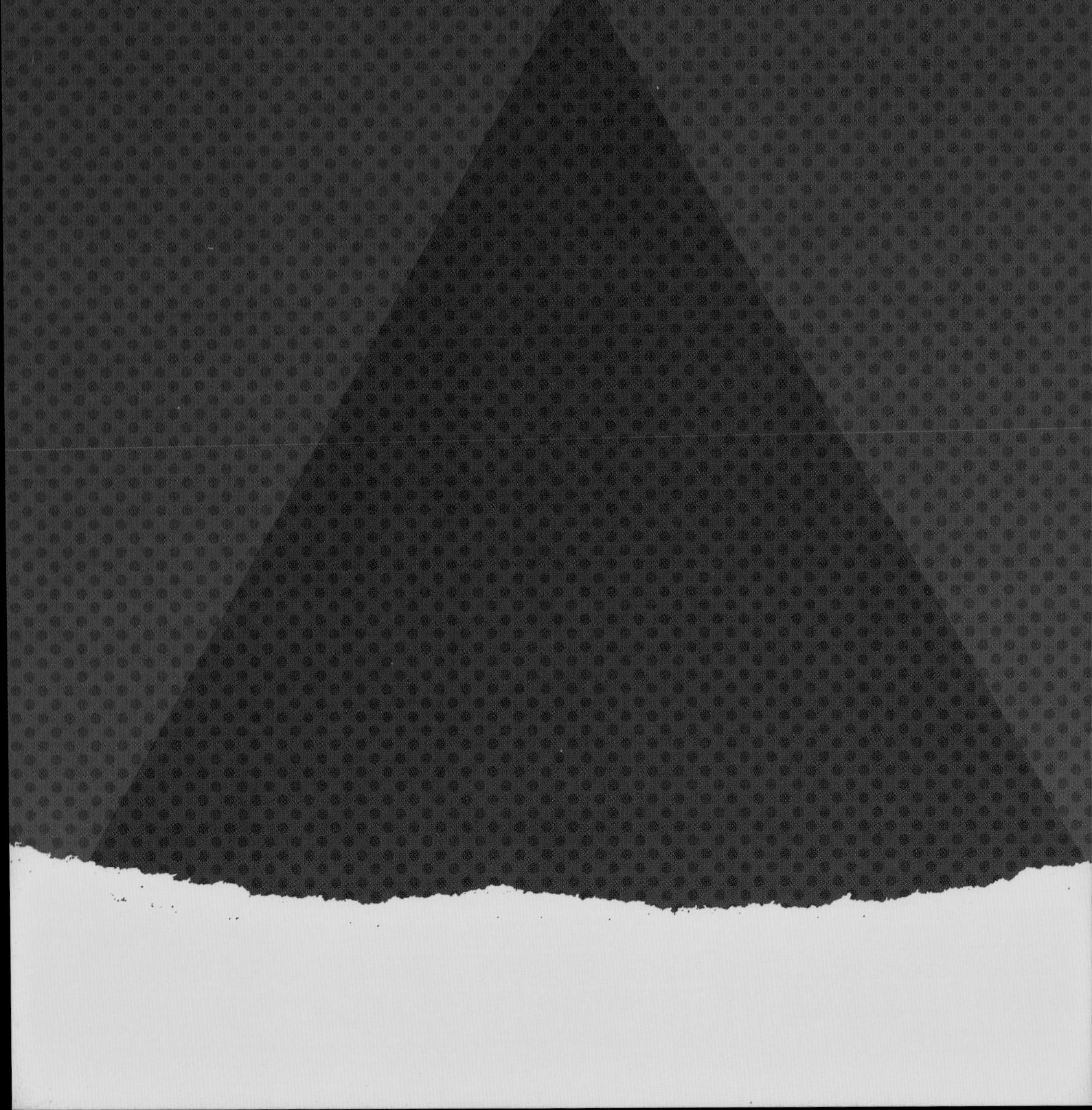

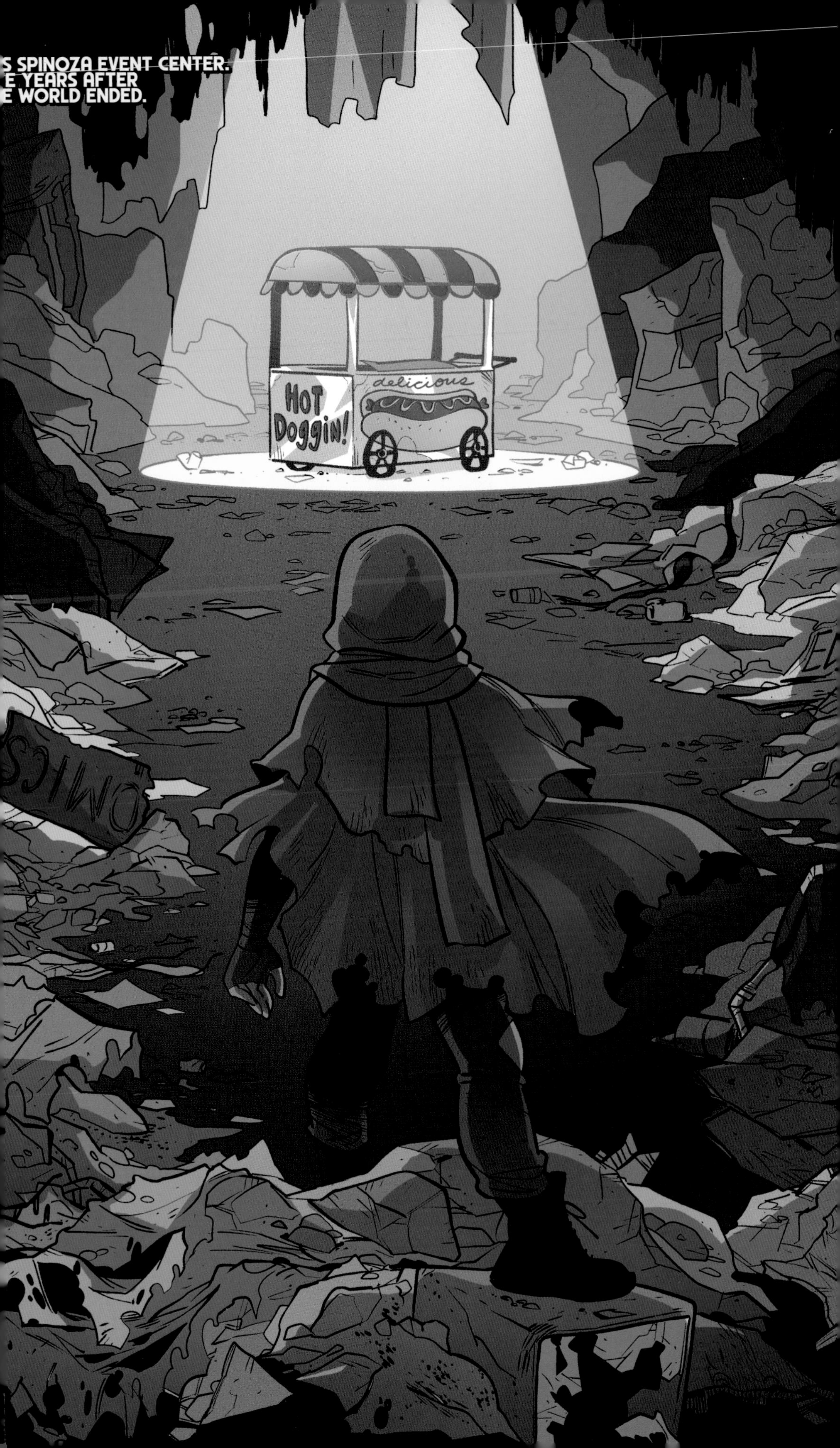
S SPINOZA EVENT CENTER.
E YEARS AFTER
E WORLD ENDED.
HOT Doggin!
delicious

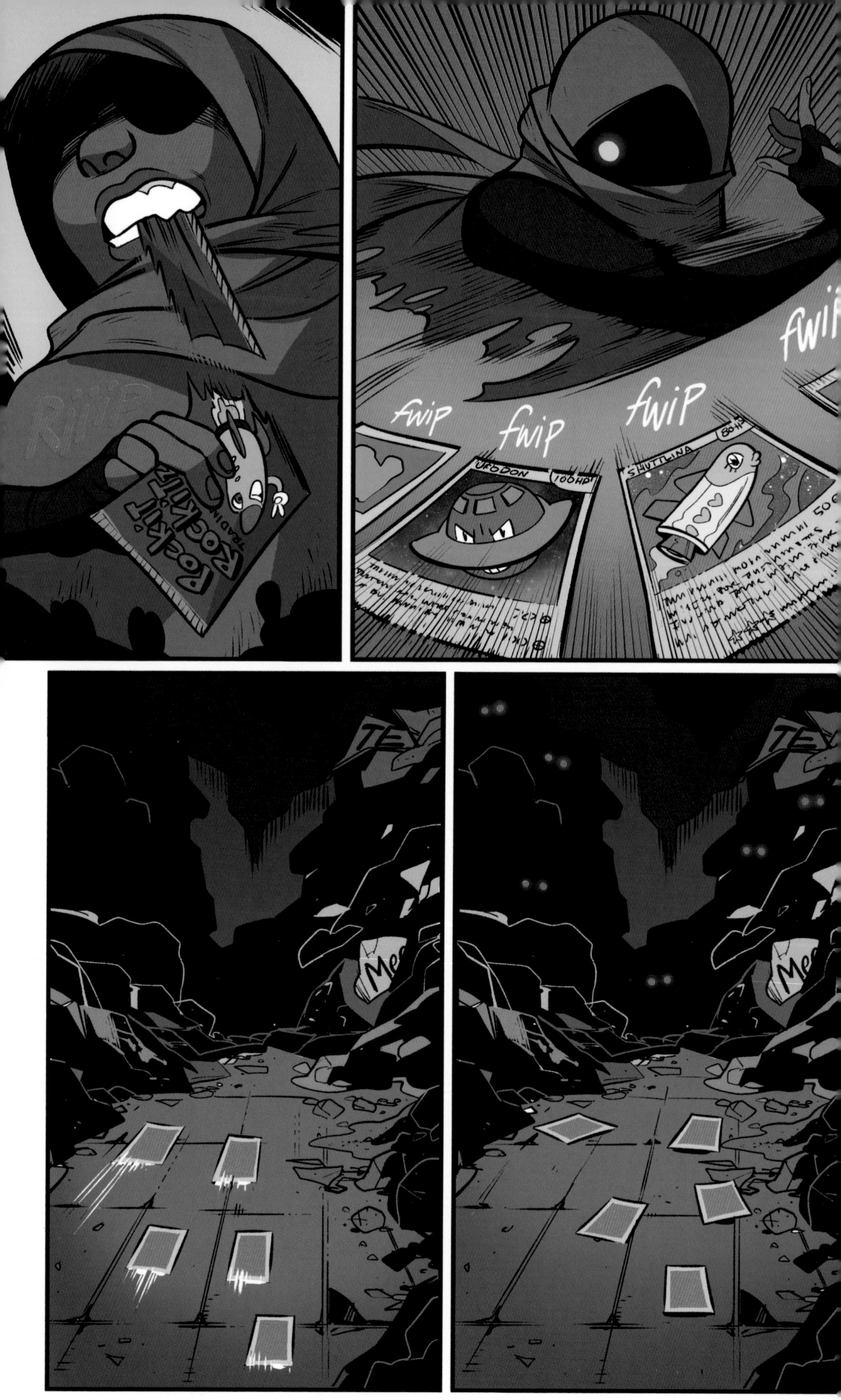
fwip
fwip
fwip
fwip
SHUTTLINA
100HP

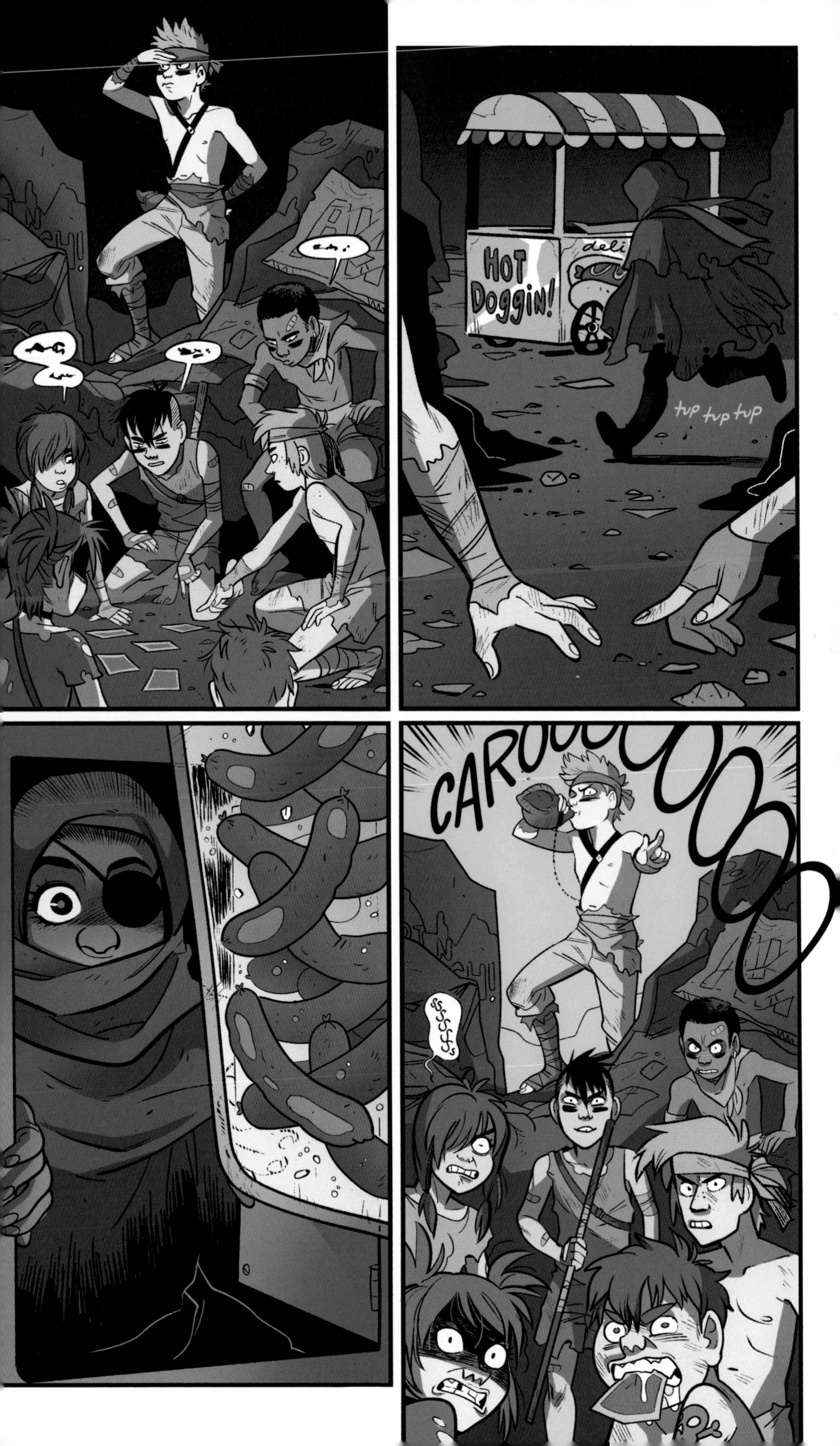
HOT DOGGIN!
deli
tup tup tup
CAROOOOOOO
SSSSSs

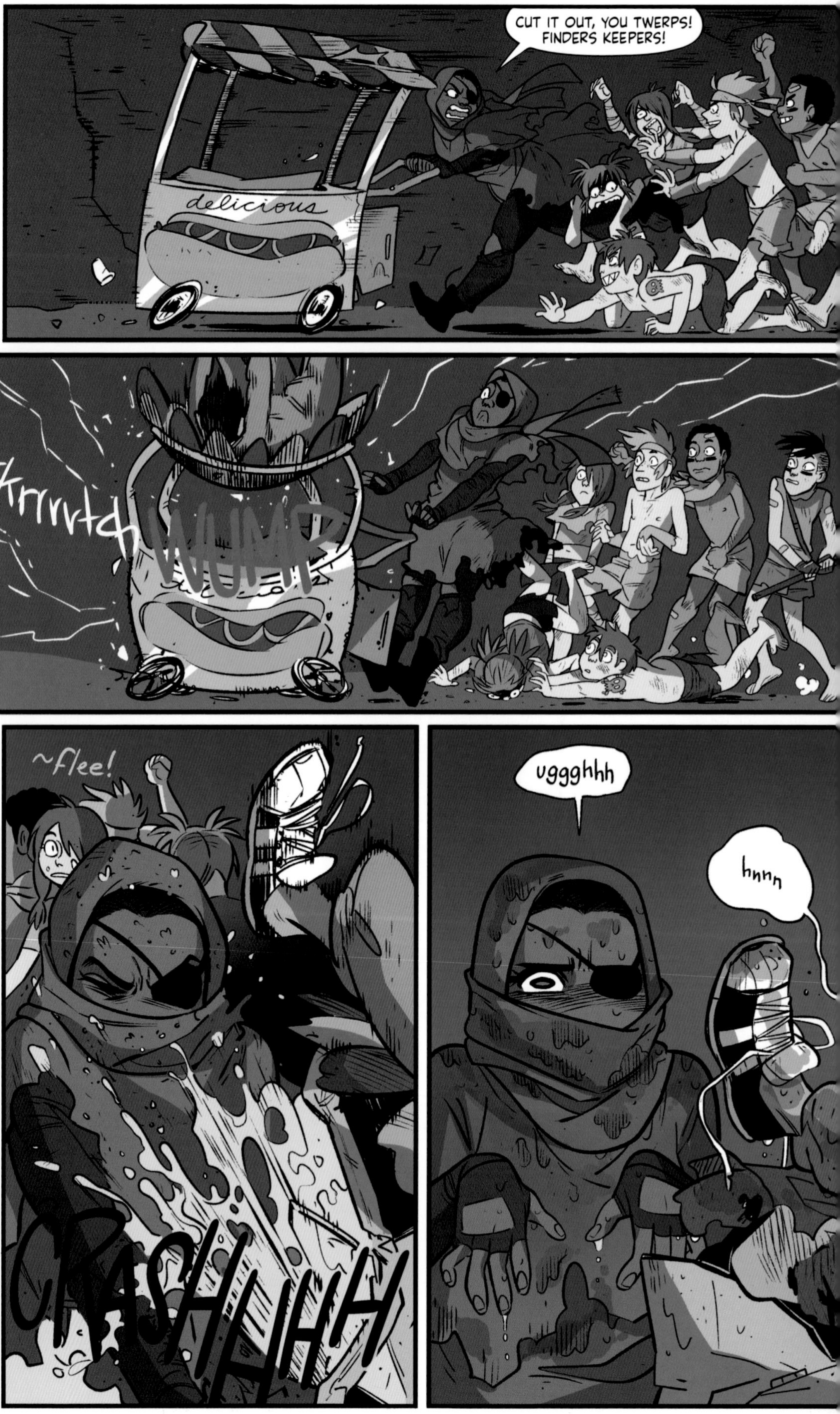
CUT IT OUT, YOU TWERPS! FINDERS KEEPERS!
delicious
Skrrrvtch
WUMP
~flee!
CRASHHHH
uggghhh
hnnn

WHERE HAVE YOU BEEN *FOR THE LAST FIVE YEARS?!*

ABOUT... THREE EXITS NORTH ON THE 5?

WOULD HAVE DROPPED BY SOONER, BUT ACCORDING TO THE AUTHORITIES--

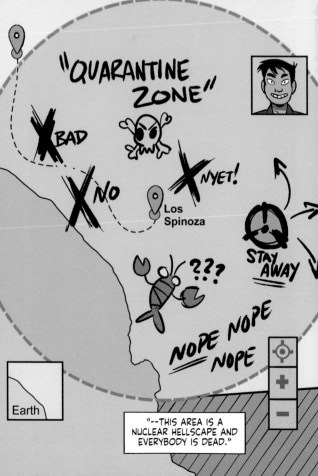

"QUARANTINE ZONE"

X BAD

X NO

X NYET!

Los Spinoza

???

STAY AWAY

NOPE NOPE NOPE

Earth

"--THIS AREA IS A NUCLEAR HELLSCAPE AND EVERYBODY IS DEAD."

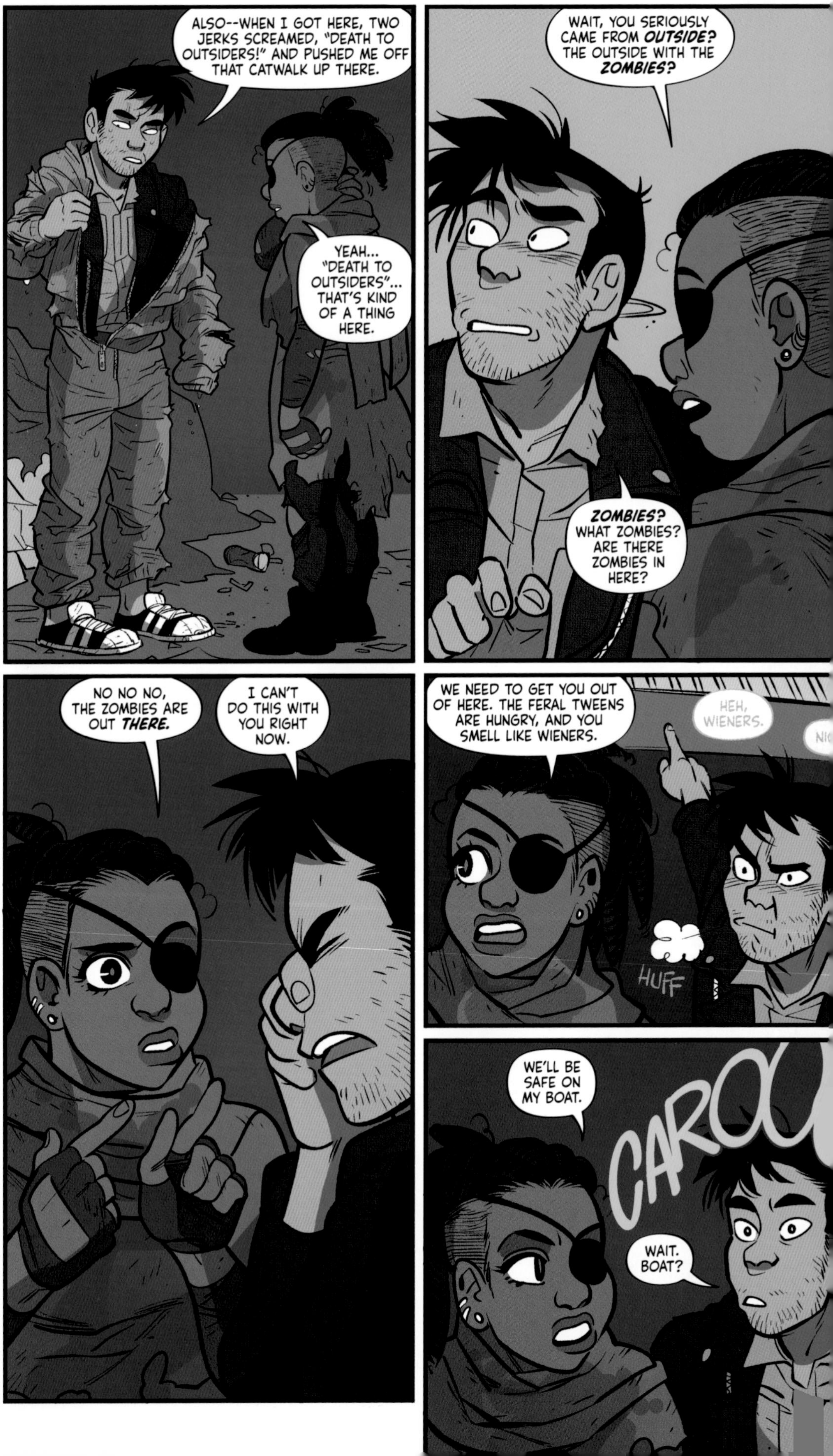
ALSO--WHEN I GOT HERE, TWO JERKS SCREAMED, "DEATH TO OUTSIDERS!" AND PUSHED ME OFF THAT CATWALK UP THERE.
YEAH... "DEATH TO OUTSIDERS"... THAT'S KIND OF A THING HERE.
WAIT, YOU SERIOUSLY CAME FROM *OUTSIDE?* THE OUTSIDE WITH THE ***ZOMBIES?***
ZOMBIES? WHAT ZOMBIES? ARE THERE ZOMBIES IN HERE?
NO NO NO, THE ZOMBIES ARE OUT ***THERE.***
I CAN'T DO THIS WITH YOU RIGHT NOW.
WE NEED TO GET YOU OUT OF HERE. THE FERAL TWEENS ARE HUNGRY, AND YOU SMELL LIKE WIENERS.
HEH, WIENERS.
HUFF
WE'LL BE SAFE ON MY BOAT.
WAIT. BOAT?

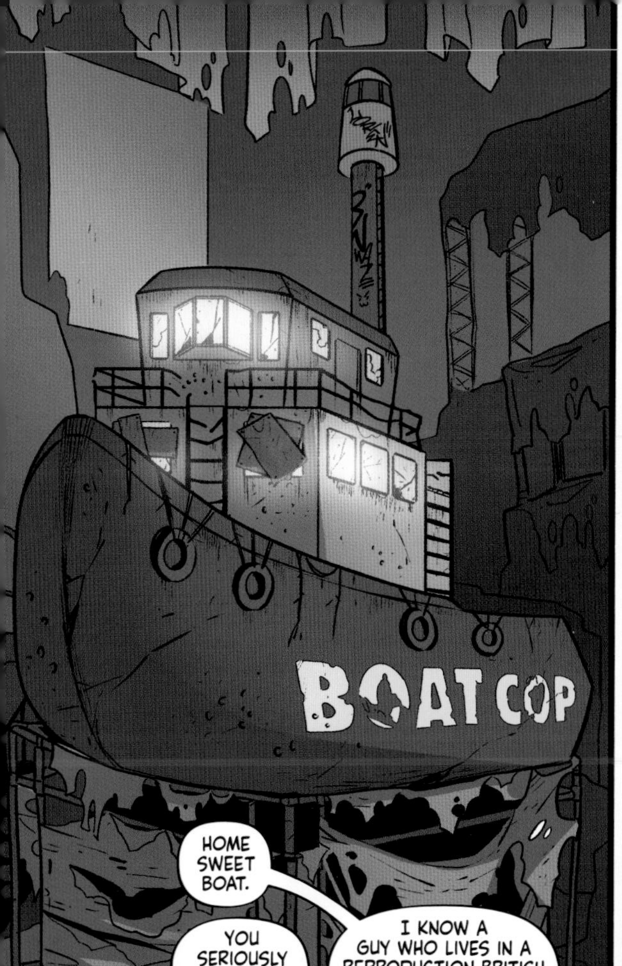
BOATCOP
HOME SWEET BOAT.
YOU SERIOUSLY LIVE IN THIS THING?
I KNOW A GUY WHO LIVES IN A REPRODUCTION BRITISH PHONE BOOTH. TRUST ME, IT IS ***NOT*** BIGGER ON THE INSIDE.

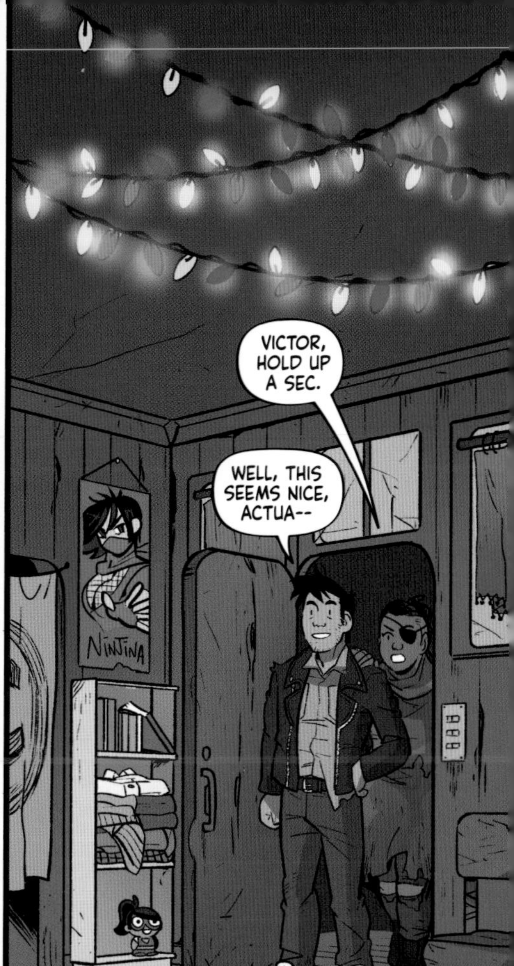
NINJINA
VICTOR, HOLD UP A SEC.
WELL, THIS SEEMS NICE, ACTUA--

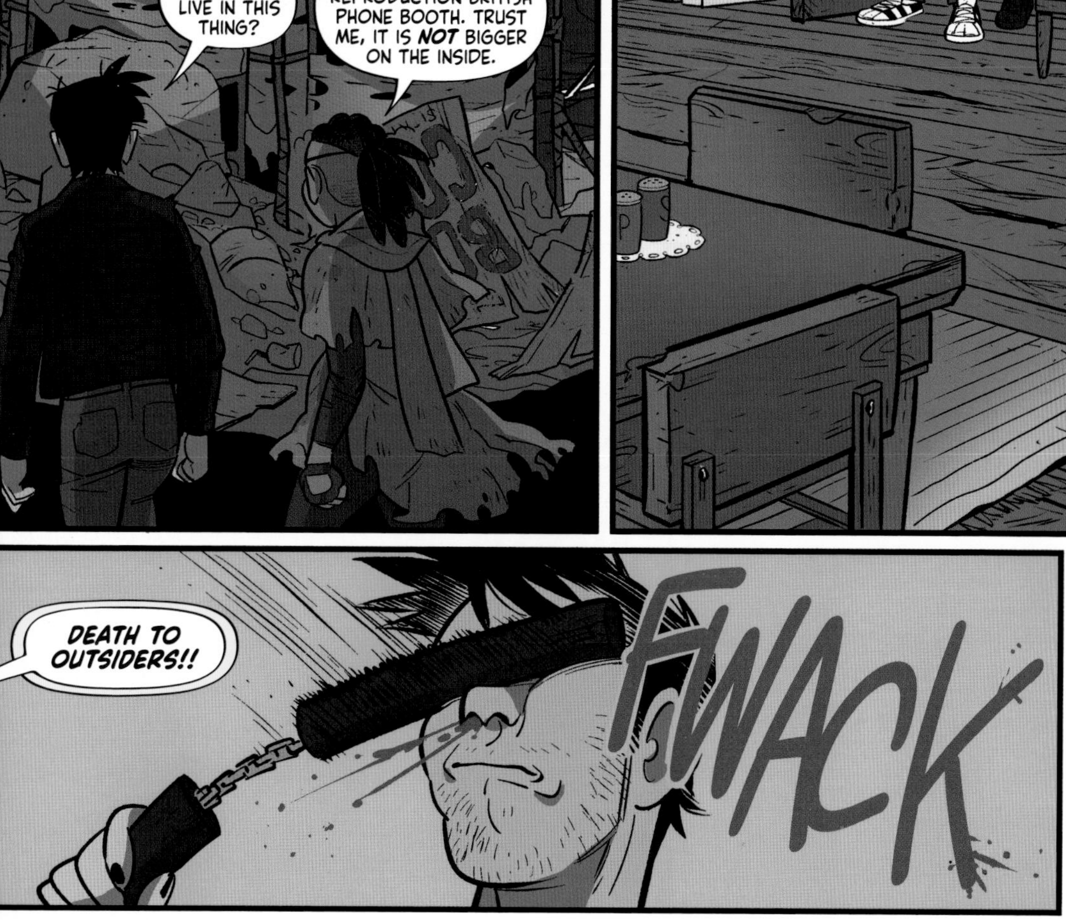
DEATH TO OUTSIDERS!!
FWACK

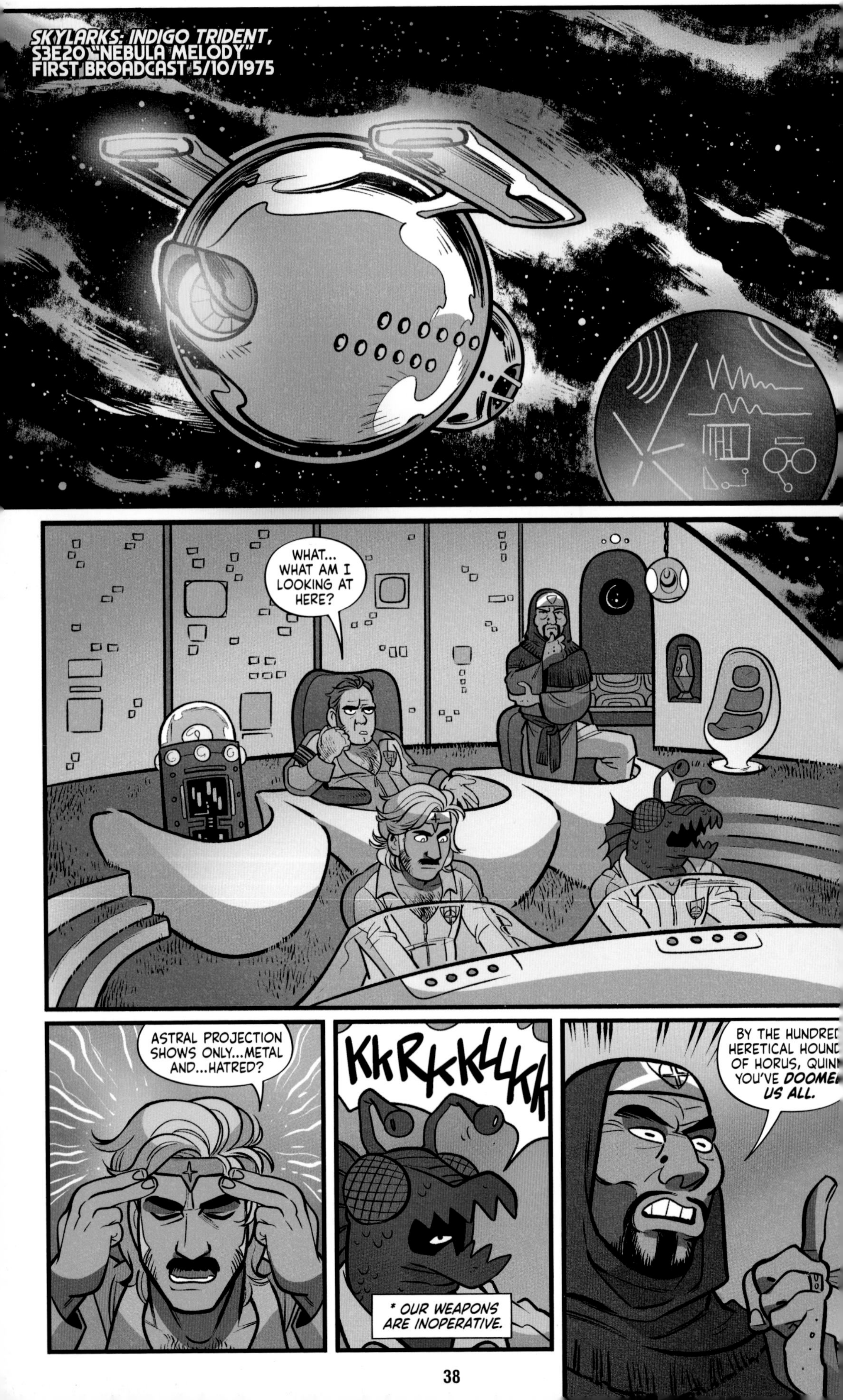
SKYLARKS: INDIGO TRIDENT,
S3E20 "NEBULA MELODY"
FIRST BROADCAST 5/10/1975
WHAT... WHAT AM I LOOKING AT HERE?
ASTRAL PROJECTION SHOWS ONLY...METAL AND...HATRED?
KKRKKLLKK
* OUR WEAPONS ARE INOPERATIVE.
BY THE HUNDRED HERETICAL HOUND OF HORUS, QUIN YOU'VE **DOOME** **US ALL.**

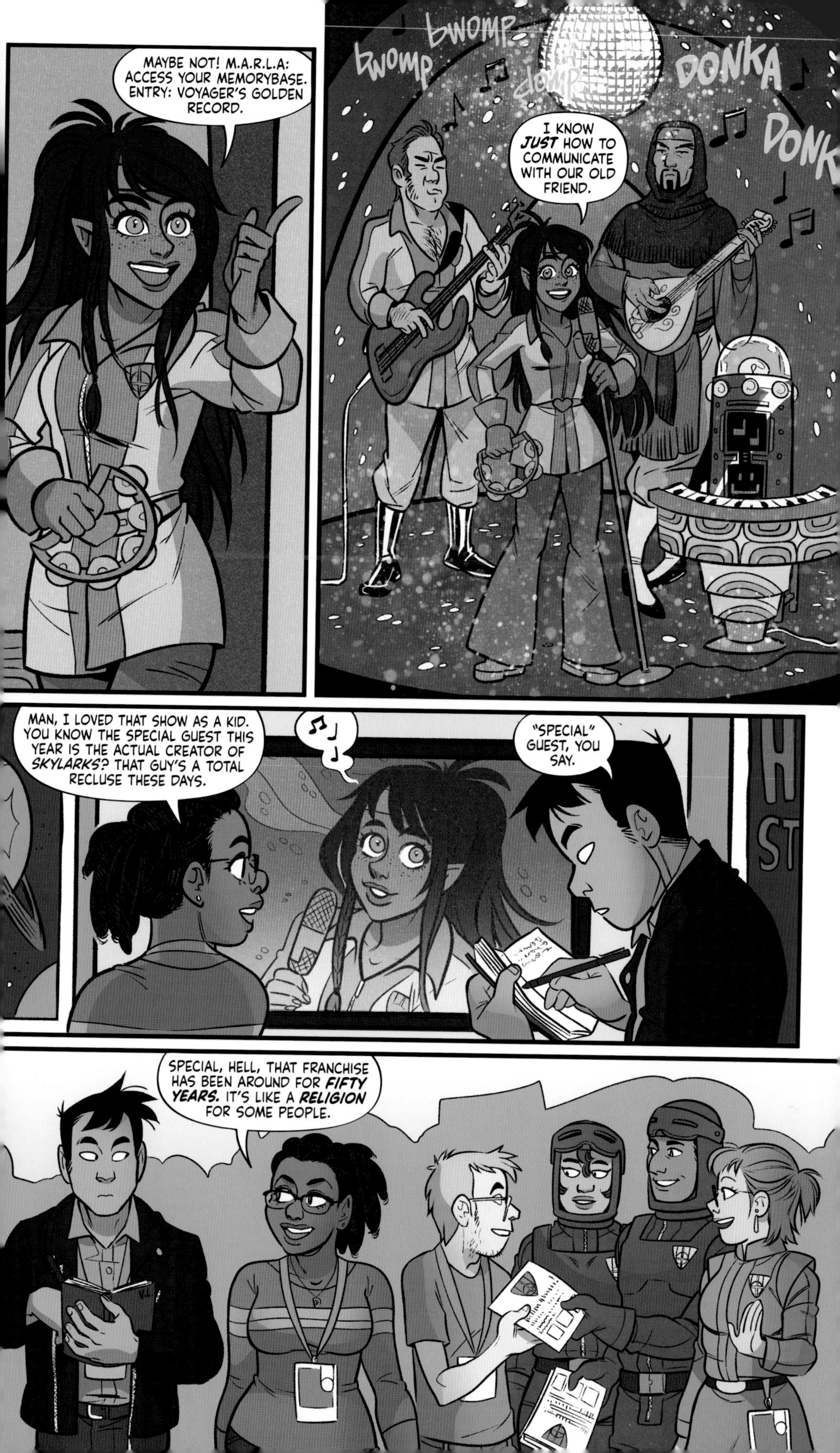
MAYBE NOT! M.A.R.L.A: ACCESS YOUR MEMORYBASE. ENTRY: VOYAGER'S GOLDEN RECORD.
BWOMP
BWOMP
DOMP
DONKA
DONK
I KNOW *JUST* HOW TO COMMUNICATE WITH OUR OLD FRIEND.
MAN, I LOVED THAT SHOW AS A KID. YOU KNOW THE SPECIAL GUEST THIS YEAR IS THE ACTUAL CREATOR OF *SKYLARKS*? THAT GUY'S A TOTAL RECLUSE THESE DAYS.
"SPECIAL" GUEST, YOU SAY.
SPECIAL, HELL, THAT FRANCHISE HAS BEEN AROUND FOR *FIFTY YEARS.* IT'S LIKE A *RELIGION* FOR SOME PEOPLE.

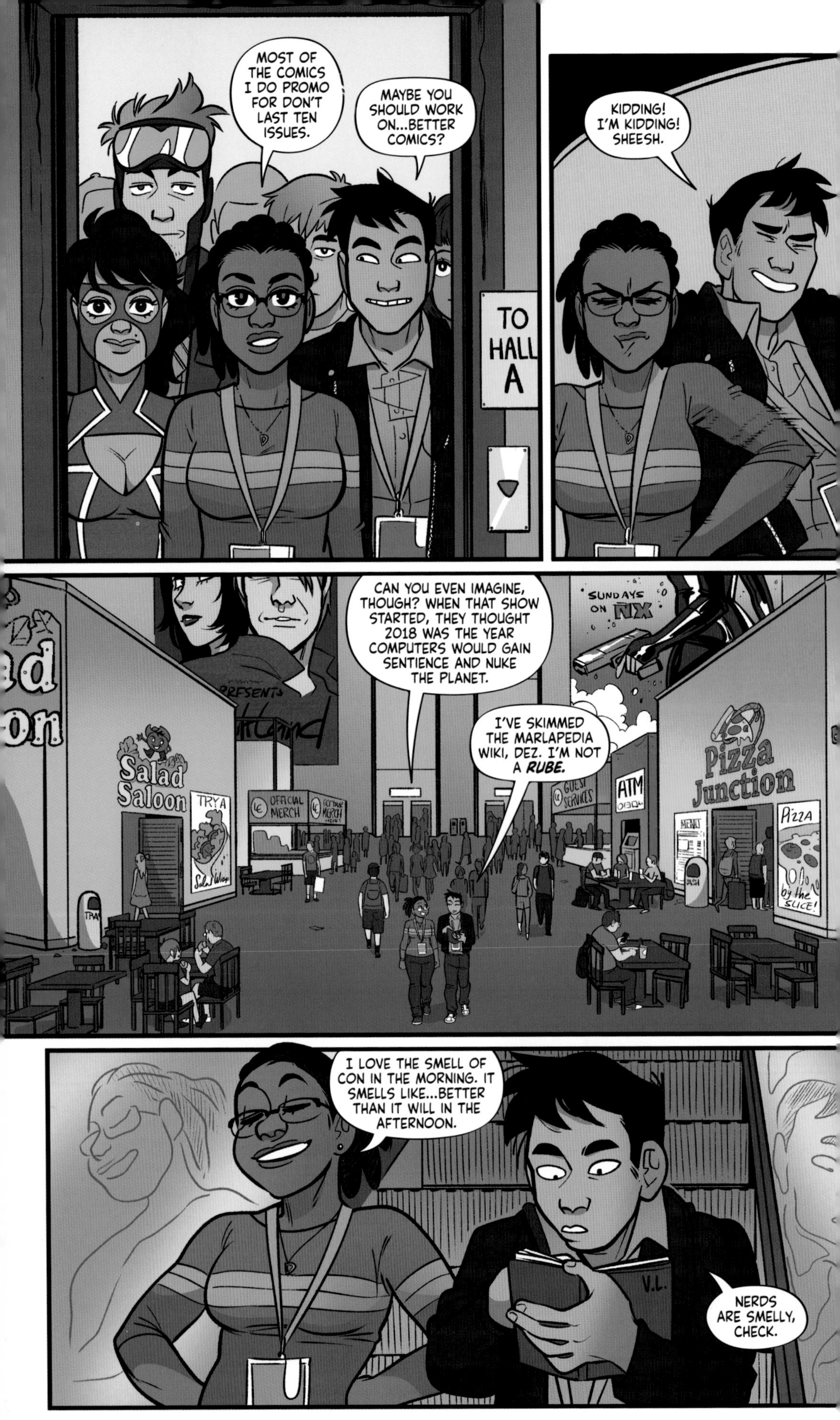
MOST OF THE COMICS I DO PROMO FOR DON'T LAST TEN ISSUES.
MAYBE YOU SHOULD WORK ON...BETTER COMICS?
TO HALL A
KIDDING! I'M KIDDING! SHEESH.
CAN YOU EVEN IMAGINE, THOUGH? WHEN THAT SHOW STARTED, THEY THOUGHT 2018 WAS THE YEAR COMPUTERS WOULD GAIN SENTIENCE AND NUKE THE PLANET.
I'VE SKIMMED THE MARLAPEDIA WIKI, DEZ. I'M NOT A ***RUBE.***
SUNDAYS ON NX
Salad Saloon
TRY A
OFFICIAL MERCH
GUEST SERVICES
ATM
Pizza Junction
MENU
PIZZA by the SLICE!
I LOVE THE SMELL OF CON IN THE MORNING. IT SMELLS LIKE...BETTER THAN IT WILL IN THE AFTERNOON.
V.L.
NERDS ARE SMELLY, CHECK.

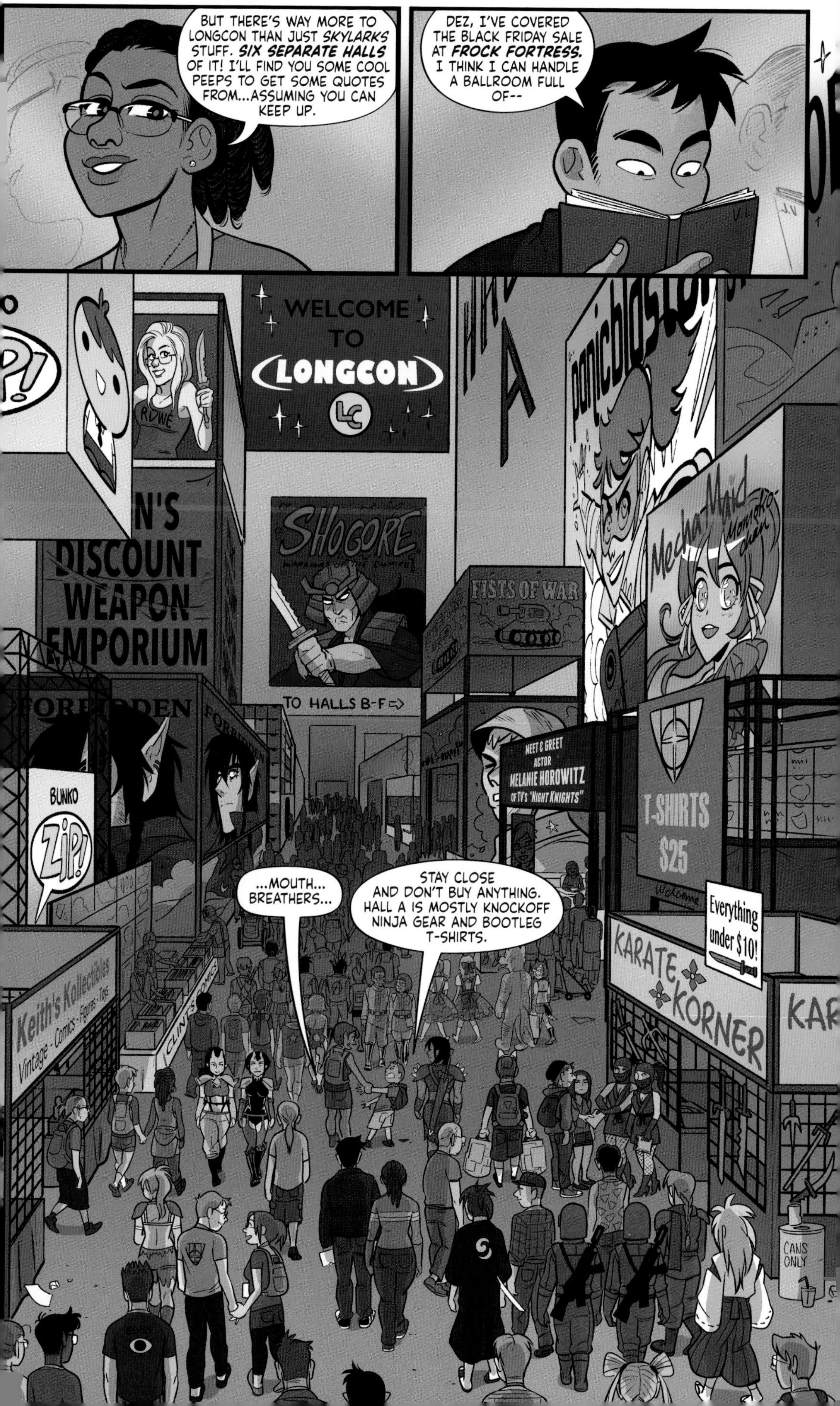
BUT THERE'S WAY MORE TO LONGCON THAN JUST SKYLARKS STUFF. SIX SEPARATE HALLS OF IT! I'LL FIND YOU SOME COOL PEEPS TO GET SOME QUOTES FROM...ASSUMING YOU CAN KEEP UP.
DEZ, I'VE COVERED THE BLACK FRIDAY SALE AT FROCK FORTRESS. I THINK I CAN HANDLE A BALLROOM FULL OF--
WELCOME TO LONGCON
LC
SHOGORE
N'S DISCOUNT WEAPON EMPORIUM
FISTS OF WAR
Mecha Maid Momoko-chan
FORBIDDEN
BUNKO
ZIP!
TO HALLS B-F
MEET & GREET ACTOR MELANIE HOROWITZ OF TV'S "NIGHT KNIGHTS"
T-SHIRTS $25
...MOUTH... BREATHERS...
STAY CLOSE AND DON'T BUY ANYTHING. HALL A IS MOSTLY KNOCKOFF NINJA GEAR AND BOOTLEG T-SHIRTS.
Everything under $10!
KARATE KORNER
Keith's Kollectibles
Vintage - Comics - Figures - Toys
CLINT'S COMICS
CANS ONLY

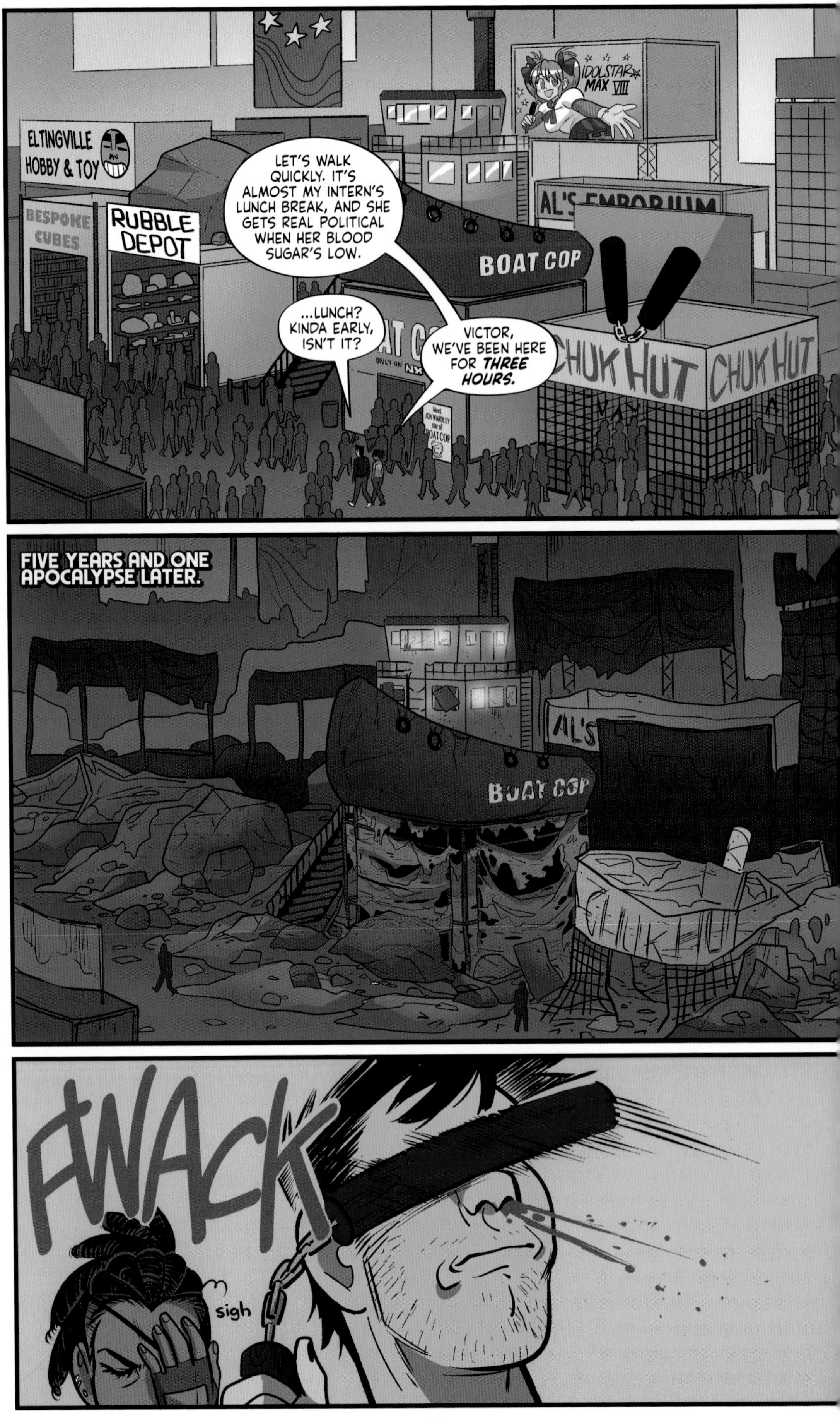
ELTINGVILLE HOBBY & TOY
BESPOKE CUBES
RUBBLE DEPOT
IDOLSTAR MAX VIII
AL'S EMPORIUM
BOAT COP
CHUK HUT
CHUK HUT
LET'S WALK QUICKLY. IT'S ALMOST MY INTERN'S LUNCH BREAK, AND SHE GETS REAL POLITICAL WHEN HER BLOOD SUGAR'S LOW.
...LUNCH? KINDA EARLY, ISN'T IT?
VICTOR, WE'VE BEEN HERE FOR ***THREE HOURS.***
FIVE YEARS AND ONE APOCALYPSE LATER.
AL'S
BOAT COP
CHUK HUT
FWACK
sigh

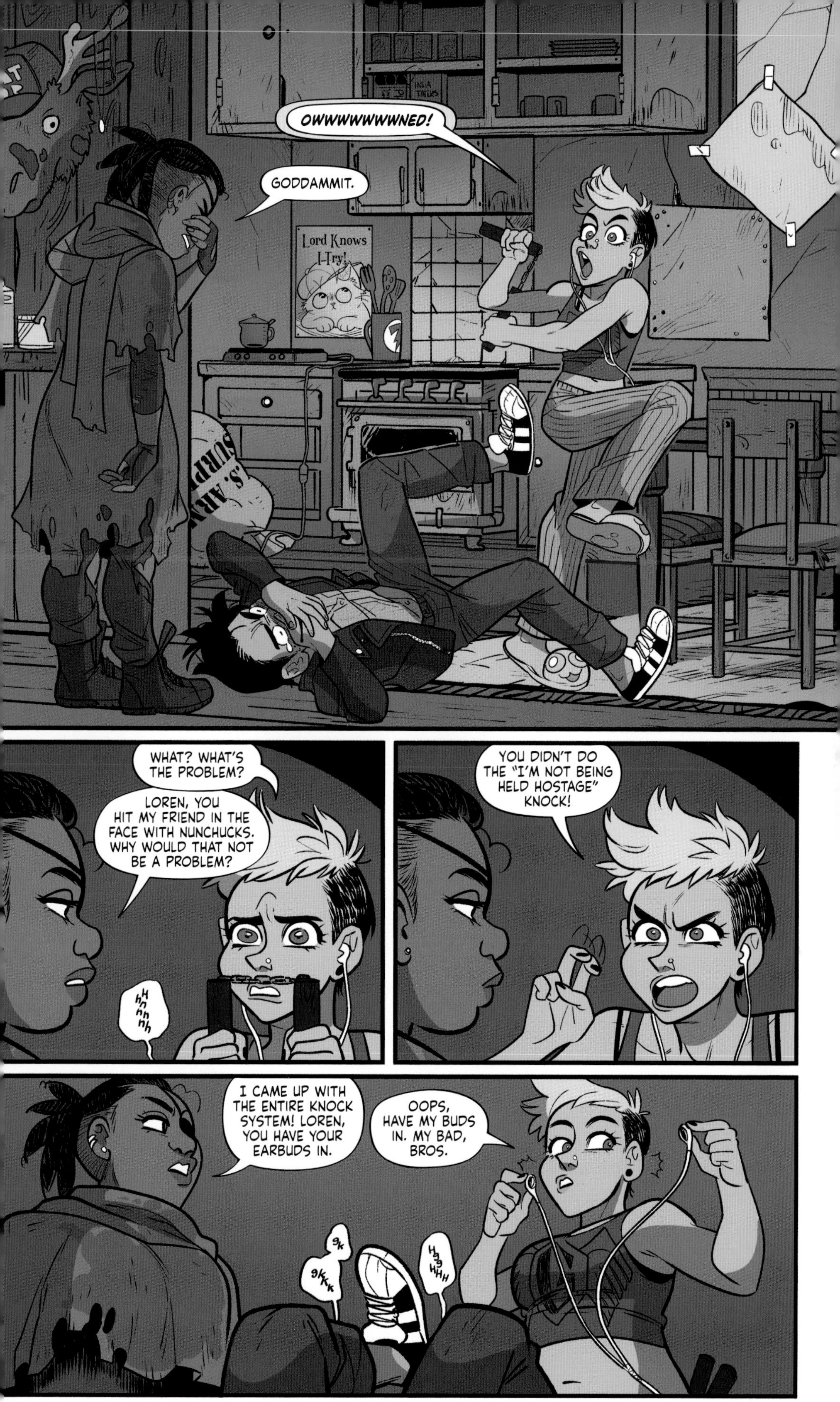
OWWWWWWWNED!
GODDAMMIT.
Lord Knows I Try!
WHAT? WHAT'S THE PROBLEM?
LOREN, YOU HIT MY FRIEND IN THE FACE WITH NUNCHUCKS. WHY WOULD THAT NOT BE A PROBLEM?
YOU DIDN'T DO THE "I'M NOT BEING HELD HOSTAGE" KNOCK!
I CAME UP WITH THE ENTIRE KNOCK SYSTEM! LOREN, YOU HAVE YOUR EARBUDS IN.
OOPS, HAVE MY BUDS IN. MY BAD, BROS.

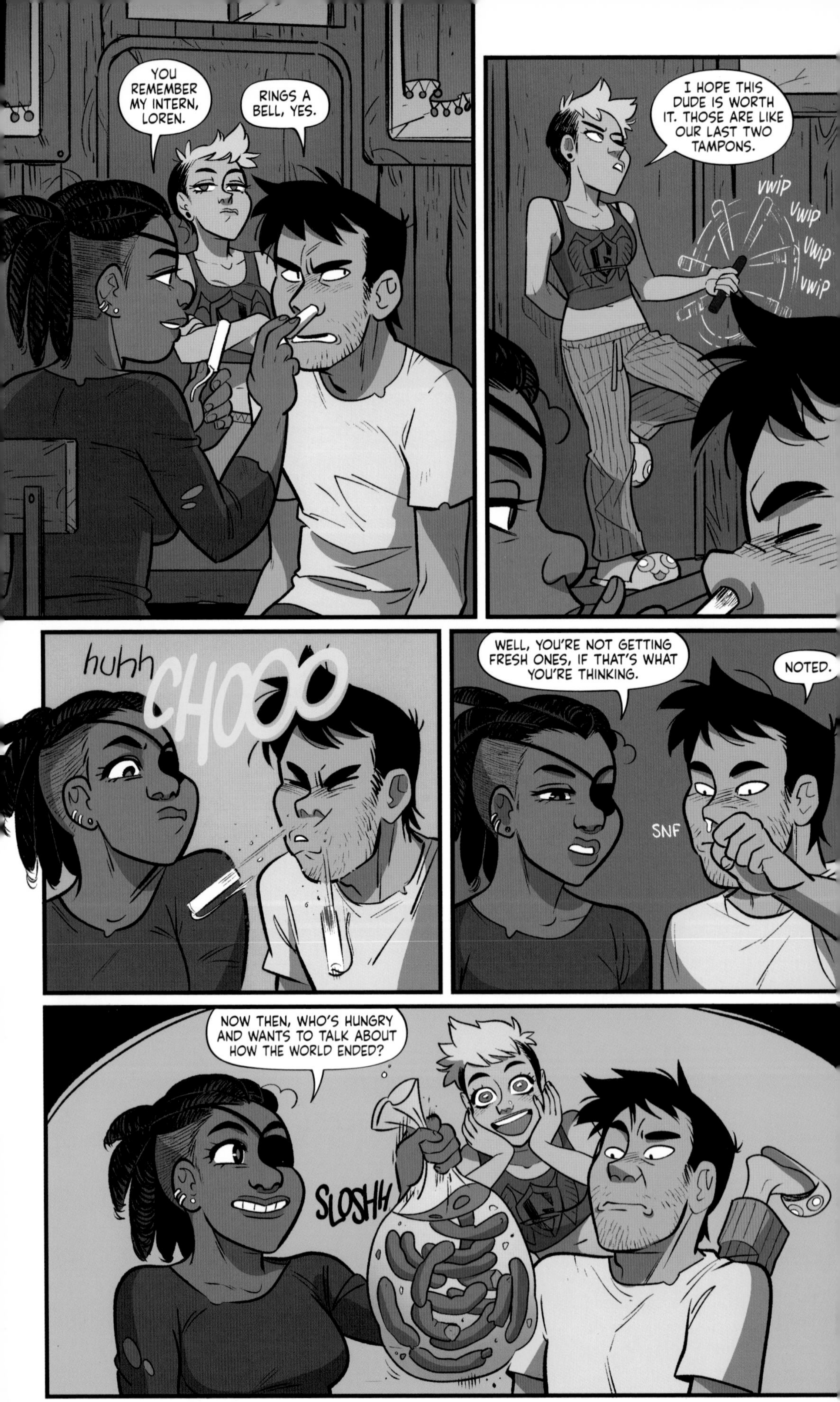
YOU REMEMBER MY INTERN, LOREN.
RINGS A BELL, YES.
I HOPE THIS DUDE IS WORTH IT. THOSE ARE LIKE OUR LAST TWO TAMPONS.
VWIP
VWIP
VWIP
VWIP
huhh
CHOOO
WELL, YOU'RE NOT GETTING FRESH ONES, IF THAT'S WHAT YOU'RE THINKING.
NOTED.
SNF
NOW THEN, WHO'S HUNGRY AND WANTS TO TALK ABOUT HOW THE WORLD ENDED?
SLOSHH

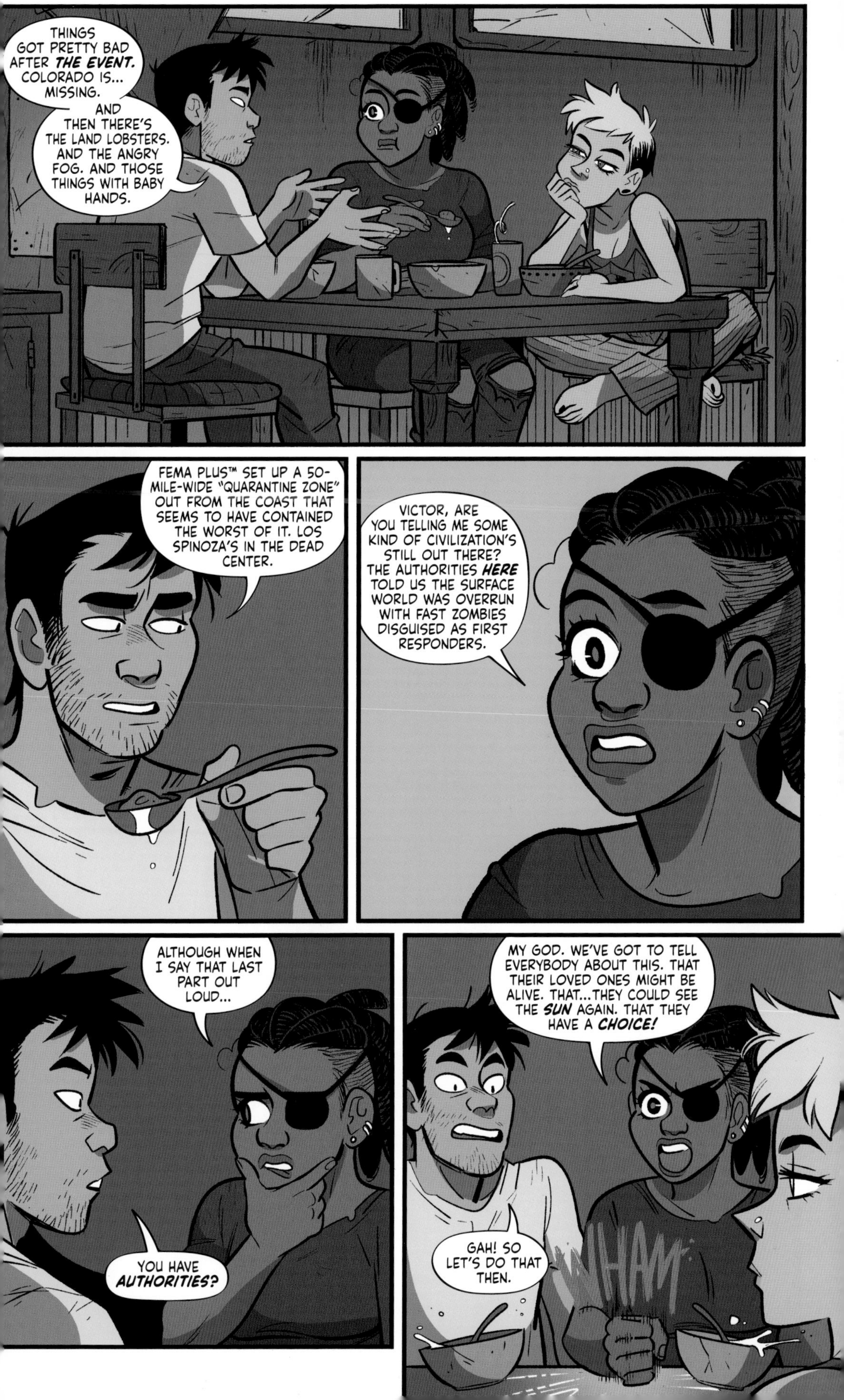
THINGS GOT PRETTY BAD AFTER ***THE EVENT.*** COLORADO IS... MISSING.
AND THEN THERE'S THE LAND LOBSTERS. AND THE ANGRY FOG. AND THOSE THINGS WITH BABY HANDS.
FEMA PLUS™ SET UP A 50-MILE-WIDE "QUARANTINE ZONE" OUT FROM THE COAST THAT SEEMS TO HAVE CONTAINED THE WORST OF IT. LOS SPINOZA'S IN THE DEAD CENTER.
VICTOR, ARE YOU TELLING ME SOME KIND OF CIVILIZATION'S STILL OUT THERE? THE AUTHORITIES ***HERE*** TOLD US THE SURFACE WORLD WAS OVERRUN WITH FAST ZOMBIES DISGUISED AS FIRST RESPONDERS.
ALTHOUGH WHEN I SAY THAT LAST PART OUT LOUD...
YOU HAVE ***AUTHORITIES?***
MY GOD. WE'VE GOT TO TELL EVERYBODY ABOUT THIS. THAT THEIR LOVED ONES MIGHT BE ALIVE. THAT...THEY COULD SEE THE ***SUN*** AGAIN. THAT THEY HAVE A ***CHOICE!***
WHAM
GAH! SO LET'S DO THAT THEN.

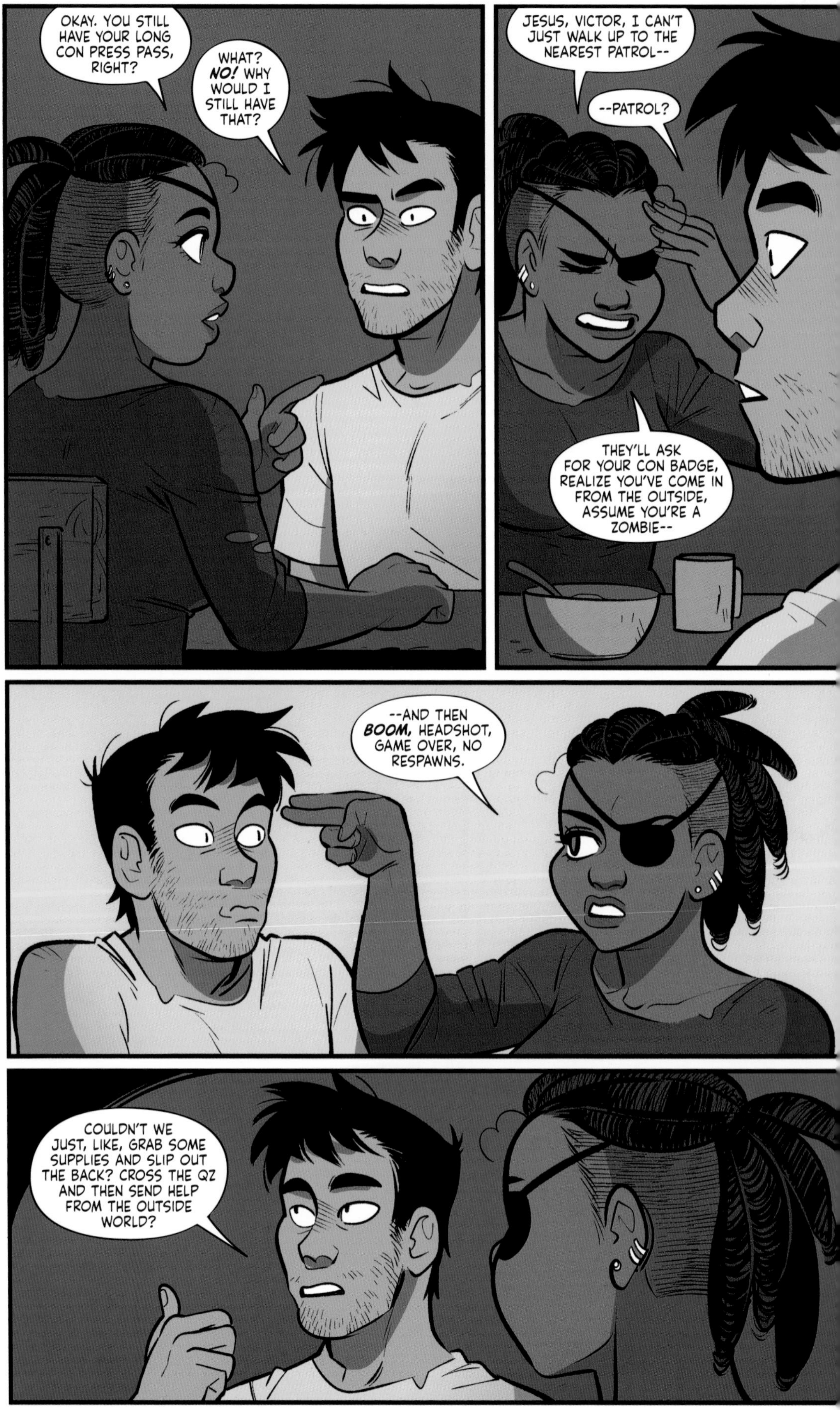
OKAY. YOU STILL HAVE YOUR LONG CON PRESS PASS, RIGHT?
WHAT? **NO!** WHY WOULD I STILL HAVE THAT?
JESUS, VICTOR, I CAN'T JUST WALK UP TO THE NEAREST PATROL--
--PATROL?
THEY'LL ASK FOR YOUR CON BADGE, REALIZE YOU'VE COME IN FROM THE OUTSIDE, ASSUME YOU'RE A ZOMBIE--
--AND THEN **BOOM,** HEADSHOT, GAME OVER, NO RESPAWNS.
COULDN'T WE JUST, LIKE, GRAB SOME SUPPLIES AND SLIP OUT THE BACK? CROSS THE QZ AND THEN SEND HELP FROM THE OUTSIDE WORLD?

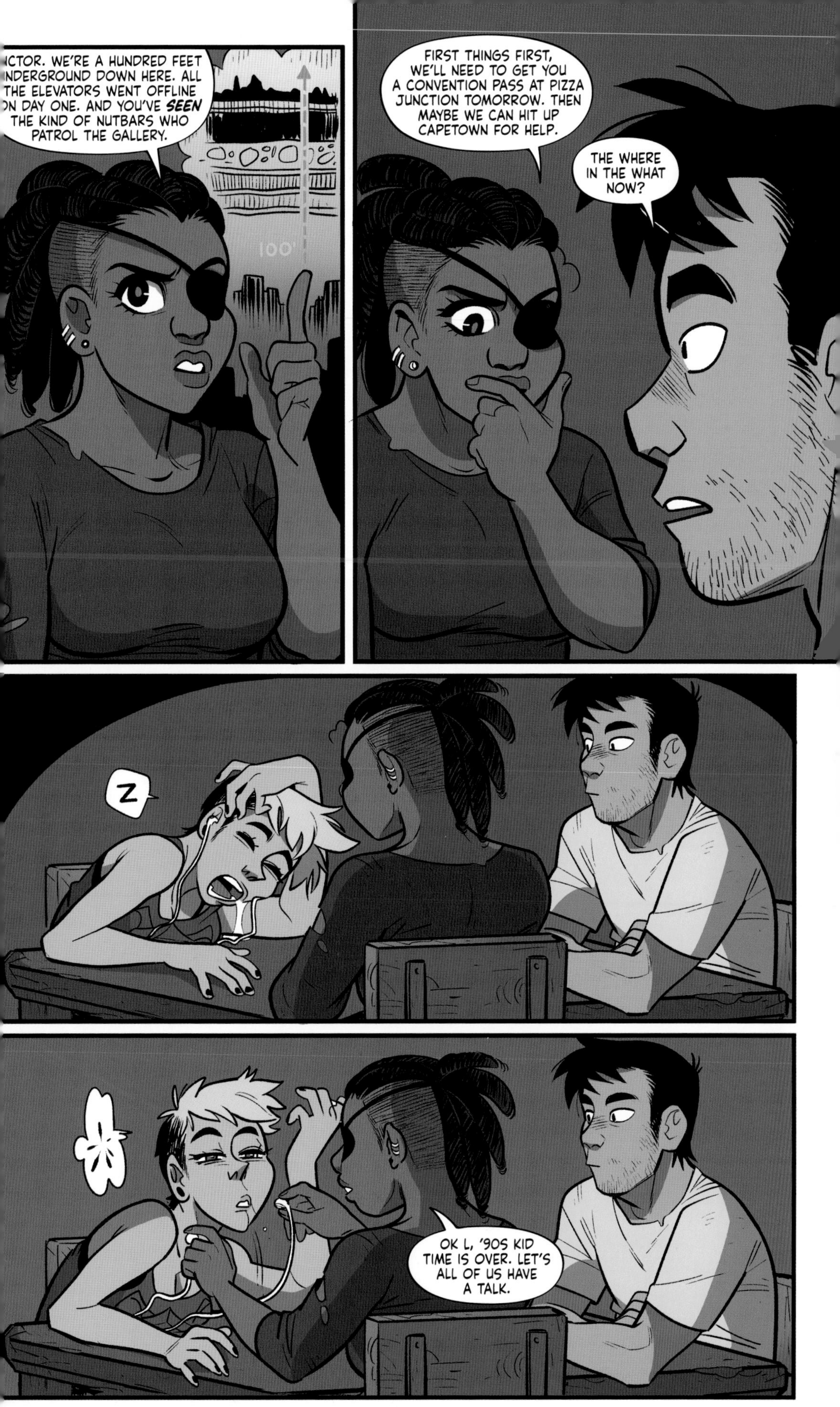

CTOR. WE'RE A HUNDRED FEET NDERGROUND DOWN HERE. ALL THE ELEVATORS WENT OFFLINE ON DAY ONE. AND YOU'VE ***SEEN*** THE KIND OF NUTBARS WHO PATROL THE GALLERY.
100'
FIRST THINGS FIRST, WE'LL NEED TO GET YOU A CONVENTION PASS AT PIZZA JUNCTION TOMORROW. THEN MAYBE WE CAN HIT UP CAPETOWN FOR HELP.
THE WHERE IN THE WHAT NOW?
Z
OK L, '90S KID TIME IS OVER. LET'S ALL OF US HAVE A TALK.

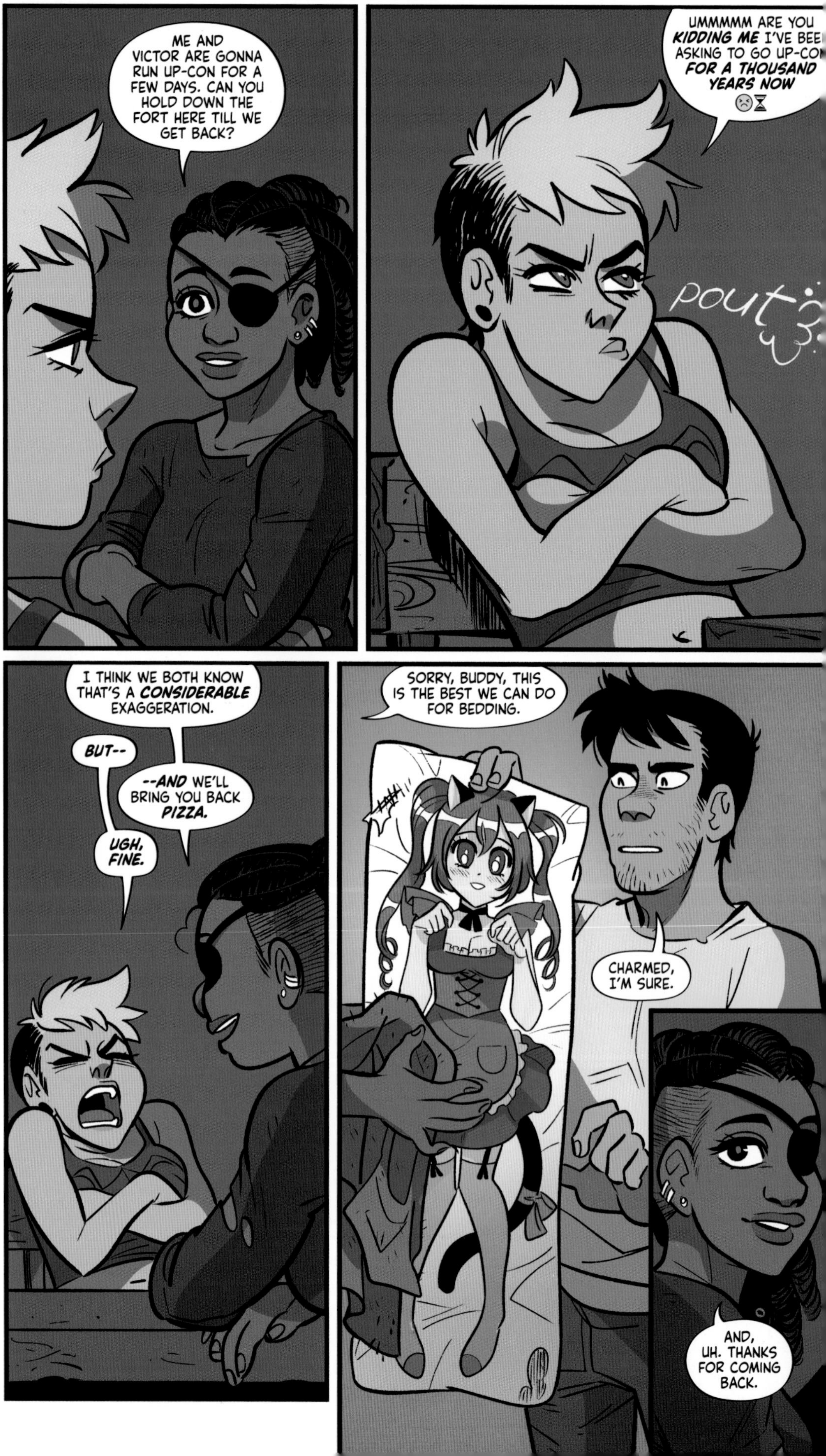

ME AND VICTOR ARE GONNA RUN UP-CON FOR A FEW DAYS. CAN YOU HOLD DOWN THE FORT HERE TILL WE GET BACK?
UMMMMM ARE YOU KIDDING ME I'VE BEEN ASKING TO GO UP-CON FOR A THOUSAND YEARS NOW
pout
I THINK WE BOTH KNOW THAT'S A CONSIDERABLE EXAGGERATION.
BUT--
--AND WE'LL BRING YOU BACK PIZZA.
UGH, FINE.
SORRY, BUDDY, THIS IS THE BEST WE CAN DO FOR BEDDING.
CHARMED, I'M SURE.
AND, UH. THANKS FOR COMING BACK.

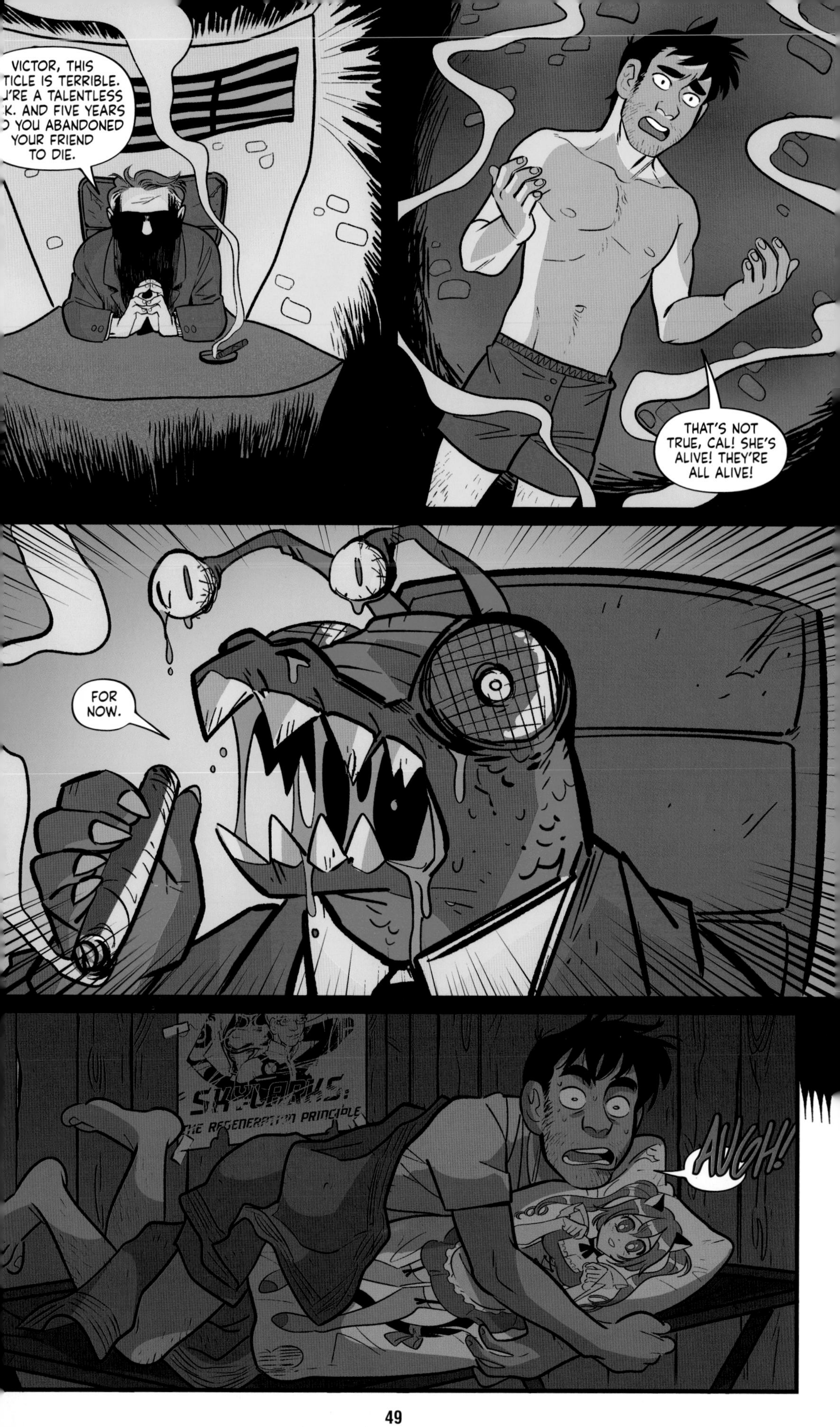
VICTOR, THIS
TICLE IS TERRIBLE.
'RE A TALENTLESS
K. AND FIVE YEARS
YOU ABANDONED
YOUR FRIEND
TO DIE.
THAT'S NOT
TRUE, CAL! SHE'S
ALIVE! THEY'RE
ALL ALIVE!
FOR
NOW.
SKYLARKS:
THE REGENERATION PRINCIPLE
AUGH!

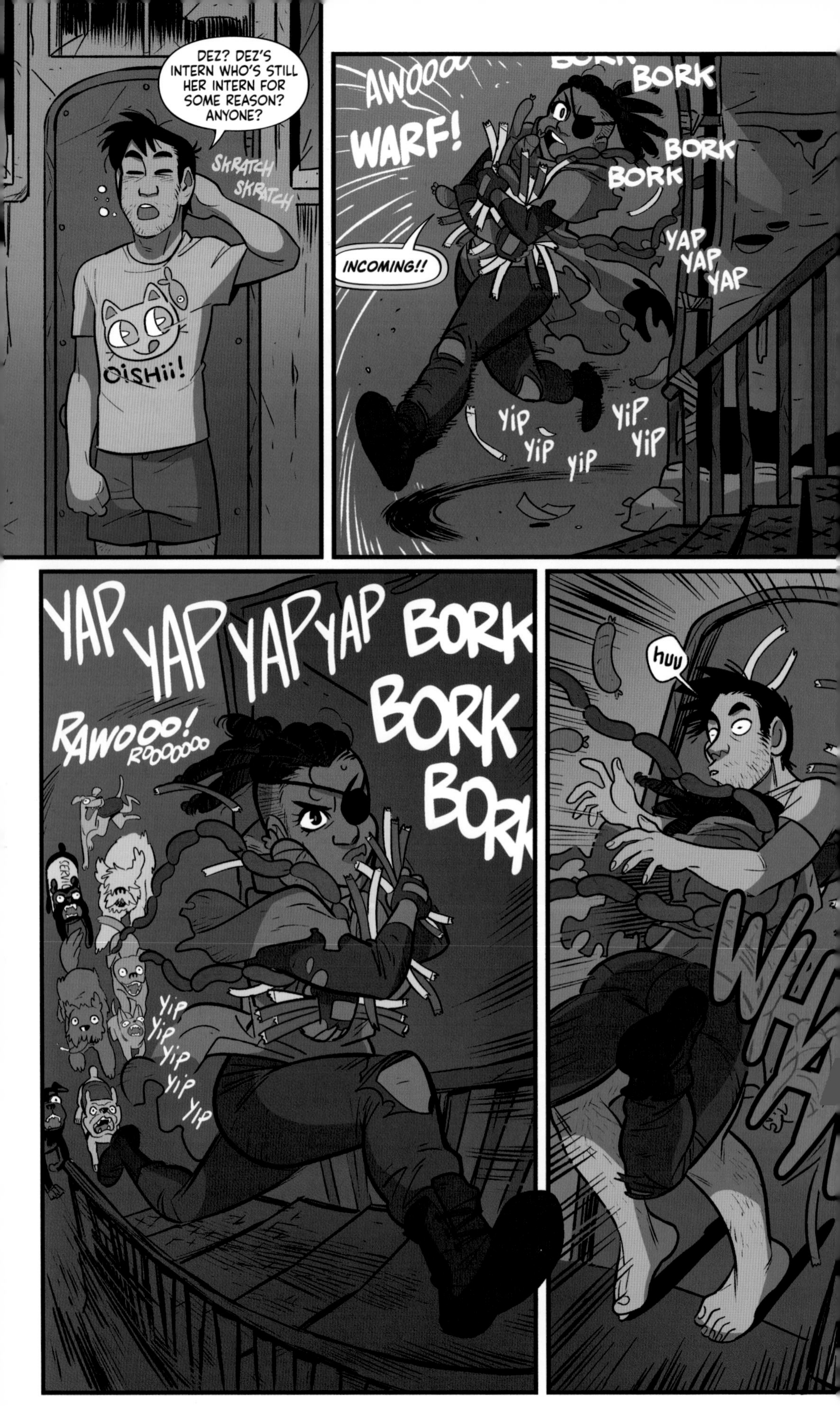
DEZ? DEZ'S INTERN WHO'S STILL HER INTERN FOR SOME REASON? ANYONE?
SKRATCH
SKRATCH
OiSHii!
WARF!
BORK
BORK
BORK
YAP
YAP
YAP
INCOMING!!
yip
yip
yip
yip
yip
YAP YAP YAP YAP
BORK
BORK
RAWOOO!
ROOOOOOO
yip
yip
yip
yip
yip
huu

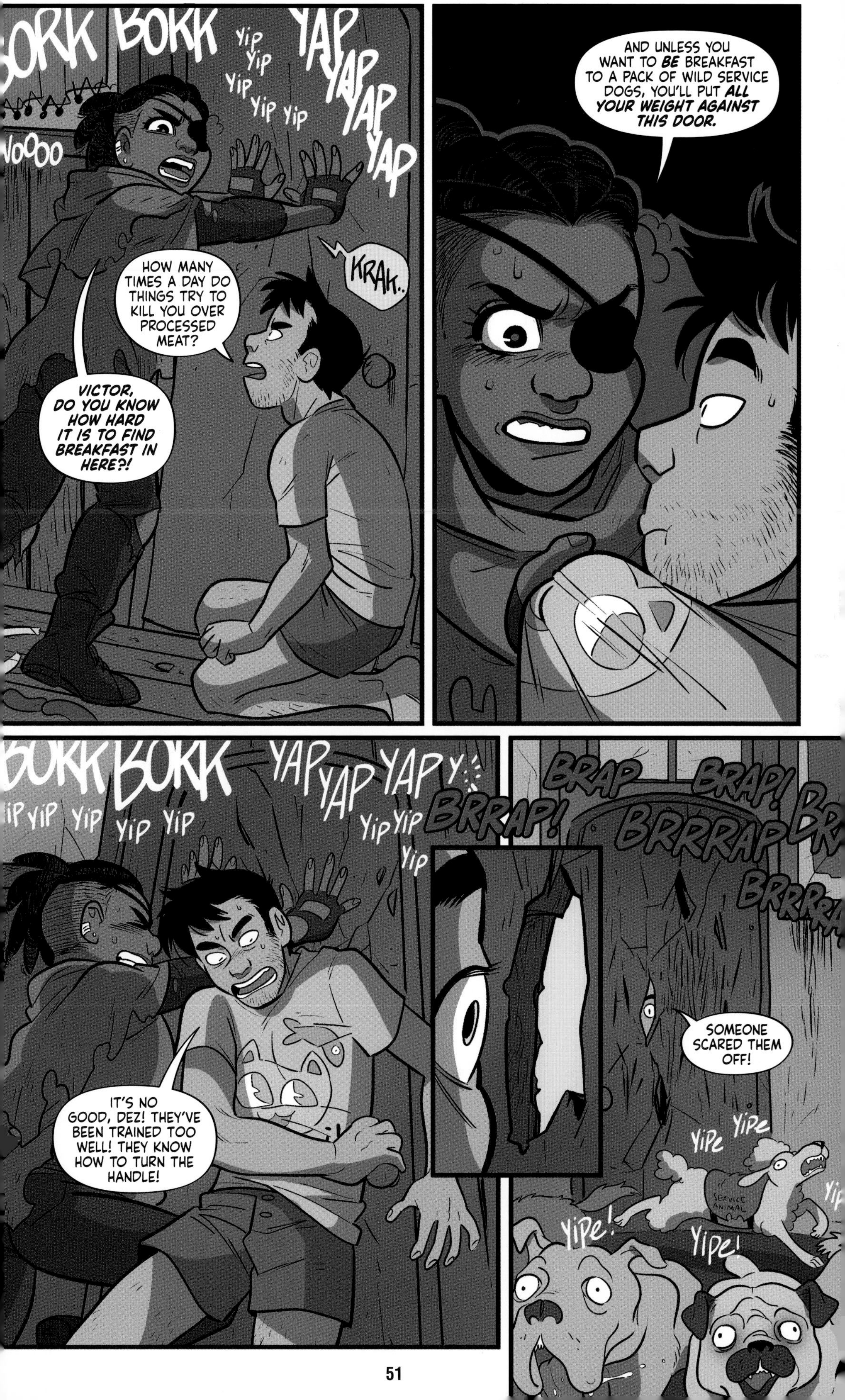

BORK BORK
YIP YIP YIP YIP YIP YIP
YAP YAP YAP YAP
NOOOO
KRAK..
HOW MANY TIMES A DAY DO THINGS TRY TO KILL YOU OVER PROCESSED MEAT?
VICTOR, DO YOU KNOW HOW HARD IT IS TO FIND BREAKFAST IN HERE?!
AND UNLESS YOU WANT TO BE BREAKFAST TO A PACK OF WILD SERVICE DOGS, YOU'LL PUT ALL YOUR WEIGHT AGAINST THIS DOOR.
BORK BORK
YAP YAP YAP
YIP YIP YIP YIP YIP YIP YIP YIP
IT'S NO GOOD, DEZ! THEY'VE BEEN TRAINED TOO WELL! THEY KNOW HOW TO TURN THE HANDLE!
BRRAP!
BRAP BRAP! BRRRAP
SOMEONE SCARED THEM OFF!
SERVICE ANIMAL
YIPE YIPE
YIPE! YIPE!

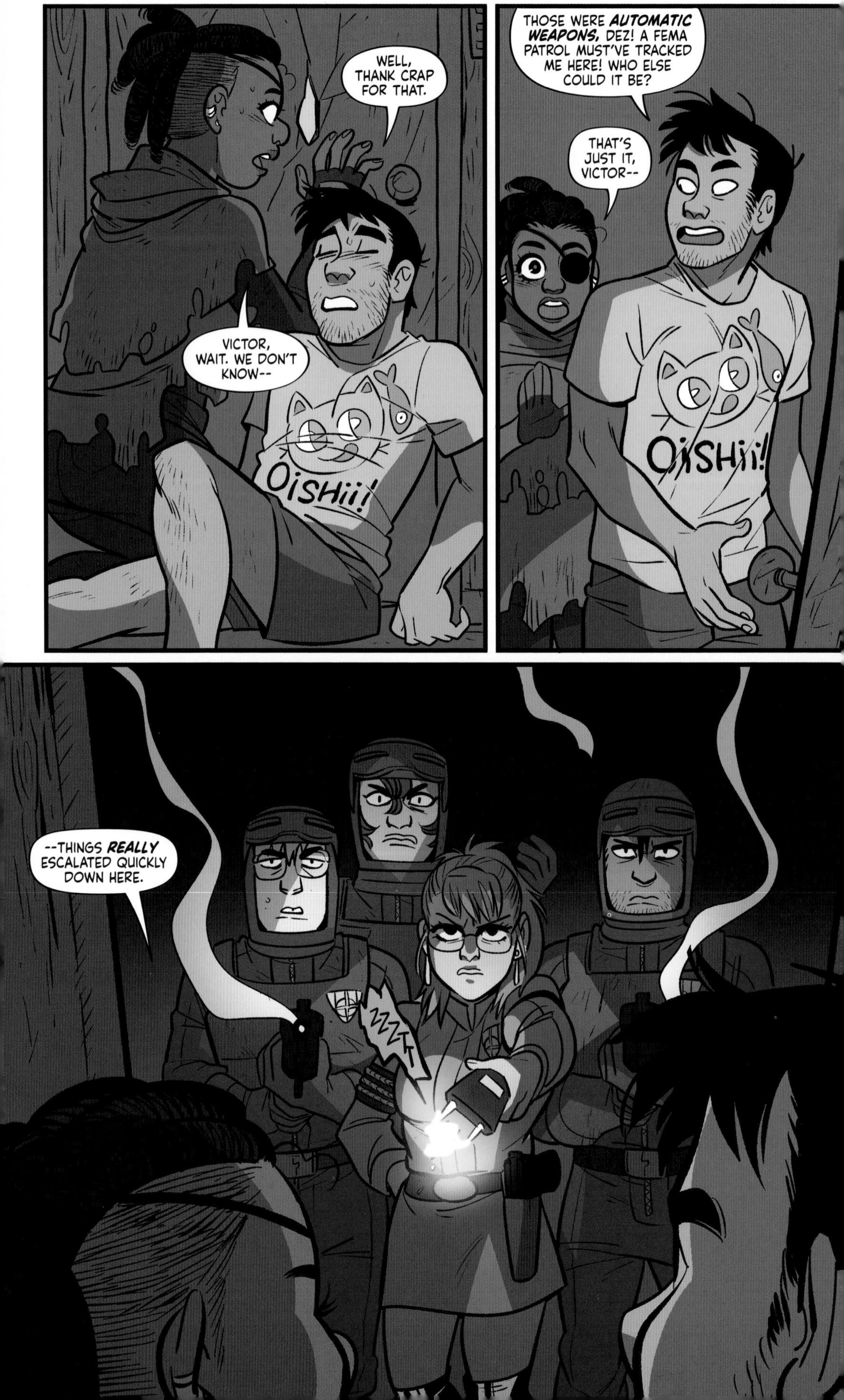

WELL, THANK CRAP FOR THAT.
VICTOR, WAIT. WE DON'T KNOW--
Oishii!
THOSE WERE ***AUTOMATIC WEAPONS,*** DEZ! A FEMA PATROL MUST'VE TRACKED ME HERE! WHO ELSE COULD IT BE?
THAT'S JUST IT, VICTOR--
Oishii!
--THINGS ***REALLY*** ESCALATED QUICKLY DOWN HERE.
ZZZZT

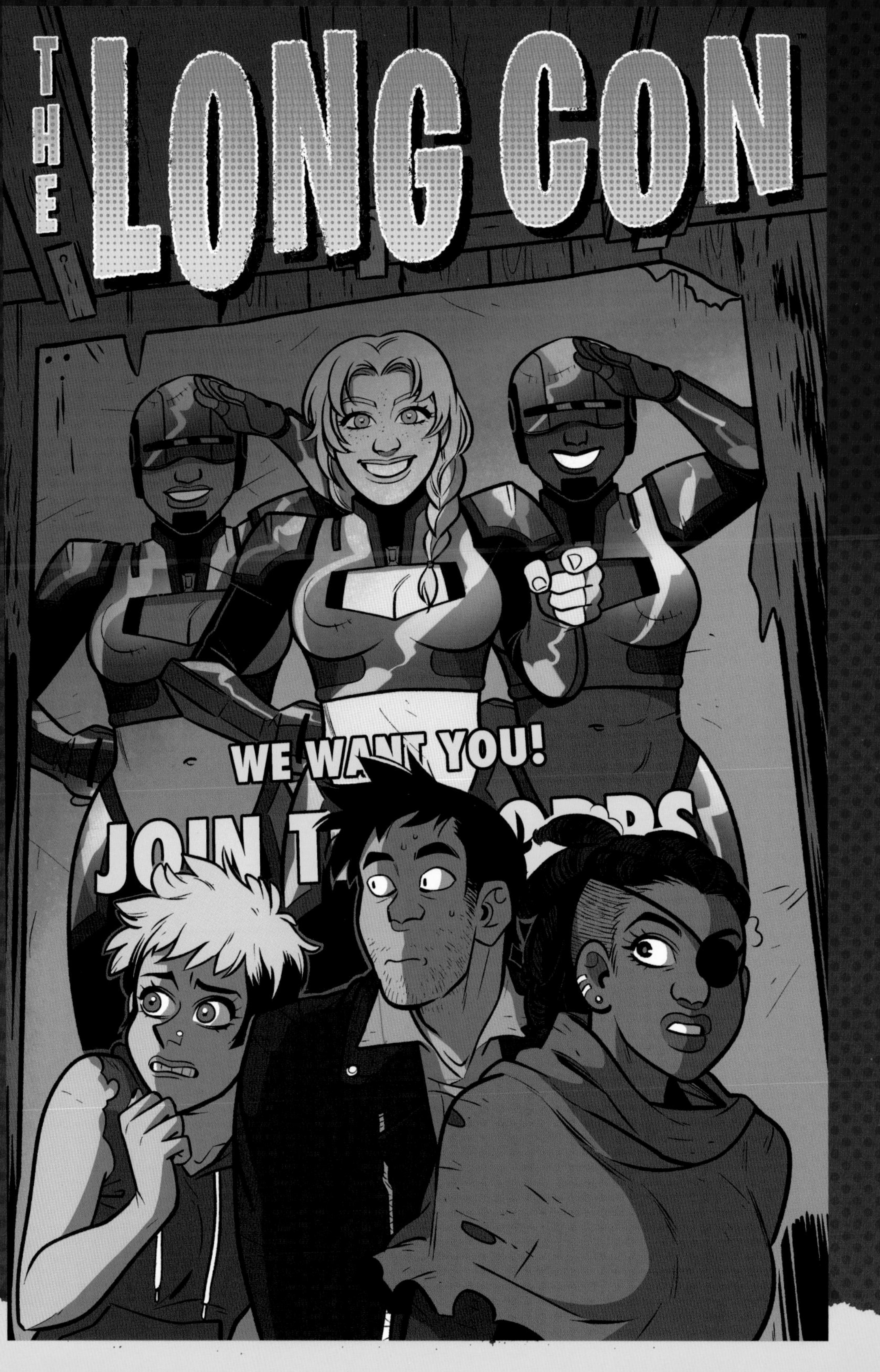
THE LONG CON
WE WANT YOU!
JOIN

CHAPTER 3: UM ACTUALLY

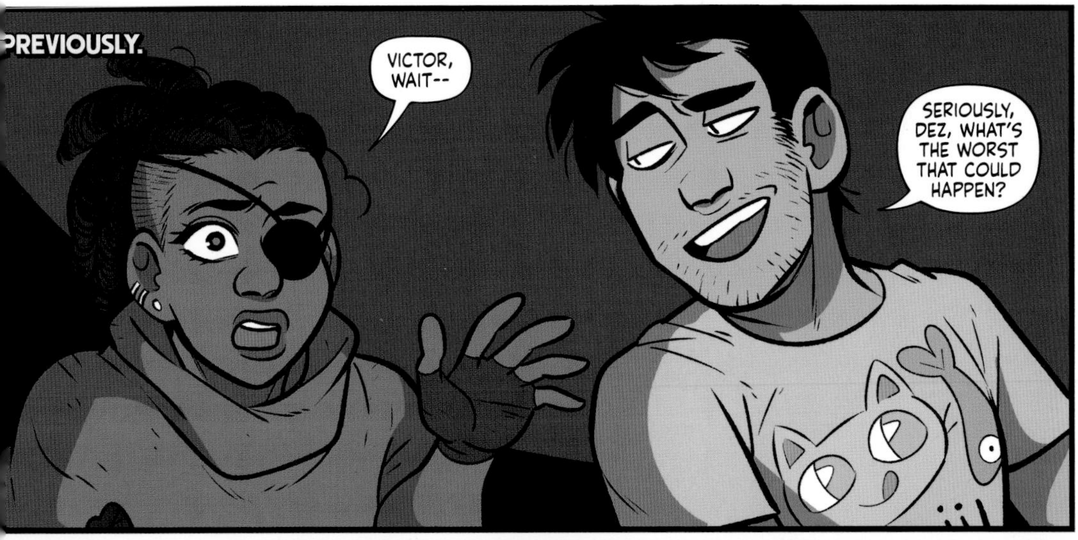
PREVIOUSLY.
VICTOR, WAIT--
SERIOUSLY, DEZ, WHAT'S THE WORST THAT COULD HAPPEN?

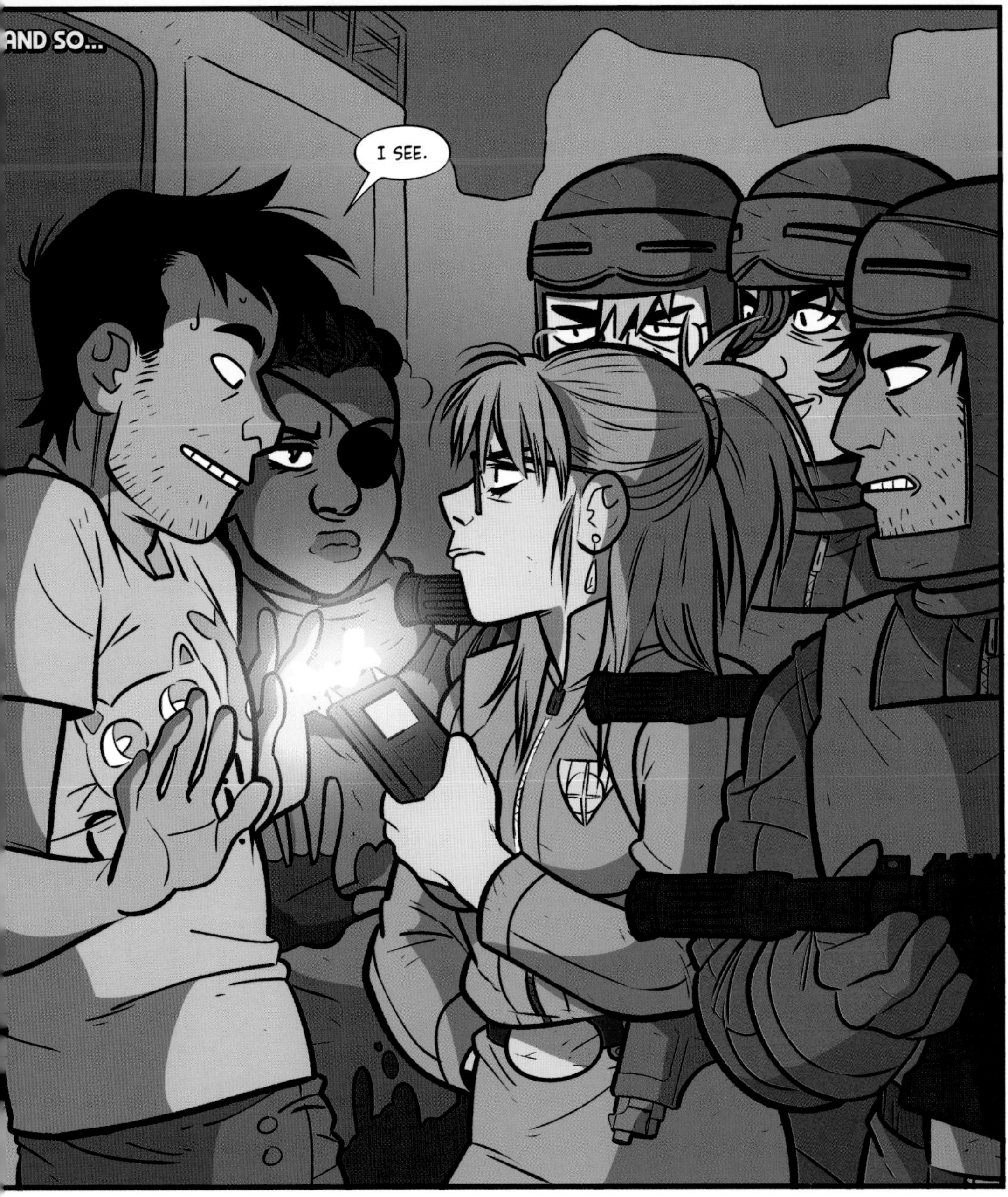
AND SO...
I SEE.

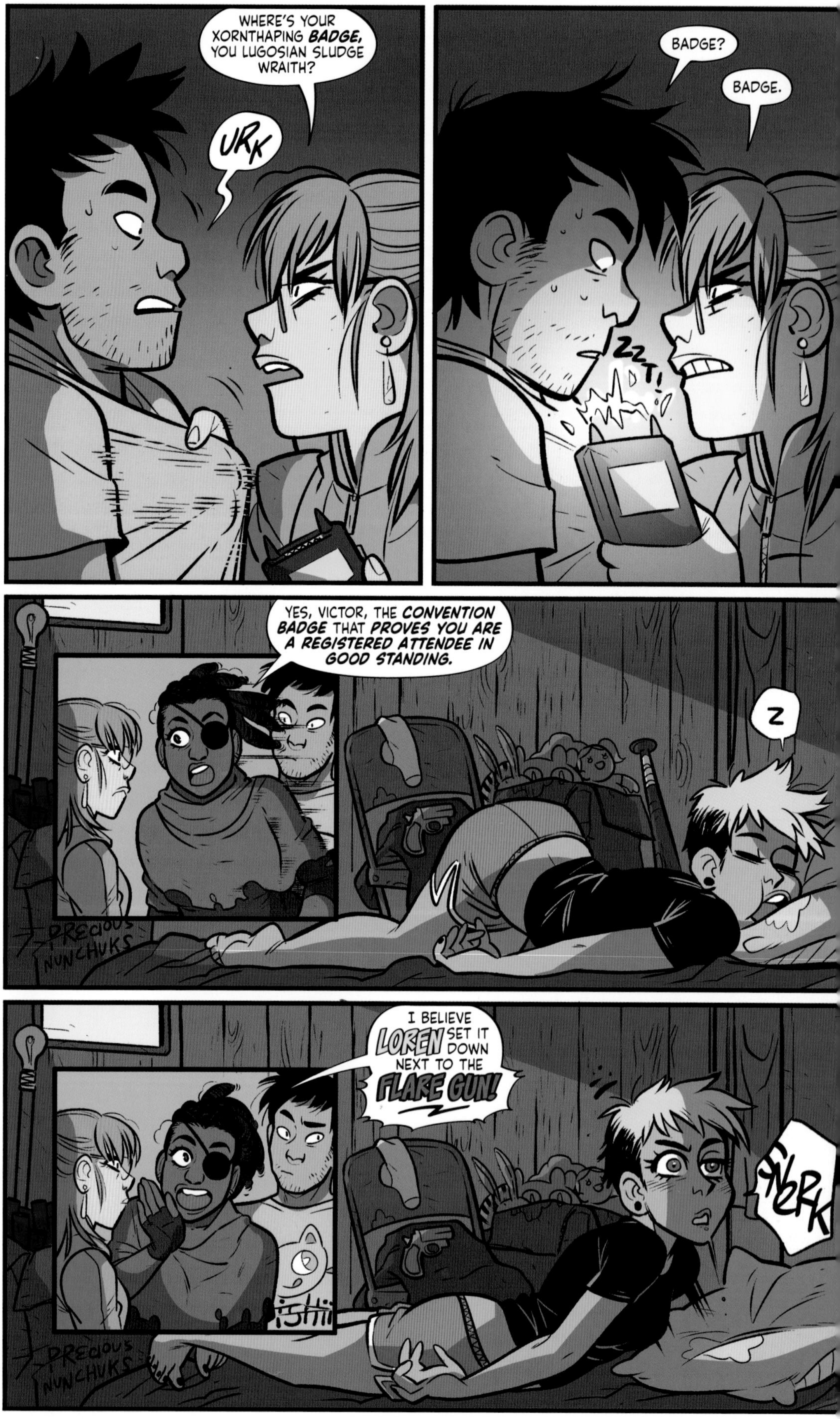
WHERE'S YOUR XORNTHAPING BADGE, YOU LUGOSIAN SLUDGE WRAITH?
URK
BADGE?
BADGE.
ZZZT!
YES, VICTOR, THE CONVENTION BADGE THAT PROVES YOU ARE A REGISTERED ATTENDEE IN GOOD STANDING.
Z
PRECIOUS NUNCHUKS
I BELIEVE LOREN SET IT DOWN NEXT TO THE FLARE GUN!
SNERK
PRECIOUS NUNCHUKS

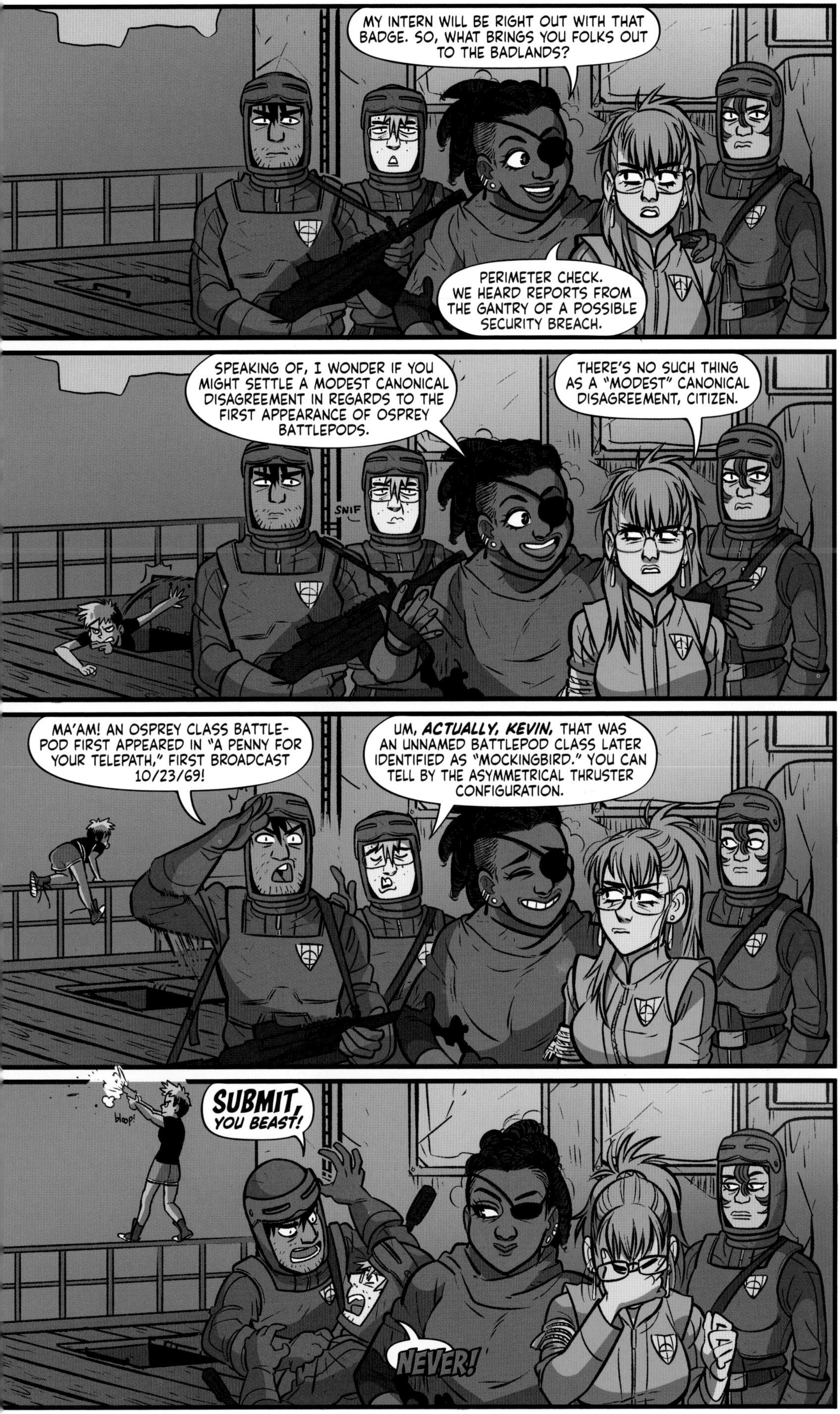
MY INTERN WILL BE RIGHT OUT WITH THAT BADGE. SO, WHAT BRINGS YOU FOLKS OUT TO THE BADLANDS?
PERIMETER CHECK. WE HEARD REPORTS FROM THE GANTRY OF A POSSIBLE SECURITY BREACH.
SPEAKING OF, I WONDER IF YOU MIGHT SETTLE A MODEST CANONICAL DISAGREEMENT IN REGARDS TO THE FIRST APPEARANCE OF OSPREY BATTLEPODS.
THERE'S NO SUCH THING AS A "MODEST" CANONICAL DISAGREEMENT, CITIZEN.
SNIF
MA'AM! AN OSPREY CLASS BATTLE-POD FIRST APPEARED IN "A PENNY FOR YOUR TELEPATH," FIRST BROADCAST 10/23/69!
UM, ***ACTUALLY, KEVIN,*** THAT WAS AN UNNAMED BATTLEPOD CLASS LATER IDENTIFIED AS "MOCKINGBIRD." YOU CAN TELL BY THE ASYMMETRICAL THRUSTER CONFIGURATION.
bloop!
SUBMIT, YOU BEAST!
NEVER!

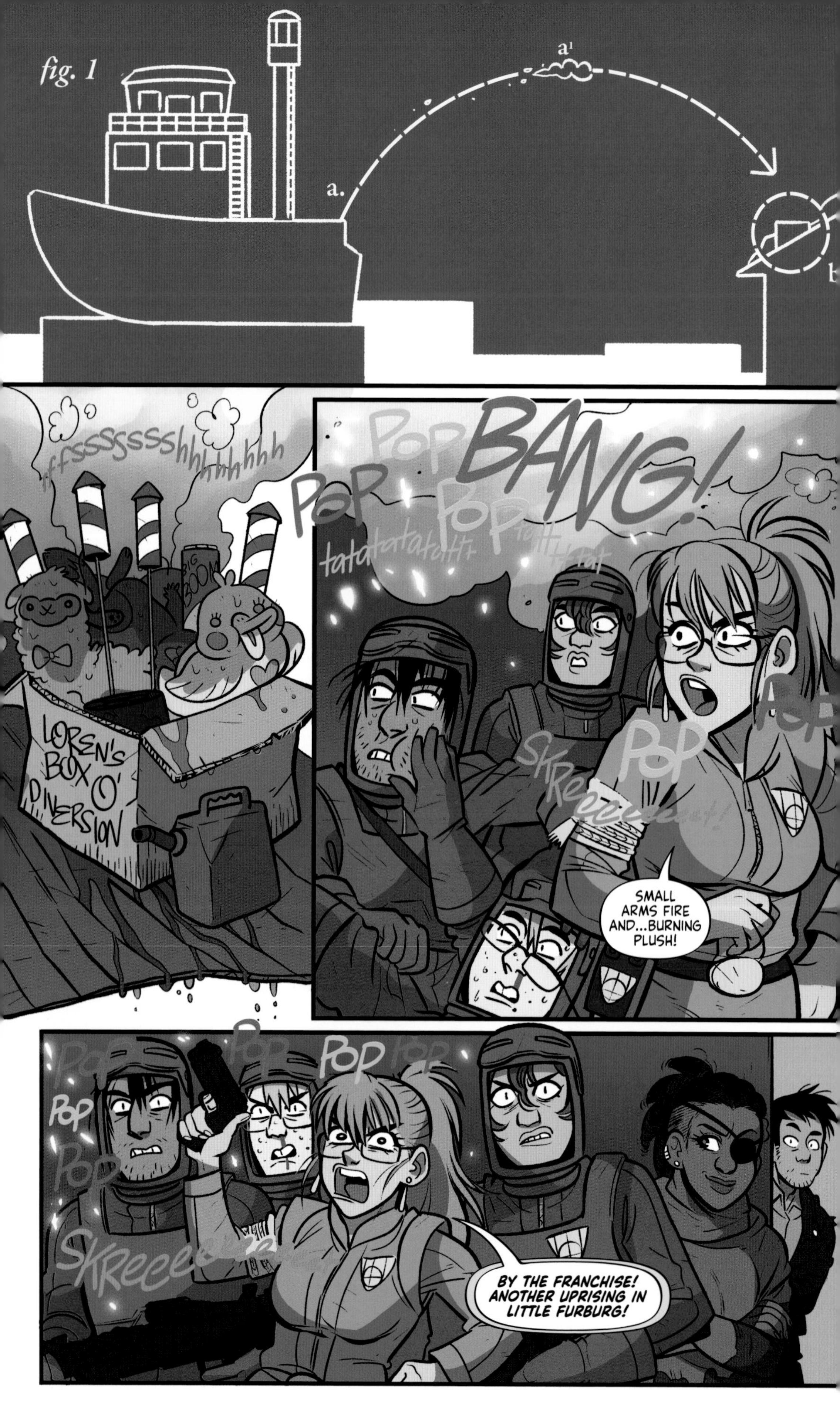
fig. 1
a.
a1
b
ffsssssssshhhhhhhhh
BIG BOOM
LOREN'S BOX 'O' DIVERSION
POP POP BANG!
POP POP
tatatatatatatt tatt tatat
SKREEEEEEEEEEEET!
POP POP
SMALL ARMS FIRE AND...BURNING PLUSH!
POP POP POP POP POP POP
SKREEEEEE
BY THE FRANCHISE! ANOTHER UPRISING IN LITTLE FURBURG!

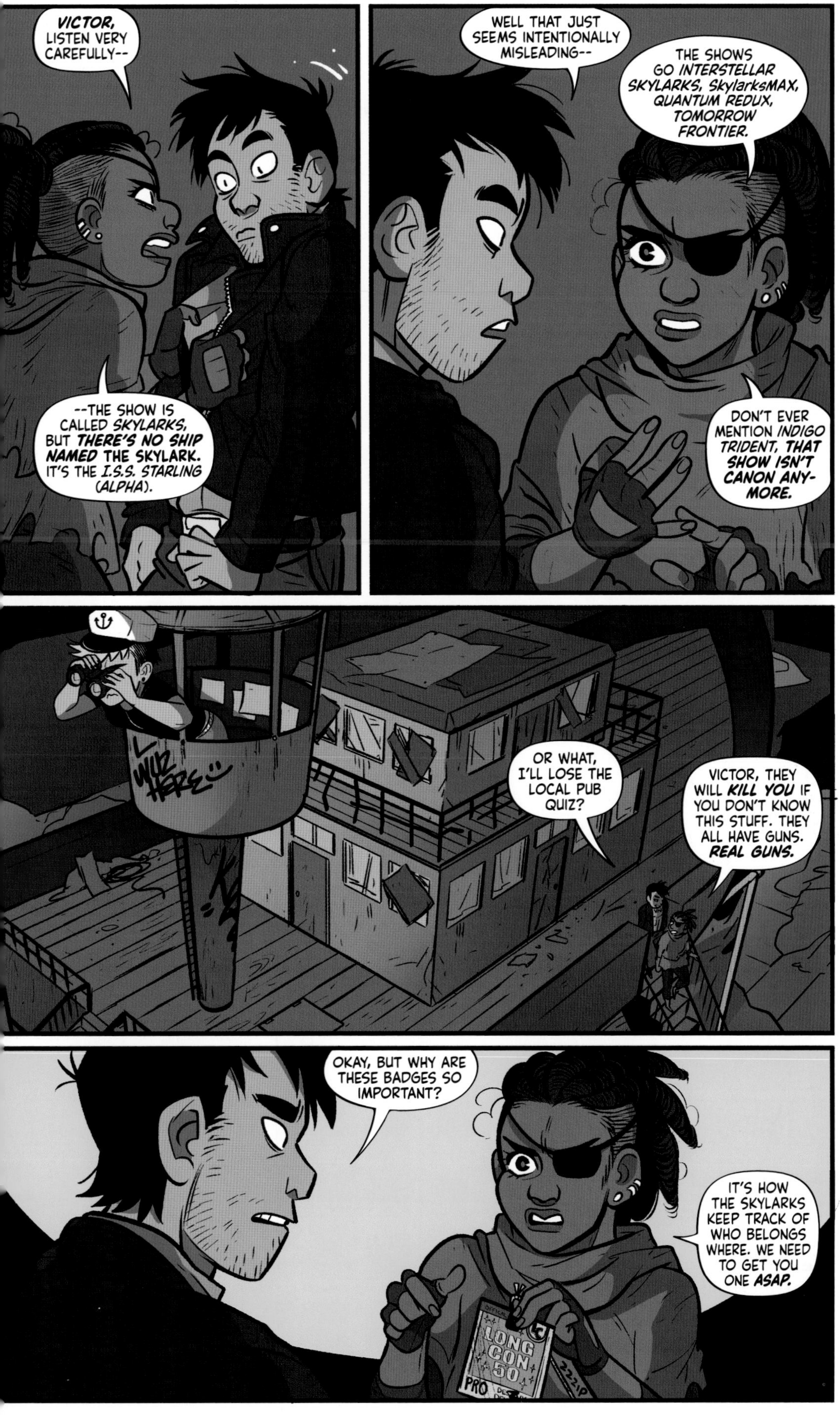
VICTOR, LISTEN VERY CAREFULLY--
--THE SHOW IS CALLED SKYLARKS, BUT THERE'S NO SHIP NAMED THE SKYLARK. IT'S THE I.S.S. STARLING (ALPHA).
WELL THAT JUST SEEMS INTENTIONALLY MISLEADING--
THE SHOWS GO INTERSTELLAR SKYLARKS, SkylarksMAX, QUANTUM REDUX, TOMORROW FRONTIER.
DON'T EVER MENTION INDIGO TRIDENT, THAT SHOW ISN'T CANON ANYMORE.
OR WHAT, I'LL LOSE THE LOCAL PUB QUIZ?
VICTOR, THEY WILL KILL YOU IF YOU DON'T KNOW THIS STUFF. THEY ALL HAVE GUNS. REAL GUNS.
OKAY, BUT WHY ARE THESE BADGES SO IMPORTANT?
IT'S HOW THE SKYLARKS KEEP TRACK OF WHO BELONGS WHERE. WE NEED TO GET YOU ONE ASAP.
LONG CON 50
PRO

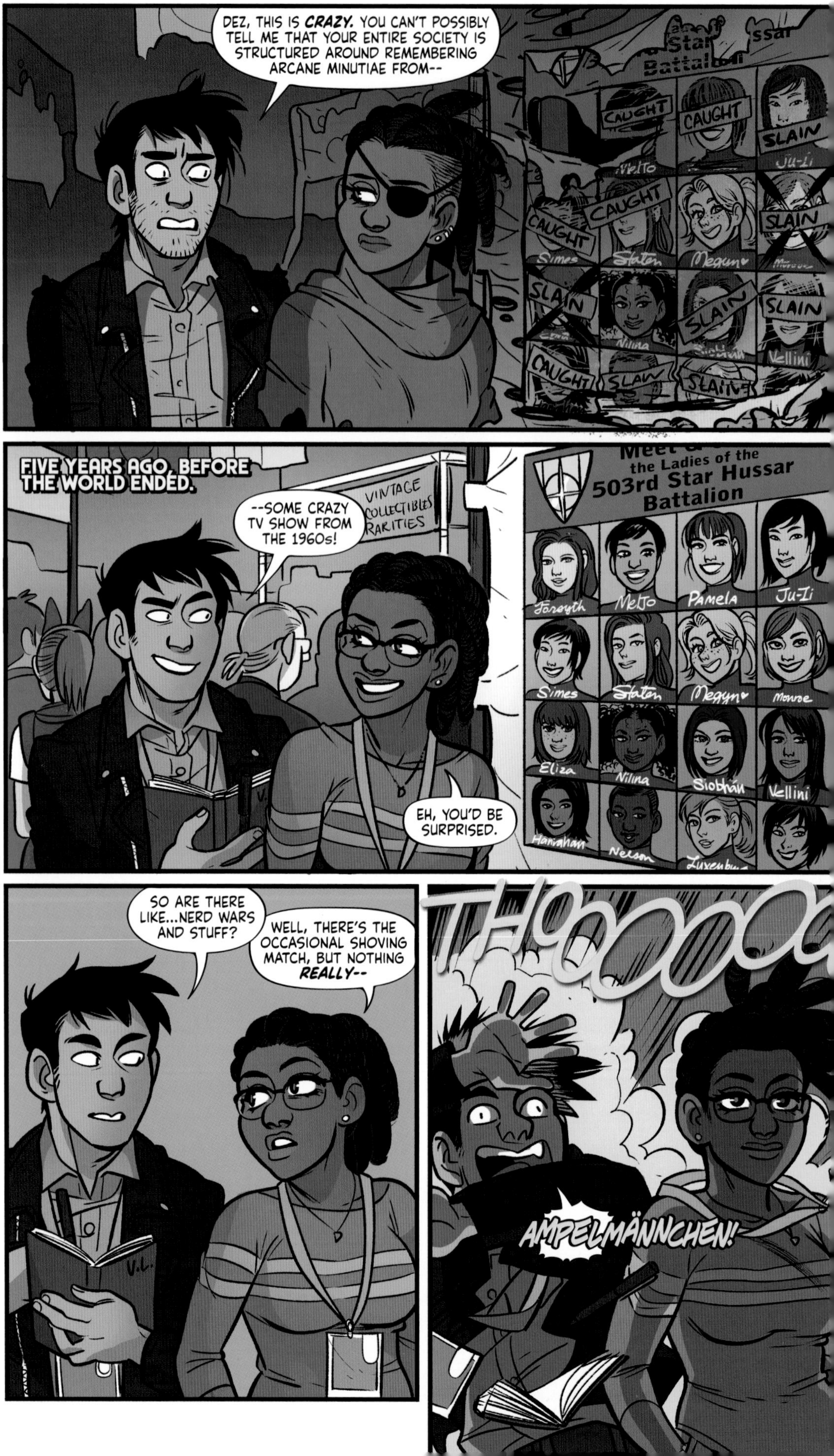
DEZ, THIS IS ***CRAZY.*** YOU CAN'T POSSIBLY TELL ME THAT YOUR ENTIRE SOCIETY IS STRUCTURED AROUND REMEMBERING ARCANE MINUTIAE FROM--
CAUGHT
CAUGHT
SLAIN
Ju-Li
CAUGHT
CAUGHT
SLAIN
Simes
Staten
Megyn
SLAIN
SLAIN
SLAIN
Nilina
Vellini
CAUGHT
SLAIN
FIVE YEARS AGO, BEFORE THE WORLD ENDED.
VINTAGE COLLECTIBLES RARITIES
--SOME CRAZY TV SHOW FROM THE 1960s!
the Ladies of the 503rd Star Hussar Battalion
Forsyth
MelJo
Pamela
Ju-Li
Simes
Staten
Megyn
Monroe
Eliza
Nilina
Siobhán
Vellini
Hanrahan
Nelson
EH, YOU'D BE SURPRISED.
SO ARE THERE LIKE...NERD WARS AND STUFF?
WELL, THERE'S THE OCCASIONAL SHOVING MATCH, BUT NOTHING ***REALLY--***
V.L.
AMPELMÄNNCHEN!

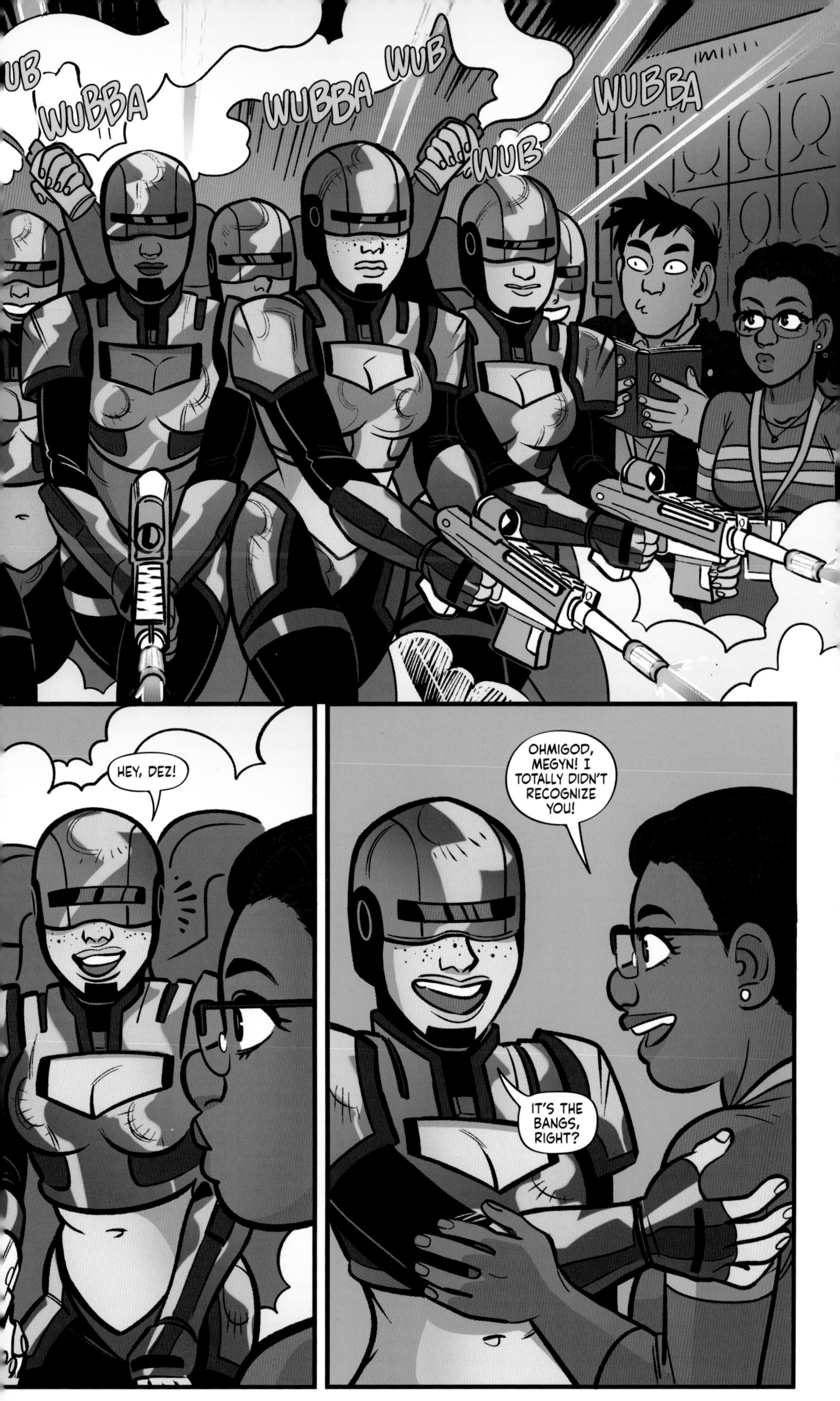
UB
WUBBA
WUBBA WUB
WUB
WUBBA
HEY, DEZ!
OHMIGOD, MEGYN! I TOTALLY DIDN'T RECOGNIZE YOU!
IT'S THE BANGS, RIGHT?

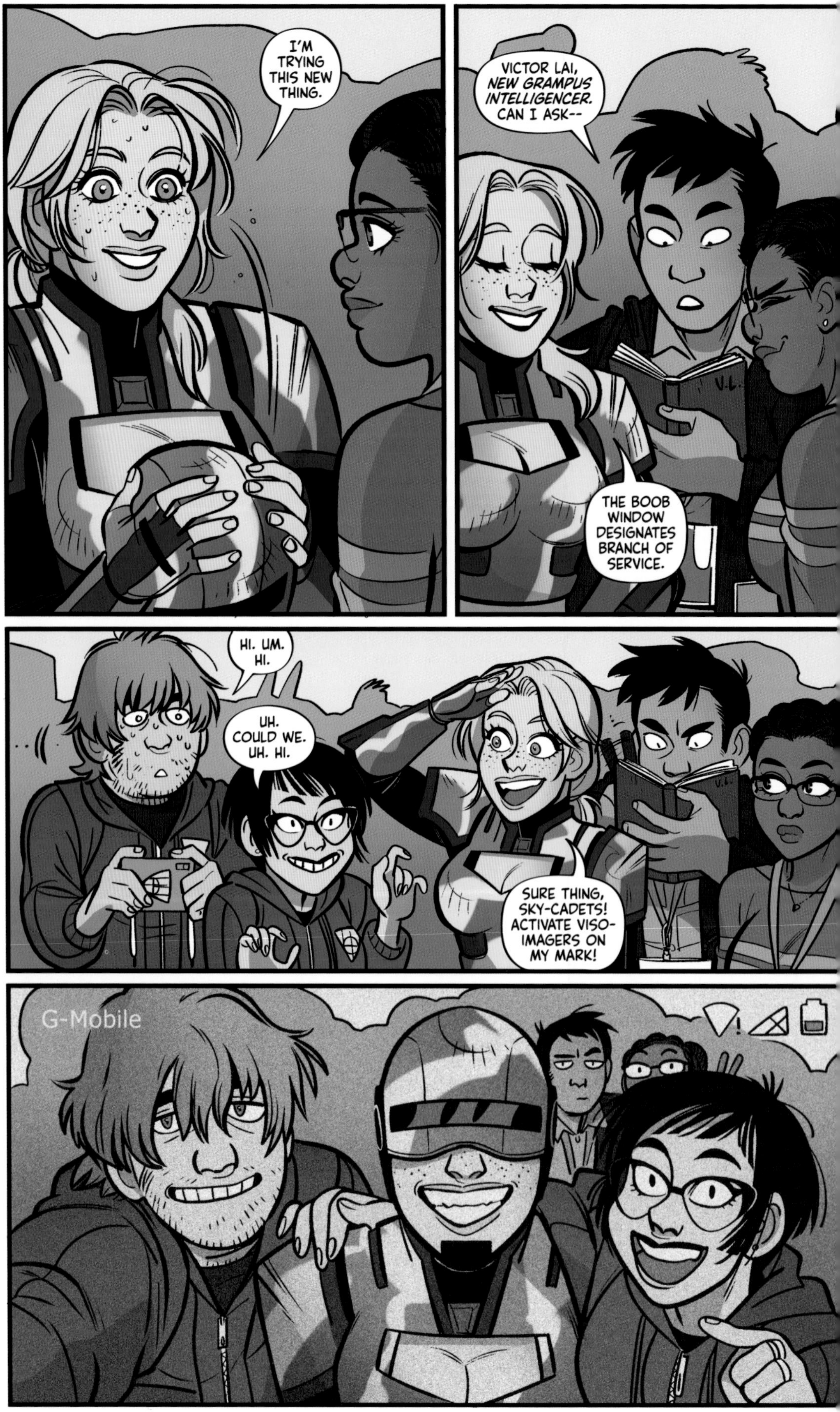

I'M TRYING THIS NEW THING.
VICTOR LAI, NEW GRAMPUS INTELLIGENCER. CAN I ASK--
V.L.
THE BOOB WINDOW DESIGNATES BRANCH OF SERVICE.
HI. UM. HI.
UH. COULD WE. UH. HI.
SURE THING, SKY-CADETS! ACTIVATE VISO-IMAGERS ON MY MARK!
G-Mobile

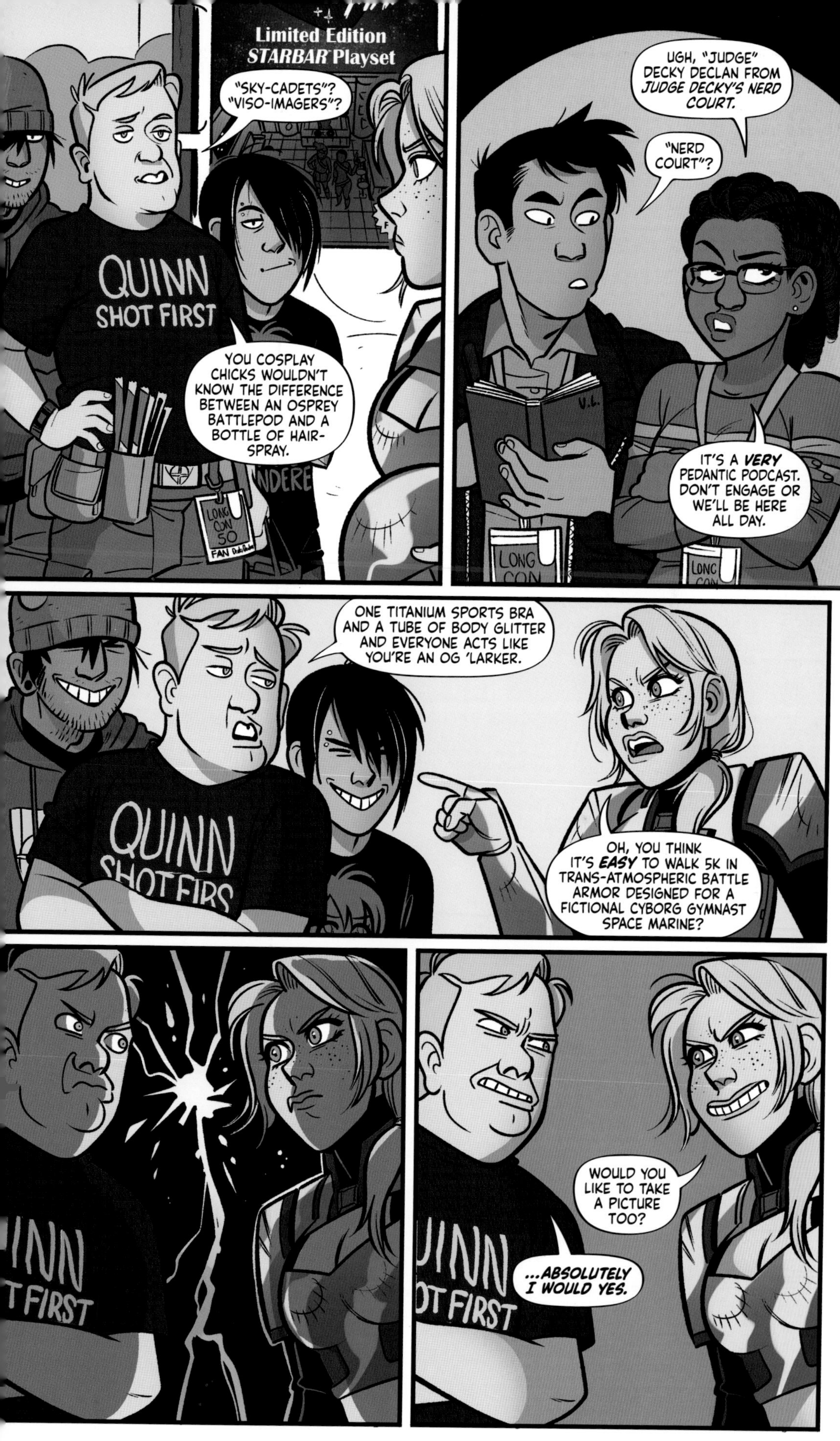
Limited Edition
STARBAR Playset
"SKY-CADETS"? "VISO-IMAGERS"?
QUINN SHOT FIRST
YOU COSPLAY CHICKS WOULDN'T KNOW THE DIFFERENCE BETWEEN AN OSPREY BATTLEPOD AND A BOTTLE OF HAIR-SPRAY.
LONG CON 50
FAN
UGH, "JUDGE" DECKY DECLAN FROM JUDGE DECKY'S NERD COURT.
"NERD COURT"?
IT'S A VERY PEDANTIC PODCAST. DON'T ENGAGE OR WE'LL BE HERE ALL DAY.
ONE TITANIUM SPORTS BRA AND A TUBE OF BODY GLITTER AND EVERYONE ACTS LIKE YOU'RE AN OG 'LARKER.
OH, YOU THINK IT'S EASY TO WALK 5K IN TRANS-ATMOSPHERIC BATTLE ARMOR DESIGNED FOR A FICTIONAL CYBORG GYMNAST SPACE MARINE?
WOULD YOU LIKE TO TAKE A PICTURE TOO?
...ABSOLUTELY I WOULD YES.

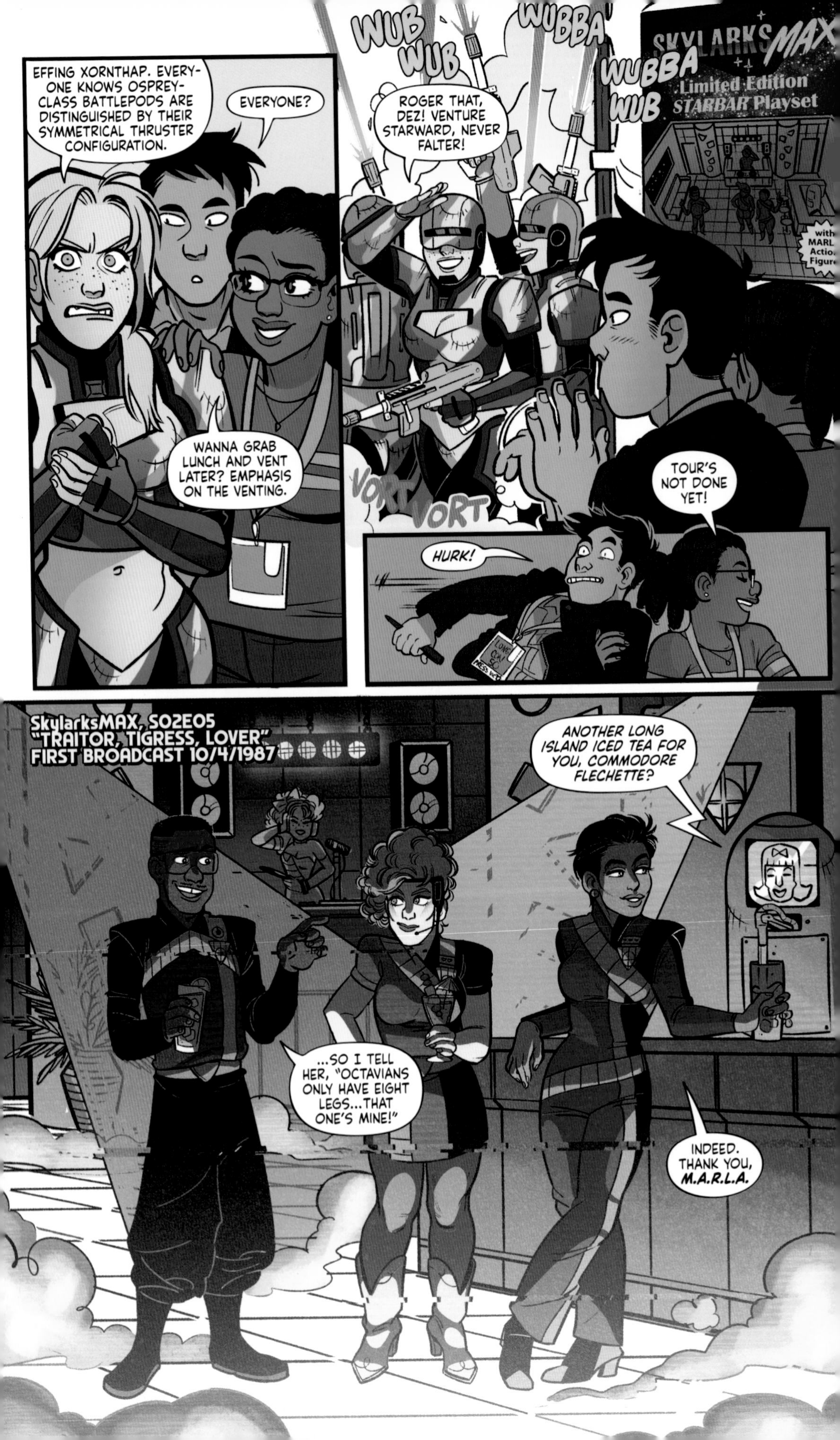
EFFING XORNTHAP. EVERYONE KNOWS OSPREY-CLASS BATTLEPODS ARE DISTINGUISHED BY THEIR SYMMETRICAL THRUSTER CONFIGURATION.
EVERYONE?
WANNA GRAB LUNCH AND VENT LATER? EMPHASIS ON THE VENTING.
WUB WUB
WUBBA WUBBA WUB
SKYLARKS MAX
Limited Edition
STARBAR Playset
ROGER THAT, DEZ! VENTURE STARWARD, NEVER FALTER!
VORT VORT
TOUR'S NOT DONE YET!
HURK!
SkylarksMAX, S02E05
"TRAITOR, TIGRESS, LOVER"
FIRST BROADCAST 10/4/1987
ANOTHER LONG ISLAND ICED TEA FOR YOU, COMMODORE FLECHETTE?
...SO I TELL HER, "OCTAVIANS ONLY HAVE EIGHT LEGS...THAT ONE'S MINE!"
INDEED. THANK YOU, M.A.R.L.A.

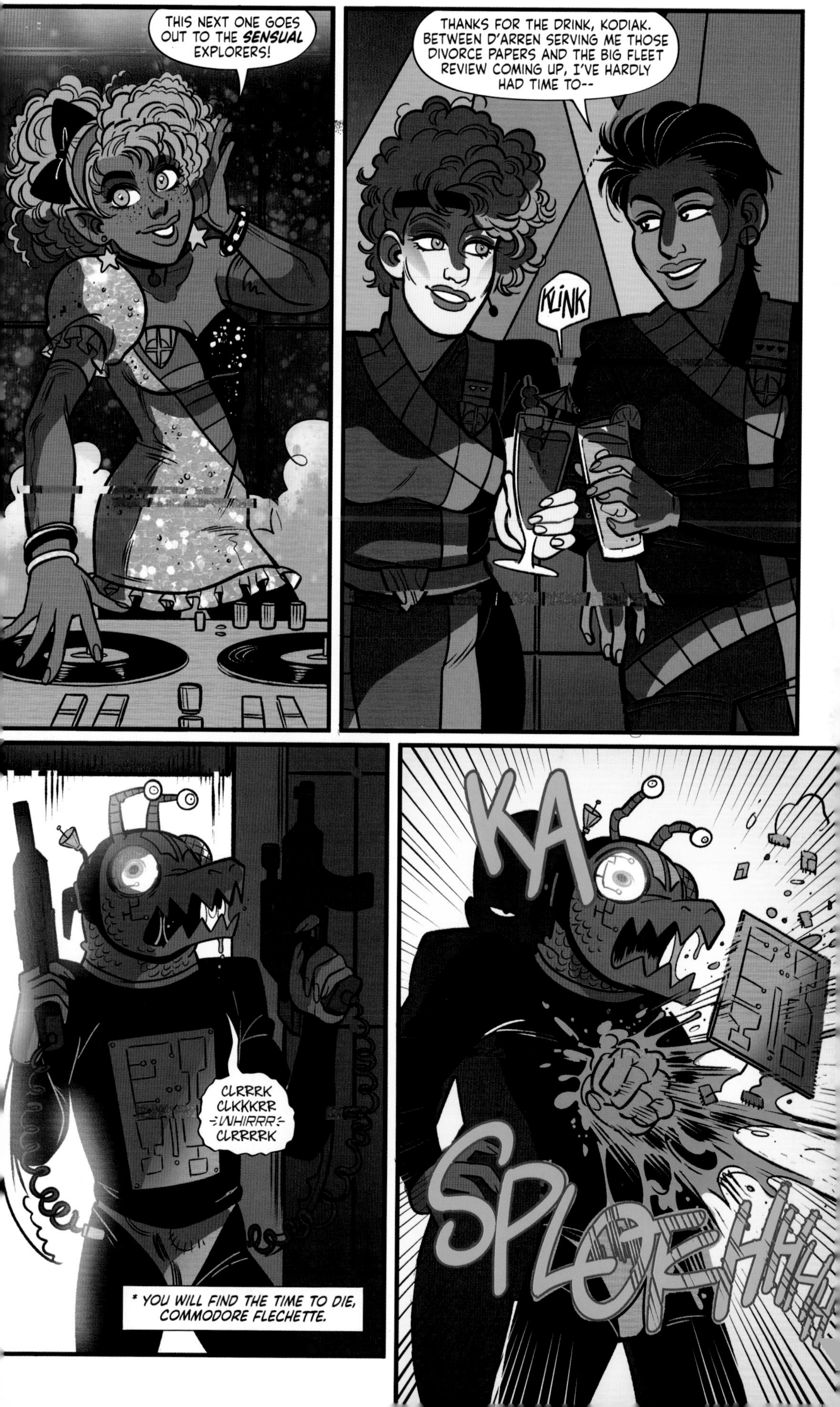
THIS NEXT ONE GOES OUT TO THE SENSUAL EXPLORERS!
THANKS FOR THE DRINK, KODIAK. BETWEEN D'ARREN SERVING ME THOSE DIVORCE PAPERS AND THE BIG FLEET REVIEW COMING UP, I'VE HARDLY HAD TIME TO--
KLINK
CLRRRK
CLKKKRR
-WHIRRR-
CLRRRRK
* YOU WILL FIND THE TIME TO DIE, COMMODORE FLECHETTE.
KA
SPLORCHHH

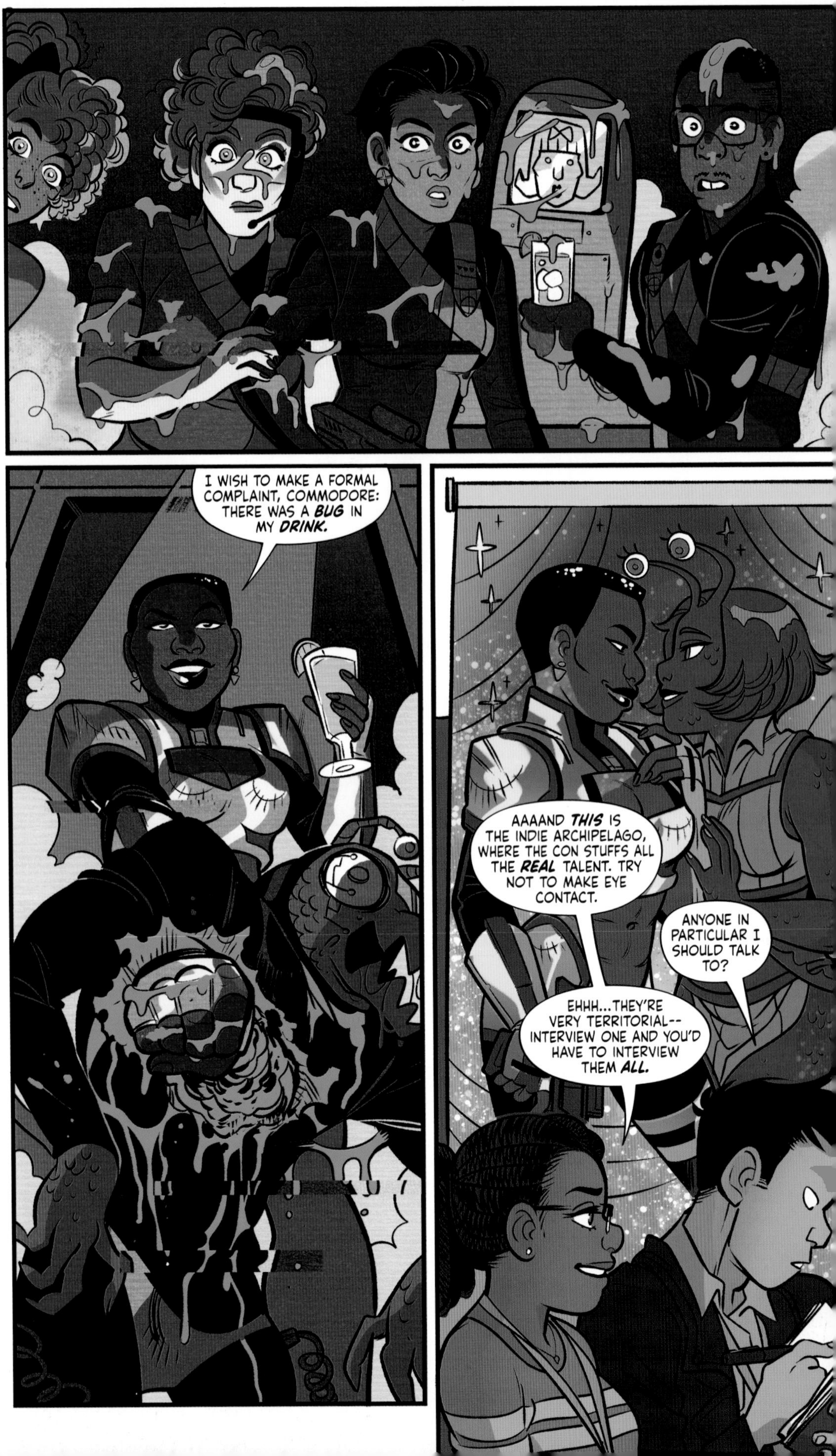
I WISH TO MAKE A FORMAL COMPLAINT, COMMODORE: THERE WAS A *BUG* IN MY *DRINK.*
AAAAND *THIS* IS THE INDIE ARCHIPELAGO, WHERE THE CON STUFFS ALL THE *REAL* TALENT. TRY NOT TO MAKE EYE CONTACT.
ANYONE IN PARTICULAR I SHOULD TALK TO?
EHHH...THEY'RE VERY TERRITORIAL--INTERVIEW ONE AND YOU'D HAVE TO INTERVIEW THEM *ALL.*

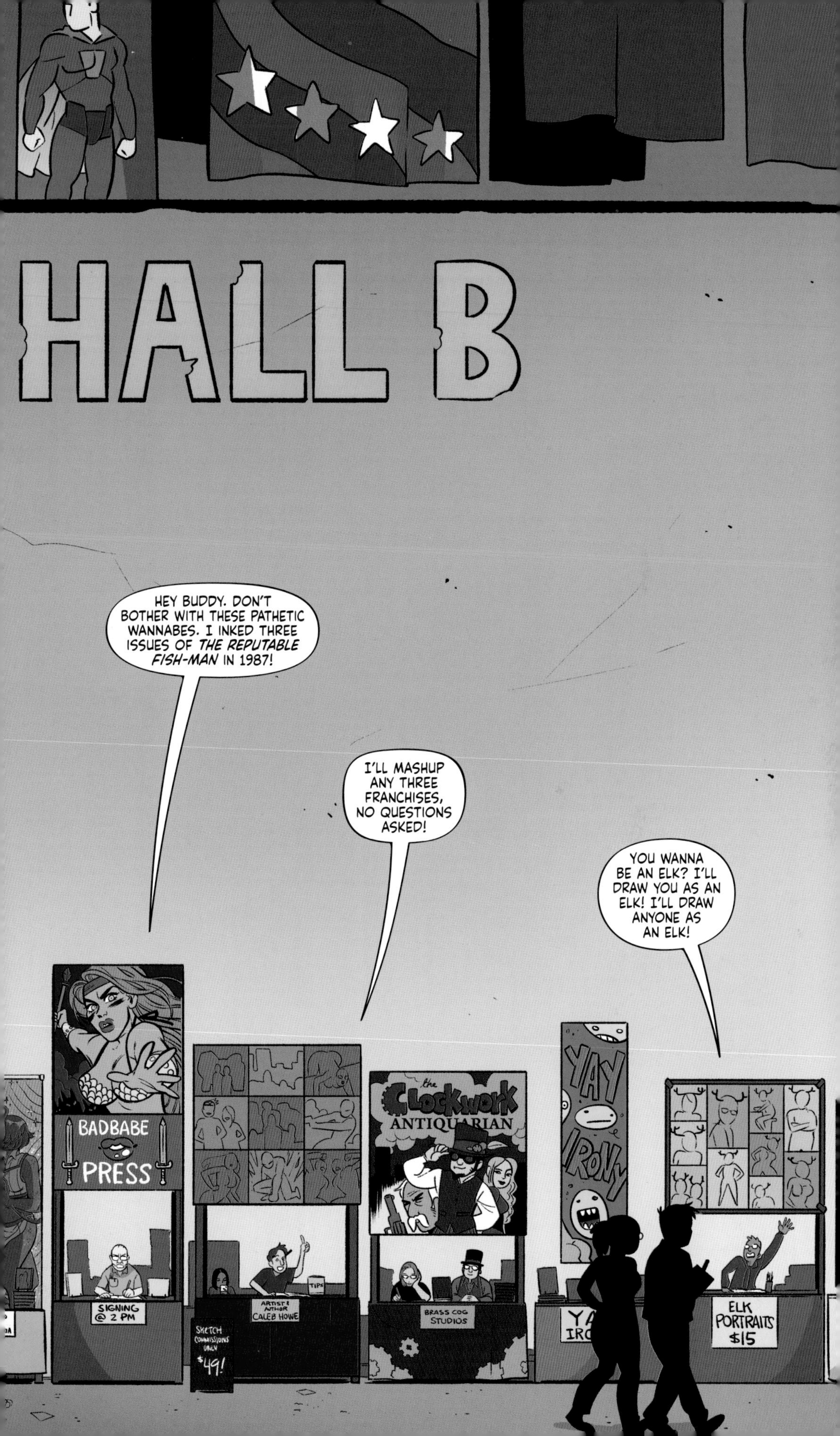
HALL B
HEY BUDDY. DON'T BOTHER WITH THESE PATHETIC WANNABES. I INKED THREE ISSUES OF *THE REPUTABLE FISH-MAN* IN 1987!
I'LL MASHUP ANY THREE FRANCHISES, NO QUESTIONS ASKED!
YOU WANNA BE AN ELK? I'LL DRAW YOU AS AN ELK! I'LL DRAW ANYONE AS AN ELK!
BADBABE PRESS
SIGNING @ 2 PM
ARTIST & AUTHOR CALEB HOWE
TIPS
SKETCH COMMISSIONS ONLY $49!
the CLOCKWORK ANTIQUARIAN
BRASS COG STUDIOS
YAY IRONY
ELK PORTRAITS $15

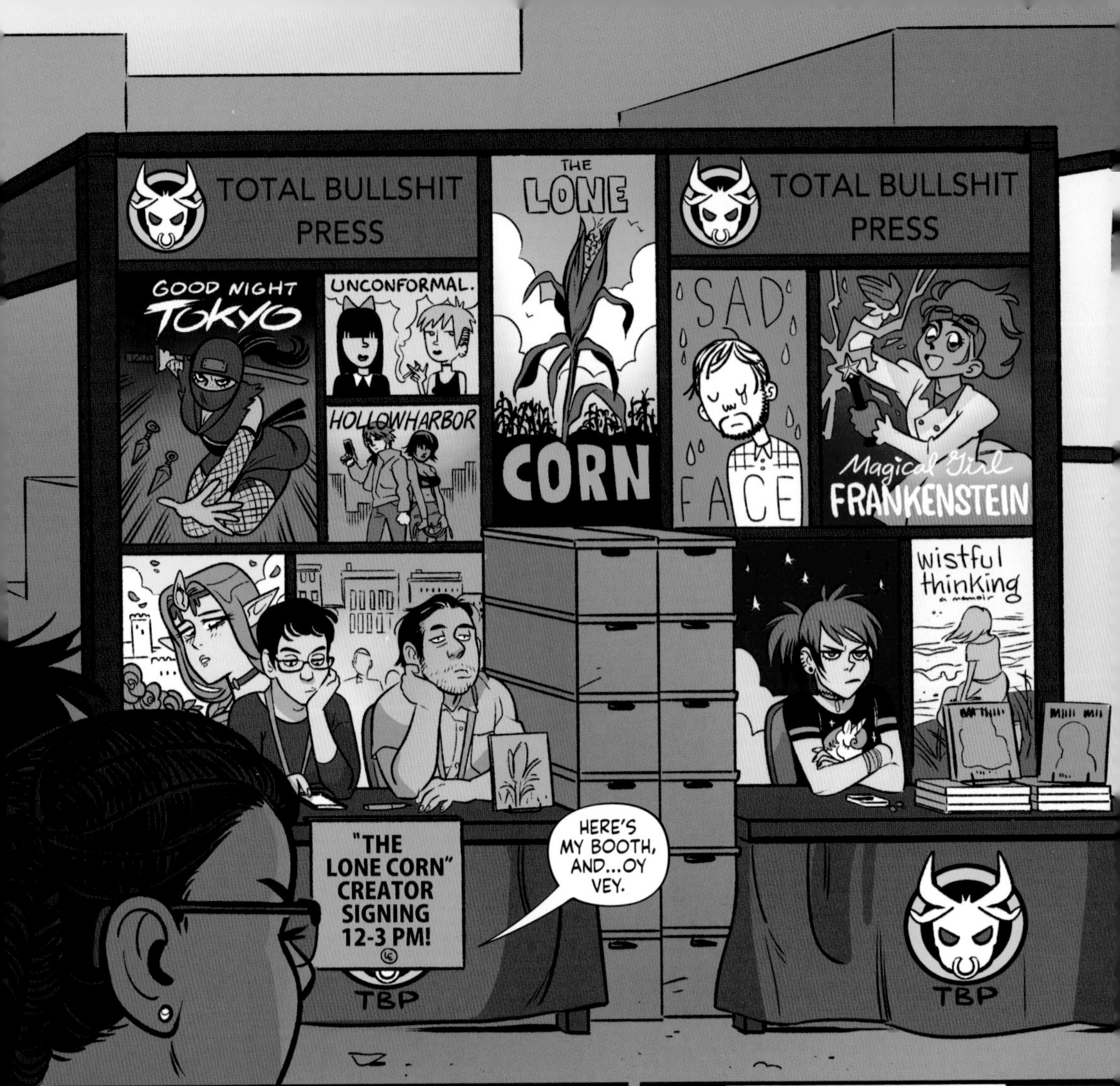
TOTAL BULLSHIT PRESS
THE LONE CORN
TOTAL BULLSHIT PRESS
GOOD NIGHT TOKYO
UNCONFORMAL.
HOLLOWHARBOR
SAD FACE
Magical Girl FRANKENSTEIN
wistful thinking
"THE LONE CORN" CREATOR SIGNING 12-3 PM!
HERE'S MY BOOTH, AND...OY VEY.
TBP
TBP

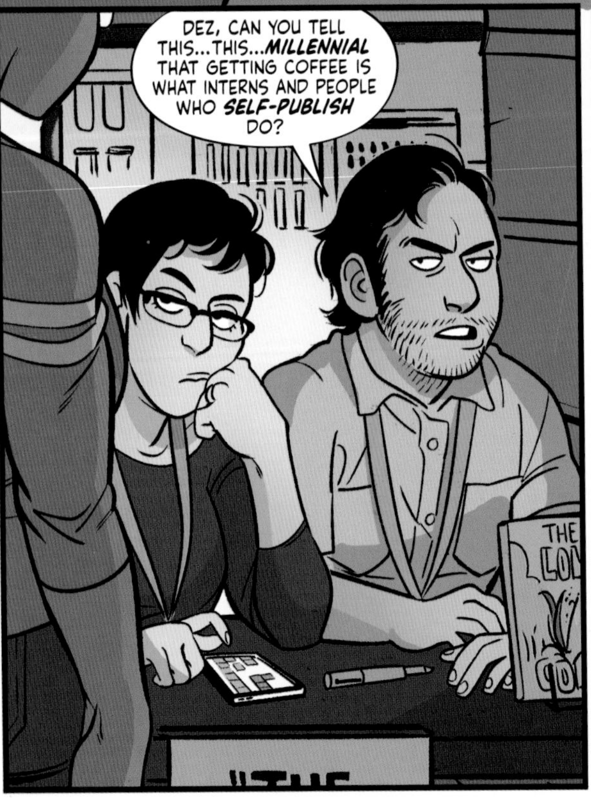
DEZ, CAN YOU TELL THIS...THIS...MILLENNIAL THAT GETTING COFFEE IS WHAT INTERNS AND PEOPLE WHO SELF-PUBLISH DO?

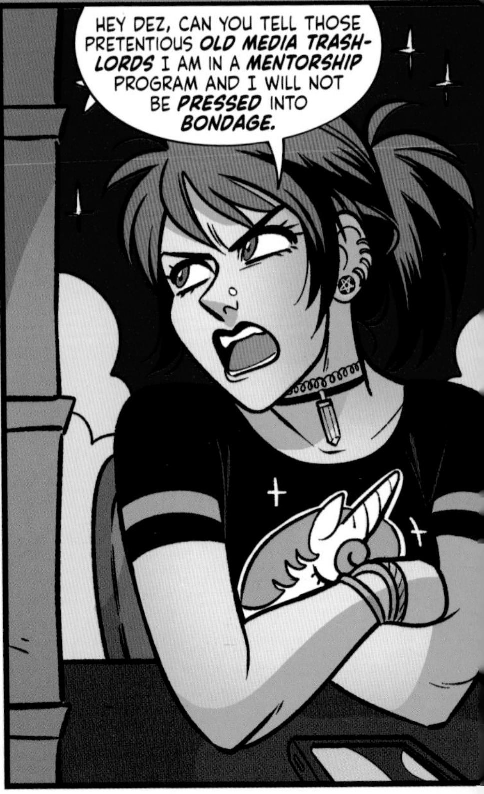
HEY DEZ, CAN YOU TELL THOSE PRETENTIOUS OLD MEDIA TRASH-LORDS I AM IN A MENTORSHIP PROGRAM AND I WILL NOT BE PRESSED INTO BONDAGE.

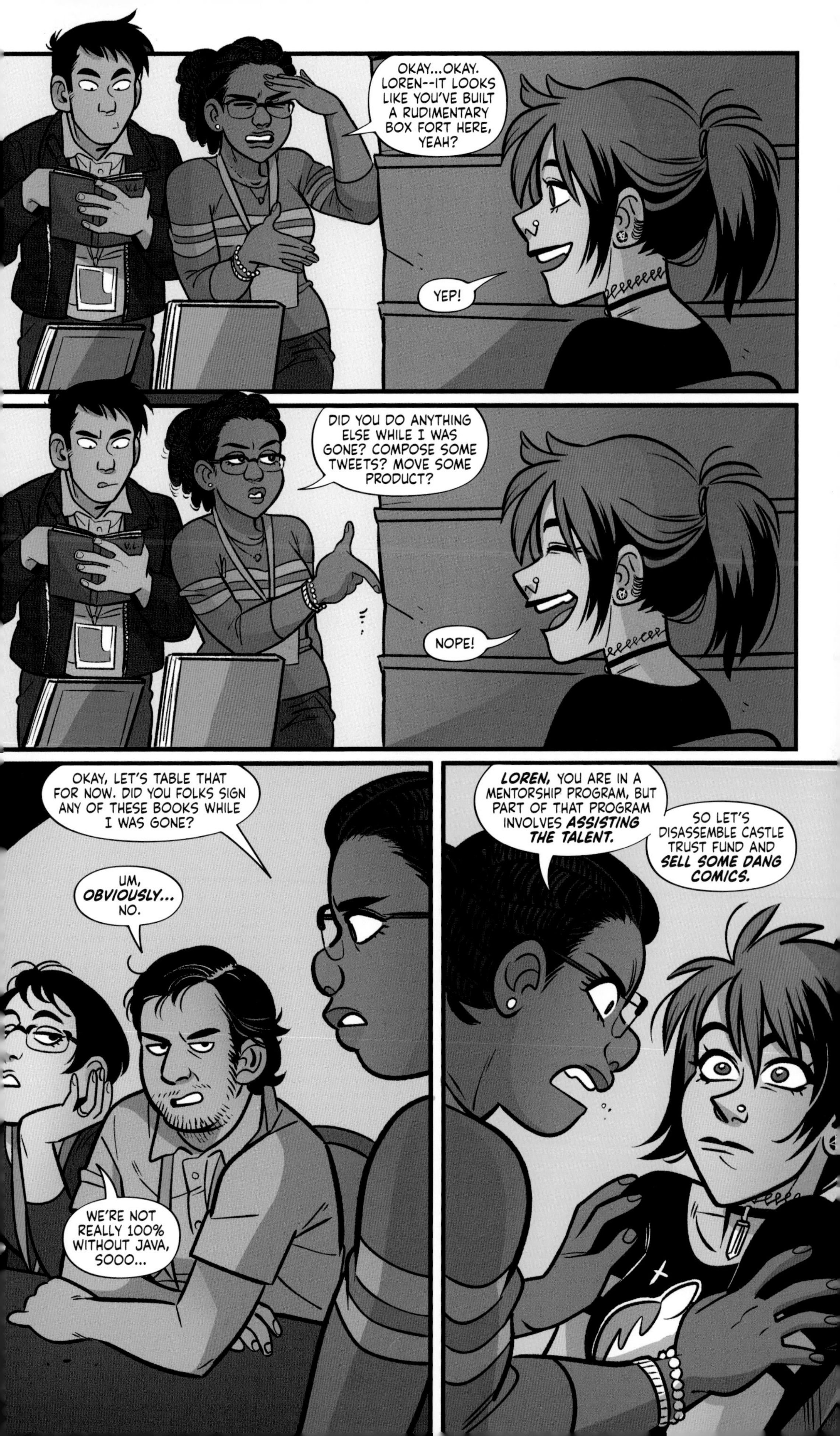
OKAY...OKAY. LOREN--IT LOOKS LIKE YOU'VE BUILT A RUDIMENTARY BOX FORT HERE, YEAH?
YEP!
DID YOU DO ANYTHING ELSE WHILE I WAS GONE? COMPOSE SOME TWEETS? MOVE SOME PRODUCT?
NOPE!
OKAY, LET'S TABLE THAT FOR NOW. DID YOU FOLKS SIGN ANY OF THESE BOOKS WHILE I WAS GONE?
UM, *OBVIOUSLY...* NO.
WE'RE NOT REALLY 100% WITHOUT JAVA, SOOO...
LOREN, YOU ARE IN A MENTORSHIP PROGRAM, BUT PART OF THAT PROGRAM INVOLVES *ASSISTING THE TALENT.*
SO LET'S DISASSEMBLE CASTLE TRUST FUND AND *SELL SOME DANG COMICS.*

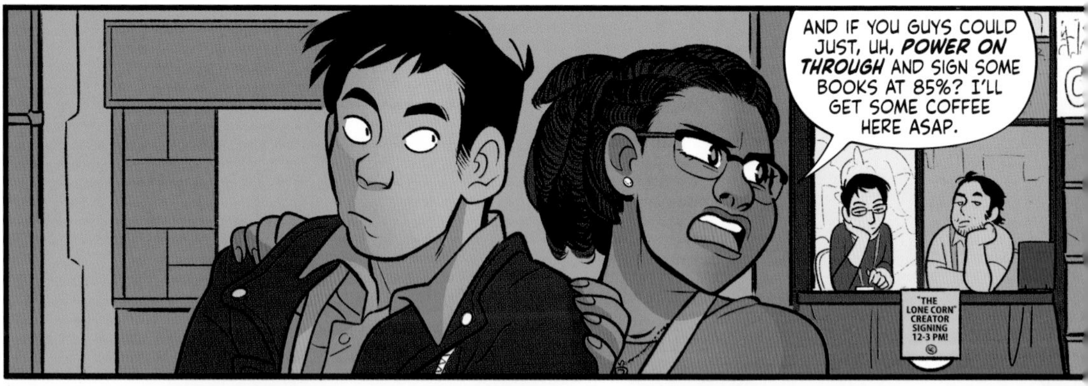
AND IF YOU GUYS COULD JUST, UH, ***POWER ON THROUGH*** AND SIGN SOME BOOKS AT 85%? I'LL GET SOME COFFEE HERE ASAP.
"THE LONE CORN" CREATOR SIGNING 12-3 PM!

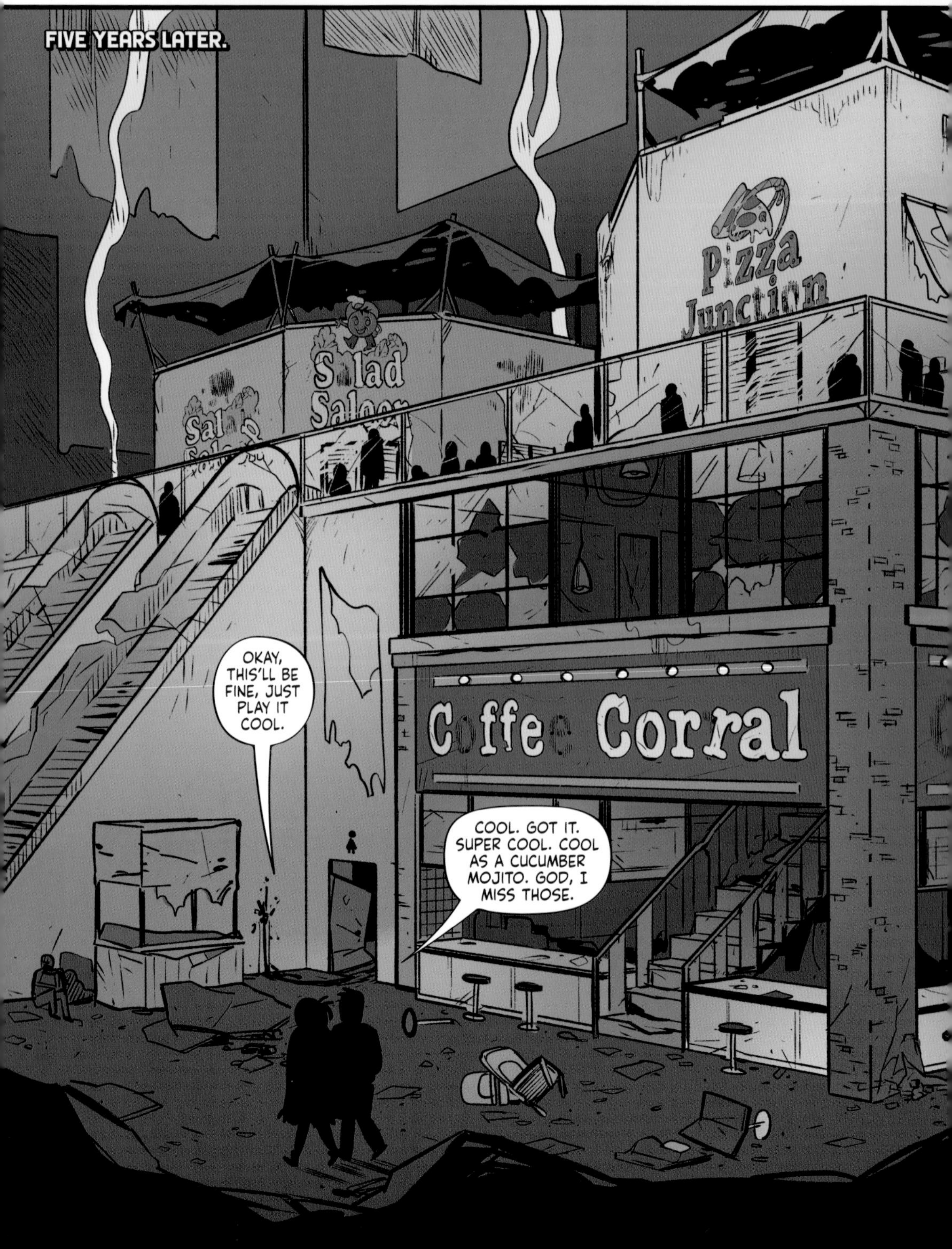
FIVE YEARS LATER.
Pizza Junction
Salad Saloon
Coffee Corral
OKAY, THIS'LL BE FINE, JUST PLAY IT COOL.
COOL. GOT IT. SUPER COOL. COOL AS A CUCUMBER MOJITO. GOD, I MISS THOSE.

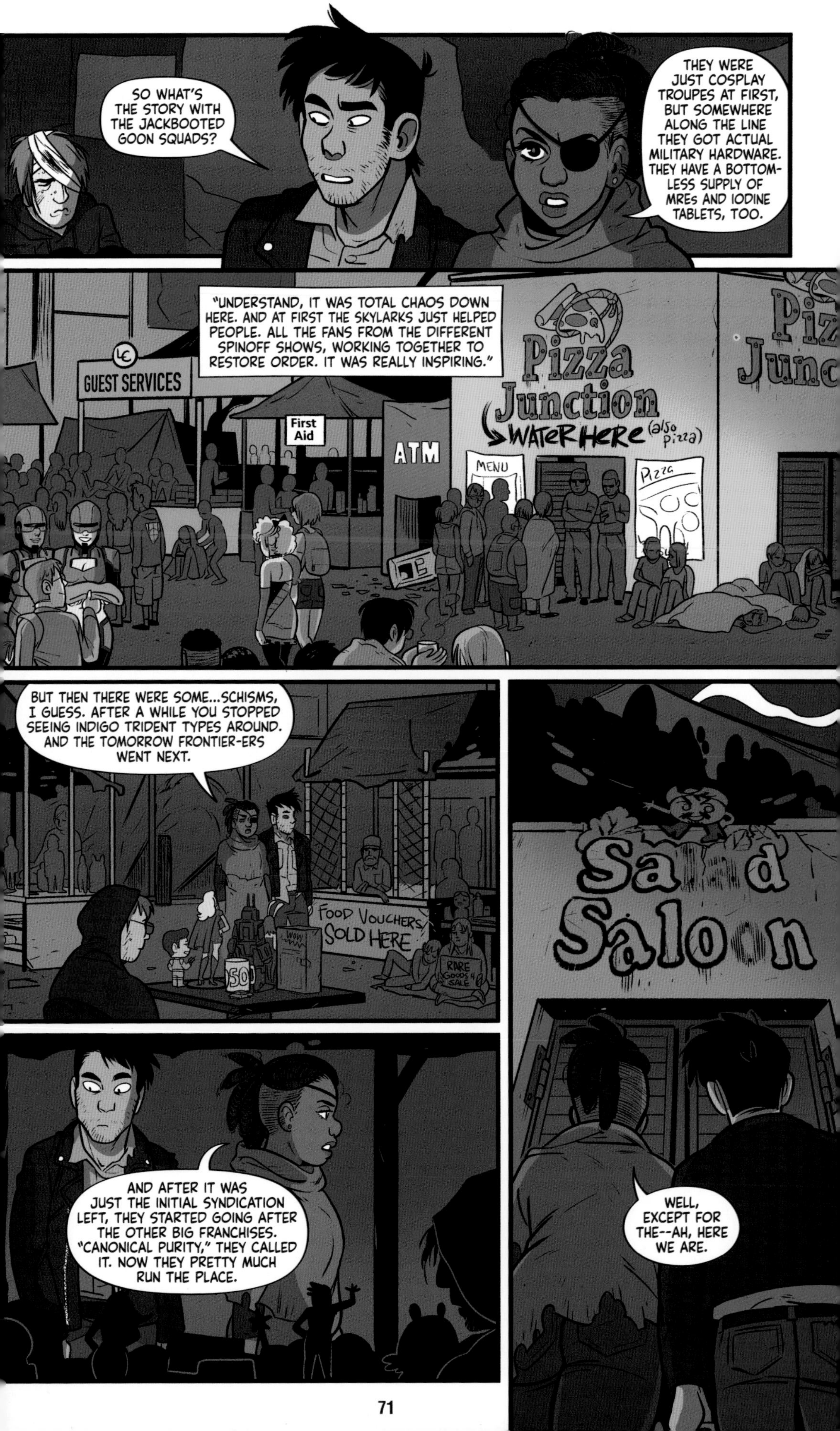
SO WHAT'S THE STORY WITH THE JACKBOOTED GOON SQUADS?
THEY WERE JUST COSPLAY TROUPES AT FIRST, BUT SOMEWHERE ALONG THE LINE THEY GOT ACTUAL MILITARY HARDWARE. THEY HAVE A BOTTOMLESS SUPPLY OF MREs AND IODINE TABLETS, TOO.
"UNDERSTAND, IT WAS TOTAL CHAOS DOWN HERE. AND AT FIRST THE SKYLARKS JUST HELPED PEOPLE. ALL THE FANS FROM THE DIFFERENT SPINOFF SHOWS, WORKING TOGETHER TO RESTORE ORDER. IT WAS REALLY INSPIRING."
GUEST SERVICES
First Aid
ATM
Pizza Junction
WATER HERE (also pizza)
MENU
Pizza
BUT THEN THERE WERE SOME...SCHISMS, I GUESS. AFTER A WHILE YOU STOPPED SEEING INDIGO TRIDENT TYPES AROUND. AND THE TOMORROW FRONTIER-ERS WENT NEXT.
FOOD VOUCHERS SOLD HERE
RARE GOODS 4 SALE
AND AFTER IT WAS JUST THE INITIAL SYNDICATION LEFT, THEY STARTED GOING AFTER THE OTHER BIG FRANCHISES. "CANONICAL PURITY," THEY CALLED IT. NOW THEY PRETTY MUCH RUN THE PLACE.
Salon
WELL, EXCEPT FOR THE--AH, HERE WE ARE.

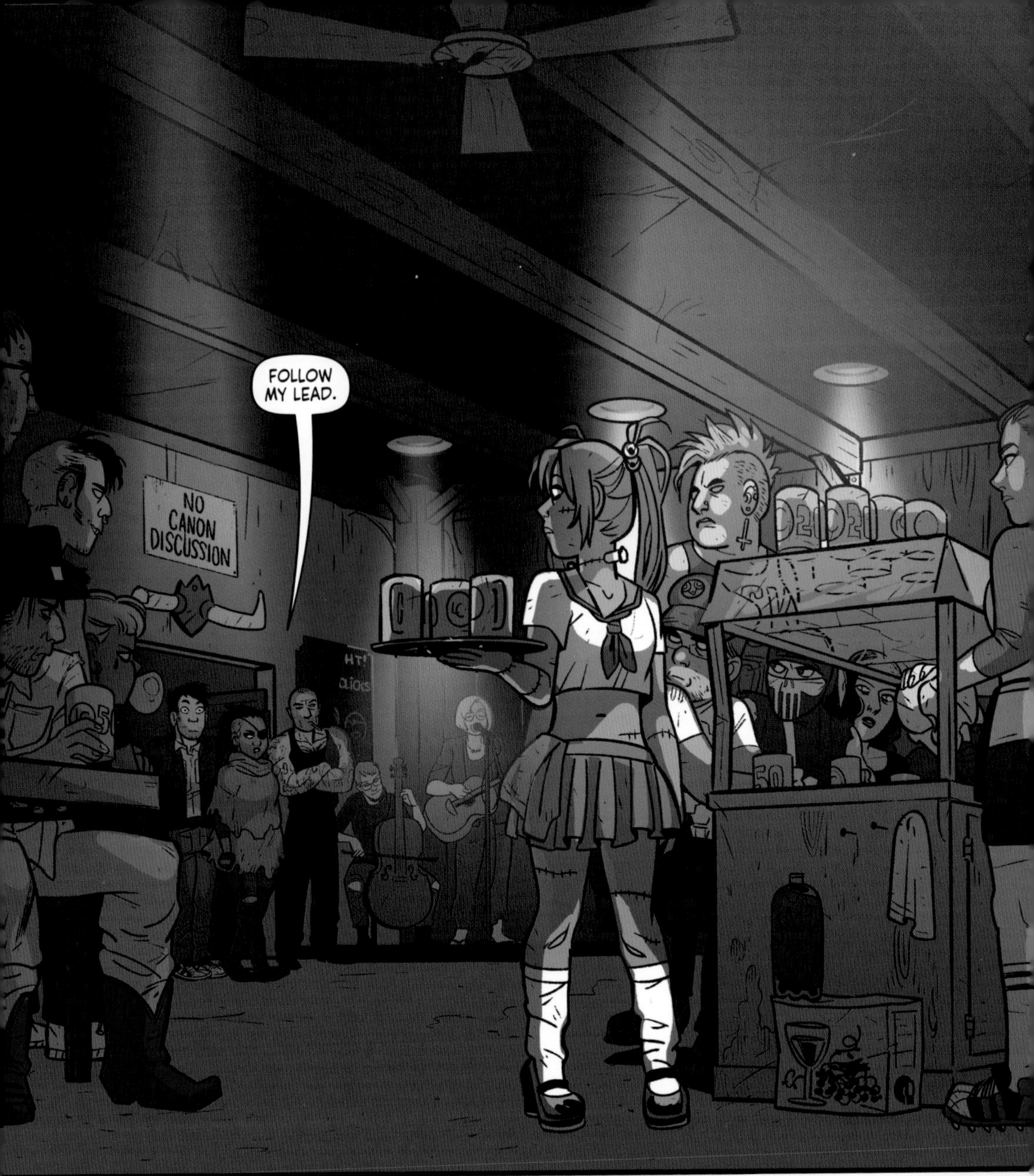
NO CANON DISCUSSION
FOLLOW MY LEAD.

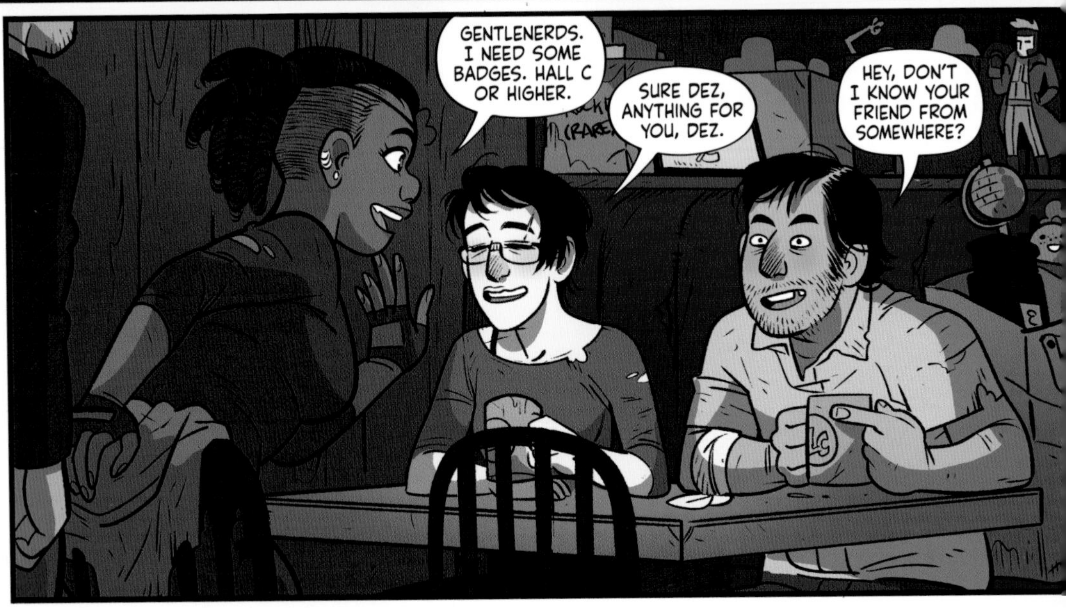
GENTLENERDS. I NEED SOME BADGES. HALL C OR HIGHER.
SURE DEZ, ANYTHING FOR YOU, DEZ.
HEY, DON'T I KNOW YOUR FRIEND FROM SOMEWHERE?

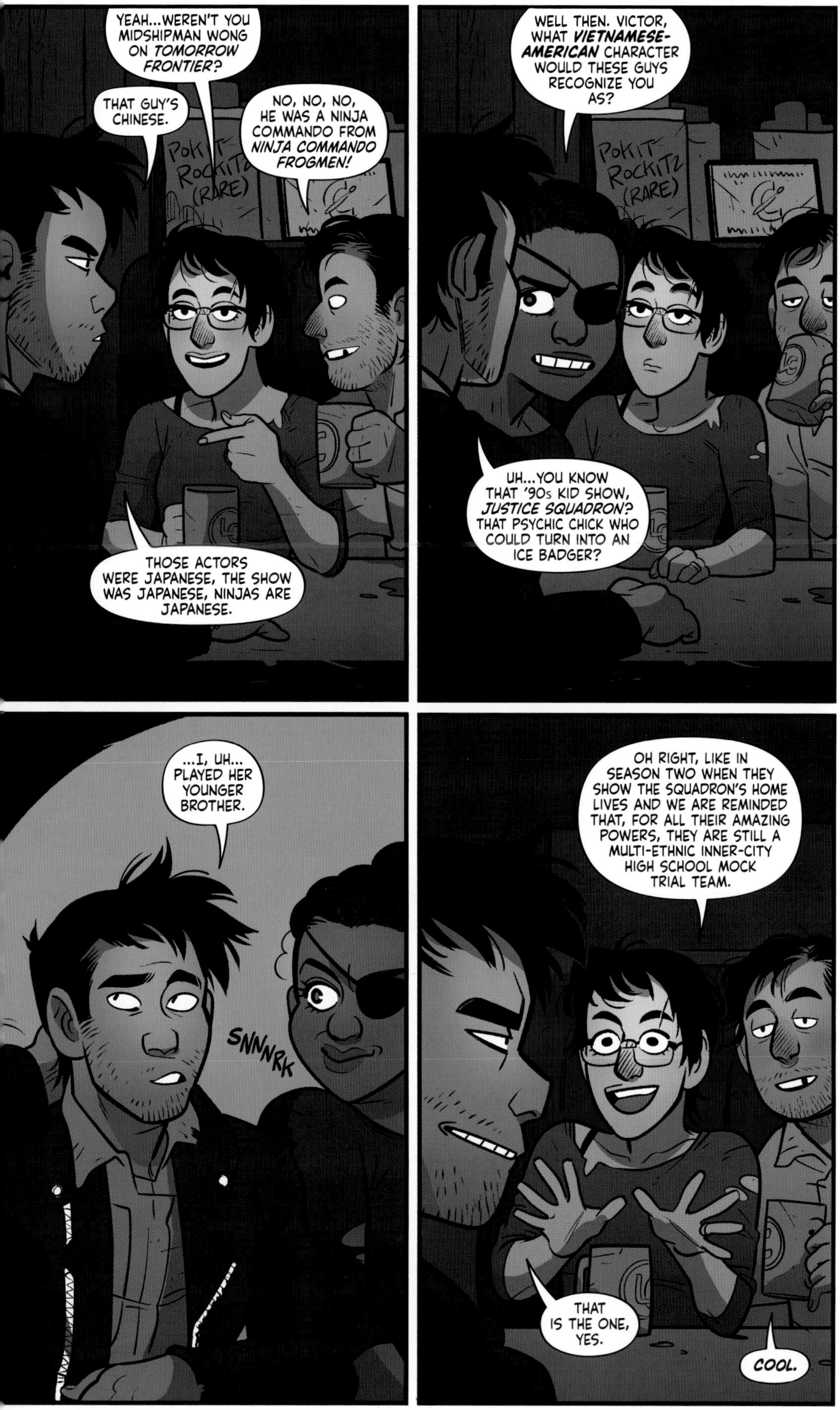
YEAH...WEREN'T YOU MIDSHIPMAN WONG ON *TOMORROW FRONTIER*?
THAT GUY'S CHINESE.
NO, NO, NO, HE WAS A NINJA COMMANDO FROM *NINJA COMMANDO FROGMEN!*
POKIT ROCKITZ (RARE)
THOSE ACTORS WERE JAPANESE, THE SHOW WAS JAPANESE, NINJAS ARE JAPANESE.
WELL THEN. VICTOR, WHAT ***VIETNAMESE-AMERICAN*** CHARACTER WOULD THESE GUYS RECOGNIZE YOU AS?
POKIT ROCKITZ (RARE)
UH...YOU KNOW THAT '90s KID SHOW, *JUSTICE SQUADRON*? THAT PSYCHIC CHICK WHO COULD TURN INTO AN ICE BADGER?
...I, UH... PLAYED HER YOUNGER BROTHER.
SNNNRK
OH RIGHT, LIKE IN SEASON TWO WHEN THEY SHOW THE SQUADRON'S HOME LIVES AND WE ARE REMINDED THAT, FOR ALL THEIR AMAZING POWERS, THEY ARE STILL A MULTI-ETHNIC INNER-CITY HIGH SCHOOL MOCK TRIAL TEAM.
THAT IS THE ONE, YES.
COOL.

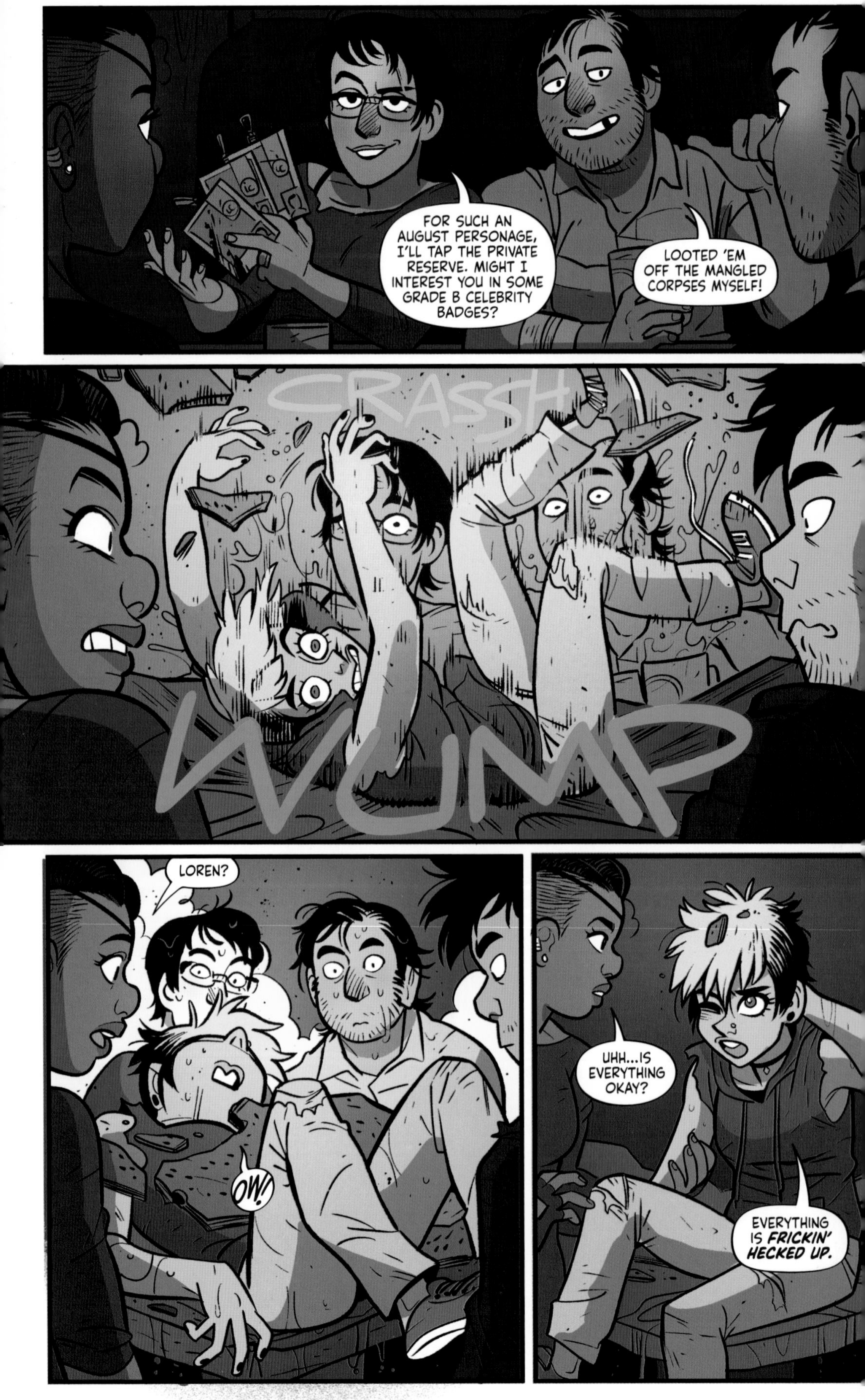
FOR SUCH AN AUGUST PERSONAGE, I'LL TAP THE PRIVATE RESERVE. MIGHT I INTEREST YOU IN SOME GRADE B CELEBRITY BADGES?
LOOTED 'EM OFF THE MANGLED CORPSES MYSELF!
CRASSH
WUMP
LOREN?
OW!
UHH...IS EVERYTHING OKAY?
EVERYTHING IS *FRICKIN'* *HECKED UP.*

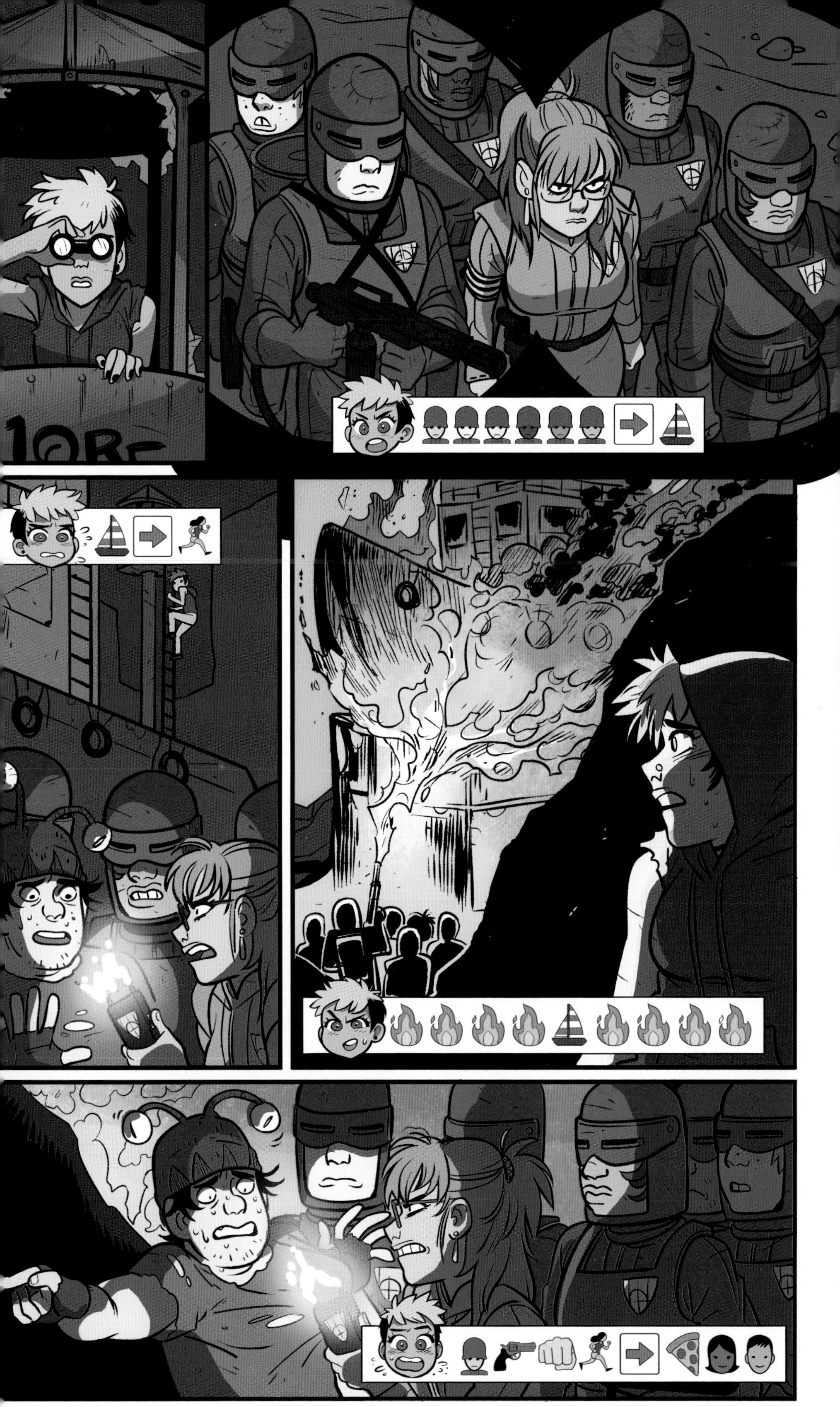

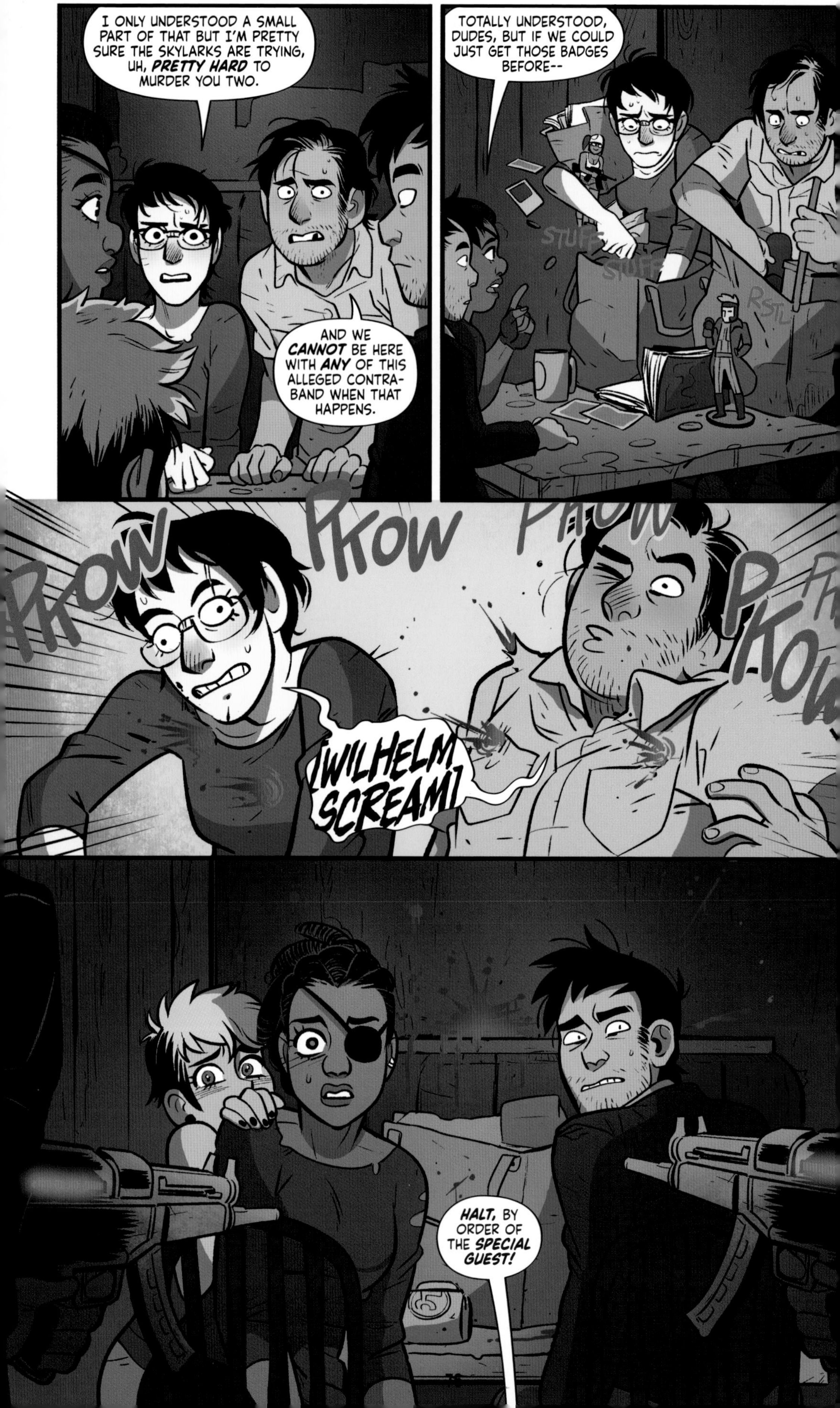
I ONLY UNDERSTOOD A SMALL PART OF THAT BUT I'M PRETTY SURE THE SKYLARKS ARE TRYING, UH, PRETTY HARD TO MURDER YOU TWO.
AND WE CANNOT BE HERE WITH ANY OF THIS ALLEGED CONTRA-BAND WHEN THAT HAPPENS.
TOTALLY UNDERSTOOD, DUDES, BUT IF WE COULD JUST GET THOSE BADGES BEFORE--
STUFF
STUFF
RSTL
PKOW
PKOW
PKOW
PKOW
[WILHELM SCREAM]
HALT, BY ORDER OF THE SPECIAL GUEST!

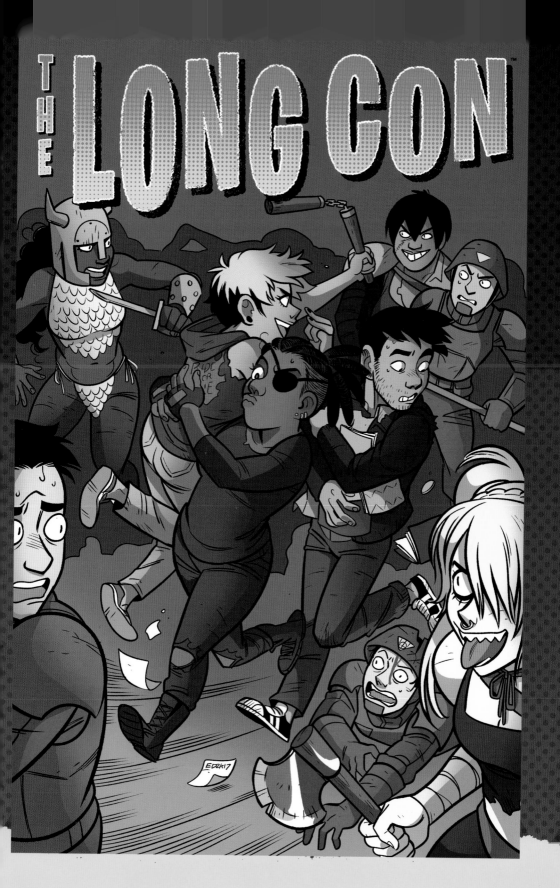

CHAPTER 4: ESCAPE FROM PIZZA JUNCTION

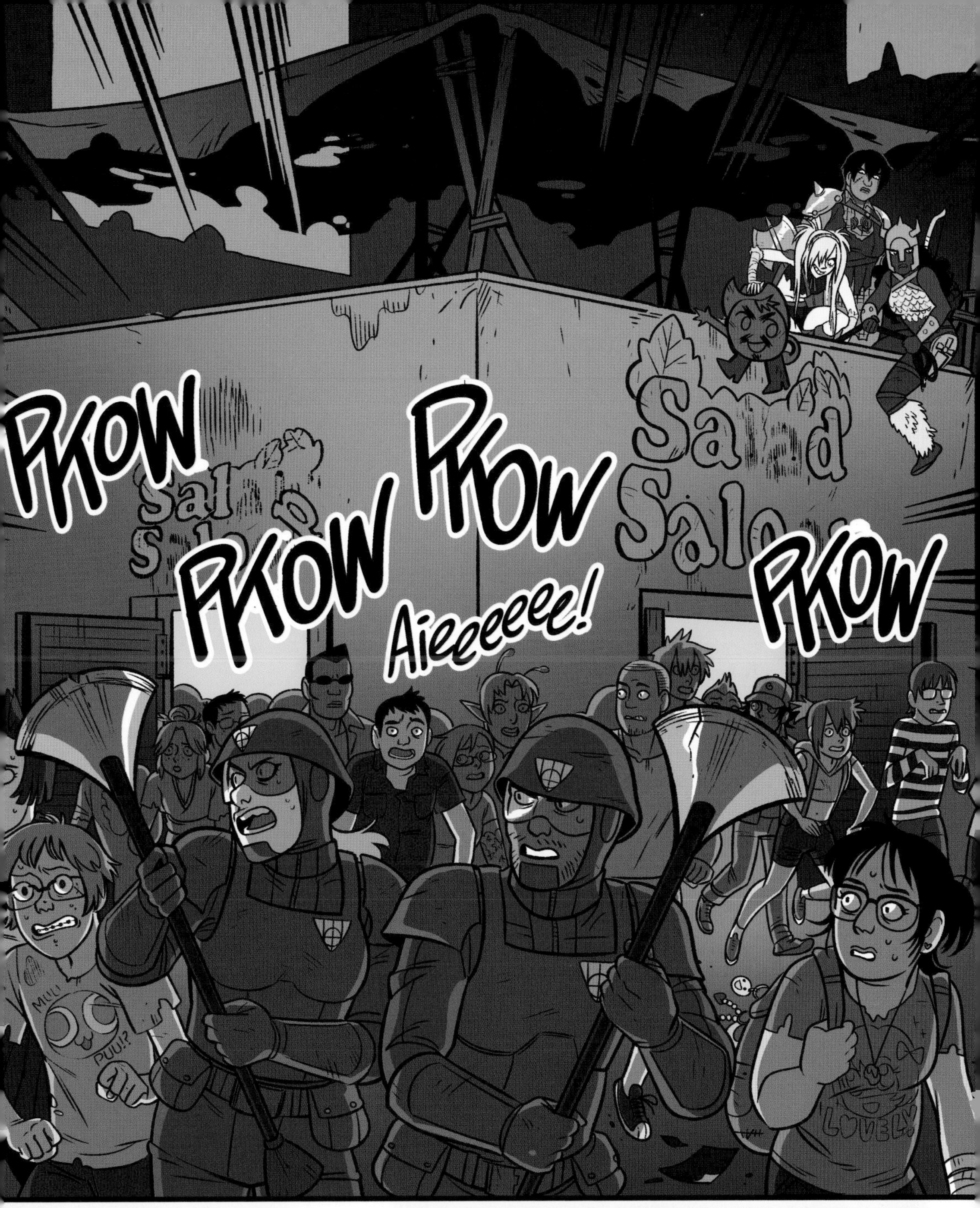
PKOW
PKOW
PKOW
Aieeeeee!
PKOW

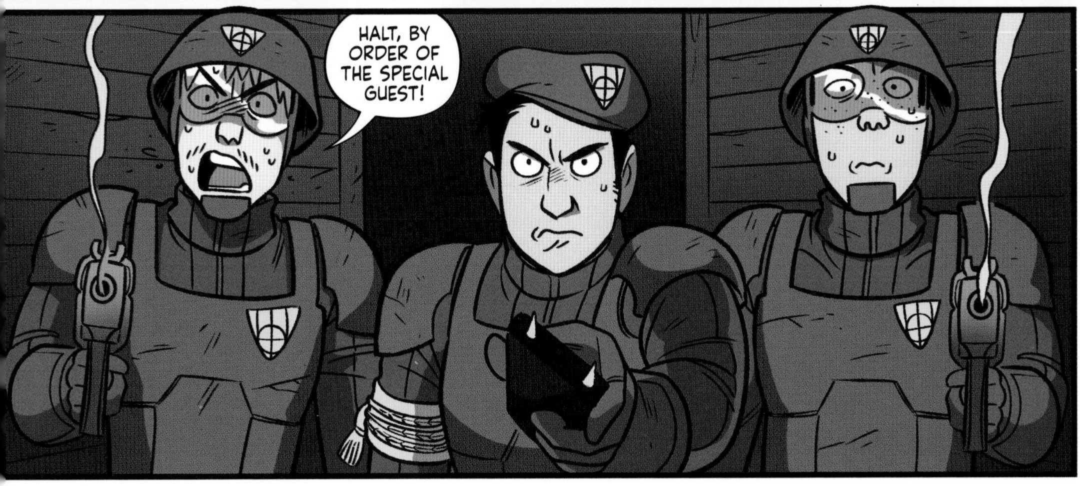
HALT, BY ORDER OF THE SPECIAL GUEST!

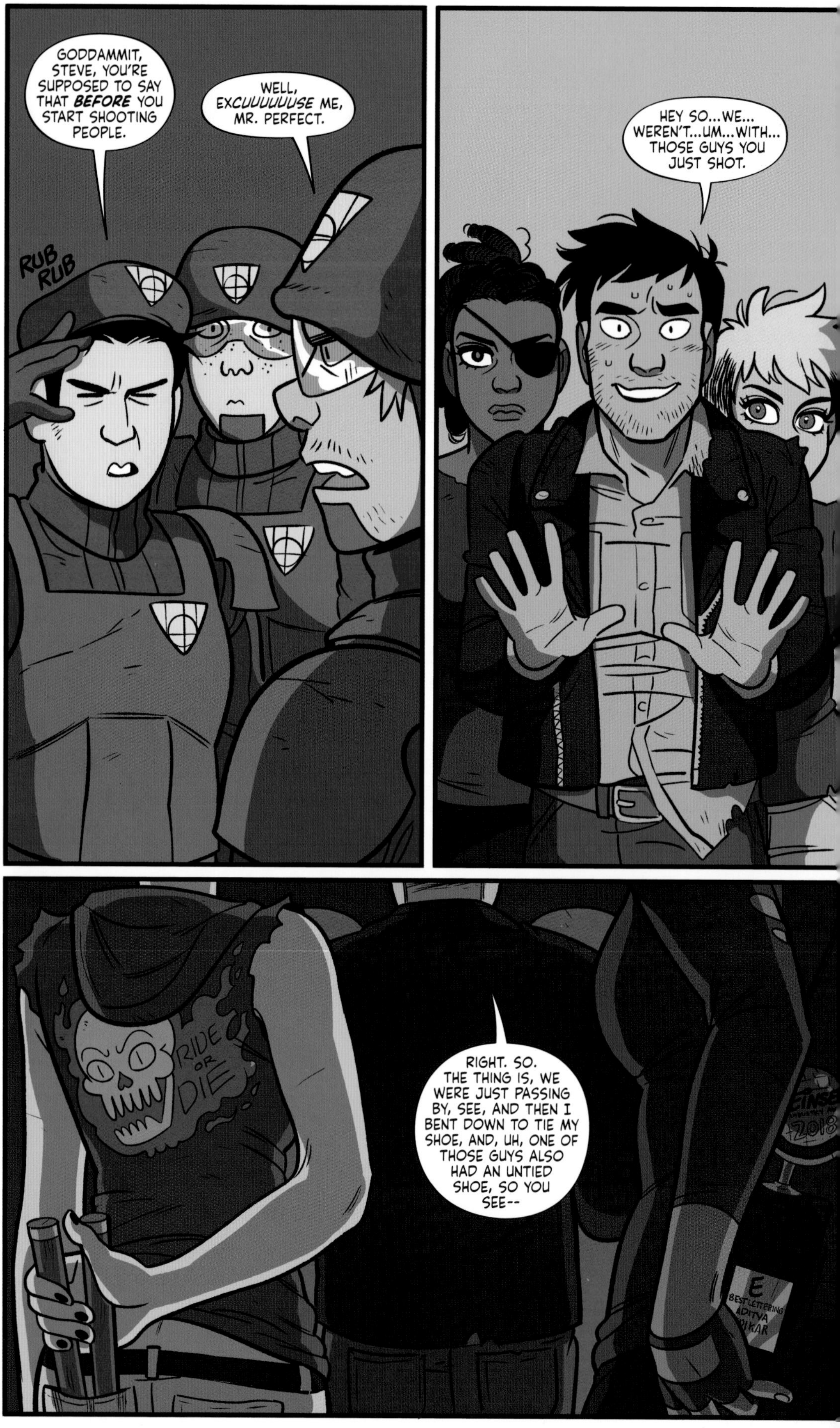
GODDAMMIT, STEVE, YOU'RE SUPPOSED TO SAY THAT **BEFORE** YOU START SHOOTING PEOPLE.
WELL, EX*CUUUUUUSE* ME, MR. PERFECT.
RUB RUB
HEY SO...WE... WEREN'T...UM...WITH... THOSE GUYS YOU JUST SHOT.
RIDE OR DIE
RIGHT. SO. THE THING IS, WE WERE JUST PASSING BY, SEE, AND THEN I BENT DOWN TO TIE MY SHOE, AND, UH, ONE OF THOSE GUYS ALSO HAD AN UNTIED SHOE, SO YOU SEE--
BEST LETTERING
ADITYA

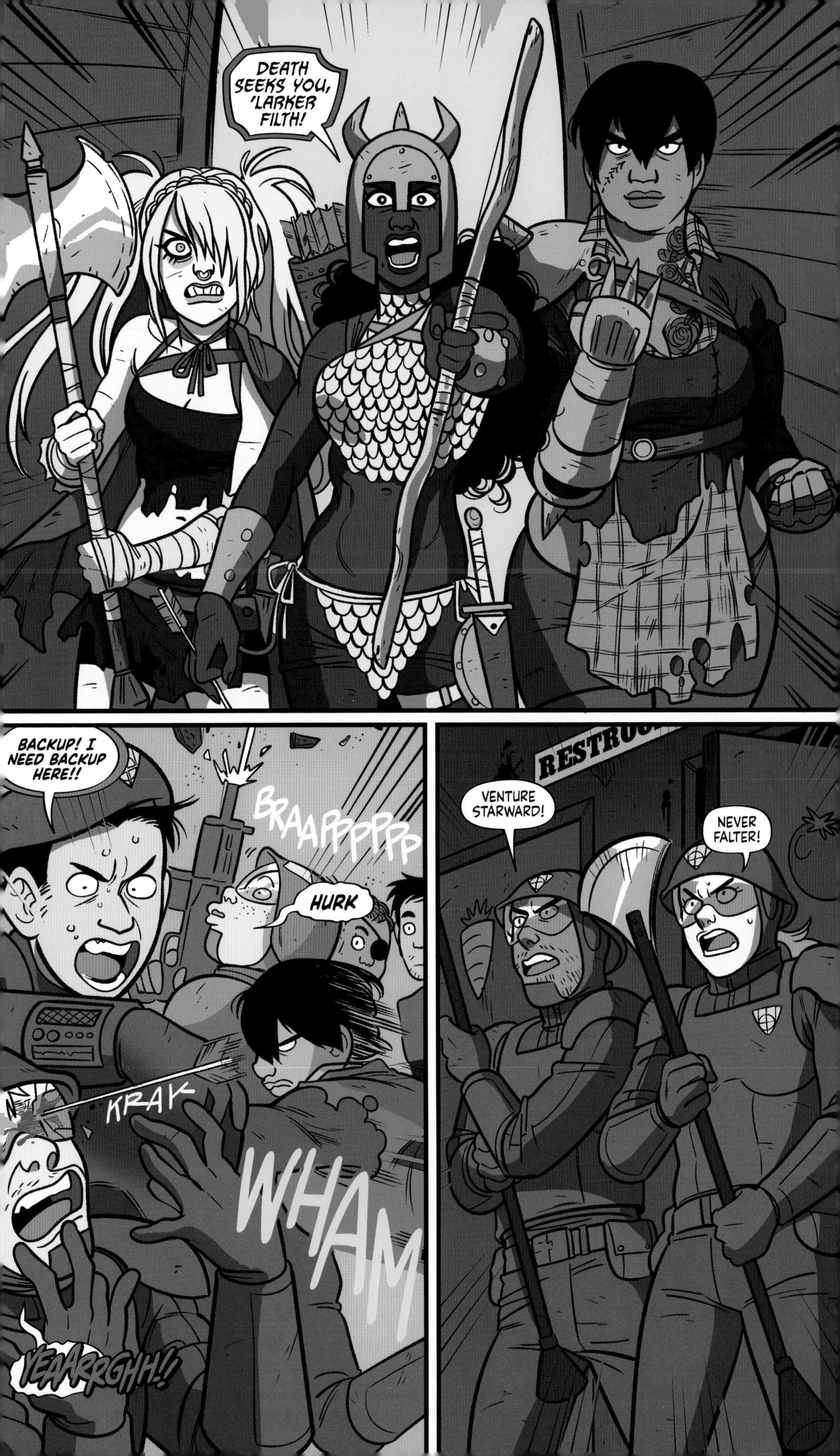
DEATH SEEKS YOU, 'LARKER FILTH!
BACKUP! I NEED BACKUP HERE!!
BRAAPPPPPP
HURK
KRAK
WHAM
YEAARRGHH!!
RESTRO
VENTURE STARWARD!
NEVER FALTER!

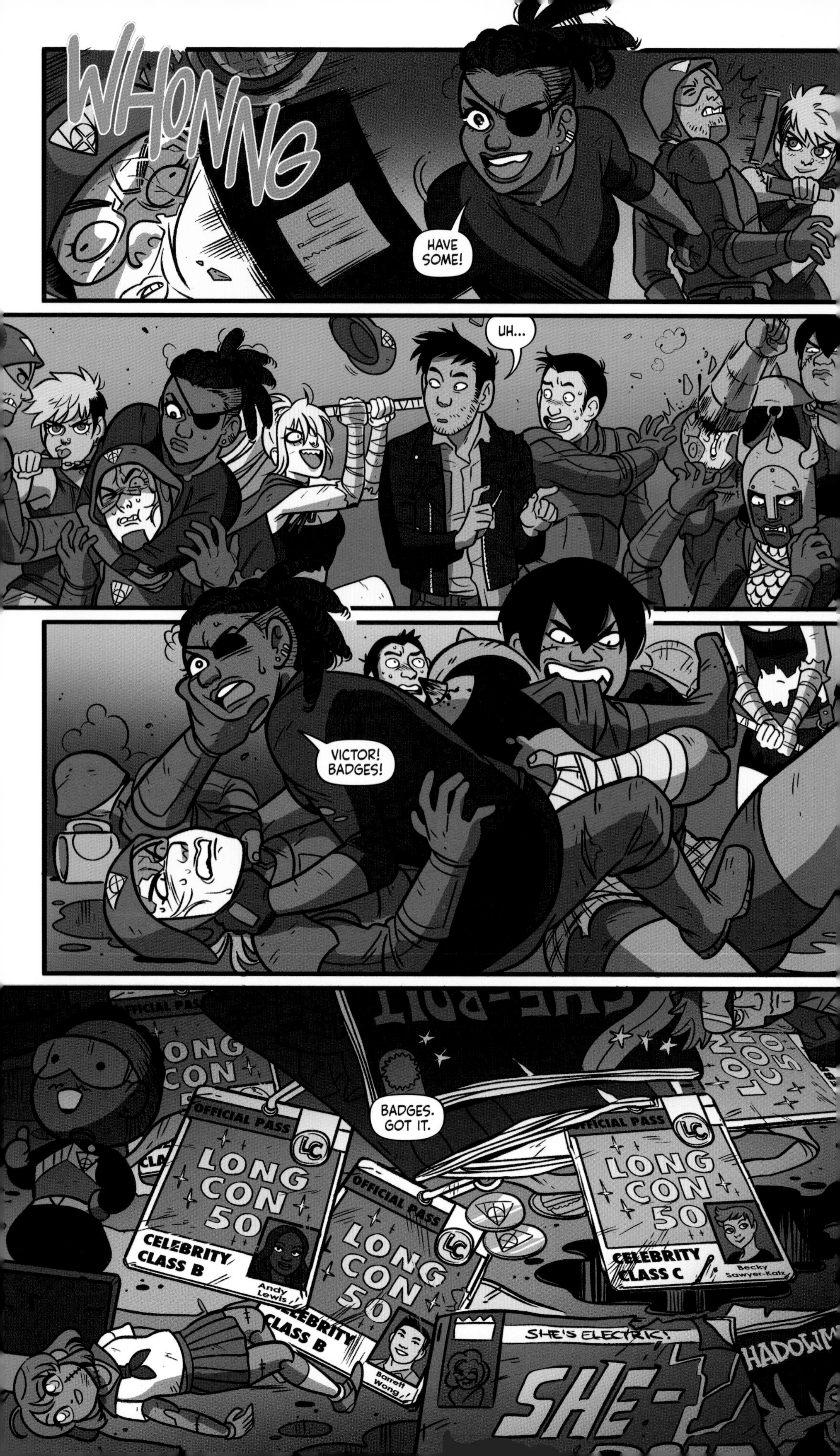
WHONNG
HAVE SOME!
UH...
VICTOR! BADGES!
BADGES. GOT IT.
OFFICIAL PASS
LONG CON 50
CELEBRITY CLASS B
Andy Lewis
OFFICIAL PASS
LONG CON 50
CELEBRITY CLASS B
Barrett Wong
OFFICIAL PASS
LONG CON 50
CELEBRITY CLASS C
Becky Sawyer-Katz
SHE'S ELECTRIC!
SHE-
HADOWM

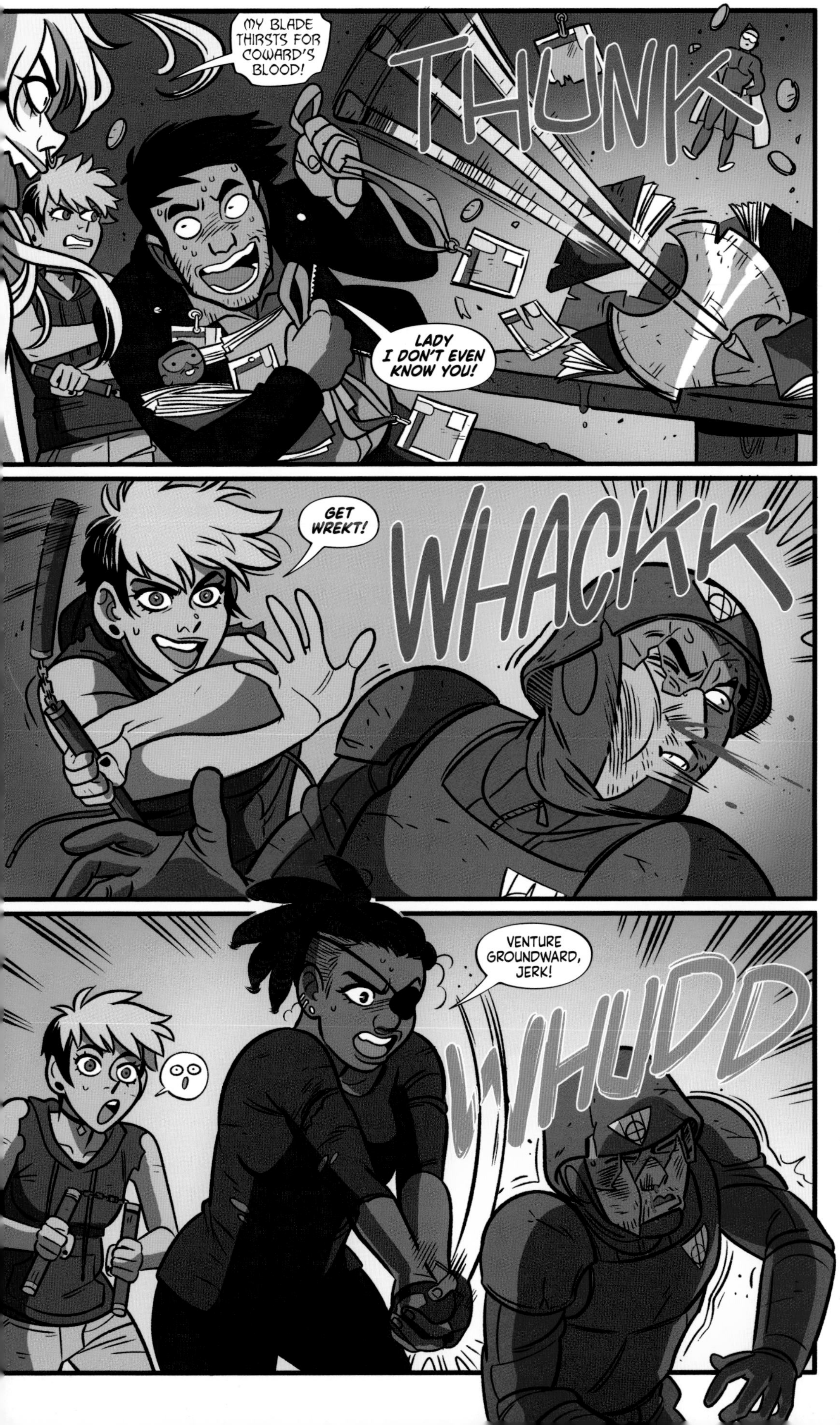
MY BLADE THIRSTS FOR COWARD'S BLOOD!
THUNK
LADY I DON'T EVEN KNOW YOU!
GET WREKT!
WHACKK
VENTURE GROUNDWARD, JERK!
WHUDD

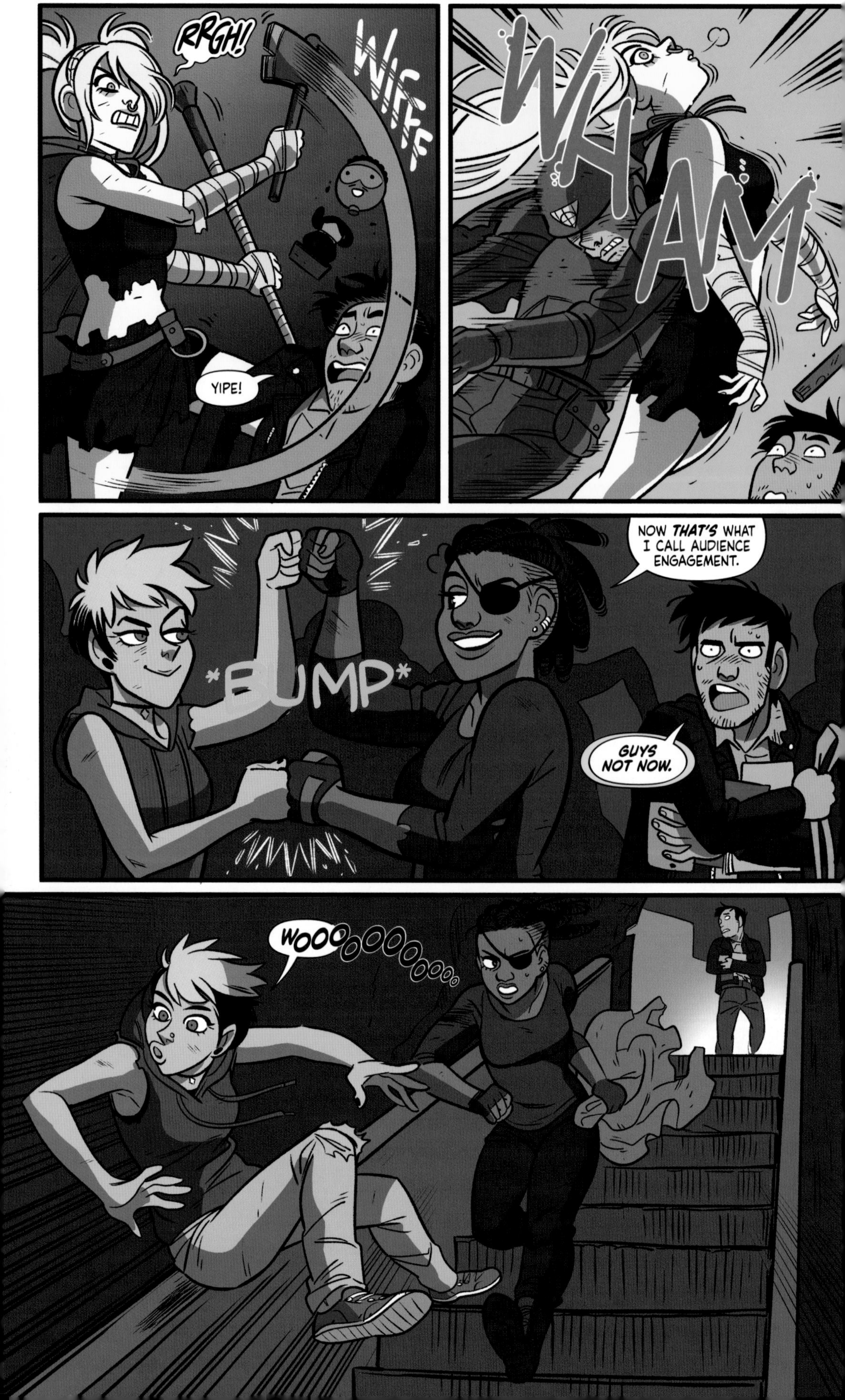
RRGH!
WIFFF
YIPE!
WHAM
NOW THAT'S WHAT I CALL AUDIENCE ENGAGEMENT.
BUMP
GUYS NOT NOW.
WOOOOOOOOOoooo

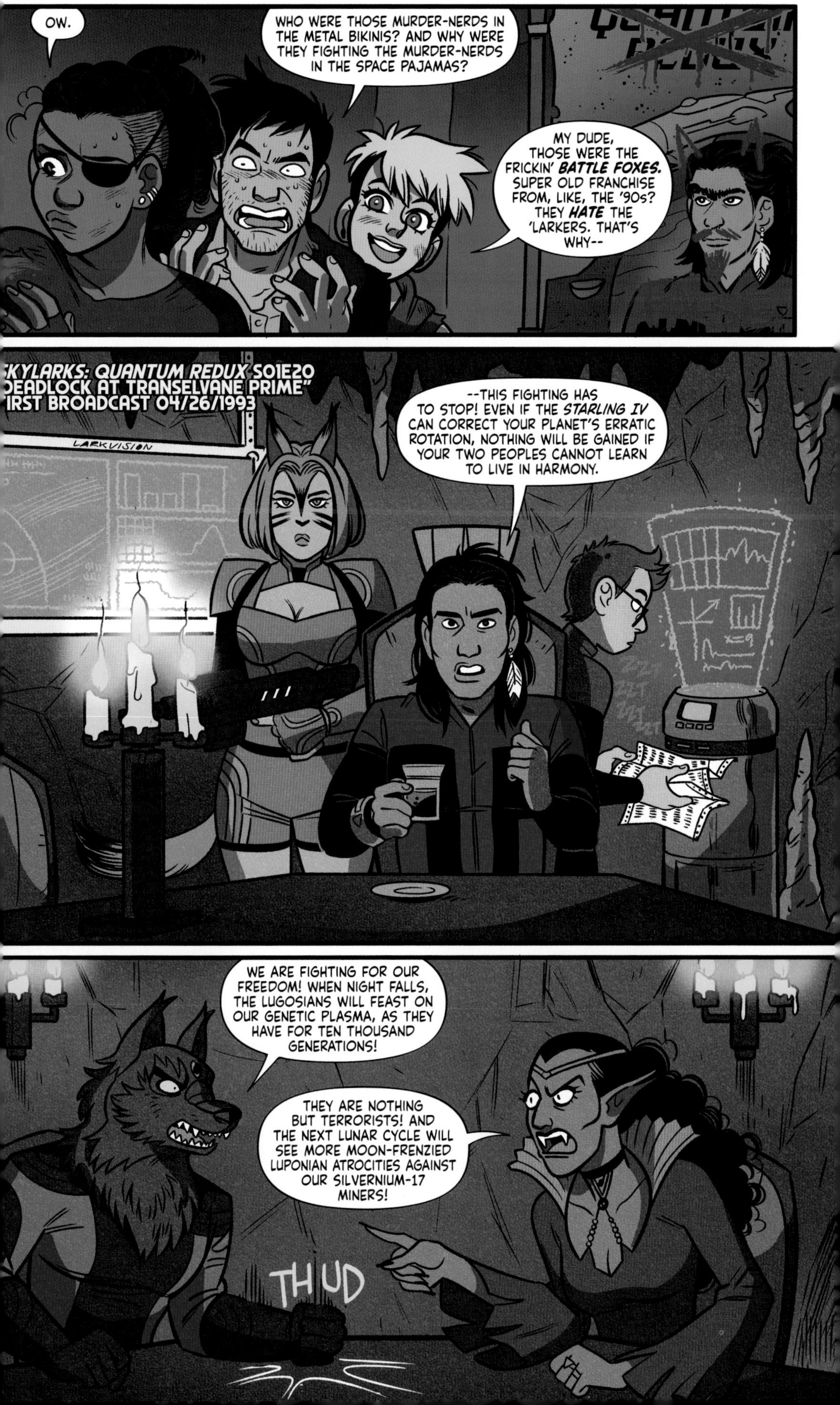
OW.
WHO WERE THOSE MURDER-NERDS IN THE METAL BIKINIS? AND WHY WERE THEY FIGHTING THE MURDER-NERDS IN THE SPACE PAJAMAS?
MY DUDE, THOSE WERE THE FRICKIN' BATTLE FOXES. SUPER OLD FRANCHISE FROM, LIKE, THE '90s? THEY HATE THE 'LARKERS. THAT'S WHY--
SKYLARKS: QUANTUM REDUX S01E20
"DEADLOCK AT TRANSELVANE PRIME"
FIRST BROADCAST 04/26/1993
LARKVISION
--THIS FIGHTING HAS TO STOP! EVEN IF THE STARLING IV CAN CORRECT YOUR PLANET'S ERRATIC ROTATION, NOTHING WILL BE GAINED IF YOUR TWO PEOPLES CANNOT LEARN TO LIVE IN HARMONY.
WE ARE FIGHTING FOR OUR FREEDOM! WHEN NIGHT FALLS, THE LUGOSIANS WILL FEAST ON OUR GENETIC PLASMA, AS THEY HAVE FOR TEN THOUSAND GENERATIONS!
THEY ARE NOTHING BUT TERRORISTS! AND THE NEXT LUNAR CYCLE WILL SEE MORE MOON-FRENZIED LUPONIAN ATROCITIES AGAINST OUR SILVERNIUM-17 MINERS!
THUD

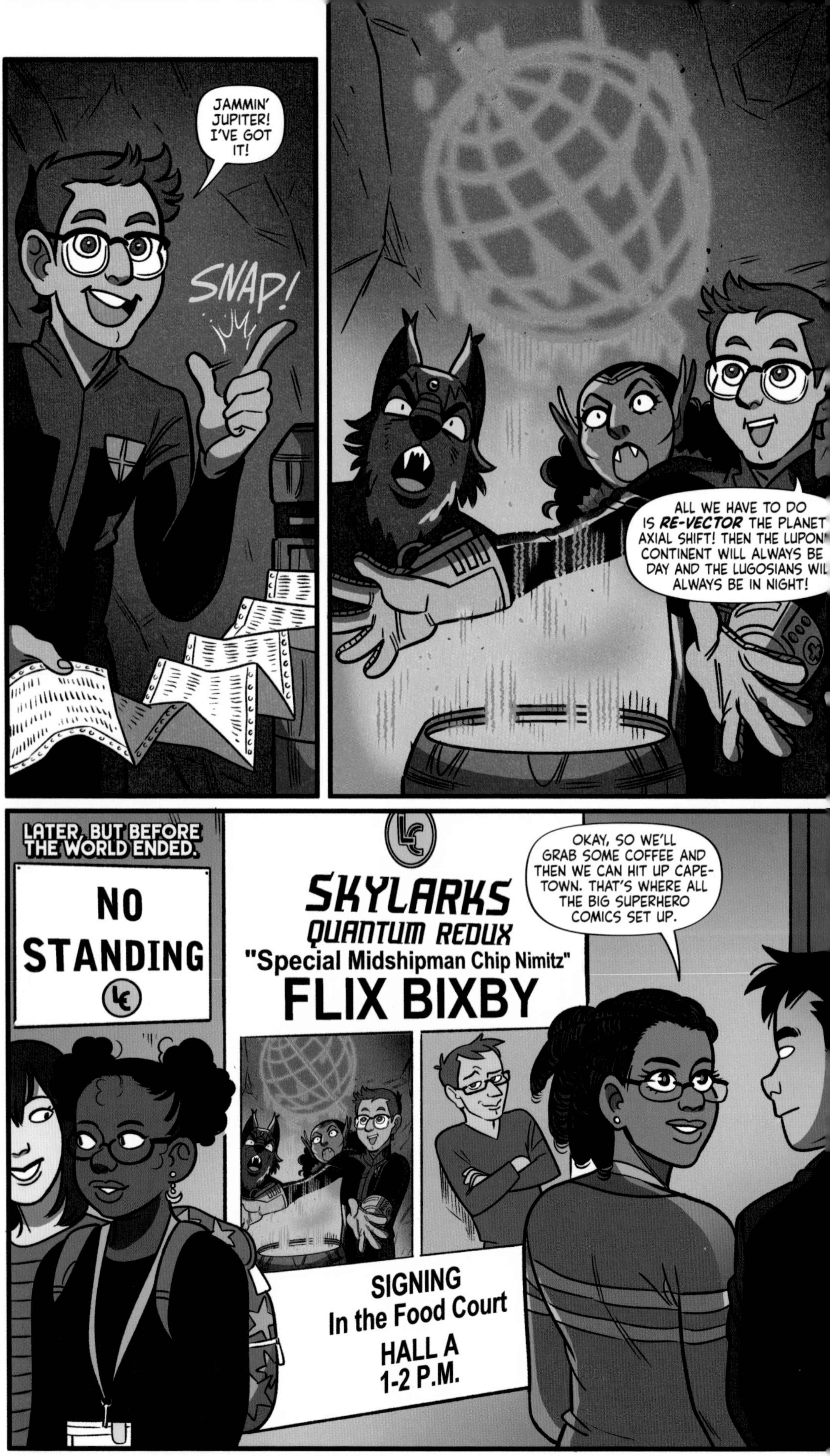
JAMMIN' JUPITER! I'VE GOT IT!
SNAP!
ALL WE HAVE TO DO IS RE-VECTOR THE PLANET AXIAL SHIFT! THEN THE LUPON CONTINENT WILL ALWAYS BE DAY AND THE LUGOSIANS WIL ALWAYS BE IN NIGHT!
LATER, BUT BEFORE THE WORLD ENDED.
NO STANDING
SKYLARKS
QUANTUM REDUX
"Special Midshipman Chip Nimitz"
FLIX BIXBY
SIGNING
In the Food Court
HALL A
1-2 P.M.
OKAY, SO WE'LL GRAB SOME COFFEE AND THEN WE CAN HIT UP CAPE-TOWN. THAT'S WHERE ALL THE BIG SUPERHERO COMICS SET UP.

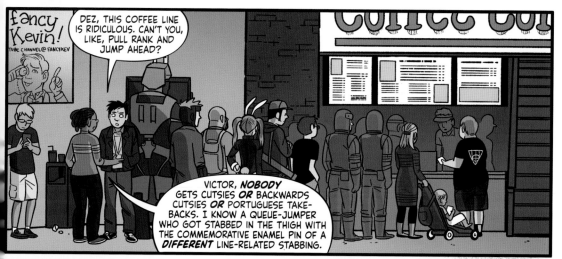

fancy Kevin!
TUBE CHANNEL @ FANCYKEV

DEZ, THIS COFFEE LINE IS RIDICULOUS. CAN'T YOU, LIKE, PULL RANK AND JUMP AHEAD?

VICTOR, *NOBODY* GETS CUTSIES *OR* BACKWARDS CUTSIES *OR* PORTUGUESE TAKE-BACKS. I KNOW A QUEUE-JUMPER WHO GOT STABBED IN THE THIGH WITH THE COMMEMORATIVE ENAMEL PIN OF A *DIFFERENT* LINE-RELATED STABBING.

STAFF ONLY

PLANET BOOM

BLUE NUMBER MFD

ALTHOUGH... THERE IS ONE POSSIBILITY...

THEY TRANSPORT CELEBRITY GUESTS THROUGH THESE OLD FREIGHT TUNNELS SO THEY DON'T GET MOBBED ON THE SHOW FLOOR.

CELEBRITIES, YOU SAY...

WHAAAAAAAT.

MOTORCYCLE MADNESS!

IS THAT--

CAT CUNNINGHAM, FROM *THE CUNNINGHAM CONUNDRUM*.

AND THAT'S--

BOAT COP'S BOAT COP.

WHO'S THAT?

OH CRAP. PLAY IT COOL.

DEZY BABY! MY AGENT'S BEEN *CRAZY* TRYING TO TRACK YOU DOWN!

FLIXY BABY! I DON'T THINK THAT'S TRUE!

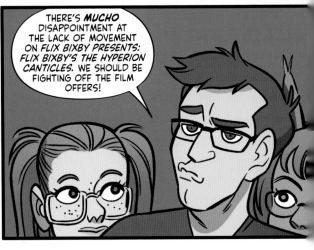

THERE'S *MUCHO* DISAPPOINTMENT AT THE LACK OF MOVEMENT ON *FLIX BIXBY PRESENTS: FLIX BIXBY'S THE HYPERION CANTICLES*. WE SHOULD BE FIGHTING OFF THE FILM OFFERS!

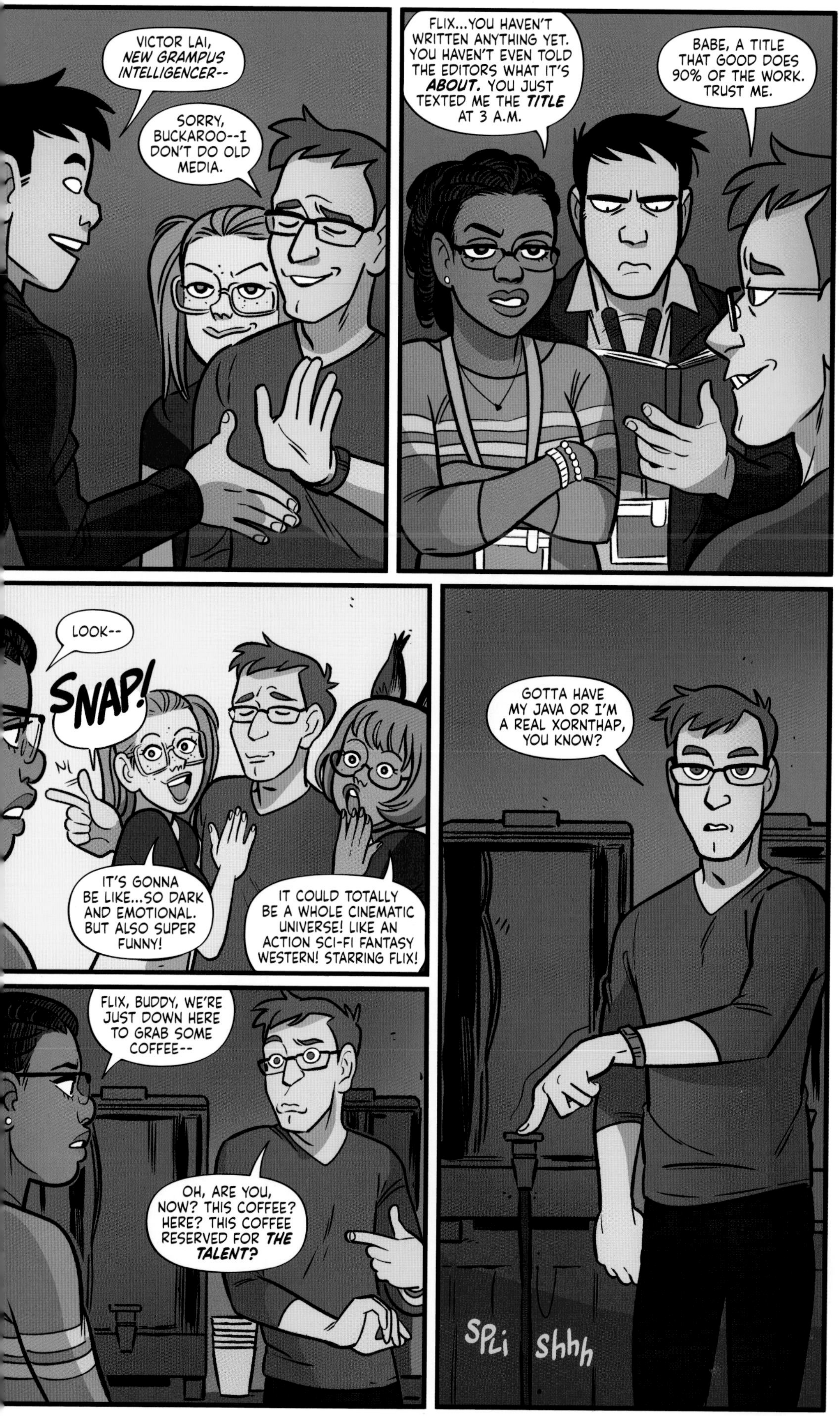
VICTOR LAI, *NEW GRAMPUS INTELLIGENCER*--
SORRY, BUCKAROO--I DON'T DO OLD MEDIA.
FLIX...YOU HAVEN'T WRITTEN ANYTHING YET. YOU HAVEN'T EVEN TOLD THE EDITORS WHAT IT'S ***ABOUT.*** YOU JUST TEXTED ME THE ***TITLE*** AT 3 A.M.
BABE, A TITLE THAT GOOD DOES 90% OF THE WORK. TRUST ME.
LOOK--
SNAP!
IT'S GONNA BE LIKE...SO DARK AND EMOTIONAL. BUT ALSO SUPER FUNNY!
IT COULD TOTALLY BE A WHOLE CINEMATIC UNIVERSE! LIKE AN ACTION SCI-FI FANTASY WESTERN! STARRING FLIX!
FLIX, BUDDY, WE'RE JUST DOWN HERE TO GRAB SOME COFFEE--
OH, ARE YOU, NOW? THIS COFFEE? HERE? THIS COFFEE RESERVED FOR ***THE TALENT?***
GOTTA HAVE MY JAVA OR I'M A REAL XORNTHAP, YOU KNOW?
SPLi Shhh

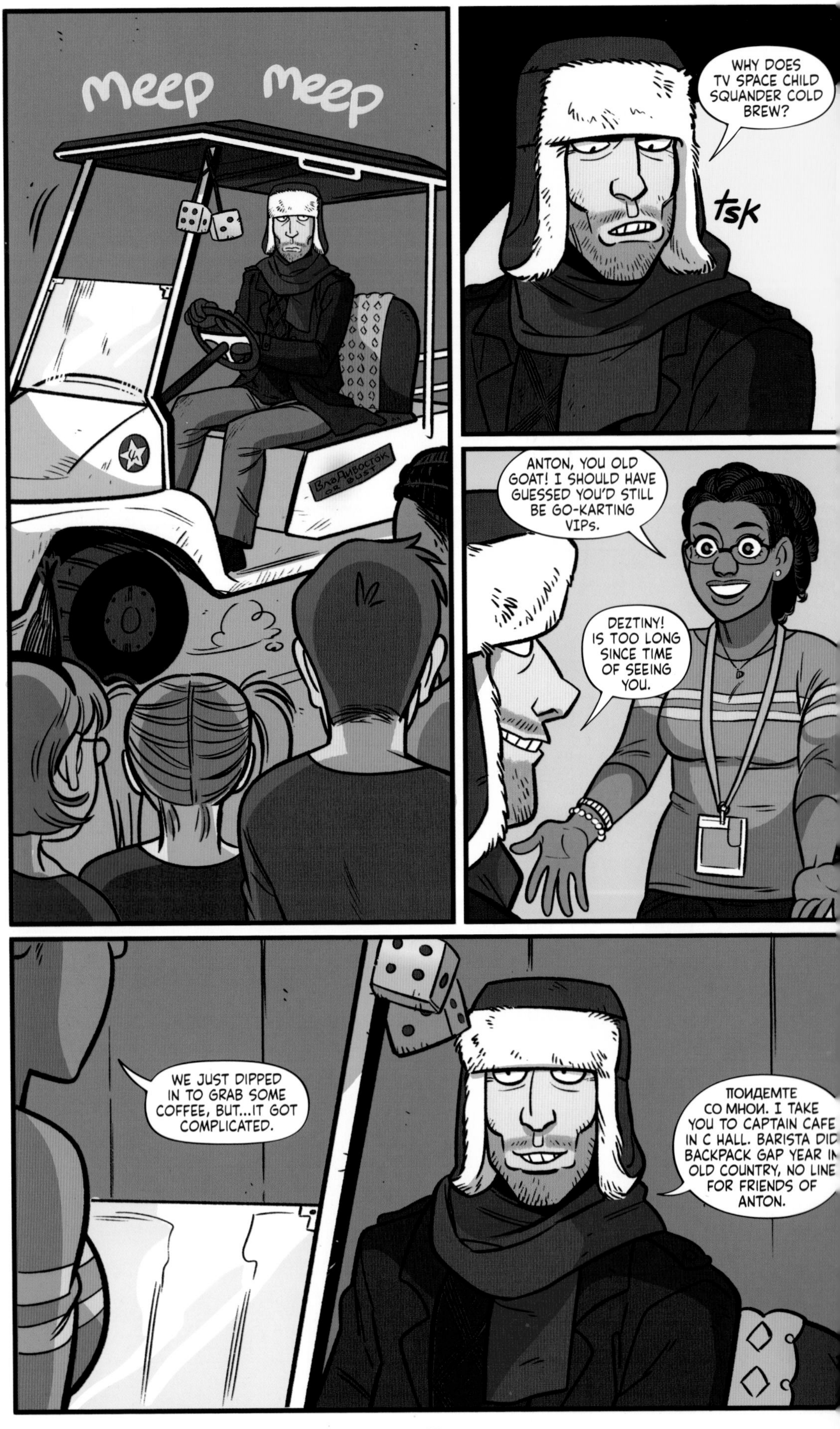
meep meep
ВлаДивосток OR BUST
WHY DOES TV SPACE CHILD SQUANDER COLD BREW?
tsk
ANTON, YOU OLD GOAT! I SHOULD HAVE GUESSED YOU'D STILL BE GO-KARTING VIPs.
DEZTINY! IS TOO LONG SINCE TIME OF SEEING YOU.
WE JUST DIPPED IN TO GRAB SOME COFFEE, BUT...IT GOT COMPLICATED.
ПОИДЕМТЕ СО МНОИ. I TAKE YOU TO CAPTAIN CAFE IN C HALL. BARISTA DID BACKPACK GAP YEAR IN OLD COUNTRY, NO LINE FOR FRIENDS OF ANTON.

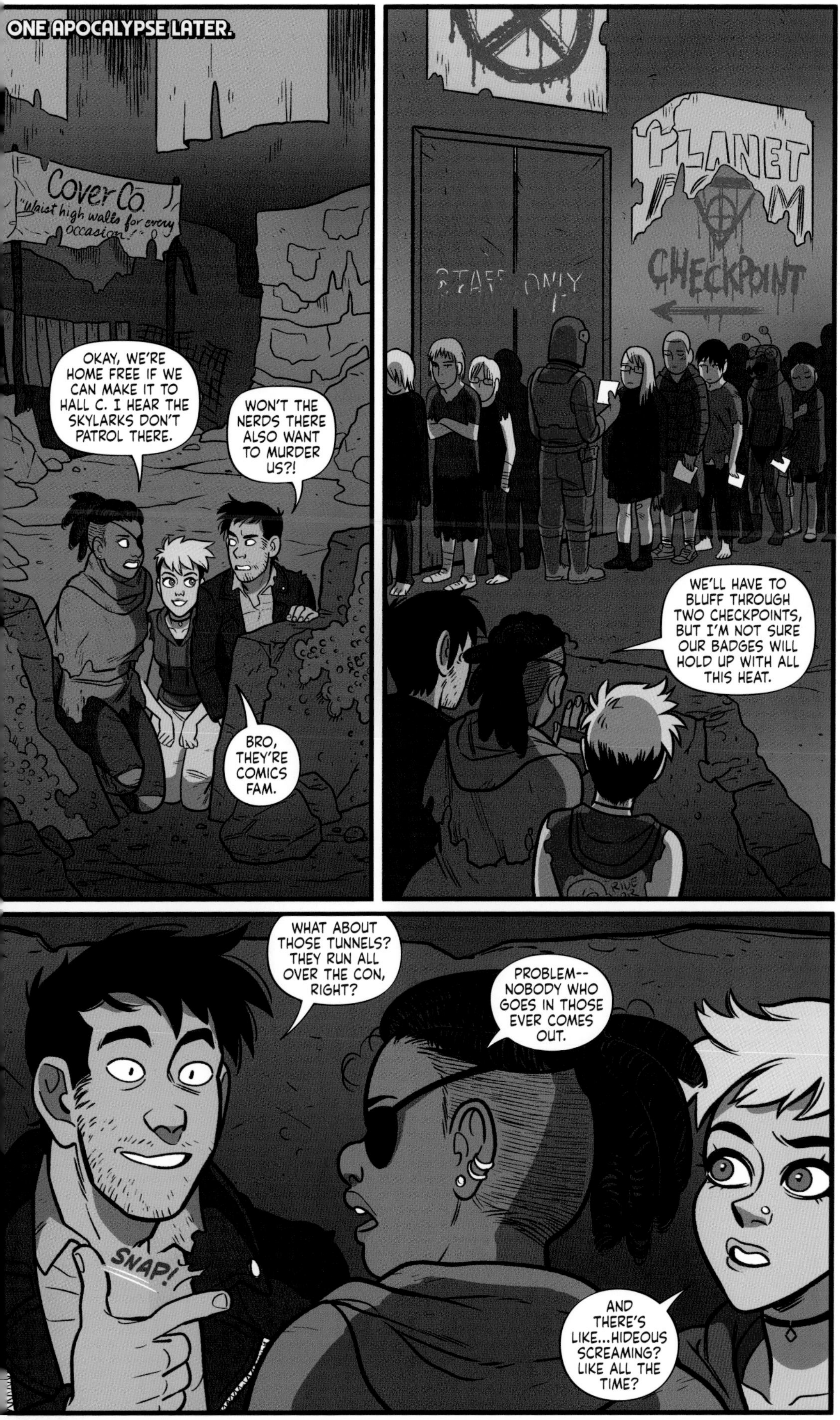
ONE APOCALYPSE LATER.
Cover Co. "Waist high walls for every occasion!"
OKAY, WE'RE HOME FREE IF WE CAN MAKE IT TO HALL C. I HEAR THE SKYLARKS DON'T PATROL THERE.
WON'T THE NERDS THERE ALSO WANT TO MURDER US?!
BRO, THEY'RE COMICS FAM.
PLANET
CHECKPOINT
WE'LL HAVE TO BLUFF THROUGH TWO CHECKPOINTS, BUT I'M NOT SURE OUR BADGES WILL HOLD UP WITH ALL THIS HEAT.
WHAT ABOUT THOSE TUNNELS? THEY RUN ALL OVER THE CON, RIGHT?
PROBLEM-- NOBODY WHO GOES IN THOSE EVER COMES OUT.
SNAP!
AND THERE'S LIKE...HIDEOUS SCREAMING? LIKE ALL THE TIME?

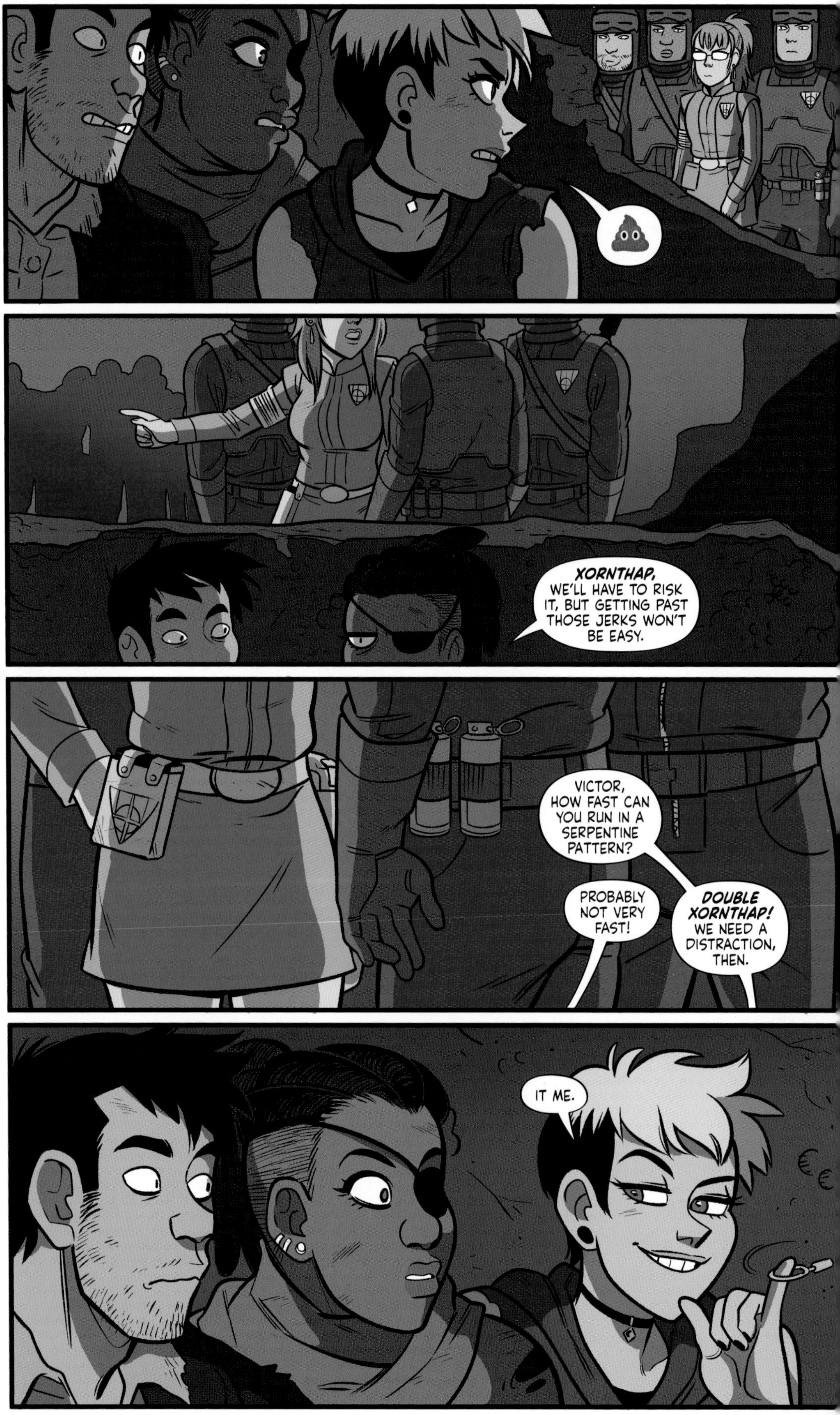
XORNTHAP, WE'LL HAVE TO RISK IT, BUT GETTING PAST THOSE JERKS WON'T BE EASY.
VICTOR, HOW FAST CAN YOU RUN IN A SERPENTINE PATTERN?
PROBABLY NOT VERY FAST!
DOUBLE XORNTHAP! WE NEED A DISTRACTION, THEN.
IT ME.

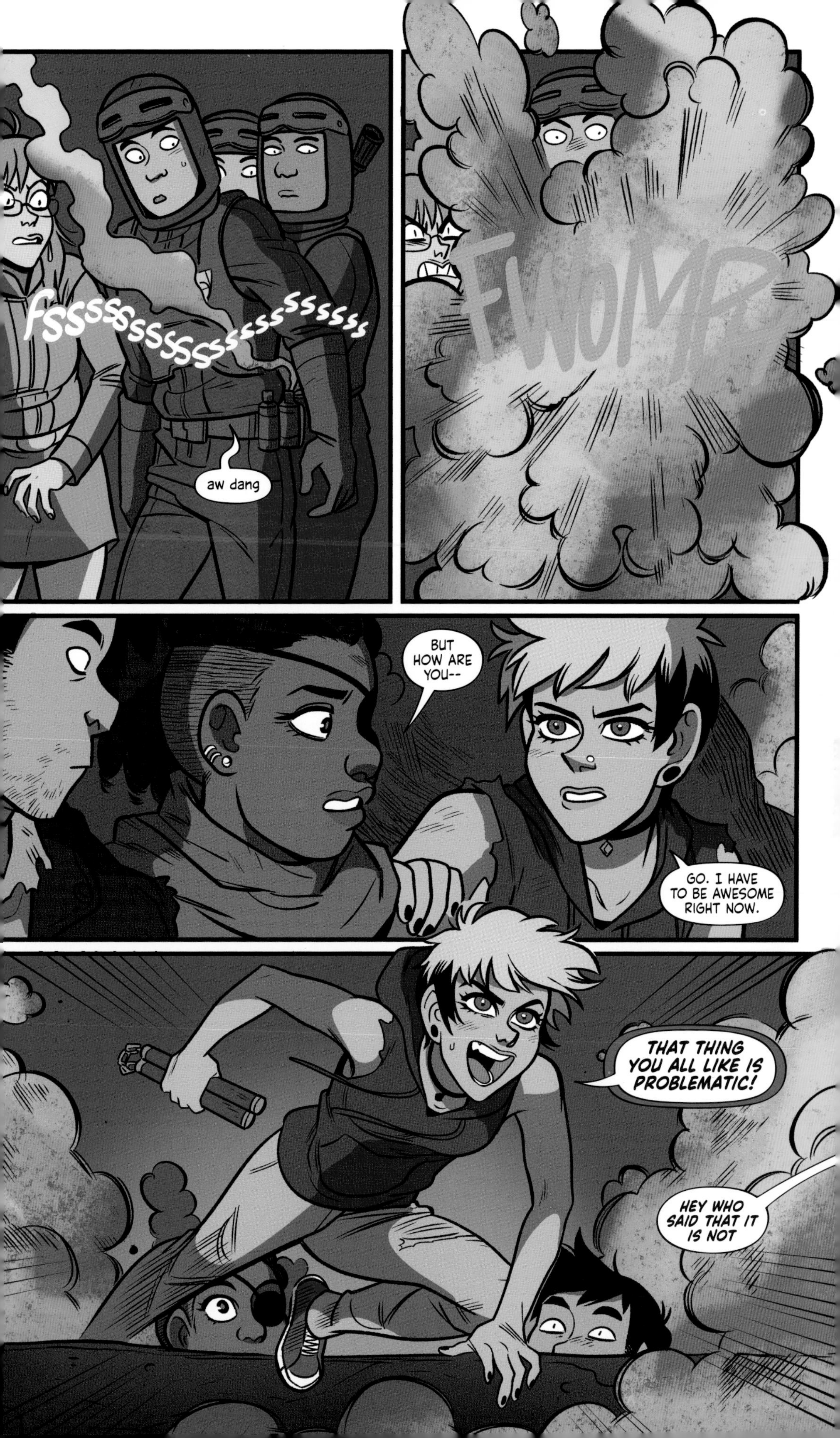
FSSSSSSSSSSSSSSSSSSSSS
aw dang
FWOMP!
BUT HOW ARE YOU--
GO. I HAVE TO BE AWESOME RIGHT NOW.
THAT THING YOU ALL LIKE IS PROBLEMATIC!
HEY WHO SAID THAT IT IS NOT

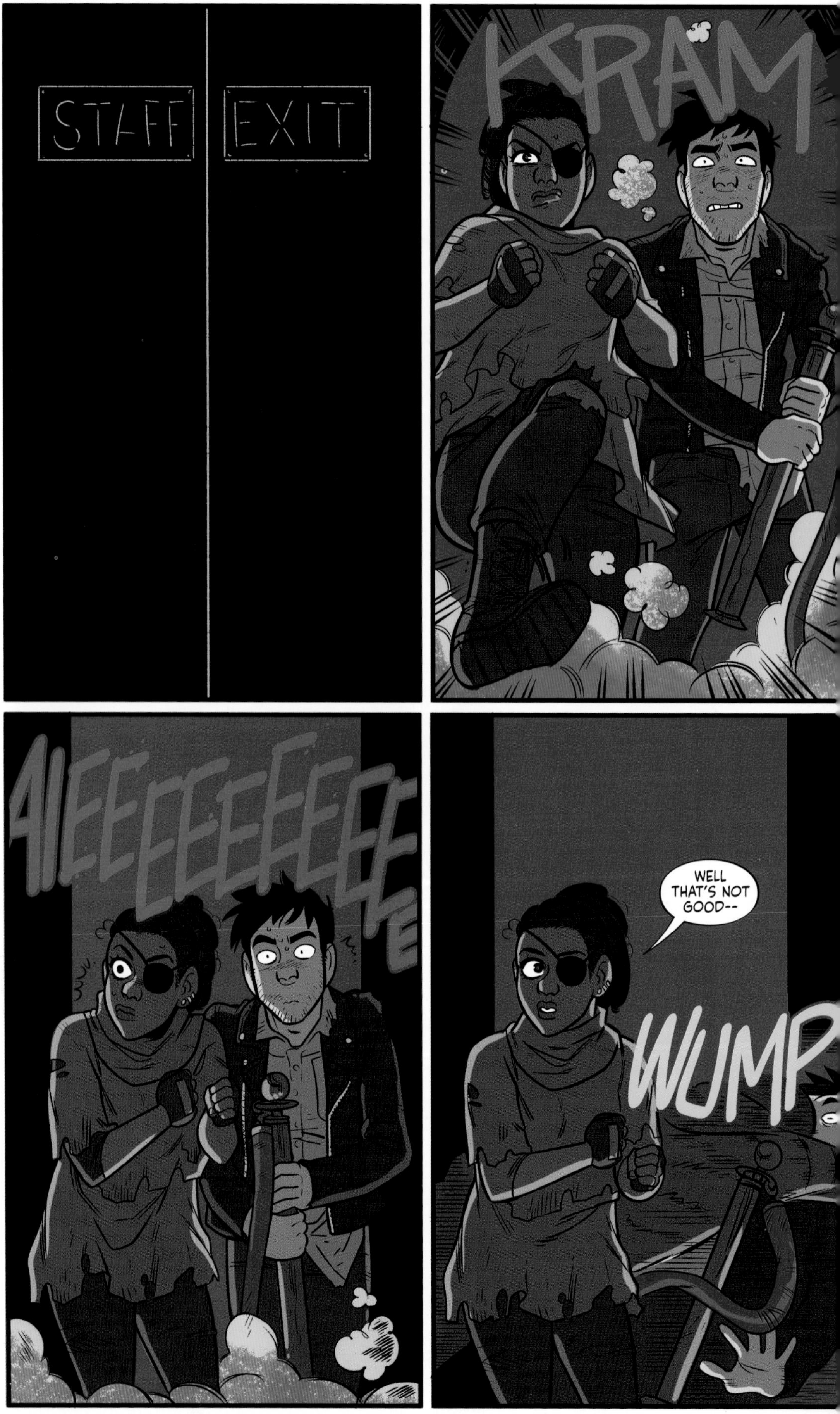
STAFF
EXIT
KRAM
AIEEEEEEEEEEEE
WELL THAT'S NOT GOOD--
WUMP

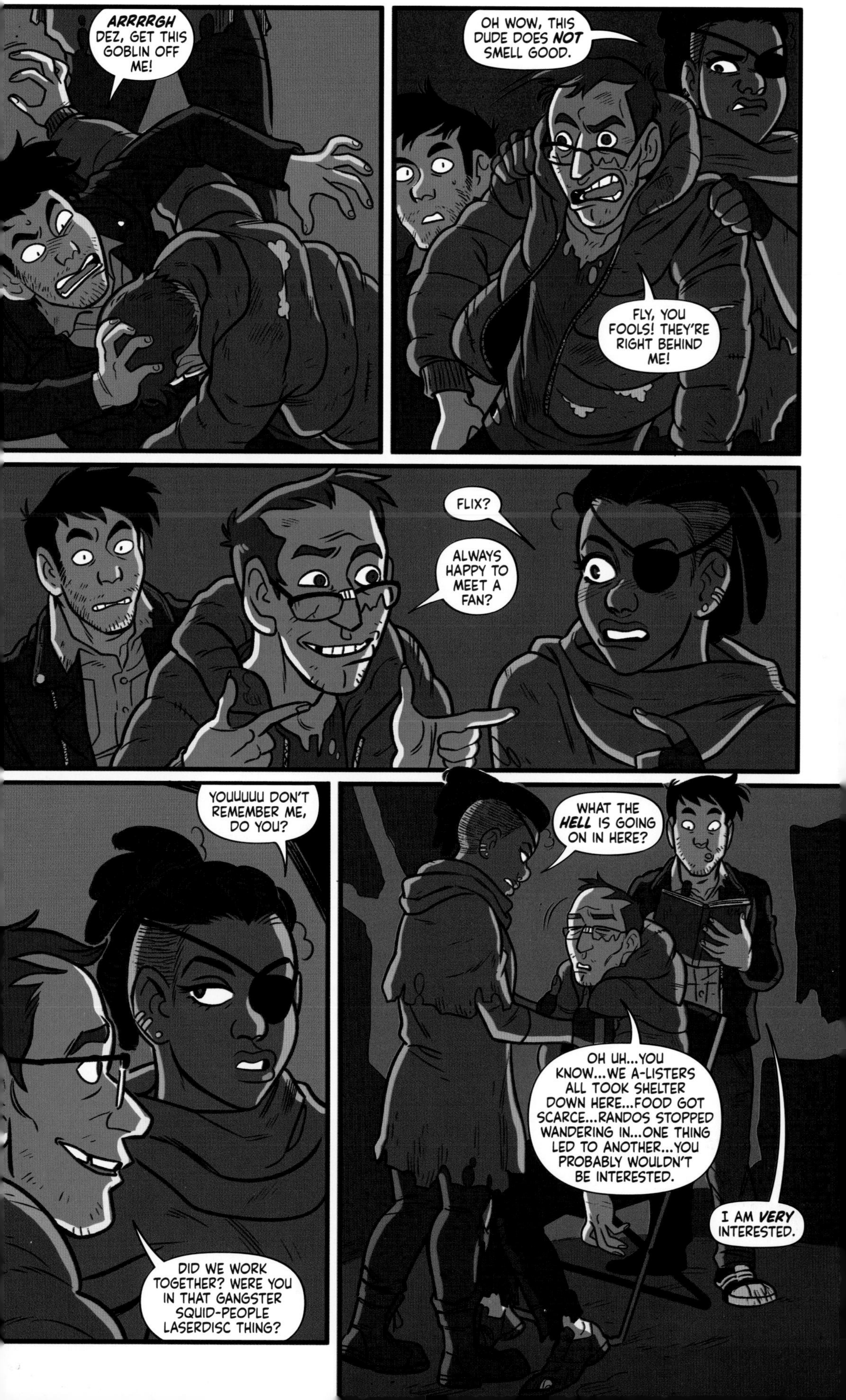

ARRRRGH DEZ, GET THIS GOBLIN OFF ME!
OH WOW, THIS DUDE DOES NOT SMELL GOOD.
FLY, YOU FOOLS! THEY'RE RIGHT BEHIND ME!
FLIX?
ALWAYS HAPPY TO MEET A FAN?
YOUUUUU DON'T REMEMBER ME, DO YOU?
DID WE WORK TOGETHER? WERE YOU IN THAT GANGSTER SQUID-PEOPLE LASERDISC THING?
WHAT THE HELL IS GOING ON IN HERE?
OH UH...YOU KNOW...WE A-LISTERS ALL TOOK SHELTER DOWN HERE...FOOD GOT SCARCE...RANDOS STOPPED WANDERING IN...ONE THING LED TO ANOTHER...YOU PROBABLY WOULDN'T BE INTERESTED.
I AM VERY INTERESTED.

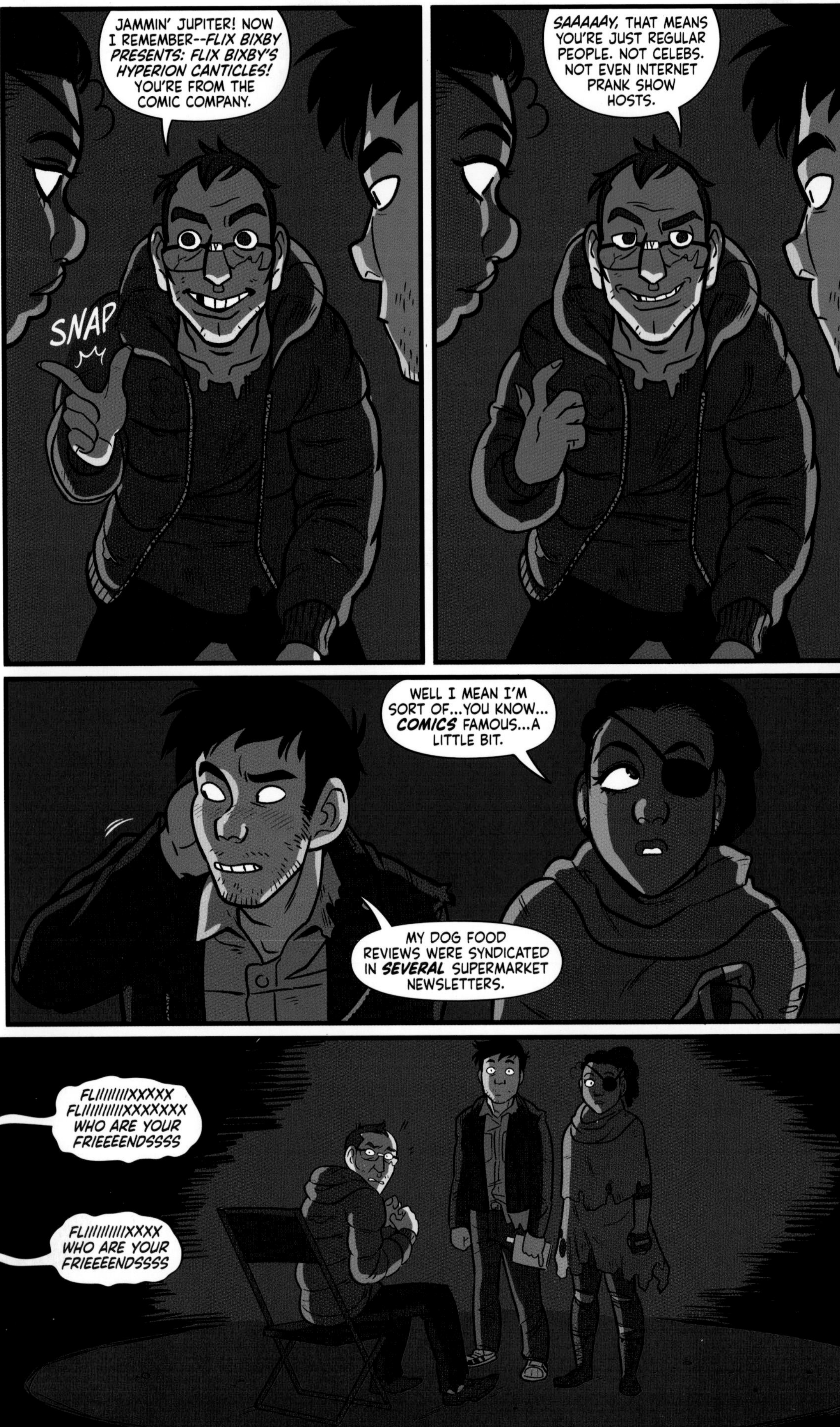
JAMMIN' JUPITER! NOW I REMEMBER--*FLIX BIXBY PRESENTS: FLIX BIXBY'S HYPERION CANTICLES!* YOU'RE FROM THE COMIC COMPANY.
SNAP
SAAAAAY, THAT MEANS YOU'RE JUST REGULAR PEOPLE. NOT CELEBS. NOT EVEN INTERNET PRANK SHOW HOSTS.
WELL I MEAN I'M SORT OF...YOU KNOW... ***COMICS*** FAMOUS...A LITTLE BIT.
MY DOG FOOD REVIEWS WERE SYNDICATED IN ***SEVERAL*** SUPERMARKET NEWSLETTERS.
FLIIIIIIIIXXXXX FLIIIIIIIIXXXXXXX WHO ARE YOUR FRIEEEENDSSSS
FLIIIIIIIIXXXX WHO ARE YOUR FRIEEEENDSSSS

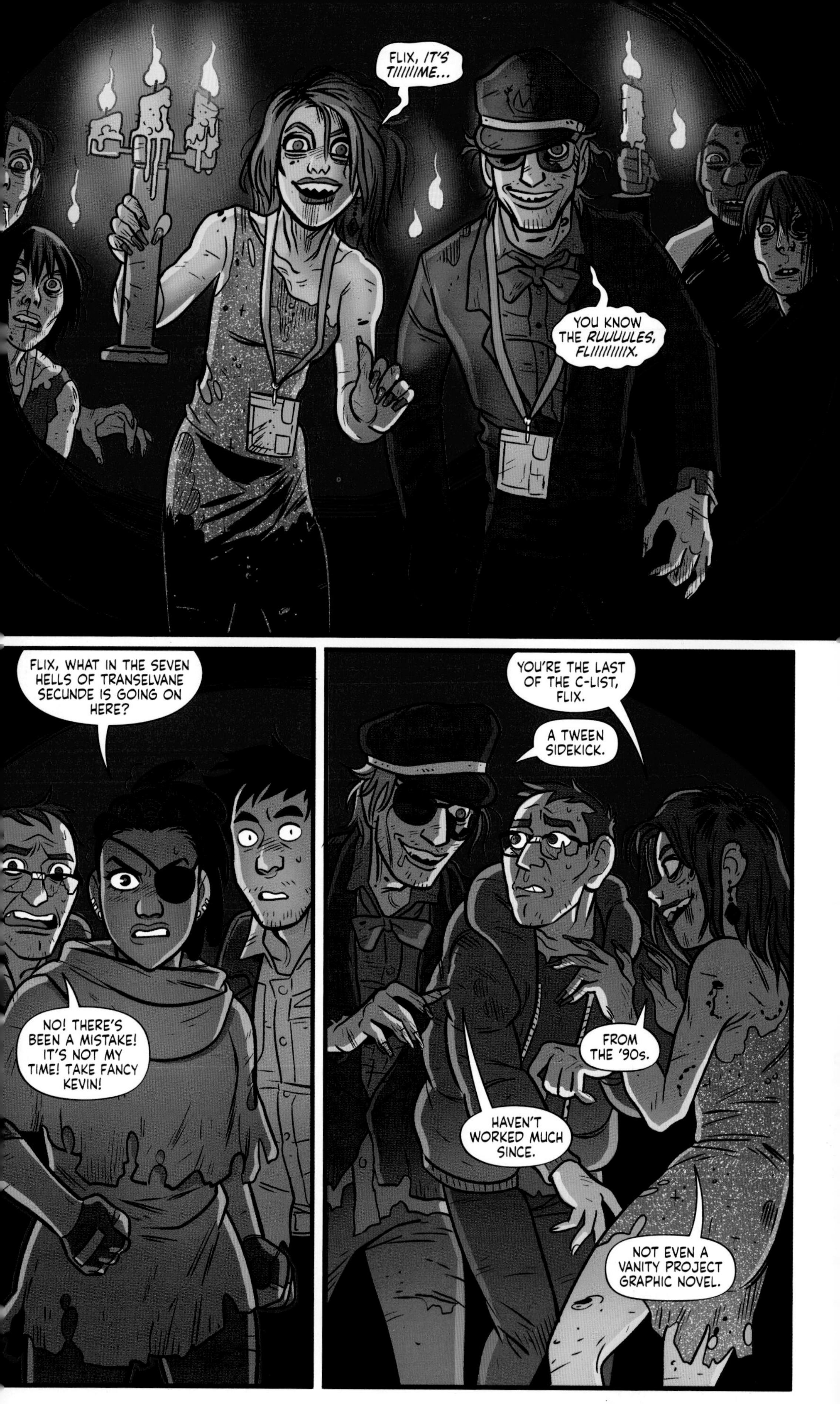
FLIX, *IT'S TIIIIIIME...*
YOU KNOW THE *RUUUULES, FLIIIIIIIIX.*
FLIX, WHAT IN THE SEVEN HELLS OF TRANSELVANE SECUNDE IS GOING ON HERE?
NO! THERE'S BEEN A MISTAKE! IT'S NOT MY TIME! TAKE FANCY KEVIN!
YOU'RE THE LAST OF THE C-LIST, FLIX.
A TWEEN SIDEKICK.
FROM THE '90s.
HAVEN'T WORKED MUCH SINCE.
NOT EVEN A VANITY PROJECT GRAPHIC NOVEL.

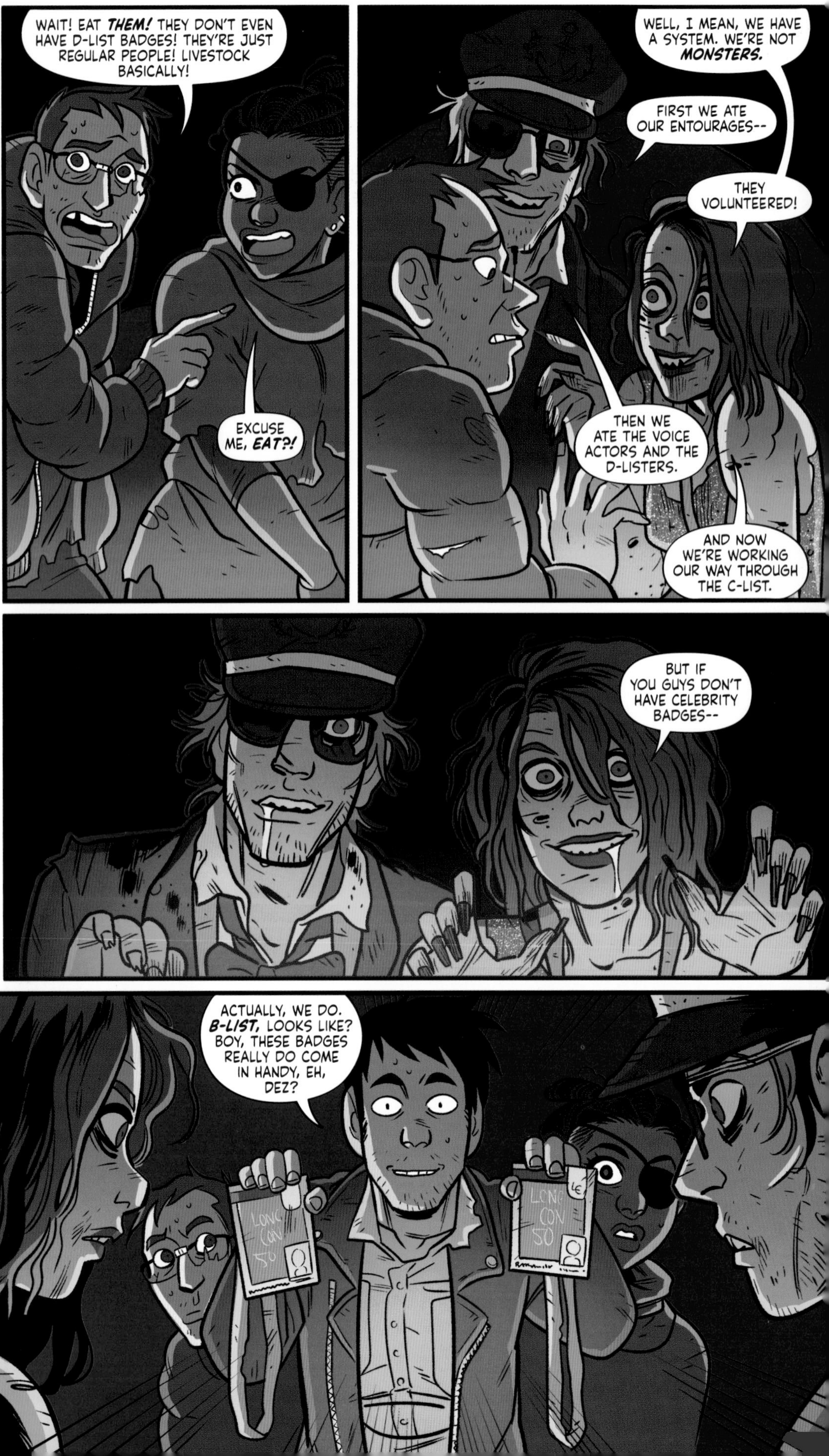
WAIT! EAT THEM! THEY DON'T EVEN HAVE D-LIST BADGES! THEY'RE JUST REGULAR PEOPLE! LIVESTOCK BASICALLY!
EXCUSE ME, EAT?!
WELL, I MEAN, WE HAVE A SYSTEM. WE'RE NOT MONSTERS.
FIRST WE ATE OUR ENTOURAGES--
THEY VOLUNTEERED!
THEN WE ATE THE VOICE ACTORS AND THE D-LISTERS.
AND NOW WE'RE WORKING OUR WAY THROUGH THE C-LIST.
BUT IF YOU GUYS DON'T HAVE CELEBRITY BADGES--
ACTUALLY, WE DO. B-LIST, LOOKS LIKE? BOY, THESE BADGES REALLY DO COME IN HANDY, EH, DEZ?
LONG CON 50
LONG CON 50

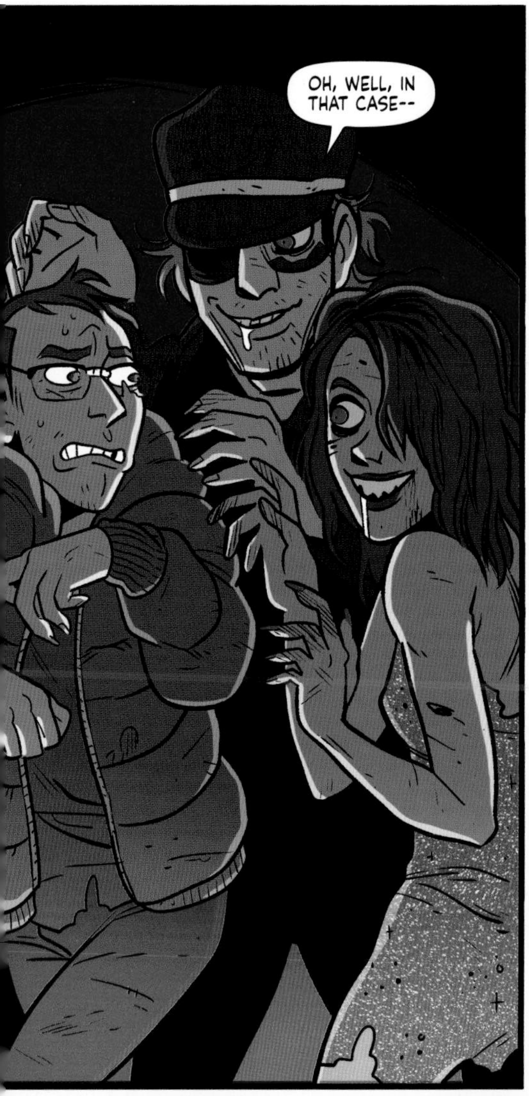
OH, WELL, IN THAT CASE--

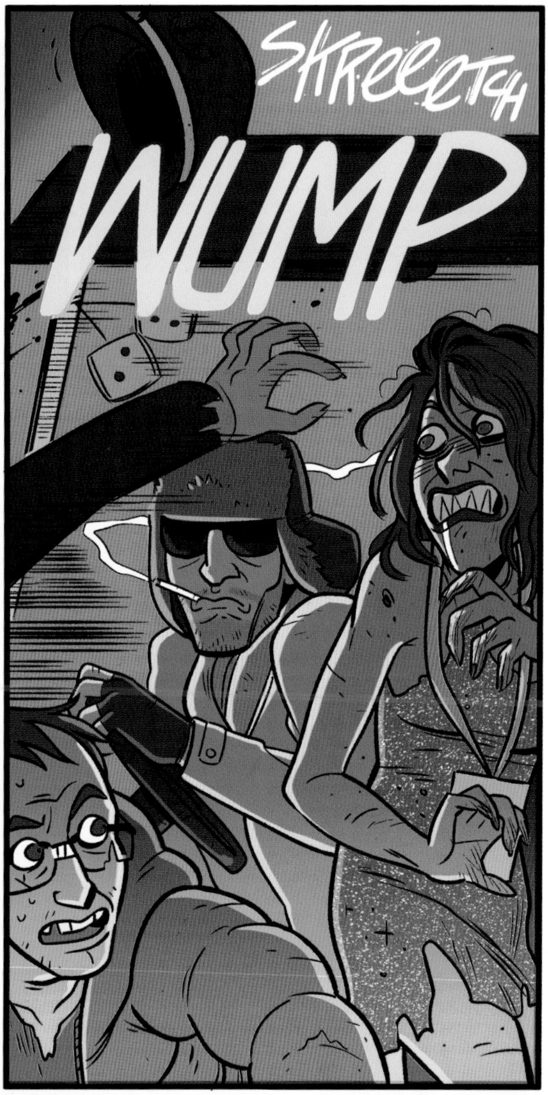
SKREEETCH
WUMP

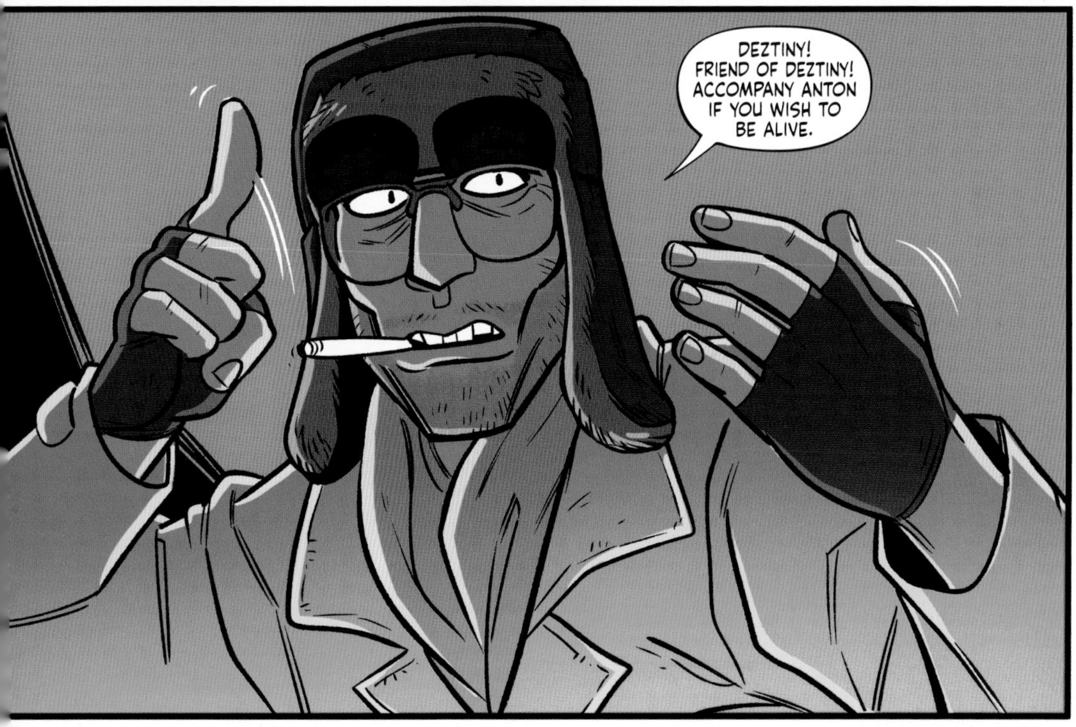
DEZTINY! FRIEND OF DEZTINY! ACCOMPANY ANTON IF YOU WISH TO BE ALIVE.

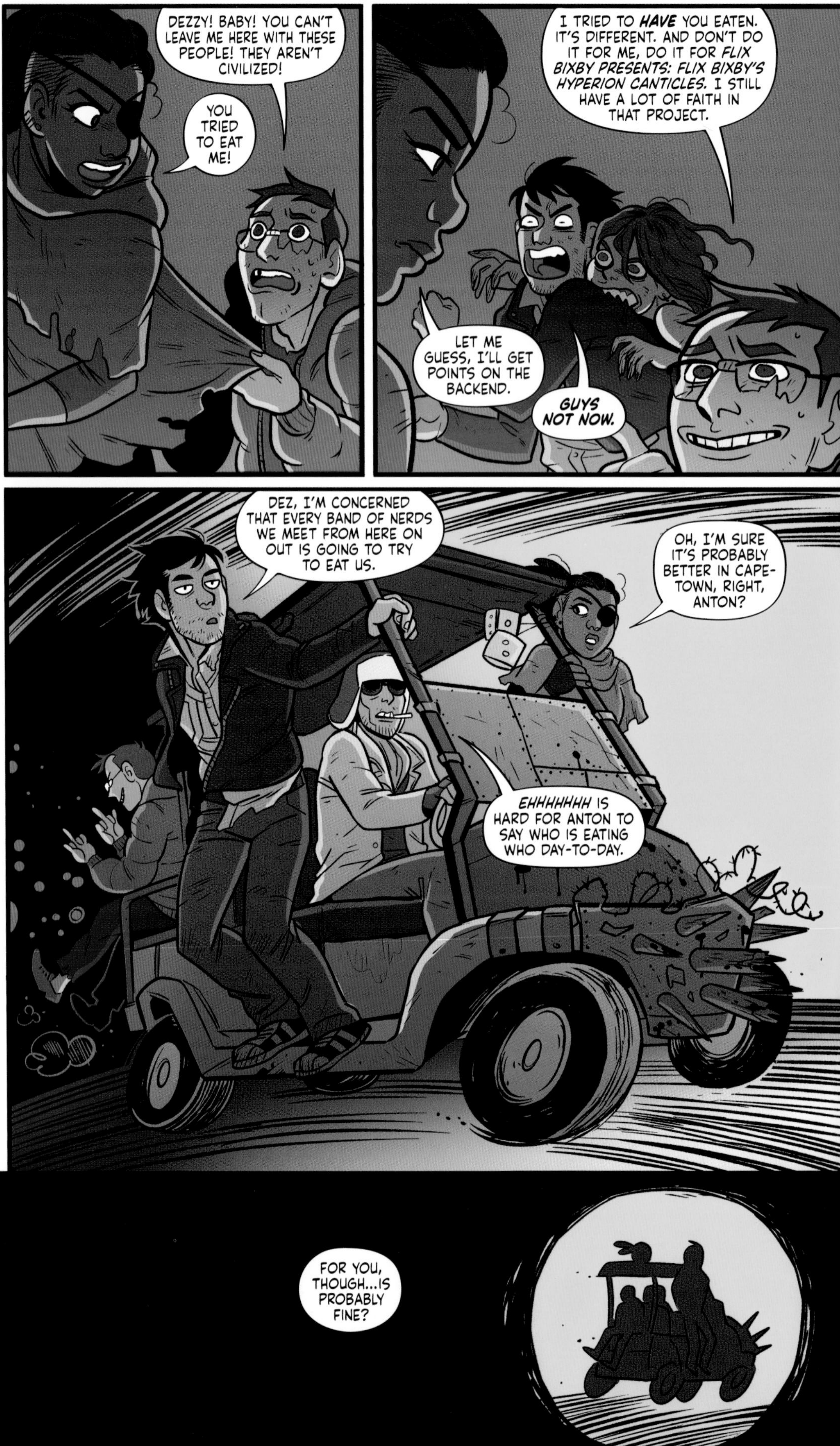
DEZZY! BABY! YOU CAN'T LEAVE ME HERE WITH THESE PEOPLE! THEY AREN'T CIVILIZED!
YOU TRIED TO EAT ME!
I TRIED TO *HAVE* YOU EATEN. IT'S DIFFERENT. AND DON'T DO IT FOR ME, DO IT FOR *FLIX BIXBY PRESENTS: FLIX BIXBY'S HYPERION CANTICLES.* I STILL HAVE A LOT OF FAITH IN THAT PROJECT.
LET ME GUESS, I'LL GET POINTS ON THE BACKEND.
GUYS NOT NOW.
DEZ, I'M CONCERNED THAT EVERY BAND OF NERDS WE MEET FROM HERE ON OUT IS GOING TO TRY TO EAT US.
OH, I'M SURE IT'S PROBABLY BETTER IN CAPE-TOWN, RIGHT, ANTON?
EHHHHHHH IS HARD FOR ANTON TO SAY WHO IS EATING WHO DAY-TO-DAY.
FOR YOU, THOUGH...IS PROBABLY FINE?

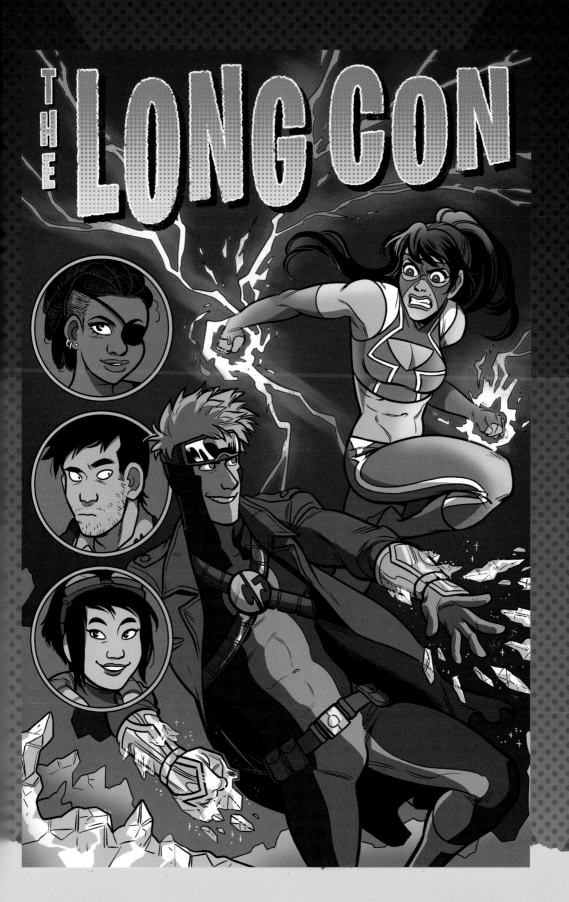

CHAPTER 5: CAPETOWN BLUES

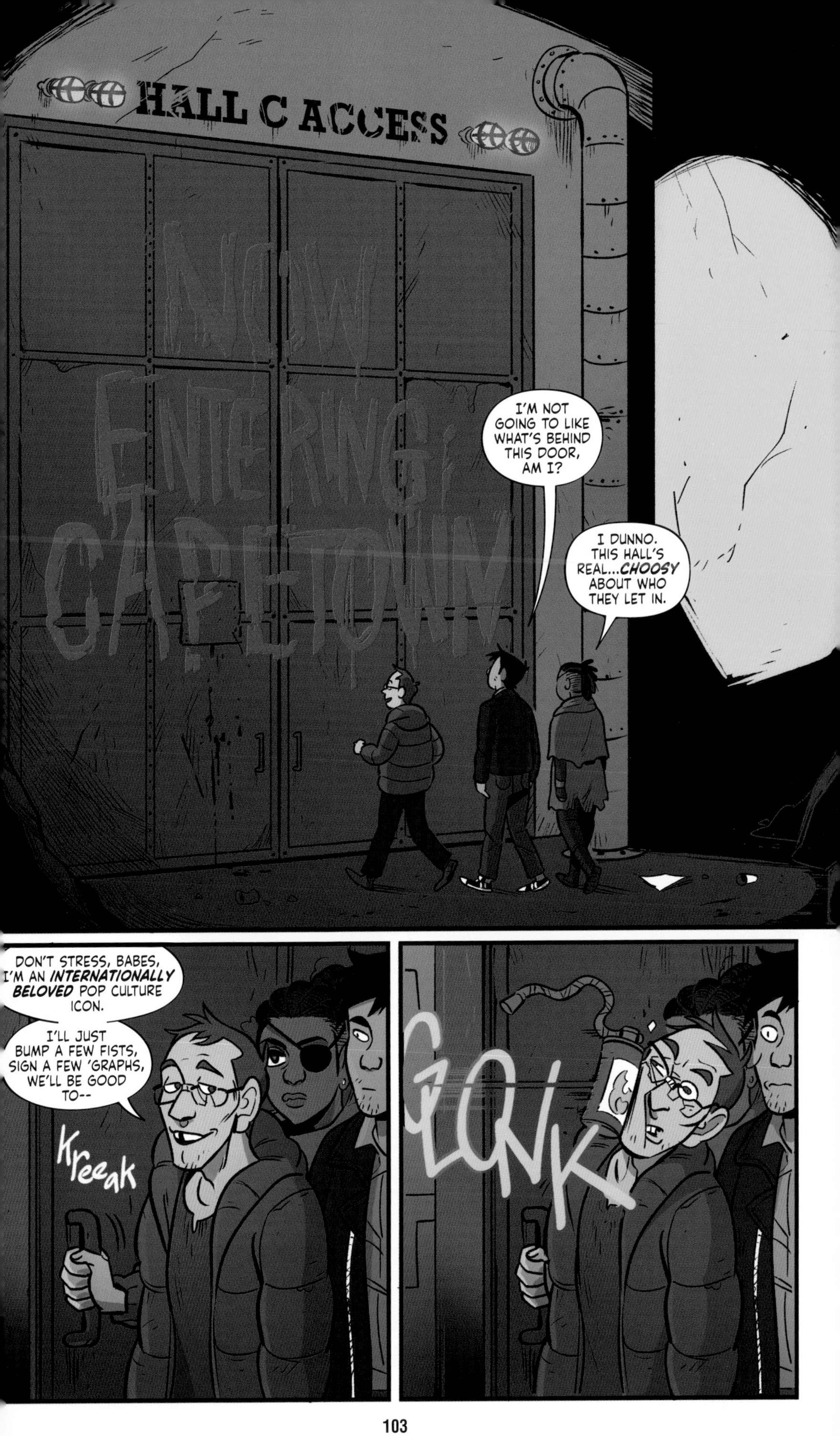
HALL C ACCESS
NOW ENTERING CAPETOWN
I'M NOT GOING TO LIKE WHAT'S BEHIND THIS DOOR, AM I?
I DUNNO. THIS HALL'S REAL...*CHOOSY* ABOUT WHO THEY LET IN.
DON'T STRESS, BABES, I'M AN *INTERNATIONALLY BELOVED* POP CULTURE ICON.
I'LL JUST BUMP A FEW FISTS, SIGN A FEW 'GRAPHS, WE'LL BE GOOD TO--
Kreeak
GLONK

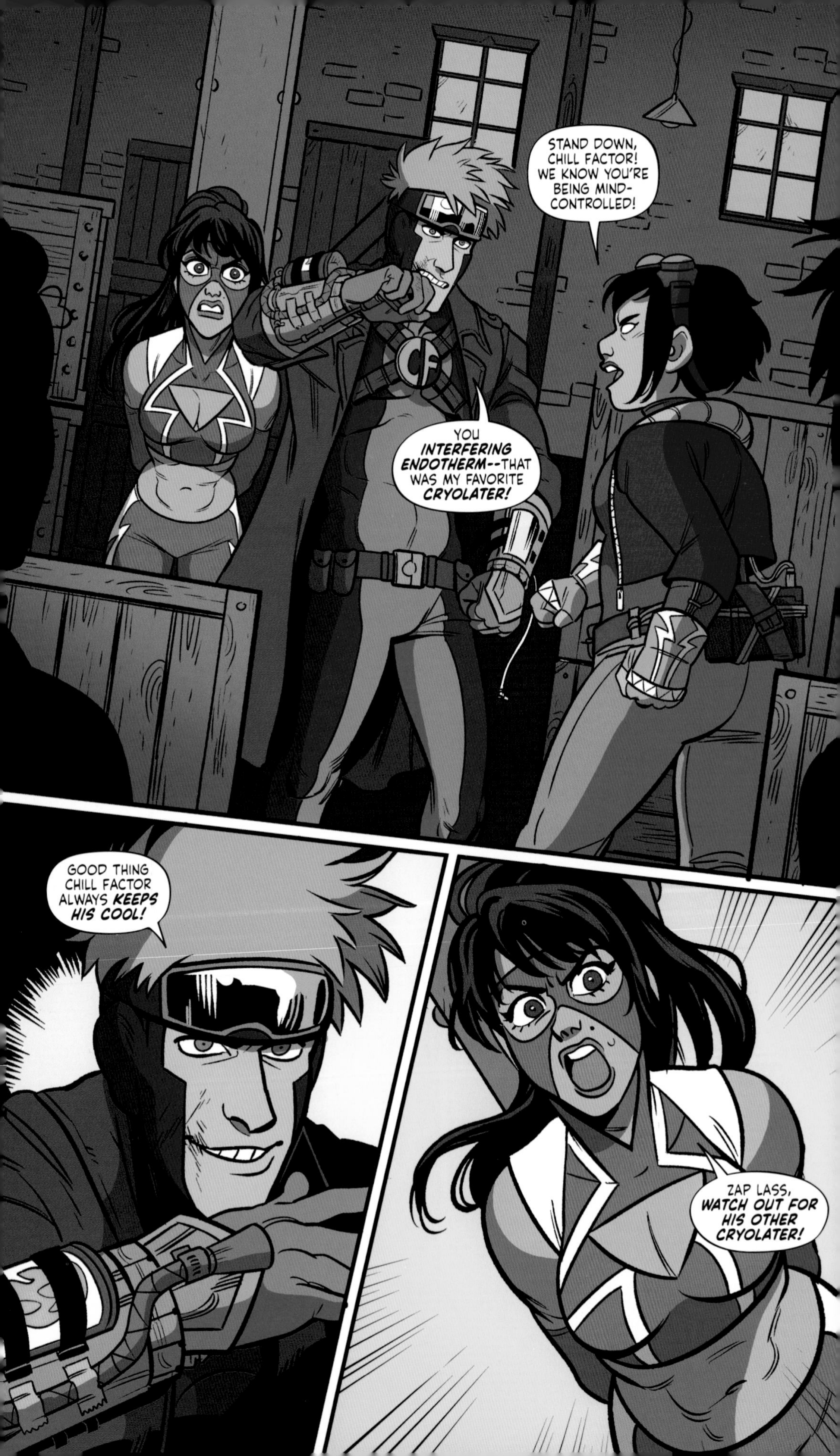
STAND DOWN, CHILL FACTOR! WE KNOW YOU'RE BEING MIND-CONTROLLED!
YOU **INTERFERING ENDOTHERM**--THAT WAS MY FAVORITE **CRYOLATER!**
GOOD THING CHILL FACTOR ALWAYS **KEEPS HIS COOL!**
ZAP LASS, **WATCH OUT FOR HIS OTHER CRYOLATER!**

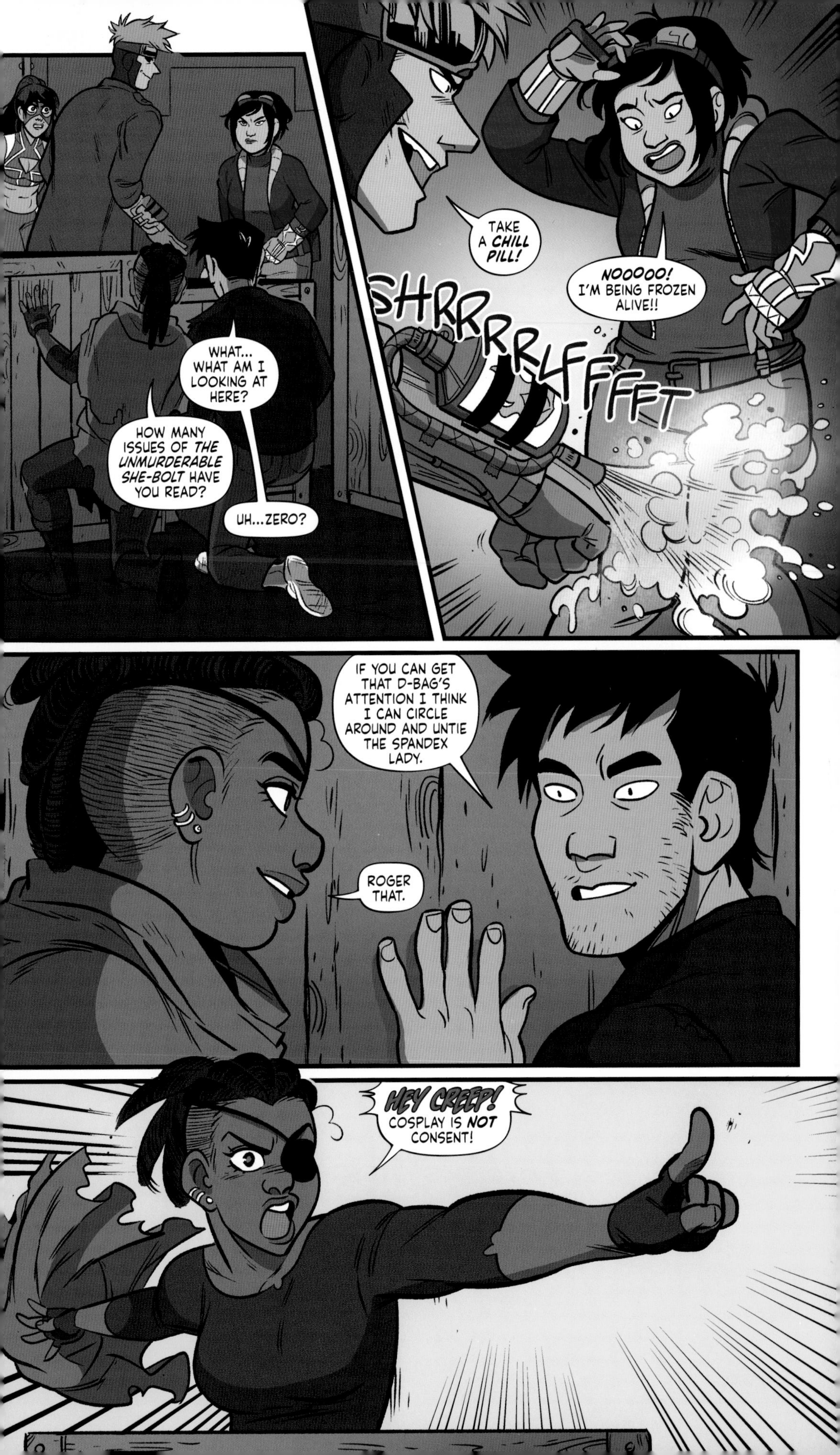

WHAT... WHAT AM I LOOKING AT HERE?
HOW MANY ISSUES OF *THE UNMURDERABLE SHE-BOLT* HAVE YOU READ?
UH...ZERO?
TAKE A *CHILL PILL!*
NOOOOO! I'M BEING FROZEN ALIVE!!
SHRRRRRLFFFFT
IF YOU CAN GET THAT D-BAG'S ATTENTION I THINK I CAN CIRCLE AROUND AND UNTIE THE SPANDEX LADY.
ROGER THAT.
HEY CREEP! COSPLAY IS *NOT* CONSENT!

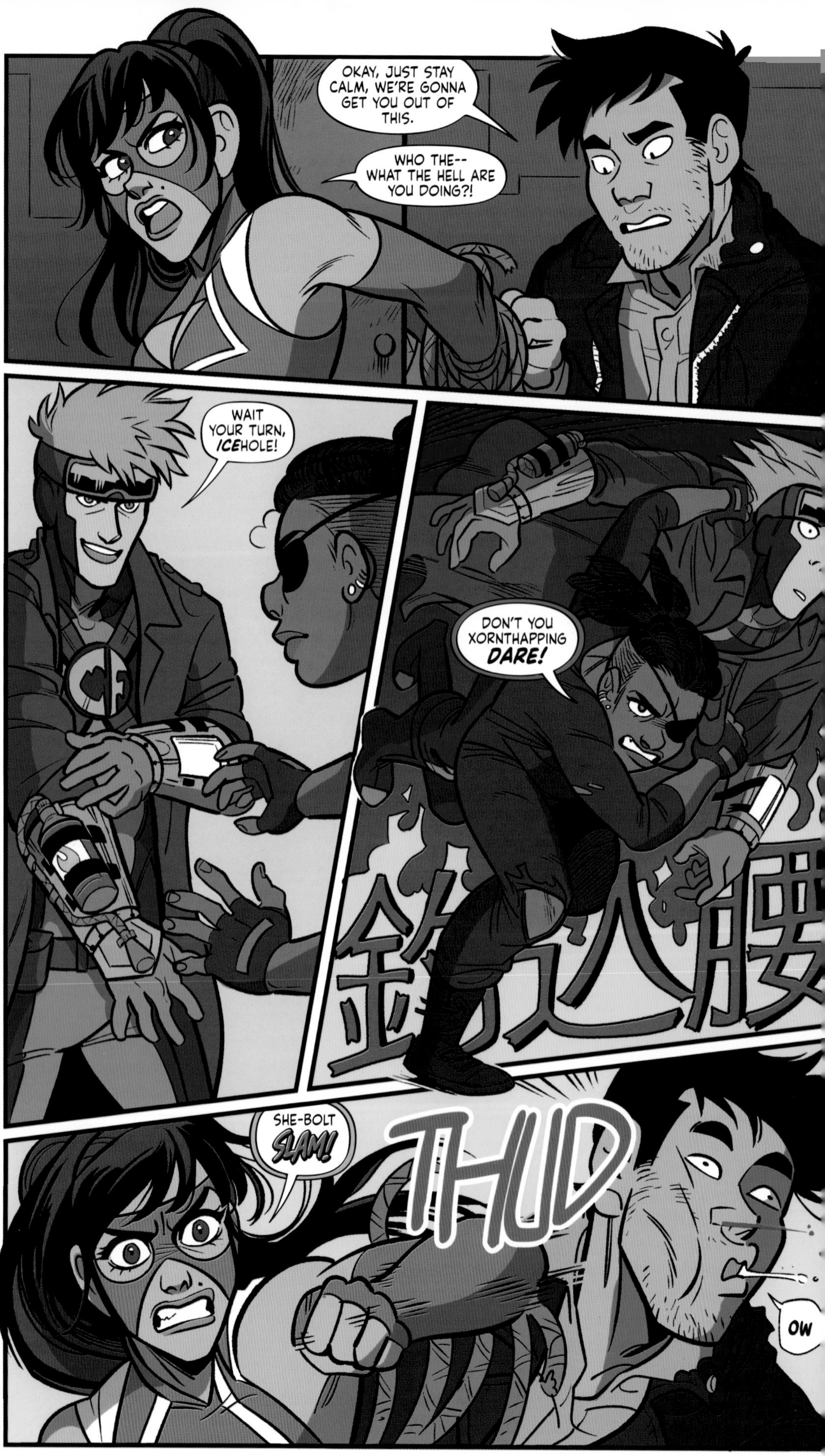
OKAY, JUST STAY CALM, WE'RE GONNA GET YOU OUT OF THIS.
WHO THE-- WHAT THE HELL ARE YOU DOING?!
WAIT YOUR TURN, ICEHOLE!
DON'T YOU XORNTHAPPING DARE!
SHE-BOLT SLAM!
THUD
OW

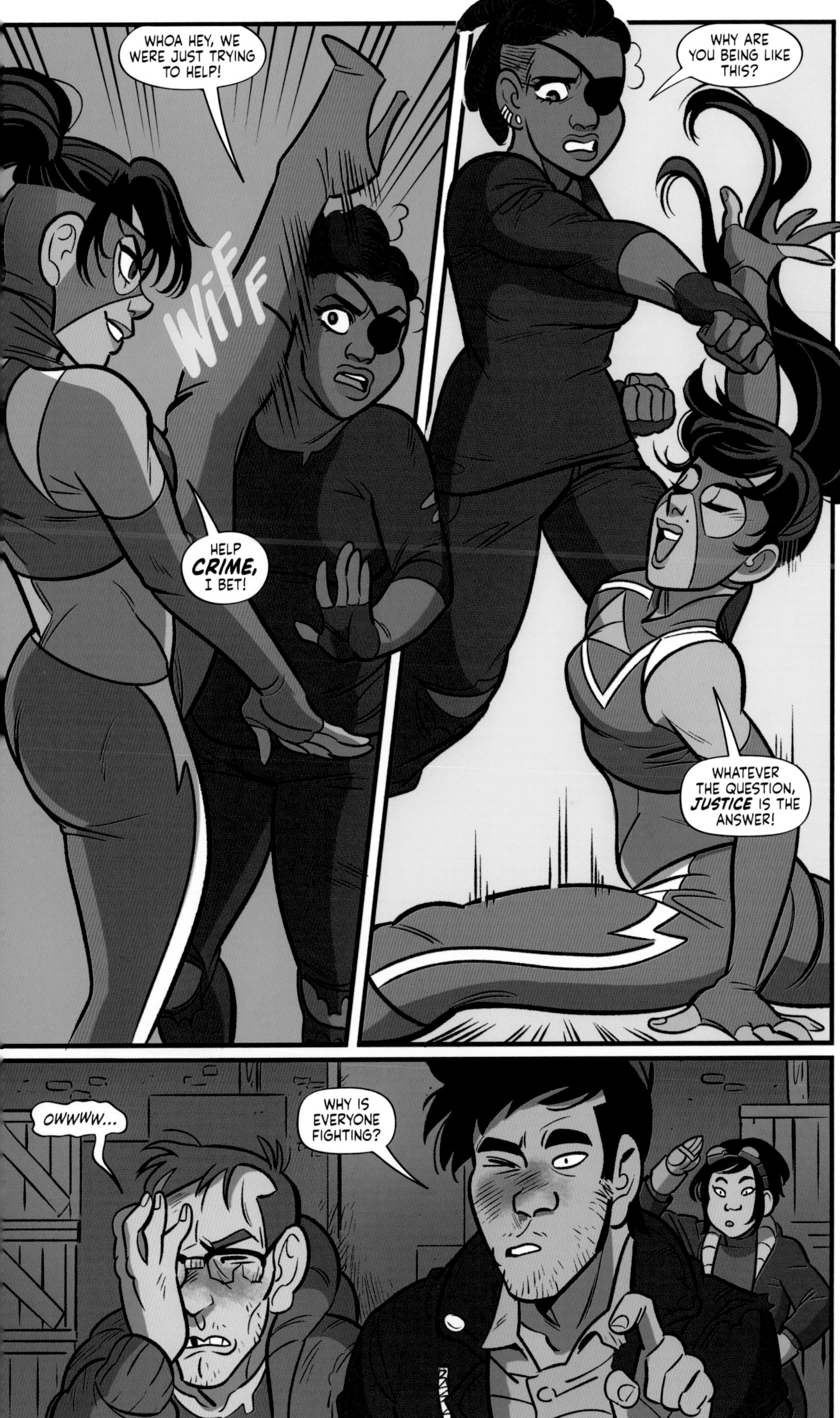
WHOA HEY, WE WERE JUST TRYING TO HELP!
WIFF
HELP CRIME, I BET!
WHY ARE YOU BEING LIKE THIS?
WHATEVER THE QUESTION, JUSTICE IS THE ANSWER!
OWWWW...
WHY IS EVERYONE FIGHTING?

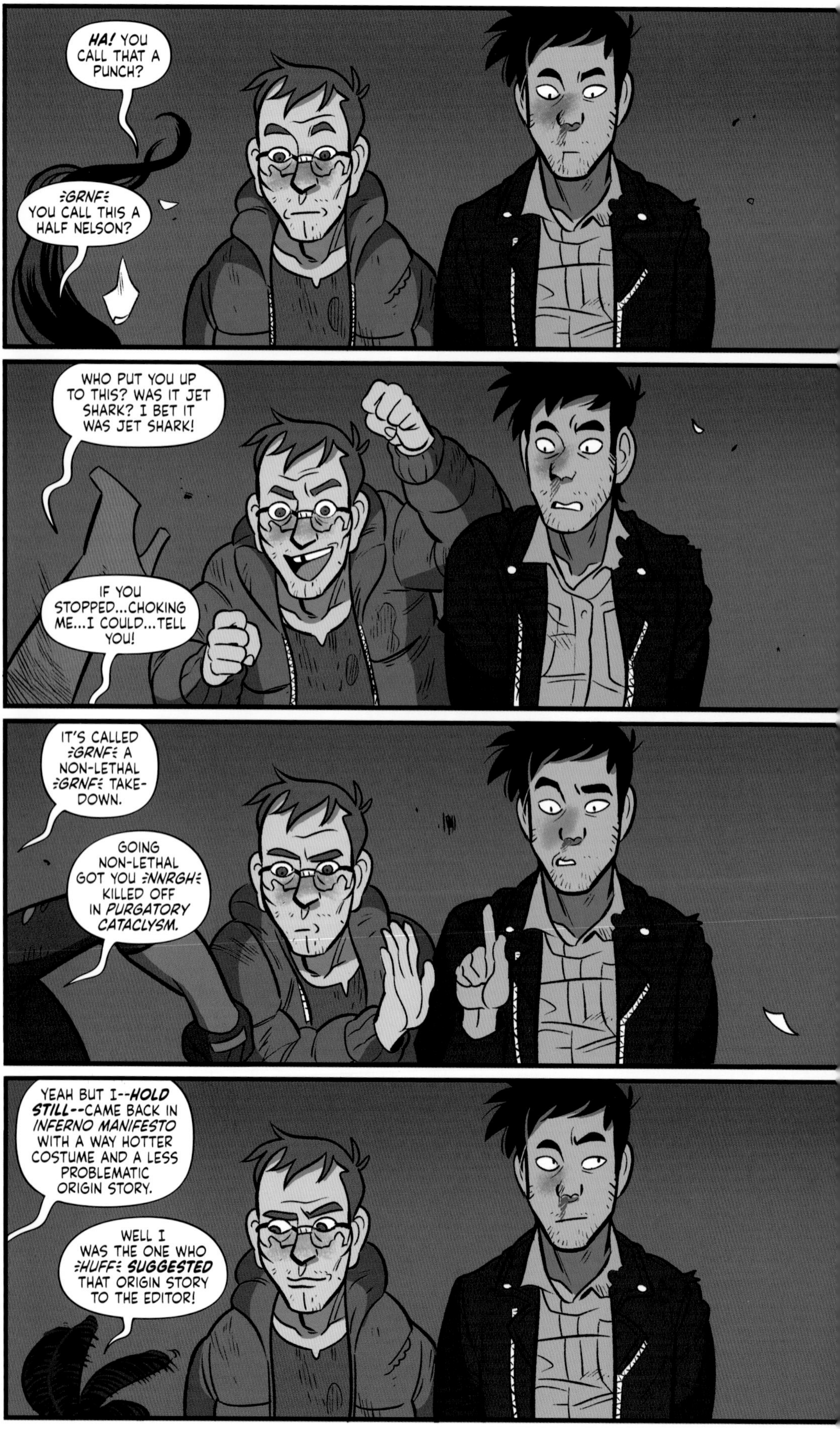
HA! YOU CALL THAT A PUNCH?
GRNF YOU CALL THIS A HALF NELSON?
WHO PUT YOU UP TO THIS? WAS IT JET SHARK? I BET IT WAS JET SHARK!
IF YOU STOPPED...CHOKING ME...I COULD...TELL YOU!
IT'S CALLED GRNF A NON-LETHAL GRNF TAKE-DOWN.
GOING NON-LETHAL GOT YOU NNRGH KILLED OFF IN PURGATORY CATACLYSM.
YEAH BUT I--HOLD STILL--CAME BACK IN INFERNO MANIFESTO WITH A WAY HOTTER COSTUME AND A LESS PROBLEMATIC ORIGIN STORY.
WELL I WAS THE ONE WHO HUFF SUGGESTED THAT ORIGIN STORY TO THE EDITOR!

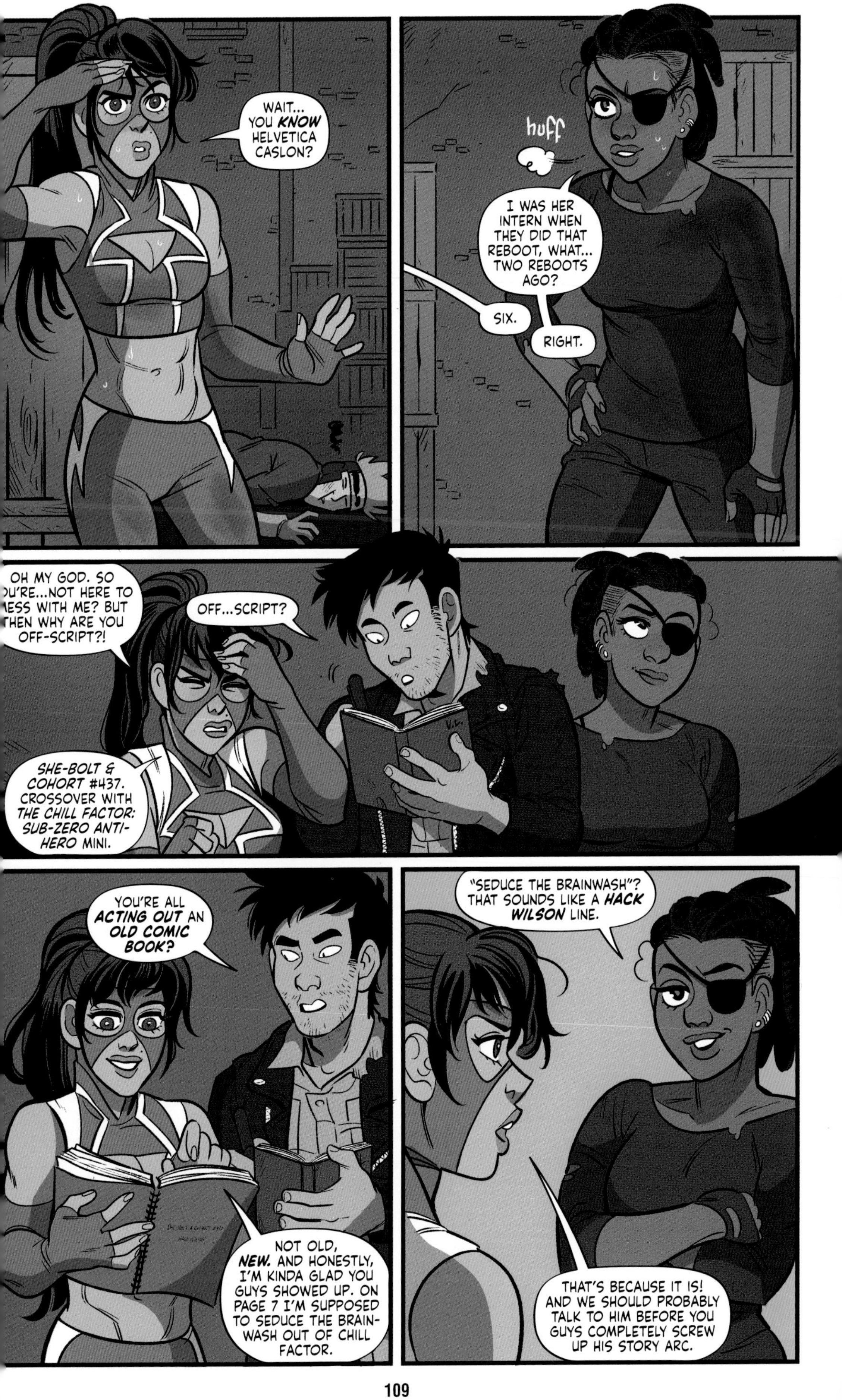
WAIT... YOU KNOW HELVETICA CASLON?
huff
I WAS HER INTERN WHEN THEY DID THAT REBOOT, WHAT... TWO REBOOTS AGO?
SIX.
RIGHT.
OH MY GOD. SO U'RE...NOT HERE TO ESS WITH ME? BUT THEN WHY ARE YOU OFF-SCRIPT?!
OFF...SCRIPT?
SHE-BOLT & COHORT #437. CROSSOVER WITH THE CHILL FACTOR: SUB-ZERO ANTI-HERO MINI.
YOU'RE ALL ACTING OUT AN OLD COMIC BOOK?
NOT OLD, NEW. AND HONESTLY, I'M KINDA GLAD YOU GUYS SHOWED UP. ON PAGE 7 I'M SUPPOSED TO SEDUCE THE BRAIN-WASH OUT OF CHILL FACTOR.
"SEDUCE THE BRAINWASH"? THAT SOUNDS LIKE A HACK WILSON LINE.
THAT'S BECAUSE IT IS! AND WE SHOULD PROBABLY TALK TO HIM BEFORE YOU GUYS COMPLETELY SCREW UP HIS STORY ARC.

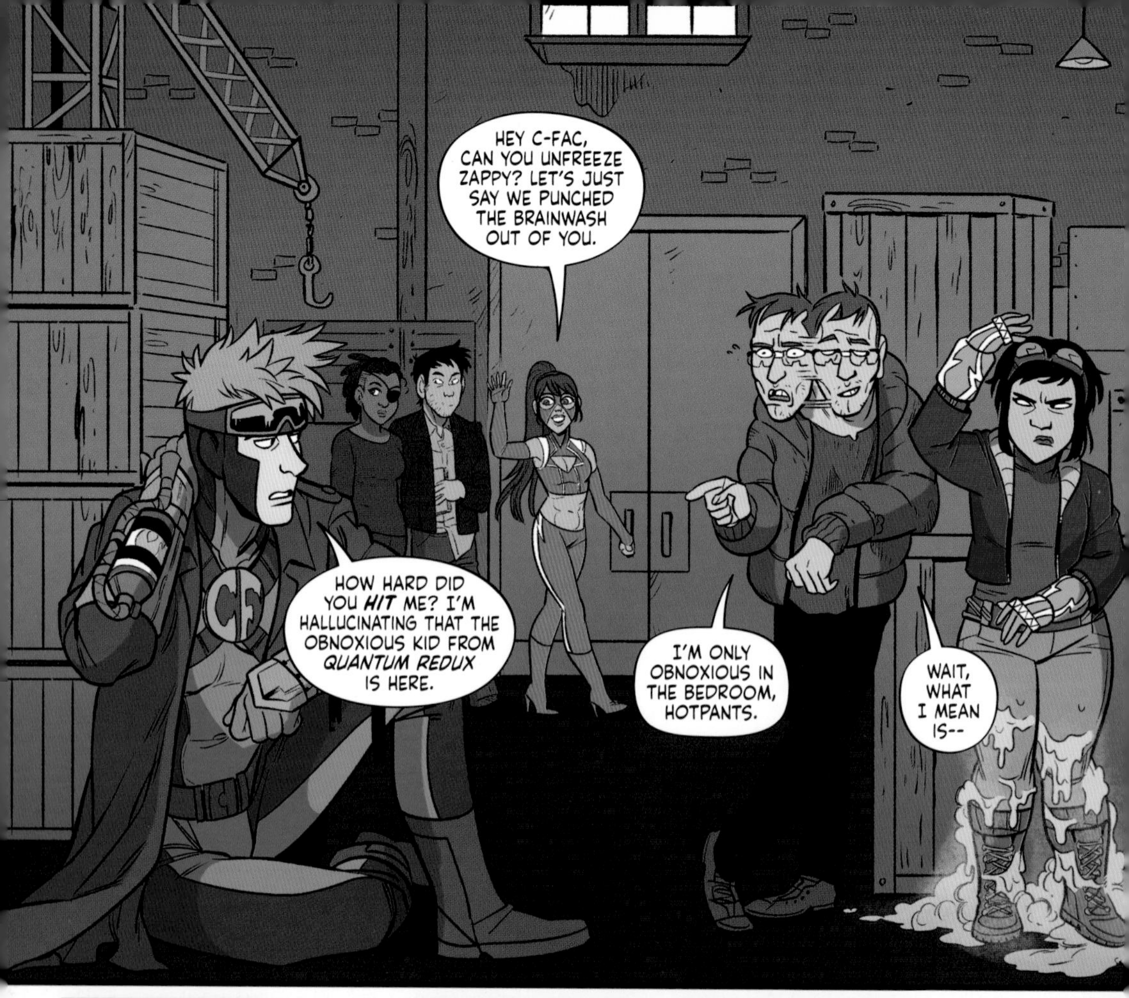
HEY C-FAC, CAN YOU UNFREEZE ZAPPY? LET'S JUST SAY WE PUNCHED THE BRAINWASH OUT OF YOU.
HOW HARD DID YOU *HIT* ME? I'M HALLUCINATING THAT THE OBNOXIOUS KID FROM *QUANTUM REDUX* IS HERE.
I'M ONLY OBNOXIOUS IN THE BEDROOM, HOTPANTS.
WAIT, WHAT I MEAN IS--

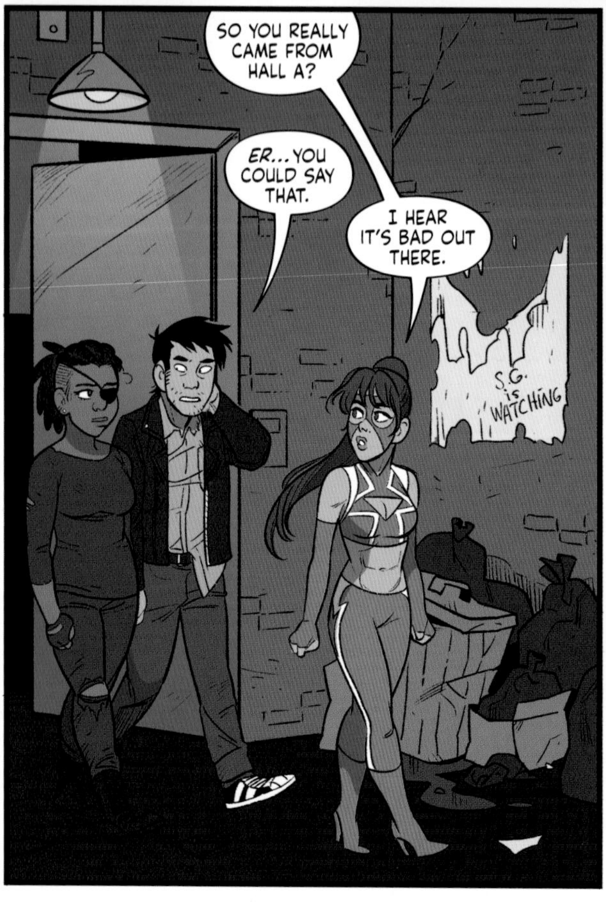
SO YOU REALLY CAME FROM HALL A?
ER...YOU COULD SAY THAT.
I HEAR IT'S BAD OUT THERE.
S.G. is WATCHING

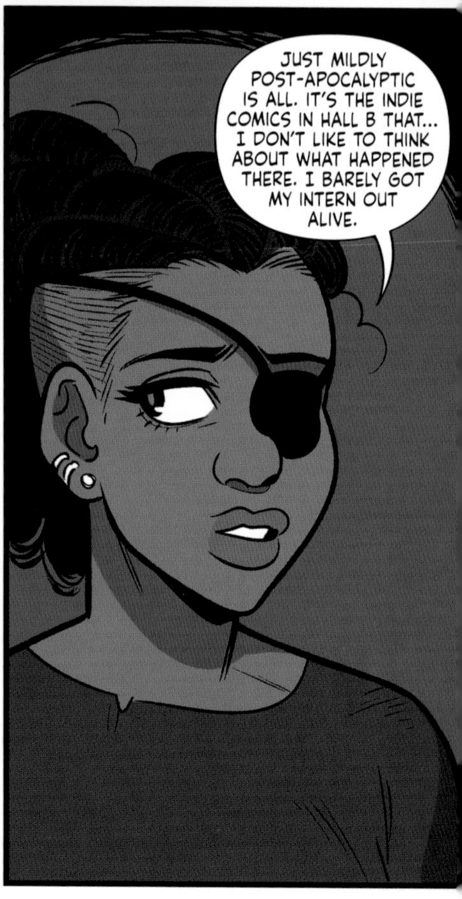
JUST MILDLY POST-APOCALYPTIC IS ALL. IT'S THE INDIE COMICS IN HALL B THAT... I DON'T LIKE TO THINK ABOUT WHAT HAPPENED THERE. I BARELY GOT MY INTERN OUT ALIVE.

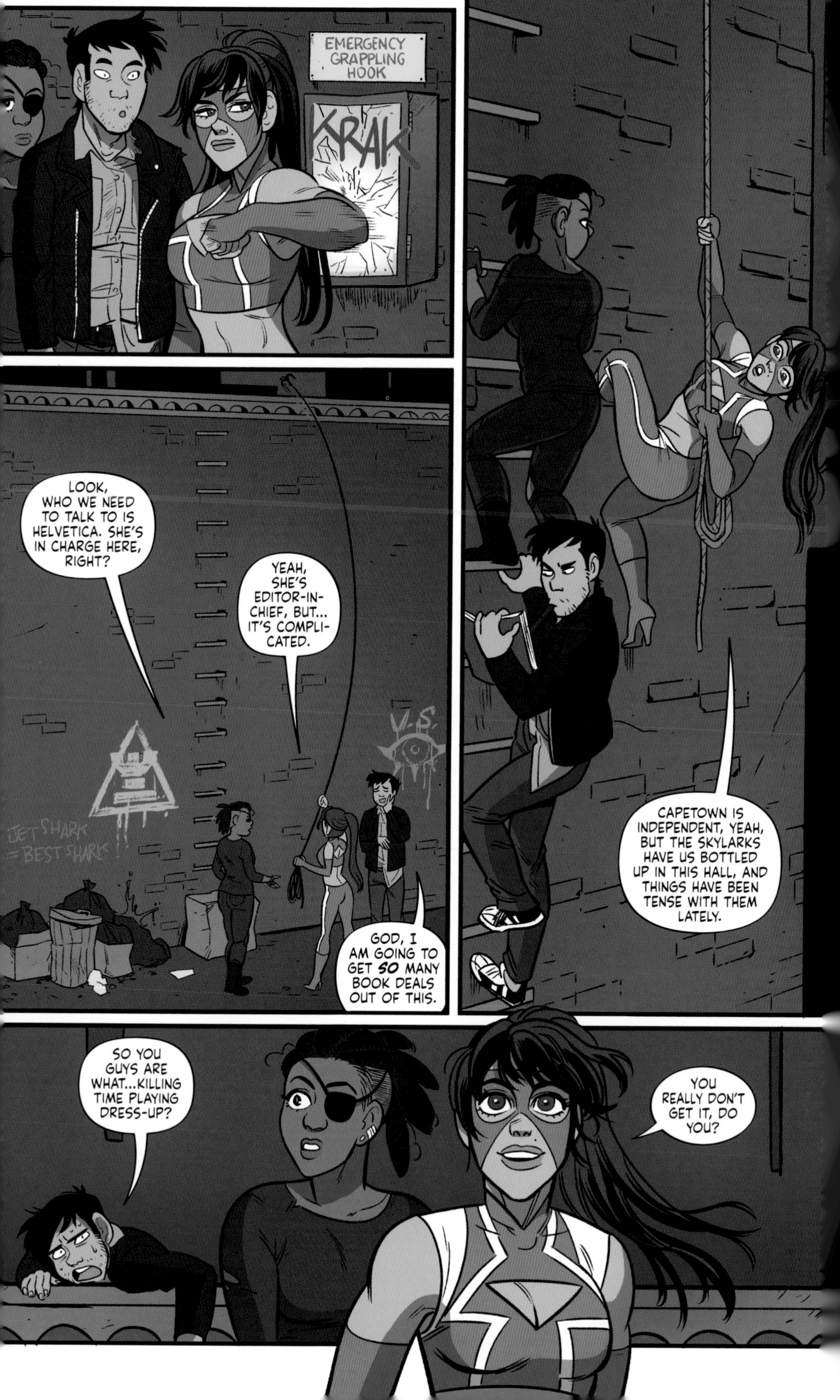
EMERGENCY GRAPPLING HOOK
KRAK
LOOK, WHO WE NEED TO TALK TO IS HELVETICA. SHE'S IN CHARGE HERE, RIGHT?
YEAH, SHE'S EDITOR-IN-CHIEF, BUT... IT'S COMPLICATED.
V.S.
JETSHARK = BESTSHARK
GOD, I AM GOING TO GET SO MANY BOOK DEALS OUT OF THIS.
CAPETOWN IS INDEPENDENT, YEAH, BUT THE SKYLARKS HAVE US BOTTLED UP IN THIS HALL, AND THINGS HAVE BEEN TENSE WITH THEM LATELY.
SO YOU GUYS ARE WHAT...KILLING TIME PLAYING DRESS-UP?
YOU REALLY DON'T GET IT, DO YOU?

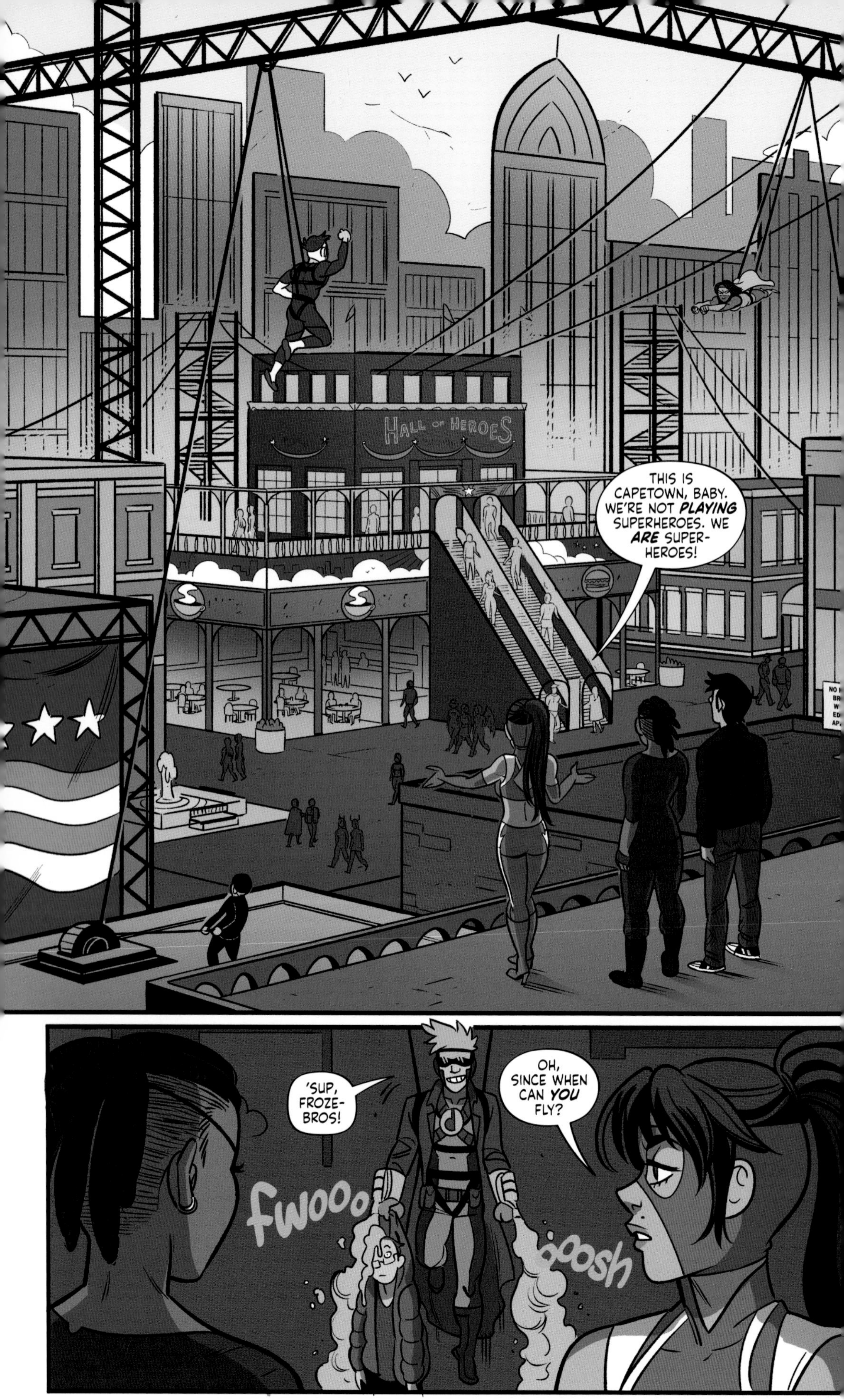
HALL OF HEROES
THIS IS CAPETOWN, BABY. WE'RE NOT *PLAYING* SUPERHEROES. WE *ARE* SUPER-HEROES!
'SUP, FROZE-BROS!
OH, SINCE WHEN CAN *YOU* FLY?
fwooo
ooosh

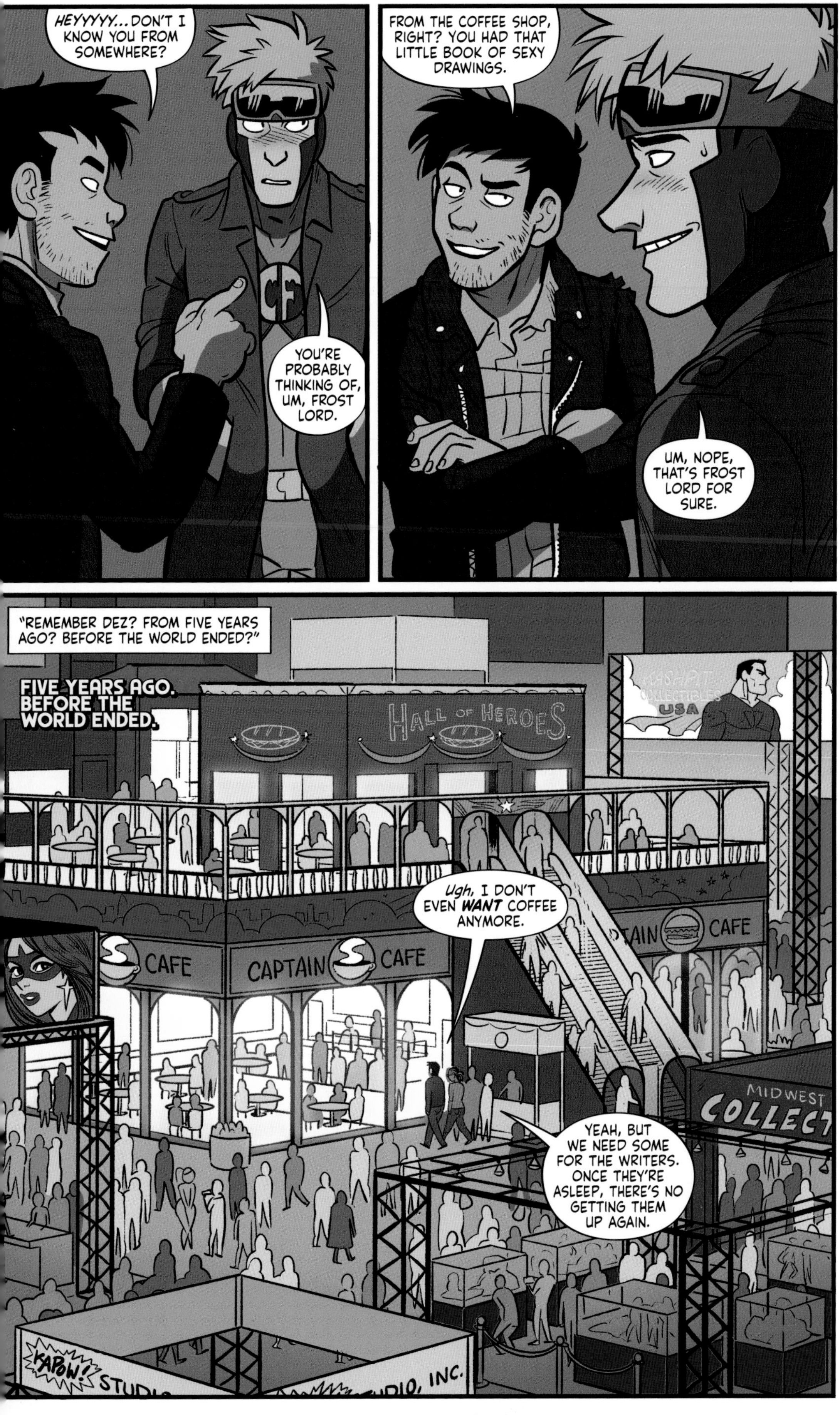
HEYYYYY... DON'T I KNOW YOU FROM SOMEWHERE?
YOU'RE PROBABLY THINKING OF, UM, FROST LORD.
FROM THE COFFEE SHOP, RIGHT? YOU HAD THAT LITTLE BOOK OF SEXY DRAWINGS.
UM, NOPE, THAT'S FROST LORD FOR SURE.
"REMEMBER DEZ? FROM FIVE YEARS AGO? BEFORE THE WORLD ENDED?"
FIVE YEARS AGO. BEFORE THE WORLD ENDED.
HALL OF HEROES
KASHPIT COLLECTIBLES USA
CAPTAIN CAFE
CAFE
Ugh, I DON'T EVEN WANT COFFEE ANYMORE.
YEAH, BUT WE NEED SOME FOR THE WRITERS. ONCE THEY'RE ASLEEP, THERE'S NO GETTING THEM UP AGAIN.
MIDWEST COLLECT
KAPOW! STUDIO, INC.

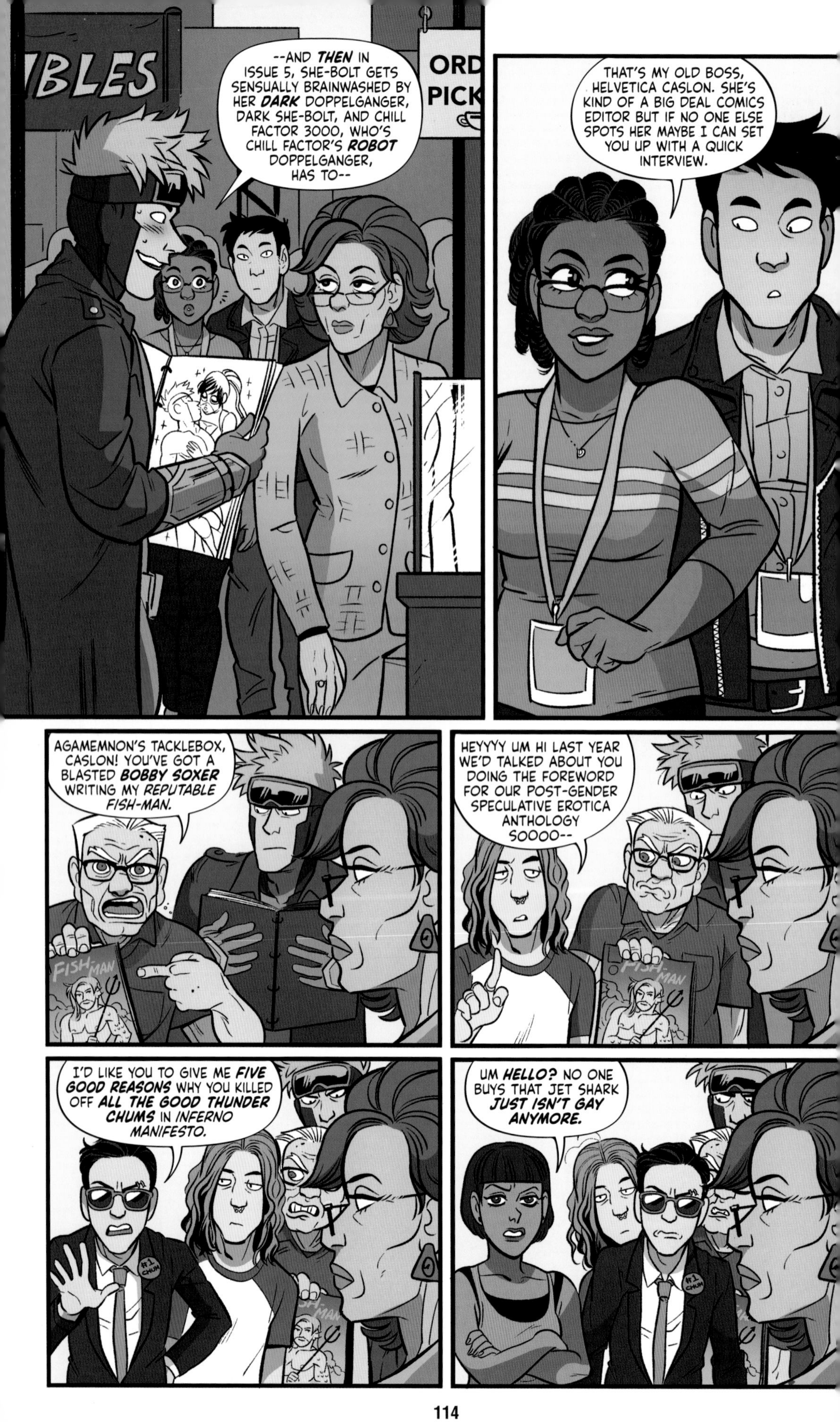

IBLES
--AND THEN IN ISSUE 5, SHE-BOLT GETS SENSUALLY BRAINWASHED BY HER DARK DOPPELGANGER, DARK SHE-BOLT, AND CHILL FACTOR 3000, WHO'S CHILL FACTOR'S ROBOT DOPPELGANGER, HAS TO--
ORD
PICK
THAT'S MY OLD BOSS, HELVETICA CASLON. SHE'S KIND OF A BIG DEAL COMICS EDITOR BUT IF NO ONE ELSE SPOTS HER MAYBE I CAN SET YOU UP WITH A QUICK INTERVIEW.
AGAMEMNON'S TACKLEBOX, CASLON! YOU'VE GOT A BLASTED BOBBY SOXER WRITING MY REPUTABLE FISH-MAN.
FISH-MAN
HEYYYY UM HI LAST YEAR WE'D TALKED ABOUT YOU DOING THE FOREWORD FOR OUR POST-GENDER SPECULATIVE EROTICA ANTHOLOGY SOOOO--
FISH-MAN
I'D LIKE YOU TO GIVE ME FIVE GOOD REASONS WHY YOU KILLED OFF ALL THE GOOD THUNDER CHUMS IN INFERNO MANIFESTO.
#1 CHUM
UM HELLO? NO ONE BUYS THAT JET SHARK JUST ISN'T GAY ANYMORE.
#1 CHUM

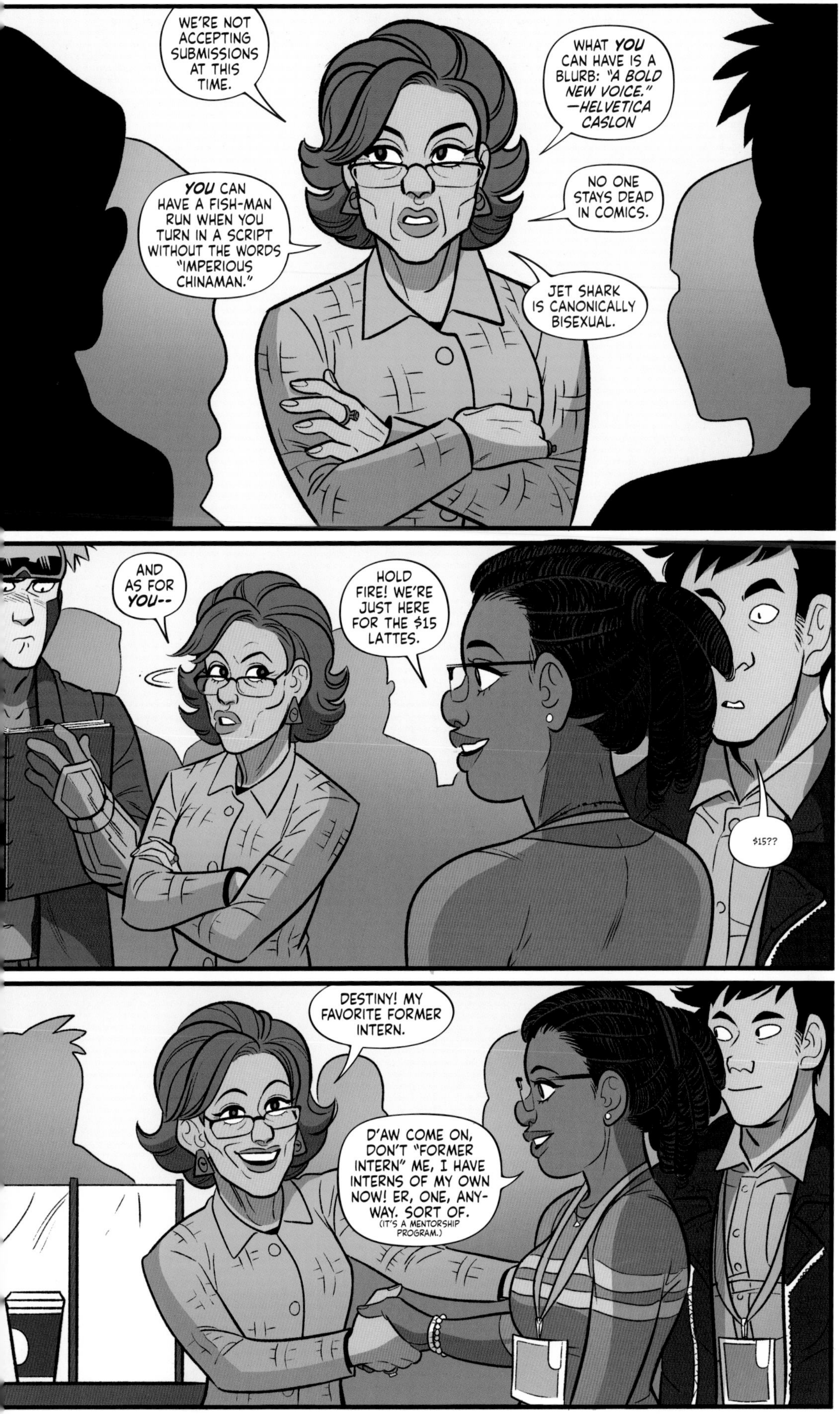
WE'RE NOT ACCEPTING SUBMISSIONS AT THIS TIME.
WHAT *YOU* CAN HAVE IS A BLURB: *"A BOLD NEW VOICE." —HELVETICA CASLON*
YOU CAN HAVE A FISH-MAN RUN WHEN YOU TURN IN A SCRIPT WITHOUT THE WORDS "IMPERIOUS CHINAMAN."
NO ONE STAYS DEAD IN COMICS.
JET SHARK IS CANONICALLY BISEXUAL.
AND AS FOR *YOU*--
HOLD FIRE! WE'RE JUST HERE FOR THE $15 LATTES.
$15??
DESTINY! MY FAVORITE FORMER INTERN.
D'AW COME ON, DON'T "FORMER INTERN" ME, I HAVE INTERNS OF MY OWN NOW! ER, ONE, ANYWAY. SORT OF.
(IT'S A MENTORSHIP PROGRAM.)

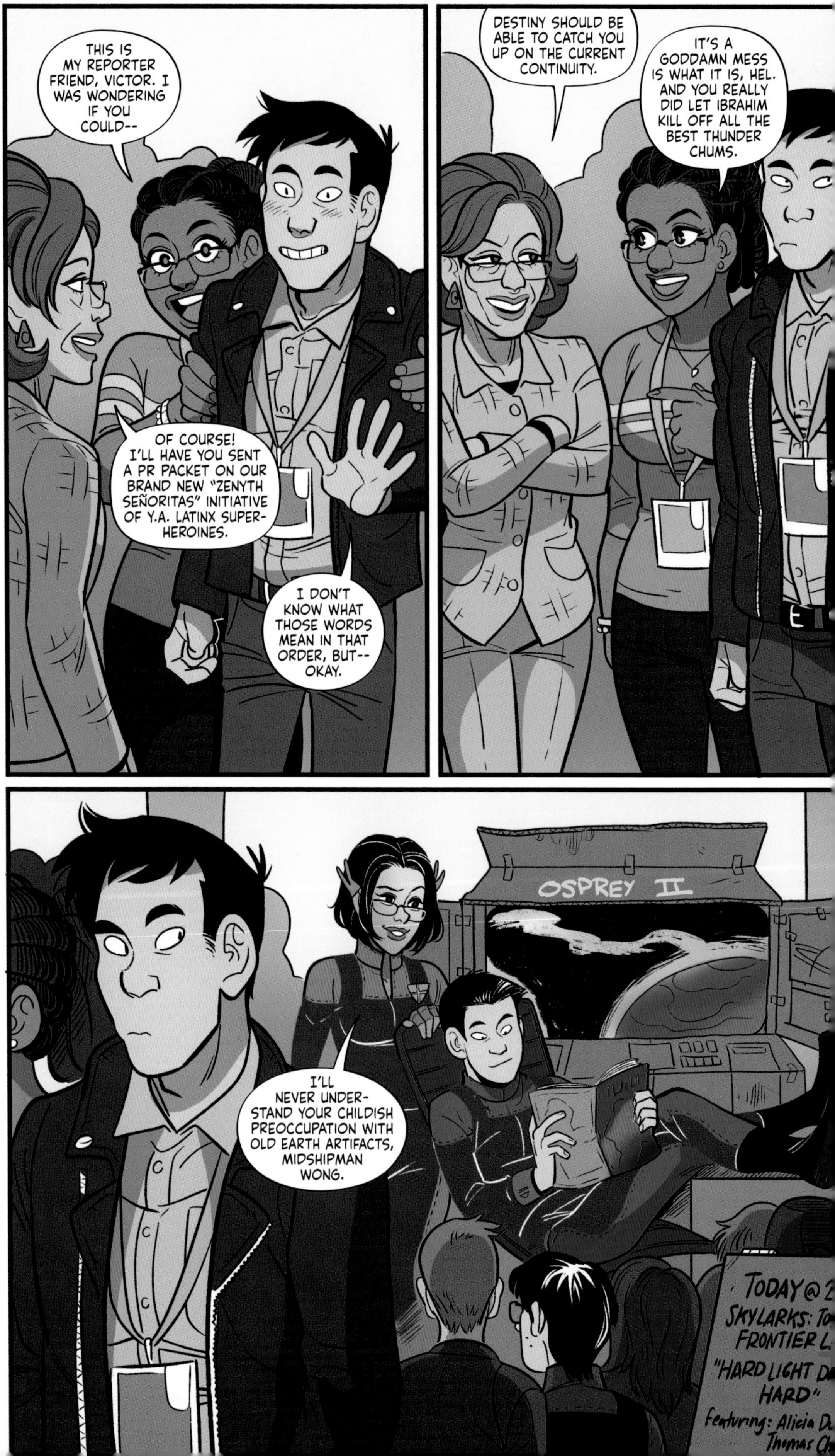
THIS IS MY REPORTER FRIEND, VICTOR. I WAS WONDERING IF YOU COULD--
OF COURSE! I'LL HAVE YOU SENT A PR PACKET ON OUR BRAND NEW "ZENYTH SEÑORITAS" INITIATIVE OF Y.A. LATINX SUPER-HEROINES.
I DON'T KNOW WHAT THOSE WORDS MEAN IN THAT ORDER, BUT-- OKAY.
DESTINY SHOULD BE ABLE TO CATCH YOU UP ON THE CURRENT CONTINUITY.
IT'S A GODDAMN MESS IS WHAT IT IS, HEL. AND YOU REALLY DID LET IBRAHIM KILL OFF ALL THE BEST THUNDER CHUMS.
OSPREY II
I'LL NEVER UNDER-STAND YOUR CHILDISH PREOCCUPATION WITH OLD EARTH ARTIFACTS, MIDSHIPMAN WONG.
TODAY @ 2
SKYLARKS: To
FRONTIER L
"HARD LIGHT D
HARD"
featuring: Alicia D
Thomas Ch

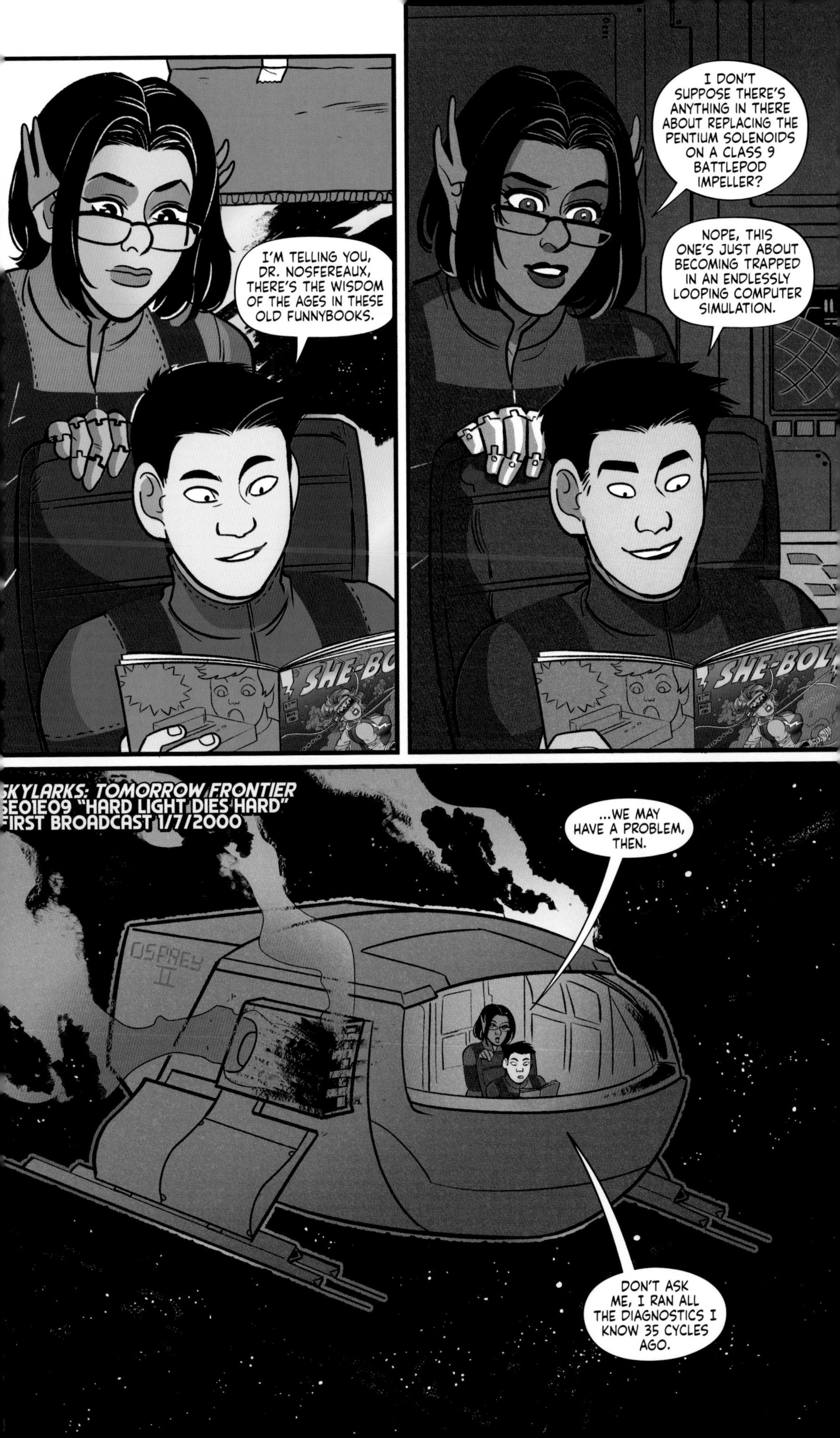
I'M TELLING YOU, DR. NOSFEREAUX, THERE'S THE WISDOM OF THE AGES IN THESE OLD FUNNYBOOKS.
SHE-BOT
I DON'T SUPPOSE THERE'S ANYTHING IN THERE ABOUT REPLACING THE PENTIUM SOLENOIDS ON A CLASS 9 BATTLEPOD IMPELLER?
NOPE, THIS ONE'S JUST ABOUT BECOMING TRAPPED IN AN ENDLESSLY LOOPING COMPUTER SIMULATION.
SHE-BOT
SKYLARKS: TOMORROW FRONTIER
SE01E09 "HARD LIGHT DIES HARD"
FIRST BROADCAST 1/7/2000
...WE MAY HAVE A PROBLEM, THEN.
OSPREY II
DON'T ASK ME, I RAN ALL THE DIAGNOSTICS I KNOW 35 CYCLES AGO.

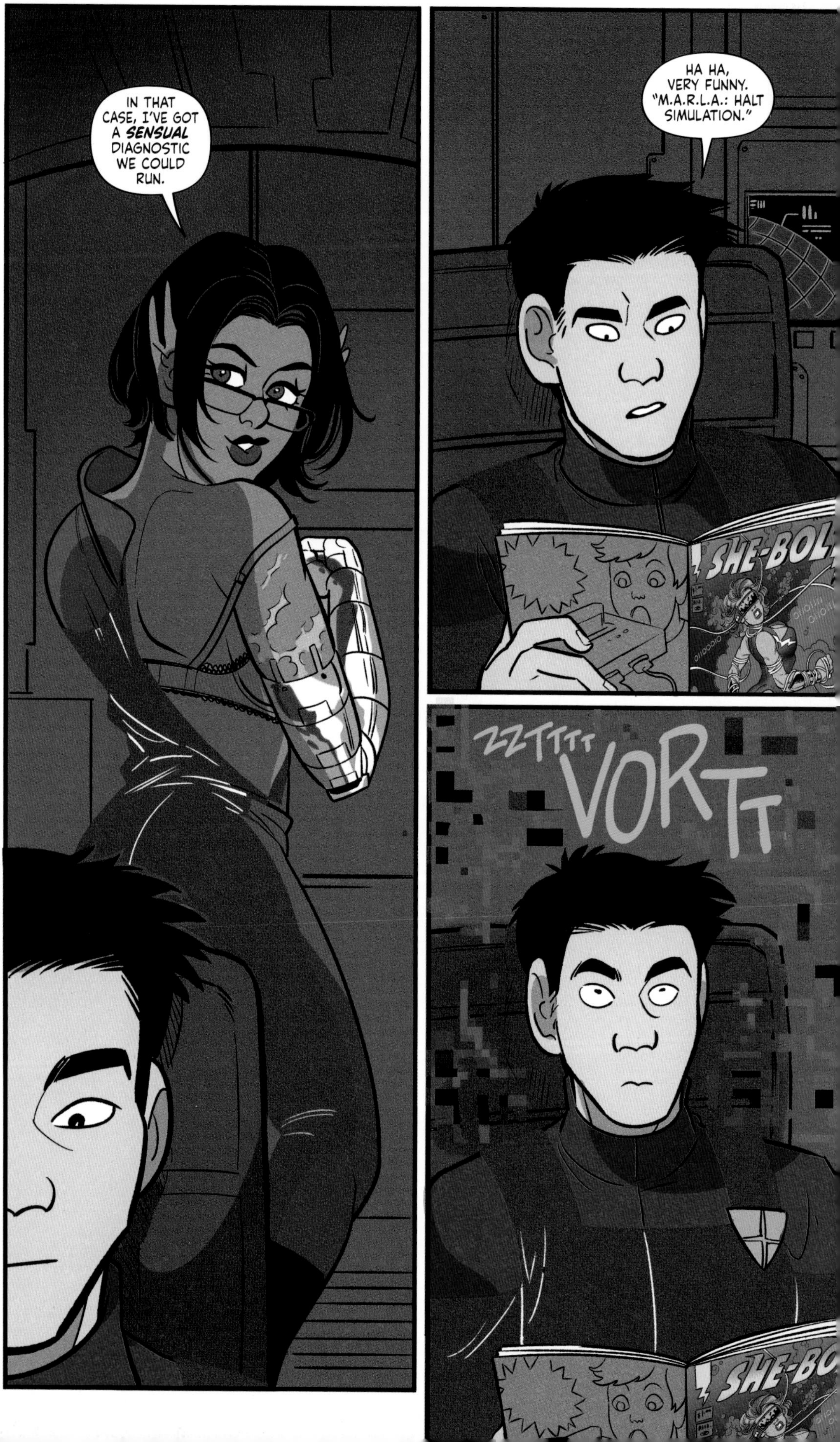
IN THAT CASE, I'VE GOT A SENSUAL DIAGNOSTIC WE COULD RUN.
HA HA, VERY FUNNY. "M.A.R.L.A.: HALT SIMULATION."
SHE-BOT
ZZTTTT VORTT
SHE-BO

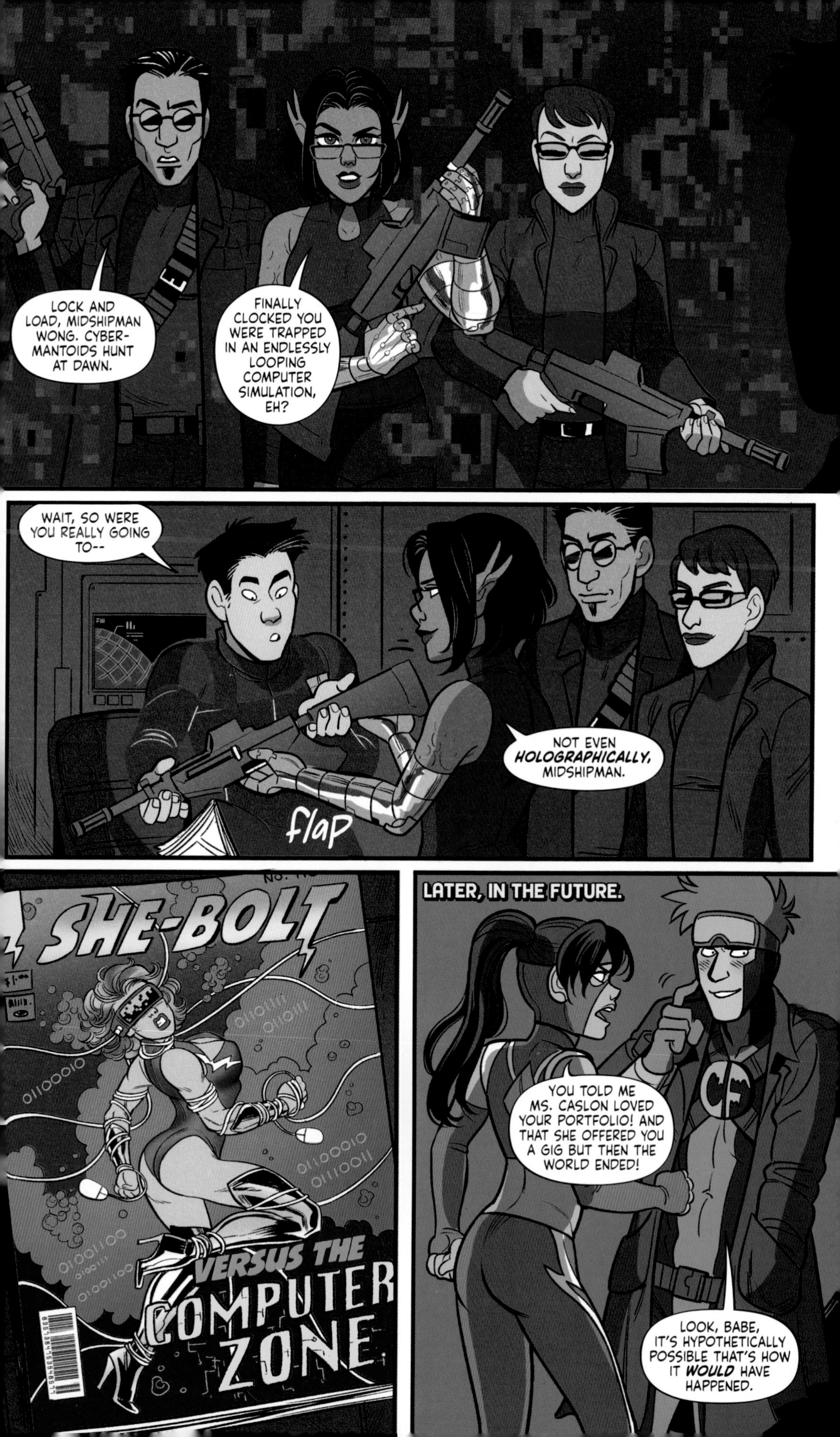
LOCK AND LOAD, MIDSHIPMAN WONG. CYBER-MANTOIDS HUNT AT DAWN.
FINALLY CLOCKED YOU WERE TRAPPED IN AN ENDLESSLY LOOPING COMPUTER SIMULATION, EH?
WAIT, SO WERE YOU REALLY GOING TO--
NOT EVEN *HOLOGRAPHICALLY,* MIDSHIPMAN.
flap
SHE-BOLT
01100010
VERSUS THE COMPUTER ZONE
LATER, IN THE FUTURE.
YOU TOLD ME MS. CASLON LOVED YOUR PORTFOLIO! AND THAT SHE OFFERED YOU A GIG BUT THEN THE WORLD ENDED!
LOOK, BABE, IT'S HYPOTHETICALLY POSSIBLE THAT'S HOW IT *WOULD* HAVE HAPPENED.

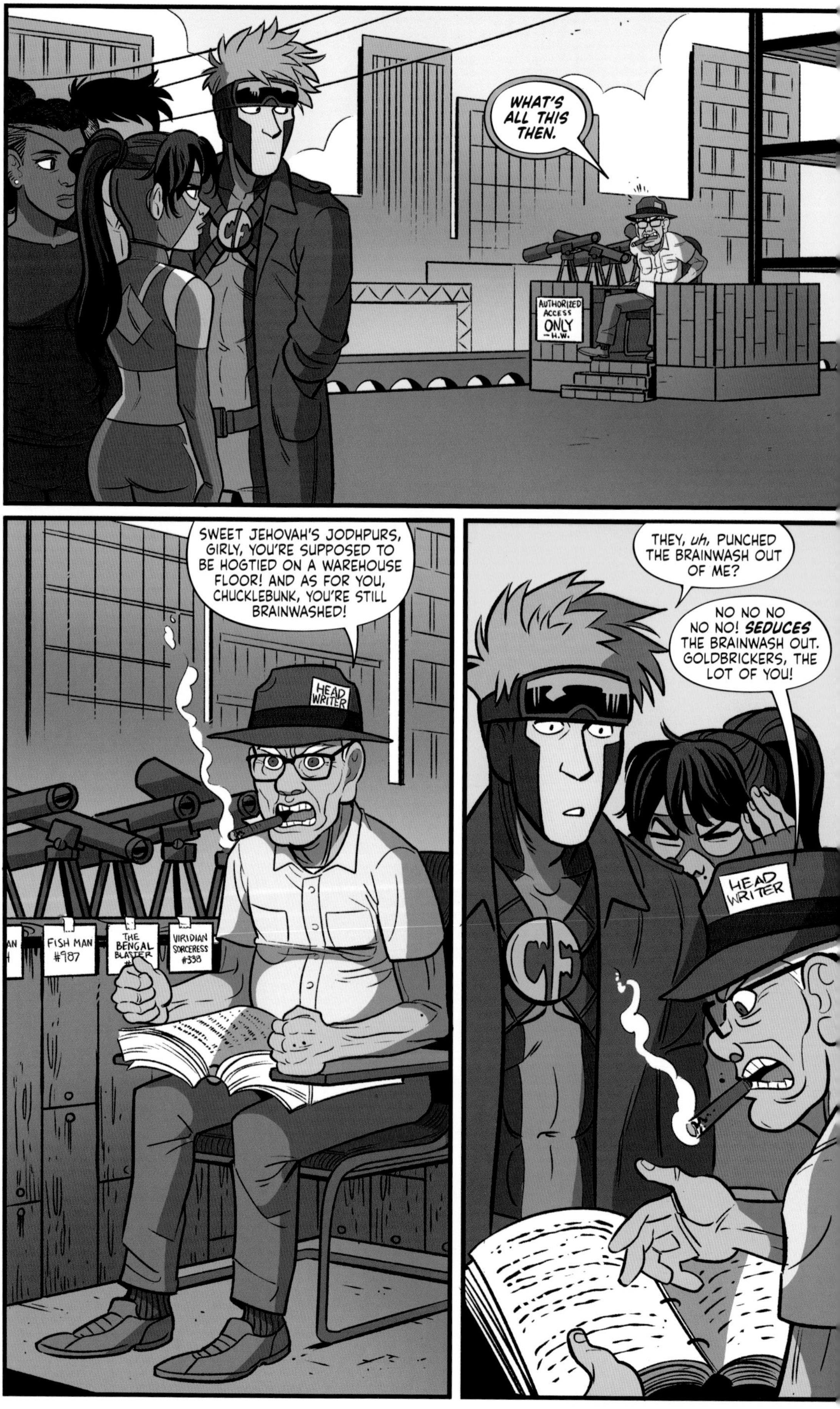
WHAT'S ALL THIS THEN.
AUTHORIZED ACCESS ONLY —H.W.
SWEET JEHOVAH'S JODHPURS, GIRLY, YOU'RE SUPPOSED TO BE HOGTIED ON A WAREHOUSE FLOOR! AND AS FOR YOU, CHUCKLEBUNK, YOU'RE STILL BRAINWASHED!
HEAD WRITER
FISH MAN #987
THE BENGAL BLASTER
VIRIDIAN SORCERESS #338
THEY, *uh,* PUNCHED THE BRAINWASH OUT OF ME?
NO NO NO NO NO! ***SEDUCES*** THE BRAINWASH OUT. GOLDBRICKERS, THE LOT OF YOU!
HEAD WRITER

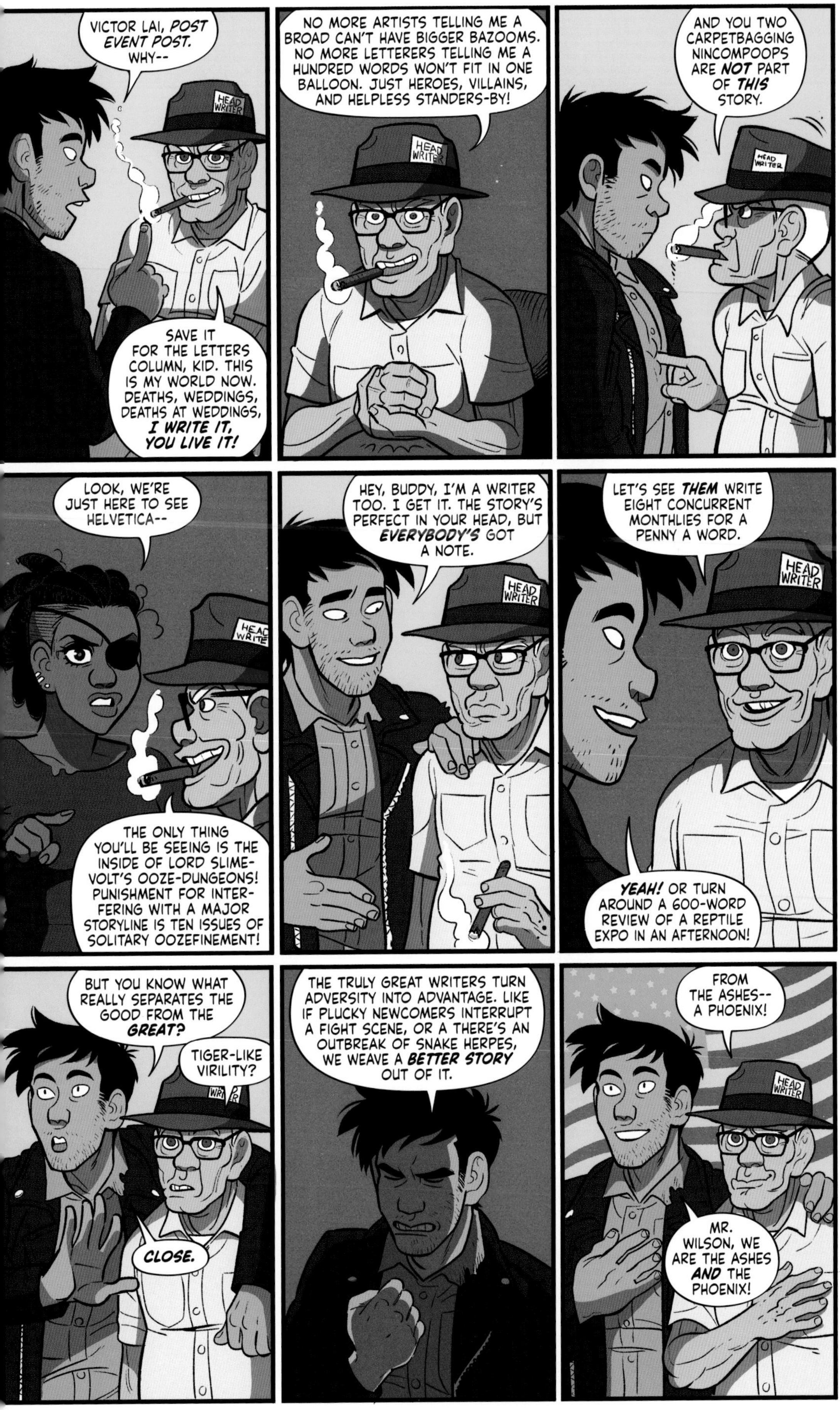
VICTOR LAI, POST EVENT POST. WHY--
SAVE IT FOR THE LETTERS COLUMN, KID. THIS IS MY WORLD NOW. DEATHS, WEDDINGS, DEATHS AT WEDDINGS, I WRITE IT, YOU LIVE IT!
HEAD WRITER
NO MORE ARTISTS TELLING ME A BROAD CAN'T HAVE BIGGER BAZOOMS. NO MORE LETTERERS TELLING ME A HUNDRED WORDS WON'T FIT IN ONE BALLOON. JUST HEROES, VILLAINS, AND HELPLESS STANDERS-BY!
AND YOU TWO CARPETBAGGING NINCOMPOOPS ARE NOT PART OF THIS STORY.
LOOK, WE'RE JUST HERE TO SEE HELVETICA--
THE ONLY THING YOU'LL BE SEEING IS THE INSIDE OF LORD SLIME-VOLT'S OOZE-DUNGEONS! PUNISHMENT FOR INTER-FERING WITH A MAJOR STORYLINE IS TEN ISSUES OF SOLITARY OOZEFINEMENT!
HEY, BUDDY, I'M A WRITER TOO. I GET IT. THE STORY'S PERFECT IN YOUR HEAD, BUT EVERYBODY'S GOT A NOTE.
LET'S SEE THEM WRITE EIGHT CONCURRENT MONTHLIES FOR A PENNY A WORD.
YEAH! OR TURN AROUND A 600-WORD REVIEW OF A REPTILE EXPO IN AN AFTERNOON!
BUT YOU KNOW WHAT REALLY SEPARATES THE GOOD FROM THE GREAT?
TIGER-LIKE VIRILITY?
CLOSE.
THE TRULY GREAT WRITERS TURN ADVERSITY INTO ADVANTAGE. LIKE IF PLUCKY NEWCOMERS INTERRUPT A FIGHT SCENE, OR A THERE'S AN OUTBREAK OF SNAKE HERPES, WE WEAVE A BETTER STORY OUT OF IT.
FROM THE ASHES-- A PHOENIX!
MR. WILSON, WE ARE THE ASHES AND THE PHOENIX!

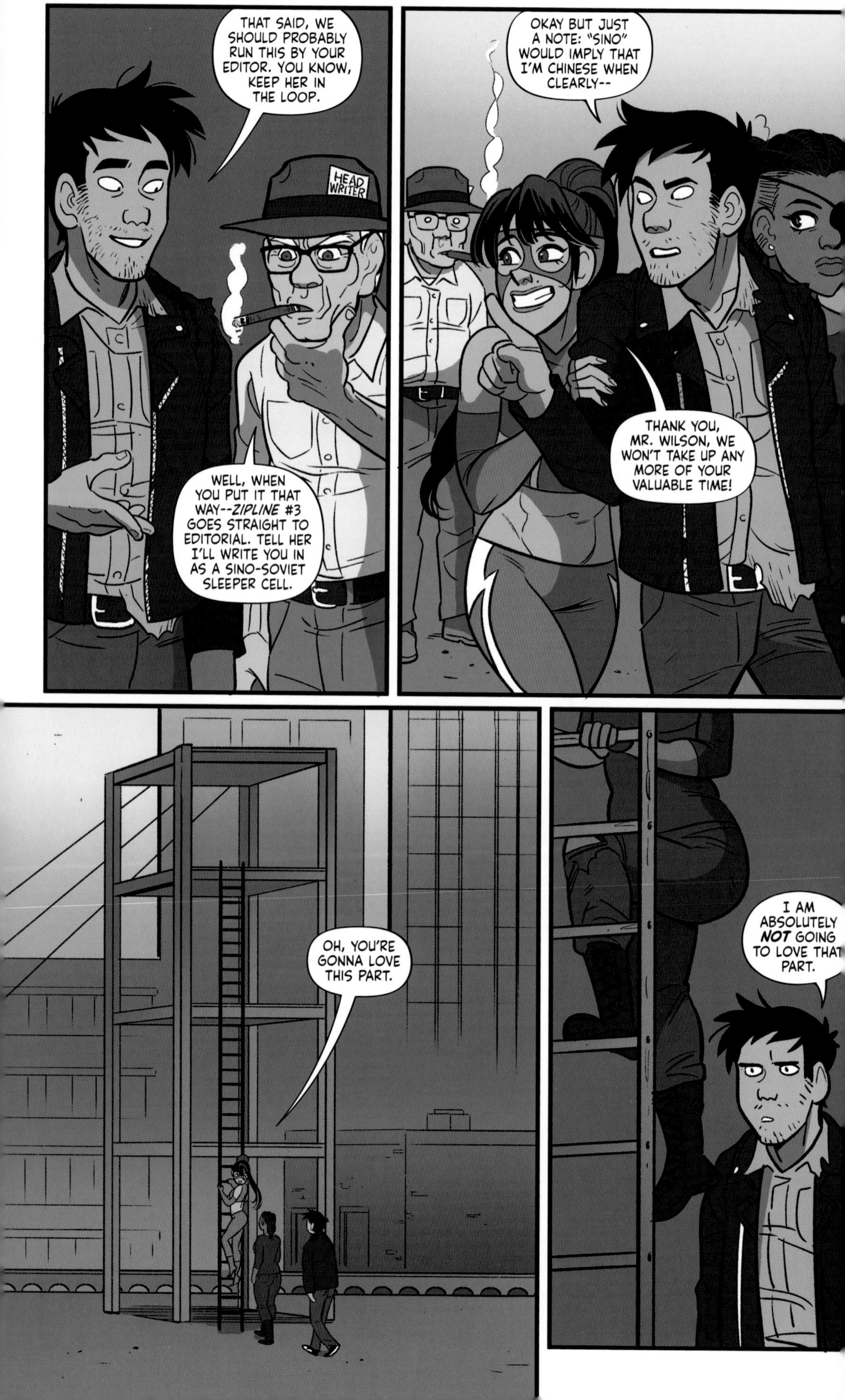
THAT SAID, WE SHOULD PROBABLY RUN THIS BY YOUR EDITOR. YOU KNOW, KEEP HER IN THE LOOP.
HEAD WRITER
WELL, WHEN YOU PUT IT THAT WAY--*ZIPLINE* #3 GOES STRAIGHT TO EDITORIAL. TELL HER I'LL WRITE YOU IN AS A SINO-SOVIET SLEEPER CELL.
OKAY BUT JUST A NOTE: "SINO" WOULD IMPLY THAT I'M CHINESE WHEN CLEARLY--
THANK YOU, MR. WILSON, WE WON'T TAKE UP ANY MORE OF YOUR VALUABLE TIME!
OH, YOU'RE GONNA LOVE THIS PART.
I AM ABSOLUTELY ***NOT*** GOING TO LOVE THAT PART.

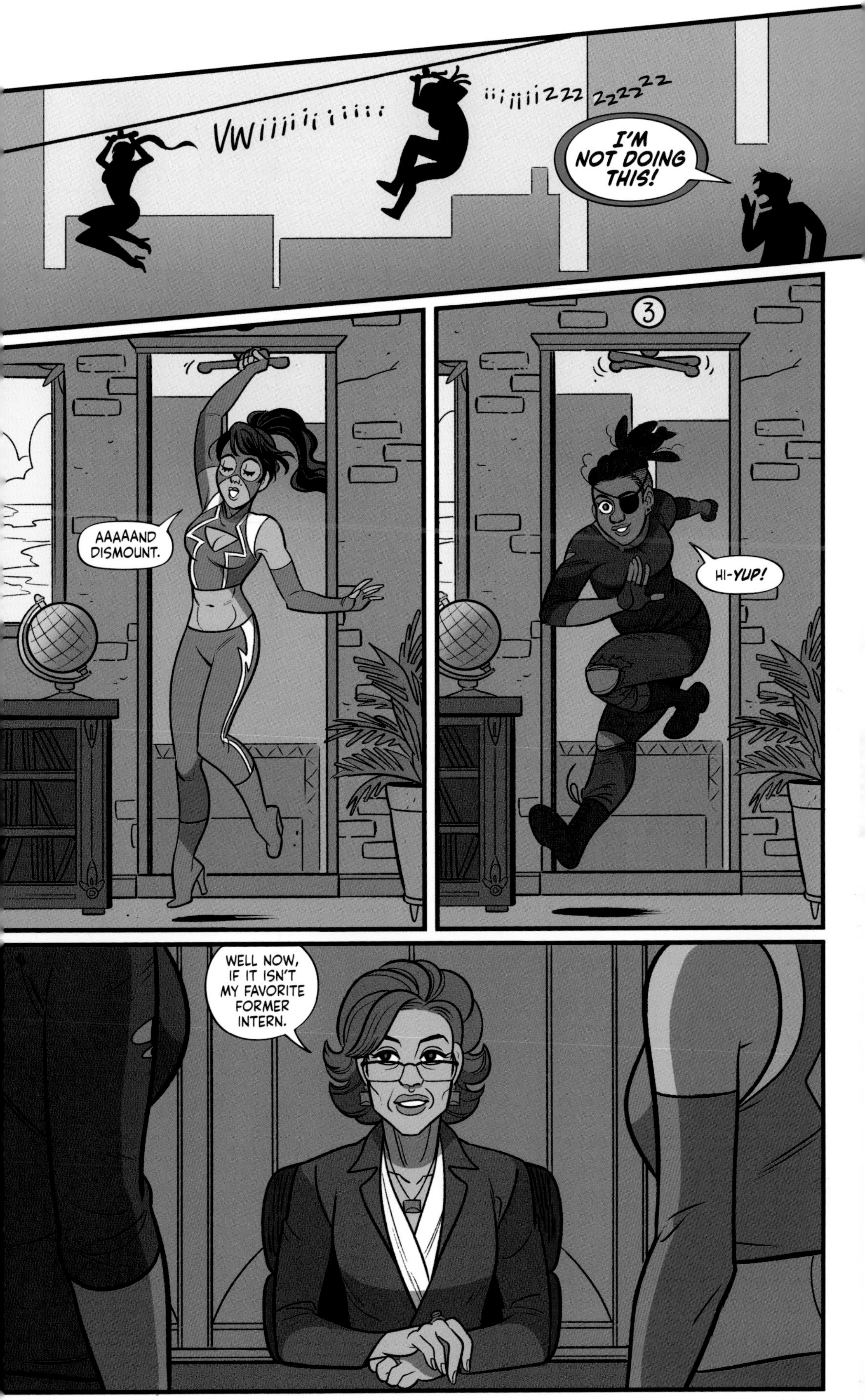
VWiiiiii iiiii
iiiiiiZZZ ZZZZZZ
I'M NOT DOING THIS!
AAAAAND DISMOUNT.
3
HI-YUP!
WELL NOW, IF IT ISN'T MY FAVORITE FORMER INTERN.

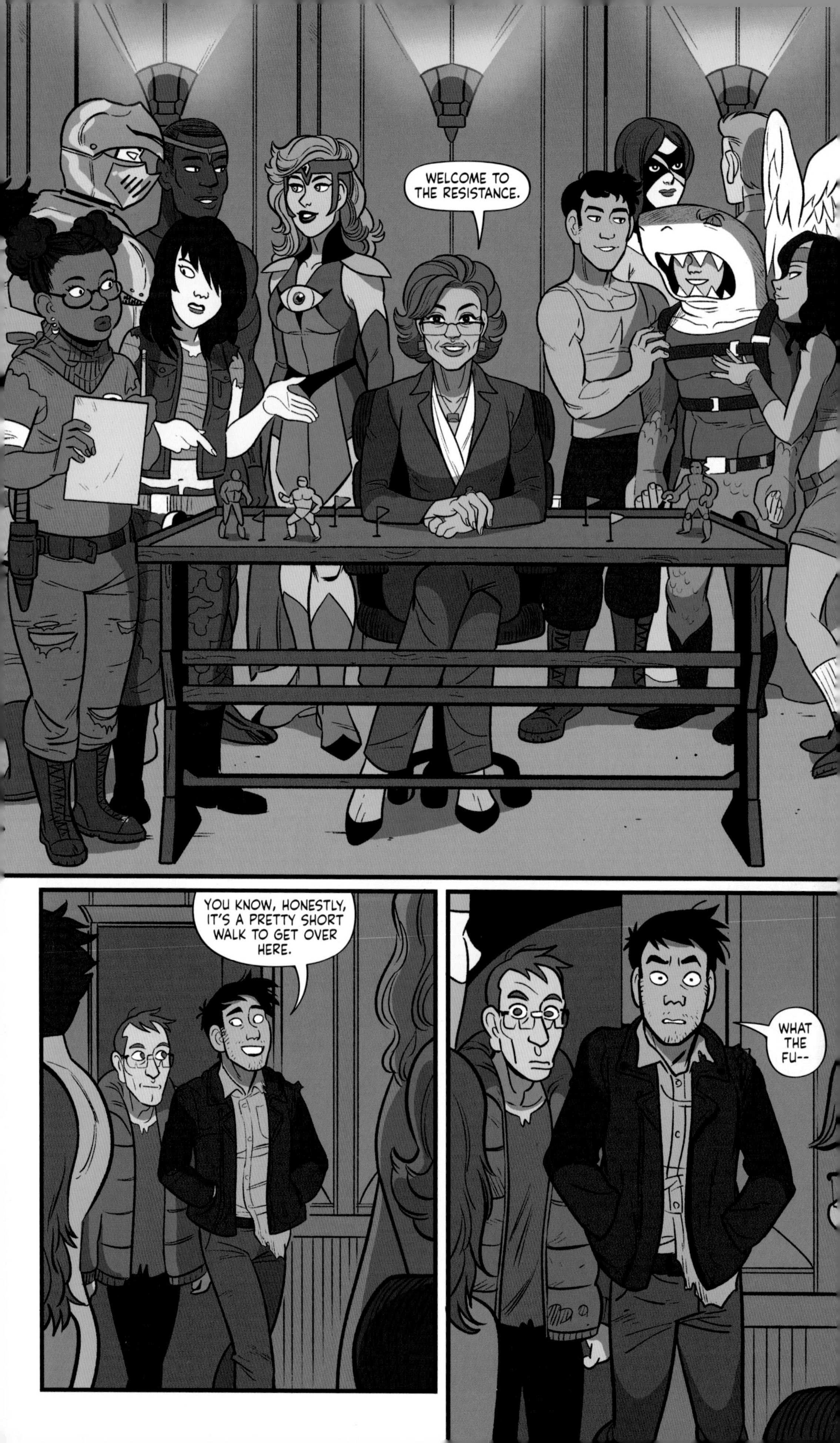
WELCOME TO THE RESISTANCE.
YOU KNOW, HONESTLY, IT'S A PRETTY SHORT WALK TO GET OVER HERE.
WHAT THE FU--

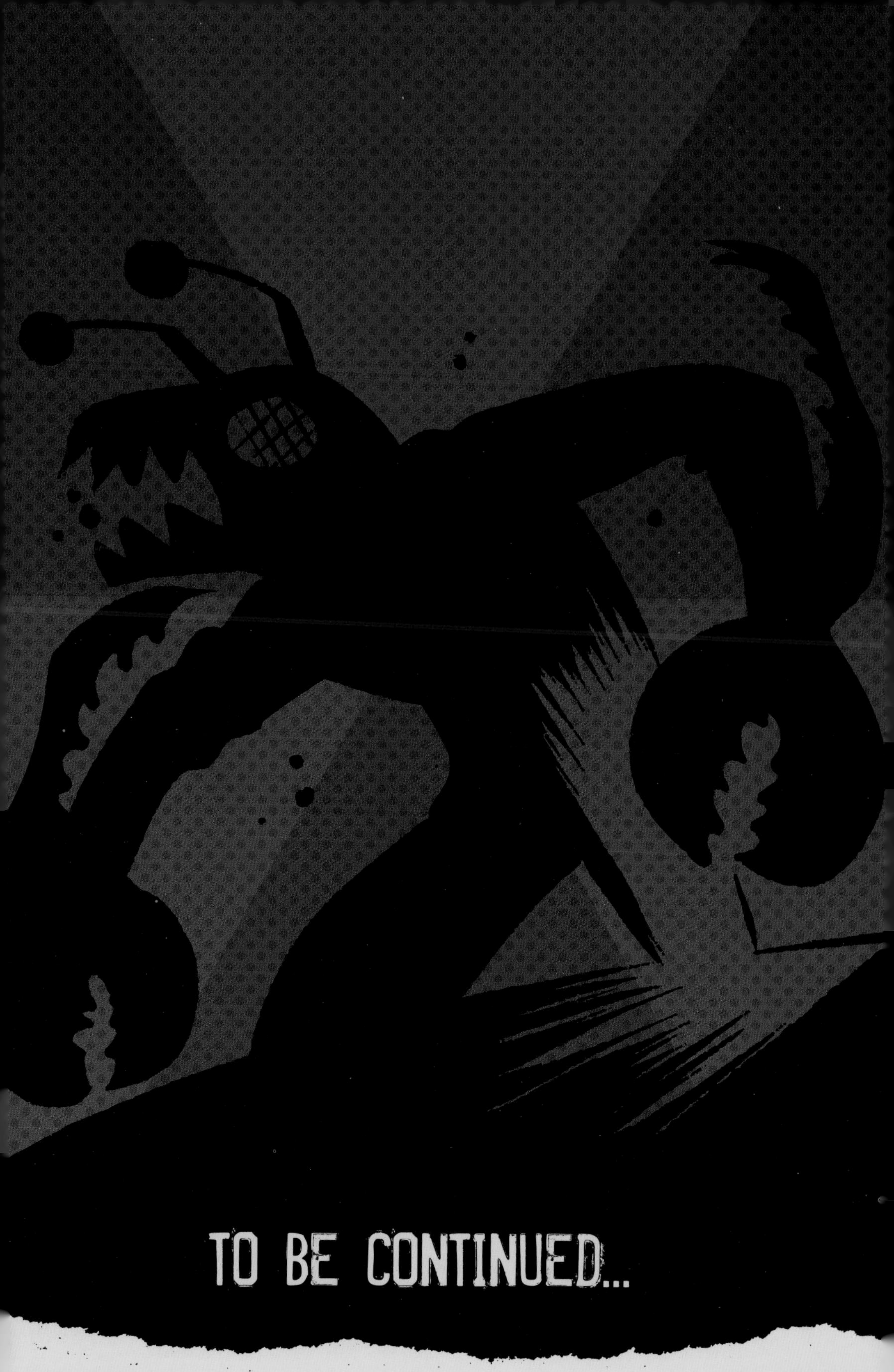

TO BE CONTINUED...

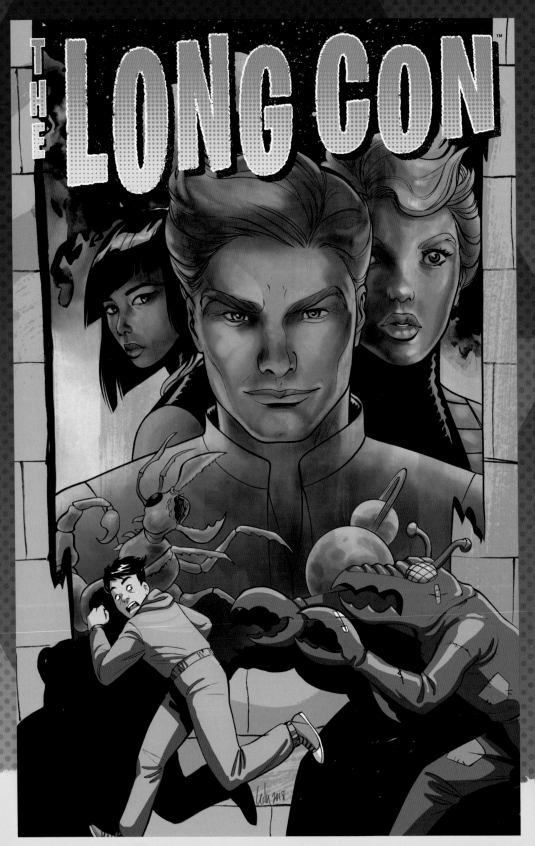

THE LONG CON #1 ALTERNATE COVER BY
LEILA DEL DUCA

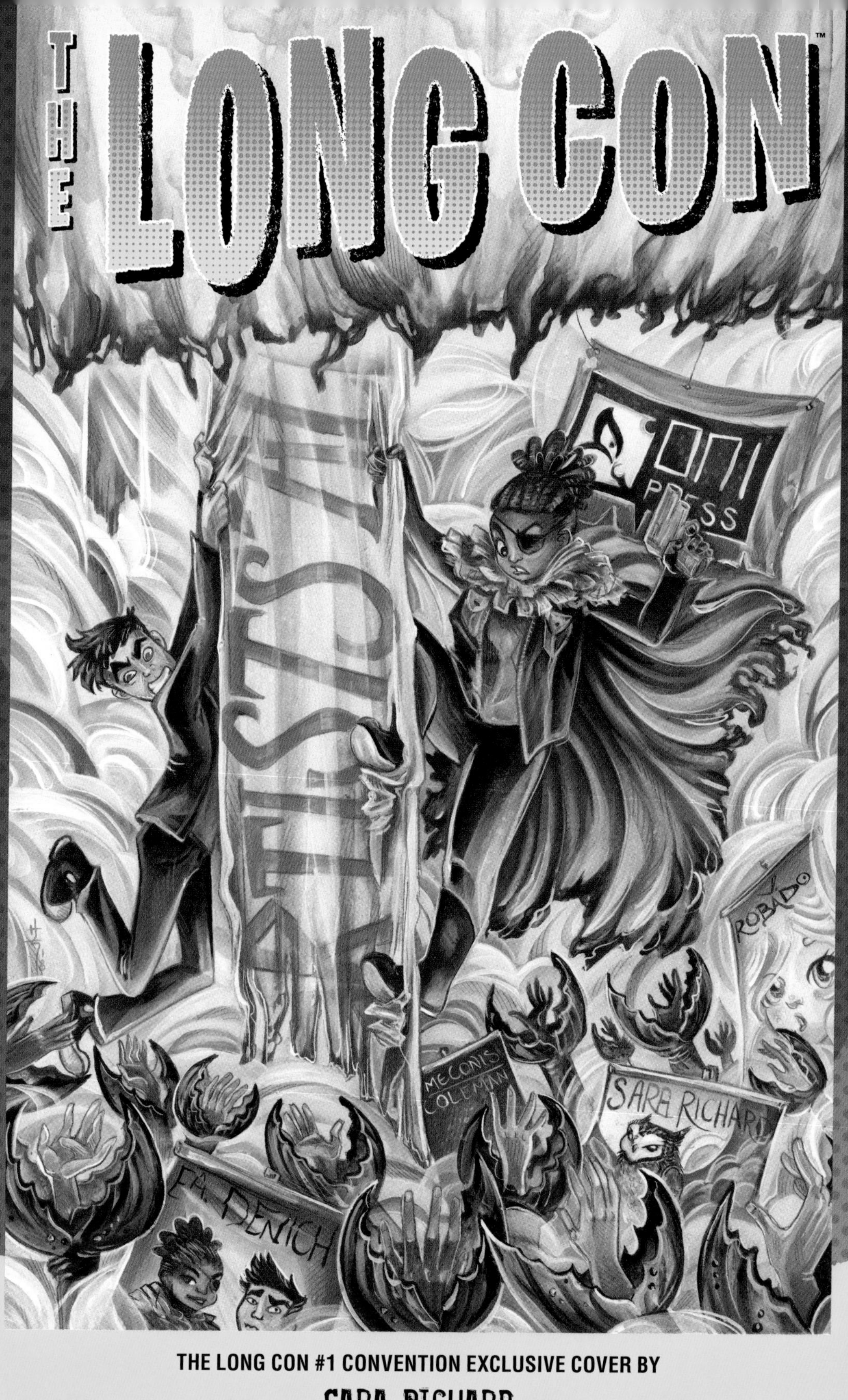
THE LONG CON™
ONI PRESS
ROBADO
MECONIS COLEMAN
SARA RICHARD
E.A. DENICH

THE LONG CON #1 CONVENTION EXCLUSIVE COVER BY

SARA RICHARD

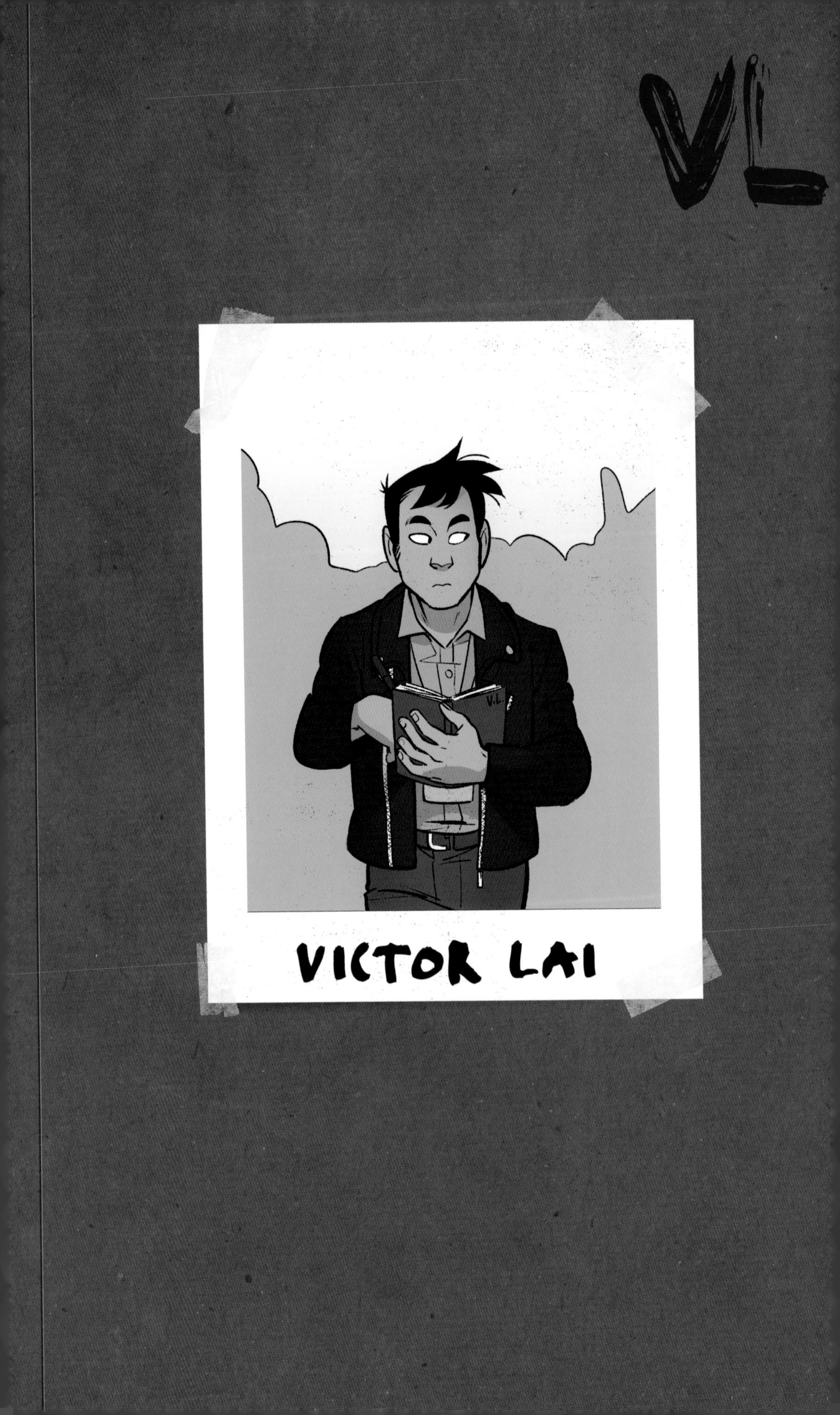
VL
VICTOR LAI

Property of <u>Victor Lai</u>, please return if found, paper is very hard to come by these days.

FEATURE PITCHES

- 15 Low-Rad Happy Hours That'll Leave You Glowing
  Note to self: invest in a working geiger counter
- "Hot" New Hazard Suit Looks: Are Glowing Green Goggles Coming Back??
  They never left, imho
- That New Stuff in the Rain That Looks Like Shampoo: It's Not Shampoo
  It's not shampoo, right? Right??
- Six New Candidates for Hot Wings, Now That All the Birds are Gone
  Not looking forward to sourcing this but Cal did love hot wings
- Those Things With The Baby Hands: What the Fuck
  Seriously, what the fuck

UPCOMING MOVIE REVIEWS

✵ **The Kids Are Yawl Right**

Set sail for Boat Cop V: Pier Pressure

Of all the Boat Cop installments to survive The Event (II, V and VI, for those keeping score at home) *Pier Pressure* is the strongest swimmer by a nautical mile. There aren't as many boat-themed gadgets this time out, but who needs gadgets when you've got a hijacked nuclear submarine full of plucky teenagers (including a fresh-faced Kimberly Elizabeth and Jon DeHaan), moon-worshiping eco-terrorists (led by legendary character actor Ace Ayling), and a late '90s power-pop soundtrack you'll be humming in the decon showers 3 weeks later.

✰ **Alas, Poor Tracking**

Hamlet 2999 will leave you melancholy

What can be said about *Hamlet 2999* that hasn't been said before? As a mid-90s direct to video re-imagining of Shakespeare's Danish drama queen aboard the crumbling interstellar generation ship DEN-MKI, it was never going to set the world on fire (though a certain *The Event* certainly did that for us). The latest re-release of that VHS tape they found in a bank vault somewhere isn't doing the film any favors either. I'm not sure what's more cringe-worthy: the writing, the production values, or the series of increasingly preposterous sex scenes featuring not one, not two, but SEVENTEEN different-

PORTRAIT OF THE ARTIST AS A ~~YOUNG~~ MAN

If you ask me self-portraiture is a perfectly good waste of precious squid ink. 5 years scrapping with scavs for canned corn and listical subjects yet not a single distinctive post-apocalyptic scar to my name. Even Hallett in HR has a claw hand. A CLAW HAND. All I've got is that persistent scowl people keep mistaking for IBS. No wonder those FEMAplus goons keep hassling me down by the QZ fence. Mark my words: next time the world ends, I'm getting a cool laser eye on the first day. **THE FIRST DAY.**

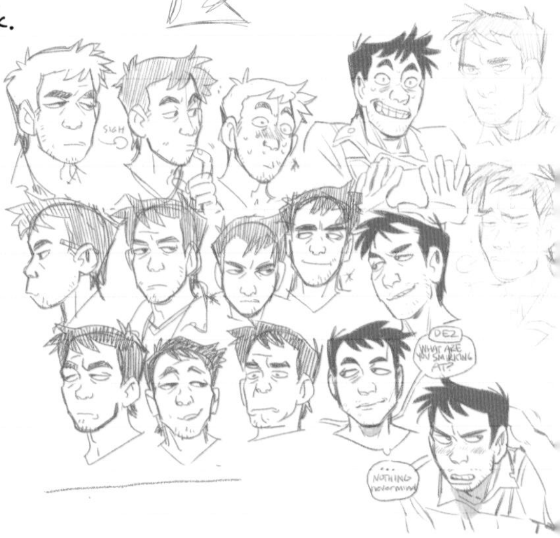
SIGH
DEZ
WHAT ARE YOU SMIRKING AT?
... NOTHING nevermind

DEZ TO THE RESCUE

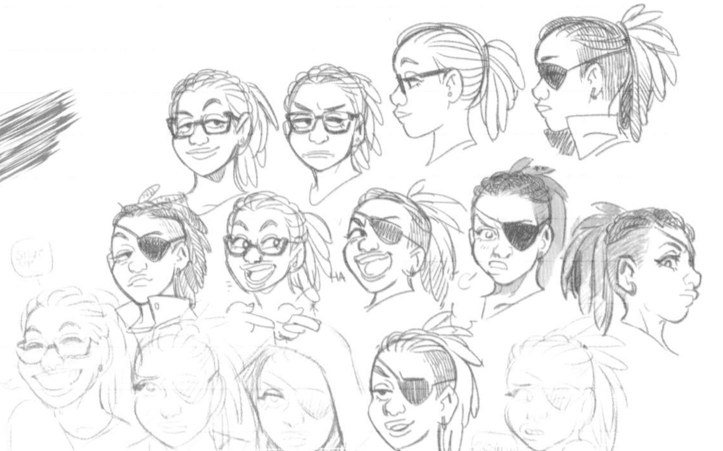

What an absolute legend! I mean, I knew Dez was a champion from the moment I met her, but 5 years in a subterranean nerd zoo really brought out her inner gladiator. It's like when that college beach weekend Went Bad and she stepped up to save our asses. I mean, my mom's van still smells like fire extinguisher when you crank the AC, but at least that manatee got the help it needed. She's managed to carve out an actual home in this chaos, keep her fighty intern alive, AND snag a cool eyepatch along the way. Who knew that some people just look better with an eyepatch? Note to self: do NOT ask what the deal is with the eyepatch.

LOREN IPSUM, FERAL INTERN

Here is what I know about Loren:

- Small, bitey
- Maintains strategic hair dye reserve, location unknown
- Can eat half her weight in rancid hot dogs and sleep standing up
- Publishes a zine, has been "well received critically", circulation unknown
- Described herself as "demi-romantic ace" then pantomimed being an airplane and said "but not that kind of ace" then shot pretend machineguns at me and said "but also yes that kind of ace"
- Nunchuck proficient

OHMYGODD
ffffff
POST EVENT

Flíx Bíxby

Ugh, just look at this goober. We get it, you were on TV in the '90s. You know who else who was on TV in the '90s? Those cartoon marmots who smelled their own farts. I don't understand how you can descend into celebrity cannibalism while still retaining a superiority complex. Things were pretty bad on the outside but we managed to get by on beans and tang. Sidebar: I do think I saw that gangster squid-people thing he was talking about. But I'll never tell him.

Category: Skylarks series

REAL WORLD ARTICLE
(written from a Production point of view)

This category lists the major *Skylarks* series.

Subcategories

This category has the following 3 subcategories, out of 3 total.

- [+] Skylarks spinoff series (1 C, 4 P)
- [+] Skylarks TV movies 3 C, 10 P)
- [+] Undeveloped projects (5 C, 15 P)

Pages in category "Skylarks series"

The following 9 pages are in this category, out of 9 total.

Interstellar Skylarks (TIS)
"Too low they dream, who dream beneath the stars," goes the immortal misquotation of 17th century poet Edward Young which begins the *Skylarks* saga. The series debuted to wide acclaim and large audience share, thanks in part to a timeslot following the wildly popular *King Cheetah Anthology Hour.* Commodore Quinn and his loyal band of soldiers-scientists would spend the next 5 seasons exploring the cosmos, safeguarding the fragile Earthling-Ellorian alliance and bedding many an alluring Ajaxian along the way.

The series was almost entirely episodic (a notable exception being "Battle Inside Time", which thanks to some clever editing used most of the same footage as "Battle Outside Time"). Other notable episodes include two stark parables on the potential risks of nuclear power ("Wherefore Atlantis" and "Night Falls on Olympus") and a moving tribute to Brown v. Board of Education in "Sky Cadet Soliloquy" (which also served to introduce the Sky Cadet training program). Less well regarded are "The Peppers Predicament" and "Commodore… Peppers?", both of which briefly placed the Commodore's prize-winning dachshund in command of the ISSS Starling.

- Episodes
- Performers

Skylarks Indigo Trident (SIT)
After several years during which *Interstellar Skylarks* reruns frequently outperformed everything they were put up against, a new series seemed inevitable. Expectations were high for "The Indigo Osiris" mini-series, which aired on 5 consecutive nights and re-launched the franchise in a distinctly 1970s direction. The new series embraced the decade's love of mysticism, dance music and Egyptology with a new ship (the titular Indigo Trident, later retconned as the ISS Kestel) and a new crew (including singing sensation Lorelai Bruderlin as Junior Midshipwoman Laxmi Aurora and teen heartthrob Daytona as CHRRRRKRRKKKRK).

- Episodes
- Performers

SkylarksMAX (SMAX)
Sex, drugs, shoulderpads. Welcome to the 80s, Skylarks style. SkylarksMAX debuted in

THE LONG CON

CREATOR CHECKLIST

DYLAN MECONIS

Dylan Meconis is an Eisner, Reuben, and Kim Yale-nominated cartoonist. She's the creator of graphic novels *Bite Me!*, *Family Man*, *Outfoxed*, and the forth-coming *Queen of the Sea* (Candlewick, 2019). She's a studio member of Helioscope in Portland, Oregon.

For all the comics pros, organizers and fans who've helped me survive 15 years of conventions.

dylanmeconis.com
@dmeconis

BEN COLEMAN

Ben Coleman is a freelance writer and a film and culture critic for the *Portland Mercury*. He was an ensemble member and contributing writer to Atomic Arts, the innovative and nationally-recognized theater company that reimagined shows like *Star Trek* for live audiences.

To my family, especially Tom and Suzy, who helped a lot. And Buzz the cat, who helped a little.

ohcoleman.com
@OhColeman

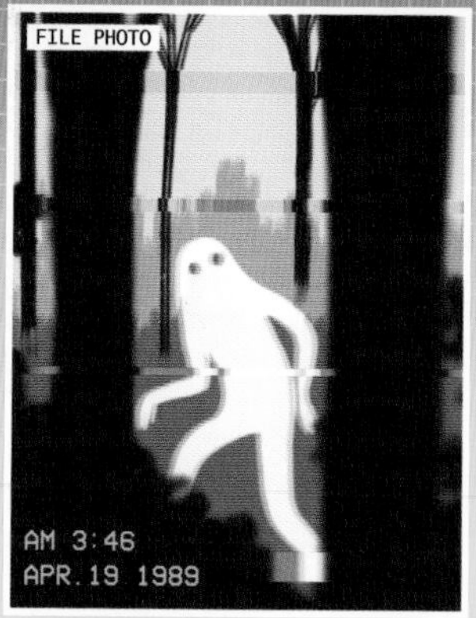
FILE PHOTO
AM 3:46
APR. 19 1989

EA Denich is a cartoonist and illustrator. She lives in Southern California.

I'd like to dedicate this book to Ryan, Mallory, and most of all, Momma. Thank you for always being my three biggest fans. And a huge thank you to Ari and Robin, our editors, and to Dylan and Ben. Thanks for all your encouragement and advice!

ghostgreen.tumblr.com
@ghostgreeen

M. VICTORIA ROBADO

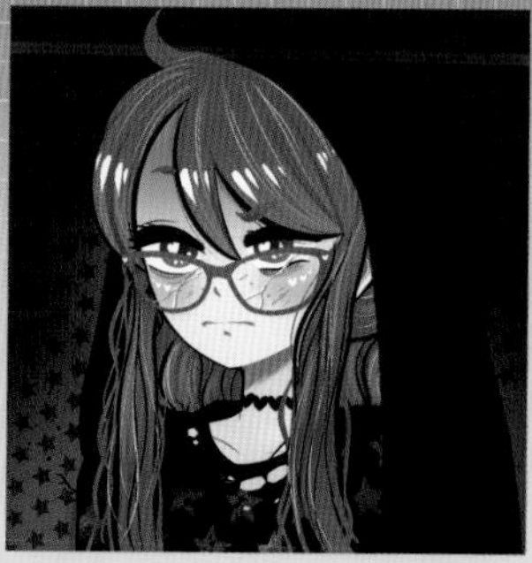

M. Victoria Robado is a comic creator and illustrator from Argentina obsessed with saturated colors, space, and cats. She writes and draws her own comics (*#Blessed*, *Never Ever Done*) and occasionally dumps her color palettes over other favorite projects.

Thanks to my Cintiq for not dying on me while flying across hemispheres.

shourimajo.com
@shourimajo

ADITYA BIDIKAR

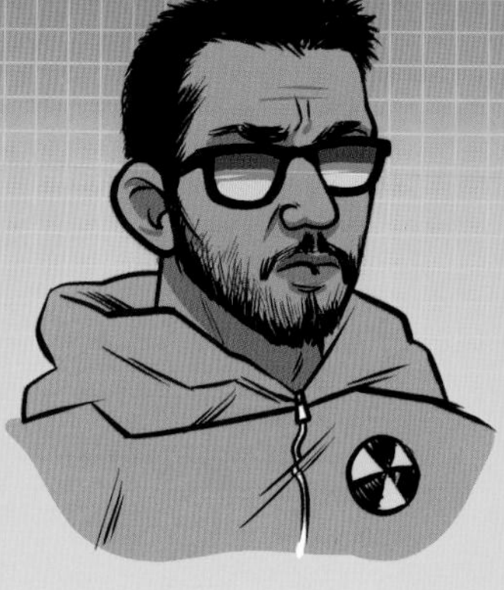

Aditya Bidikar is a comics letterer based in India. Apart from *The Long Con*, he is currently working on *Black Cloud*, *VS*, *Motor Crush*, *Paradiso* and *Kid Lobotomy*, among others.

To my cat Loki, who did his best to not let me work on this book.

adityab.net
@adityab

MORE GREAT BOOKS FROM ONI PRESS!

PAMELA RIBON ♥ CAT FARRIS
My Boyfriend
IS A
BEAR

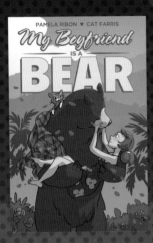

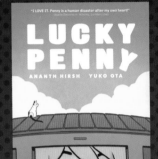

MY BOYFRIEND IS A BEAR
By Pamela Ribon &
Cat Farris

PIZZASAURUS
REX
JUSTIN
WAGNER
WARREN
WUCINICH

PIZZASAURUS REX
By Justin Wagner &
Warren Wucinich

"I LOVE IT. Penny is a human disaster after my own heart!"
LUCKY
PENNY
ANANTH HIRSH
YUKO OTA

LUCKY PENNY
By Ananth Hirsh &
Yuko Ota

KIM REAPER
GRIM
BEGINNINGS
BY SARAH GRALEY

KIM REAPER, VOLUME 1: GRIM BEGINNINGS
By Sarah Graley

LETTER
44
VOLUME I ESCAPE VELOCITY

LETTER 44, VOLUME 1: ESCAPE VELOCITY
By Charles Soule,
Alberto Jiménez Alburquerque,
Guy Major, & Dan Jackson

THE
BUNKER
JOSHUA HALE FIALKOV JOE INFURNARI
VOLUME 1

THE BUNKER, VOLUME 1
By Joshua Hale Fialkov
& Joe Infurnari

ONI PRESS